Our Davie Pepper

THE FAMOUS PEPPER BOOKS
by Margaret Sidney
IN ORDER OF PUBLICATION

Our Davie Pepper

By

MARGARET SIDNEY

Grosset & Dunlap

PUBLISHERS

NEW YORK

Preface

I OFTEN RUN down to Badgertown and into the Little Brown House to talk things over with the Peppers, and every single time they one and all tell me they don't think I have told enough about David.

It quite cut me to the heart the other day to hear Polly say mournfully, "You've made a book about Ben and one about Phronsie, and you've told all about Joel's adventures, and stories that I made up; and you never let Davie have a book— and he is *our Davie*."

"Oh, I will, Polly—I will!" I promised. And she laughed gleefully, and Ben smiled in great satisfaction, and Joel said: "Whickets! Now, Dave, you're going to have a book all to yourself." And Phronsie crowed and gurgled, and made a cheese right in the middle of the old kitchen floor. As for Mother Pepper, the look she gave me, well—wasn't I glad that I had promised!

But David ran up to me and whispered, "I'd rather you made another book about Joel."

"I can't, Davie," I whispered back, "the children all over the country have been teasing me for years to give them a book about you. And now as all the rest of the Pepper family want it, why, you see, I just *must* write it."

"Oh, dear!" said David.

Polly ran over to our corner. "Dear Margaret Sidney," she begged, clasping her hands, *"please* tell all about Davie when he was a little boy. That's what we want; because you see you told ever so much more about the rest of us than you did about him. And Davie was always just splendid! Why, he was our Davie!"

So now here is "Our Davie Pepper," just as the Little Brown House people wanted me to write it.

MARGARET SIDNEY

Contents

Davie and Old Man Peters

"MY SAKES! David Pepper, you can't get it in."

"Perhaps I can, Mrs. Peters."

"No, you can't. There, give it to me. You're all het up, runnin' on arrants for Mr. Atkins. He shouldn't 'a' told you to hurry clear down here from th' store."

David sank down on the wooden box turned upside down outside the Peters kitchen door and watched Mrs. Peters's vigorous efforts to crowd a long woolen coat, very much frayed on the edge, one sleeve gone, and various other dilapidations that might be noticed, into a round, splint-bottomed basket. "Your ma c'n do th' mendin' better'n me," she said, during the process, and dropping her voice as her eyes roved anxiously. "I put th' pieces underneath. Oh, my!" she whirled around suddenly, her back to the basket, and brought up a red face. "How you scar't me, Tildy!" as the kitchen door was flung wide and a head thrust out.

" 'Tain't Pa—you needn't be afraid." Yet Tildy looked over her shoulder and grasped her apron tighter over something huddled up within its folds, as she skipped over the big flat stone. "You know as well as I do that he's well off toward the south medder."

" 'Tain't nothin' to be certain sure of, if your pa is headed for th' south medder, that he won't see what we're doin' here," said her mother hopelessly. "Well, what you got in your apron?"

Matilda knelt down by the basket on the grass and flung her apron wide. "It's some o' my quince sass."

"You ain't goin' to give that away!" cried Mrs. Peters in alarm, and resting both hands on her knees. "Gracious, your pa—"

"Let Pa alone, can't you?" cried Matilda lifting the coat edge to tuck in the big glass jar. "I guess he won't rage an' ramp no more at th' sass, than your lettin' Mis Pepper mend this coat."

"Well, I d'no. Sass is sass, an' your pa knows how many jars you put up— Oh, dear me, Matilda!" She gazed helplessly off toward the south meadow.

Davie got off from the wooden box. "Oh don't, Mrs. Peters," he begged in great distress, "send the jelly to Mamsie."

" 'Tain't jell—it's sass," said Matilda, pushing the jar in further, and flapping the coat till it bulged over the basket. "An' I guess I ain't goin' to let your ma have all them measles to your house, an' not do nothin'. There—" She jumped to her feet. "You got to carry it careful, Davie. It's too bad there ain't no handle." She twitched the frayed cord that served as one, "I'll get another string."

"Come back here, Tildy," cried her mother. "Ain't you crazy! Your pa'll be back. Let Davie go."

Matilda turned away from the kitchen door. "Ain't you silly, Ma!" yet she came back. "Well there, run along, Davie, an' carry it careful."

"An' you tell your ma," said Mrs. Peters, "we're sorry she's got all the measles to her house, an' she c'n mend my coat better'n me, an' she mustn't tell no one it's for Mis Peters, an'—"

"Land, Ma, th' boy can't remember all that," said Matilda, giving David a little push.

"I guess I can—I'll try to," said David, grasping the old worn string with both hands.

"You go along," said Matilda, with another push, "an' if you see Pa comin' along anywhere, you set th' basket in behind th' bushes till he gits by. Remember, David Pepper!"

"Yes," said David. "I'll remember."

"Well, now come along, Ma. Peters," said Matilda; "he hain't spilled th' things yit, an' he's turned th' road. We've got to git back to work."

" 'Twouldn't be so bad ef you hadn't put in that quince sass, Tildy," mourned her mother, picking up her worn calico gown to step over a puddle of water from a broken drainpipe. "But I'm awful skeered about that."

"Oh, Ma, you make me sick." Matilda gave her a little push into the kitchen, slipped in after her, and slammed the door; but her hand shook as she took up the broom. "I'm goin' to work anyhow. You c'n set an' worry about Pa, ef you want to. I'm glad, for my part, that Mis Pepper's goin' to have that basket o' things."

"So be I," cried Mrs. Peters. "Land sakes! I guess I'm as glad as you be, Tildy Peters. An' I s'pose Davie's gettin' along toward home pretty fast by this time."

Matilda shook her head and pursed up her lips as she went out to sweep the back entry. "All the same, I wish Davie Pepper was safe home to the Little Brown House," she said to herself.

The old cord cut into Davie's fingers as he trudged along

the winding road, the basket wobbling about from side to side; but every step was bringing him home to Mamsie, and he smiled as he went along.

"Hey there!" a sudden turn of the road brought him squarely before a tall, gaunt old man leaning against the stone wall on the other side of a scrub oak.

"Where you ben?" demanded Old Man Peters.

"Just—just—" began David.

"Jest where? Stop your hemmin' an' hawin'. Where you ben?"

Davie clutched the basket with trembling fingers and a wild despair that it was now too late to consider bushes.

"You ben down to my house, I know." Old Man Peters's little eyes gleamed fiercely. "Well, what you got in that basket?" pointing to it.

"It's—it's—"

"It's—it's— Didn't I tell you to stop hemmin' an' hawin', you Pepper Boy! I'll give you somethin' to hem an' haw for pretty soon, ef you don't look out." He broke off a stick from the scrub oak.

Davie clutched the old string tighter yet.

"Let's see," said Old Man Peters, drawing close to poke up a corner of the coat with the stick.

"You mustn't," said Davie, drawing back, and putting one hand over the top of the basket.

"Mustn't," roared Old Man Peters, shaking the stick at him.

"No," said Davie. "You mustn't," and he tried to edge off farther; but the stick came down across his little calico blouse.

"I'll give you somethin' to make you see that you can't say 'mustn't' to me," said Mr. Peters, bringing the stick down again. "There, you take that!"

Davie was whirling around now so fast that Old Man Peters preferred to try the stick on the little legs instead of the small shoulders in the calico blouse, while he roared, "I'll make you dance. Drop that basket, will you!"

"Here—what you doin'?" somebody called out, and a young man leaped the stone wall. "Hulloa, Old Peters, you stop that!"

Old Man Peters turned around. He would have dropped the stick, but the young man saved him the trouble by seizing it to break it into two pieces and toss them into the dusty road.

"He's ben a-sassin' me," cried the old man, pointing to David, who had sunk down on the grass by the side of the road, still hanging to the basket.

"Well, you ain't a-goin' to beat up any boy in Badgertown. Now I tell you, Peters! And who wouldn't sass you, I wonder. Here you, get up," he said, going over to David.

But David showing no inclination to get up, the man turned his face over.

"Well, I'll be blowed, ef tain't one o' th' Pepper children," he exclaimed, starting back. "You've got to take somethin' from me, now I tell you, Old Man Peters!" He pushed up his gray cotton shirt sleeves and advanced on the old man, "for beatin' up one o' Mis Pepper's boys."

"You git away—tain't nothin' to you, Jim Thompson," cried Mr. Peters, "an' I'll have th' law on you ef you tetch me!" He put up both horny hands and tried to huddle back of the scrub oak.

"Th' law's got to deal with you, Old Peters, first, an' it'll fall pretty heavy for hurtin' one o' them Pepper children," declared Thompson, dragging him by an angry hand back to the roadside.

"David—David Pepper!" screamed the old farmer, "you

tell him I ain't hurt ye. Tell him, David. Ow! you let me be, Jim Thompson!"

David looked up and tried to speak. Oh, if Mamsie were only here! Then his head fell down on the dusty road.

"Look at that boy, you old scoundrel!" roared Thompson, cuffing Old Man Peters wherever he got a good chance. Then he flung him to the middle of the road. "Lie there till I can 'tend to you." But the old farmer preferred to attend to himself, and without waiting to pick up his hat that had fallen off in the scuffle, he slunk off as fast as he conveniently could.

"Don't hurt him," begged Davie feebly, as Thompson bent over him. "Oh, I want Mamsie!"

"You're a-goin' to her—I'll take you." The young man lifted him up to his shoulder, Davie still clinging to the basket. "Where did he hurt you?" he asked anxiously.

"I'm not hurt much," said Davie, trying not to cry.

Jim Thompson set his teeth hard. "Here, give me that basket," and holding Davie fast by one arm, he strode off, first kicking Old Man Peters's hat into a neighboring field where it landed in a bog.

"Mamsie—somebody's coming, and he's got a big bundle —how funny," cried Polly, looking out of the window.

"A peddler, most likely," said Mrs. Pepper, over in the window, trying to finish a coat to go back to Mr. Atkins at the store. The measles were making it extra hard to keep the wolf from the door.

"Well, he won't sell anything here," said Polly with a laugh, and running to the old green door. "Why—" as she flung it open.

It was all over in a minute, and Mrs. Pepper had her boy in her arms. Davie trying to say, "I'm not much hurt," and Polly running for the camphor bottle, while Jim Thompson set down the basket on the floor, where it rolled over and out flew the "quince sass" from the protecting folds of the coat.

"Old Man Peters was a-beatin' him up," said the young farmer, working his hands awkwardly together and wishing he could help.

"Mamsie," said Davie, both hands around her neck, and cuddling up to lay his white cheek against her face, "I didn't let him have the basket—and you are to mend the coat. You can do it so much better, she says, than she can."

"Mrs. Peters, Davie?"

"Yes, and Miss Matilda sent the jelly—no, it isn't jelly—but—I forget—"

"Yes, I know, dear. Now let Mother see where you are hurt."

"Oh, Mamsie!" Polly, flying back with the camphor bottle, was aghast as Mrs. Pepper stripped off the calico blouse.

"Put down the camphor, Polly," said Mother Pepper. Her lips were set very tightly together, and a bright spot burned on either cheek. "Bring Mother the oil bottle and get the roll of old cotton in the lower bureau drawer. Be careful not to wake up Phronsie. Thank you, Mr. Thompson, for bringing home my boy," as Polly ran off.

"I guess I'll go back an' lick Old Man Peters," said the young farmer, turning off to the door.

"Oh, no," Mother Pepper spoke quickly. "Say nothing to him. I'll take care of the matter."

"I'd love to," said Mr. Thompson longingly.

"No—no—" Mrs. Pepper shook her head decidedly. And he went off.

"Oh, Mamsie, that wicked Old Man Peters!" Polly clasped her hands, and her brown eyes blazed. "I just want something dreadful to happen to him," and she hovered over

David bolstered up in Mamsie's rocking chair, his legs and little shoulders bound up in old cotton bandages.

"Polly," said Mother Pepper sternly, "never let me hear you say anything like that again."

"I can't help it," said Polly, fighting with the tears. Then she gave it up and ran over to throw herself down on the floor and lay her head in Mother Pepper's lap, "to think of Davie being hurt. Oh, Mamsie!"

"I'm not much hurt," said Davie, poking up his head from the pillow against his back, "only my legs—they're a little bad. Don't cry, Polly," he begged, dreadfully distressed.

"Our Davie!" sobbed Polly, huddling down further in her mother's lap, "just think, Mamsie—our *Davie!*"

Mrs. Pepper shut her lips together, but she smoothed Polly's brown head. "Mother will see to it," she said, "and you must never say anything like that again, Polly. Now wipe your eyes; here comes Dr. Fisher."

"Well—well—well—" cried the little doctor, coming in cheerily. He was very happy as Ben was getting along splendidly, while as for Phronsie, why she just got better and better every day. Oh, the measles wasn't so very bad after all to fight. But now, here was Davie bolstered up in the big calico-covered chair. Oh, dear, that was too bad!

"Well, my boy," the little doctor got over to the chair and looked down at him with keen eyes behind the big spectacles, "what's the matter with you?"

"I'm not much hurt," said Davie, "only my legs—they feel the worst."

"Eh?" said Dr. Fisher. Then he set down his bag and looked over at Mrs. Pepper. So then the story had to come out. When it was all told and Dr. Fisher became quiet, for he was almost as bad as Polly in his indignation, and Davie's legs and shoulders had been taken care of, "You don't need to do anything, Mrs. Pepper," he said, "I'll take care of that brute of a man."

And Mother Pepper said just as she had told the young farmer, "Oh no, I will see to the matter myself."

"Oh, goody—I got the wood all piled at Deacon Blodgett's." In rushed Joel. "Come on, Dave," and he was scurrying over to Mamsie's big chair, when he spied the basket on the floor, for nobody had thought or cared about it. And there was the jar of Matilda's "quince sass" that had rolled off by itself. "Oh," he pounced upon it, "may I have some— may I?" He ran with it to Mrs. Pepper, nearly upsetting the little doctor on the way.

"Look out there," cried Dr. Fisher; "here, don't run me down, Joe," and then Joel saw Davie propped against the pillows. Down went Matilda's "quince sass" on the kitchen floor, and he threw himself into the chair on top of Davie, poor bandaged legs and all.

The little old kitchen then was in a hubbub. It all had to be explained to Joel, who made things so very dreadful that finally Dr. Fisher said, "I'll take him off, Mrs. Pepper. Hold on to that boy, Polly, till I've had a look at Ben up in the loft. If Phronsie is asleep, she's all right. Then, Joel Pepper, you shall hop into my gig."

II

Mrs. Pepper Attends to the Matter

PARSON HENDERSON shut the gate with a firm hand and stepped out into the road.

The parsonage door opened and the minister's wife ran down the path. "Here, Jotham, take this to Mrs. Pepper." She put a clean folded napkin, from which came a nice smell of something newly baked, into his hand. "Oh, I do hope Mrs. Pepper will let you see that horrible Mr. Peters," she began anxiously.

"Mrs. Pepper always knows her own mind," said the parson, "and if she wants to attend to the matter, it's not for us, Mehitable, to interfere." He handled the napkin bundle gingerly and moved off.

"It was perfectly dreadful, Jim Thompson said, and you know he tells the truth, husband." She pattered after him. "Do see if you can't persuade her to let you see Mr. Peters. You know you want to."

"That I do!" declared the parson, his eyes flashing. "Well, don't you worry, Mehitable; it will be attended to."

"He ought to be driven out of town—that old creature had," cried his wife, with very red cheeks. "Everybody hates him. Now I hope this will make him leave Badgertown."

"Softly there, Mehitable," the parson patted one of the

10

red cheeks. "Badgertown must be careful what it does. There are his poor wife and Matilda to consider."

"Oh, I know it," groaned Mrs. Henderson. "Well, do try and get Mrs. Pepper to let you fix the matter up." She hurried over the old flat stone. There in the doorway stood Miss Jerusha.

"I sh'd think Jotham had enough to do, without taking up with Mis Pepper's troubles," she said tartly.

"Oh, it's his business to do what he can for Badgertown people, Jerusha," said Mrs. Henderson.

"Badgertown people!" sniffed Miss Jerusha. She set her spectacles straighter and glared at the parson's wife. "You've all gone mad over that Little Brown House family," she said. "For my part, I hate shiftless folks who expect to be looked out for all the while."

"Don't you ever call the Little Brown House people shiftless again in my presence." The parson's wife got as tall as she could, even up to her tiptoes. "Anybody with a heart would be sorry for that poor brave woman and those dear children who are trying to help her. I can't think, Jerusha, how you can be so—so—"

She left the last word to look out for itself, her voice trailing off. But she marched with a high head past the long angular figure, and the door of her husband's study closed with a snap.

"Let me see 'em—let me see 'em!" Joel prancing around in the Little Brown House kitchen, stopped suddenly and twitched the small calico sleeve.

"No," said David, edging off. "I don't want anybody to see 'em."

"I'm going to," declared Joel, holding on with both hands to the blouse as David whirled around. "I saw 'em yesterday, and I'm going to see 'em again. Hold still, Dave. *Zip!*"

"There, now you've torn it!" Davie cried in distress.

Joel's stubby hands dropped and he stood still in dismay.

" 'Tisn't torn—torn—much," he said, quite aghast.

"It's torn—and now Mamsie will have to work and mend it. Oh, dear!"

With that the tears fell, and Davie threw himself on the floor, and sobbed as if his heart would break.

"What *is* the matter?" cried Polly, rushing in from the bedroom, where she had been giving Phronsie her breakfast of mush. For once there was some real milk, for Dr. Fisher had set a bottle on the kitchen table after his visit to see how the measles were coming on. "Oh, Davie!" She threw herself down beside him. "Where are you hurt?"

Mrs. Pepper hurried over the steps from the Provision Room, where she had been looking over the potatoes to see how long they would last.

"I tore—tore—" said Joel, in the middle of the kitchen floor. His face was working dreadfully and he twisted his hands together trying not to cry.

"What did you do, Joe?" cried Polly, running over to him.

"Mamsie," cried Davie, throwing his arms around her, "he didn't mean to."

"There—there," said Mrs. Pepper, taking him up to her lap. "Joel, come here and tell Mother all about it."

"He didn't mean to," began Davie again, wiping up his tears.

"I don't believe Joey did mean to, Mamsie, whatever it is," said Polly, pulling him along. He was digging one small fist into first one eye and then the other, and saying at every step, "I didn't mean to, Mamsie," and he threw himself down and burrowed his face on top of Davie's legs in Mrs. Pepper's lap.

"Stop saying you didn't mean to, Joel, and tell Mother what you did to Davie," said Mrs. Pepper firmly.

Joel put out a shaking hand and felt for the torn place in the little calico blouse, Polly hanging over them in great anxiety. "There," he said, "I didn't mean to do it, Mamsie."

"He means he's torn Davie's jacket," said Polly with a little gasp. "Oh, dear me, Joel, you've scared us almost to death!"

"Mamsie will have to work and mend it," howled Joel. With that Davie began again to cry, and to burrow deeper against Mrs. Pepper's neck.

"For shame, Joel!" cried Polly. "It's ever so much worse to cry now than it was to tear Davie's jacket."

"Is it?" cried Joel, bringing up his head suddenly and gazing at her out of two black eyes; the tears trailed down over his snubby nose. "Is it really, Polly?"

"Indeed it is, Joe," she said decidedly.

"Then I'm not going to cry any more," declared Joel, wiping off the last tear with the back of one brown hand and jumping up.

"Now, that's Mother's good boy," said Mrs. Pepper approvingly.

"Whatever made you tear Davie's jacket, Joe?" cried Polly, very much puzzled and running after him.

"I wanted to see the red things on his legs," said Joel. "Oh, I'd 'a' made Old Man Peters squinge and squinge if I'd been there! This is the way I'd have done." Joel ran over to the corner and seized the broom, and landed about him so savagely that Polly flew off laughing, and Davie joined in with a merry shout, until the little old kitchen fairly rang with the noise.

"Yes—sir-ee!" said Joel, prancing madly around, "that's the way I'd 'a' squinged him if I'd been there."

Davie slid out of Mother Pepper's lap and ran after him, the torn bit of calico flapping at the end of his blouse.

"Let me, Joel," he cried, trying to reach the broom as Joel pranced on.

"You couldn't do it," said Joel. "I must squinge Old Man Peters myself," holding the broom very high. Then he saw Davie's face. "You may have it," he said.

Polly ran into the bedroom and came back on her tiptoes. "Phronsie's asleep," she said. "Now I'm awfully glad, for I can clean out the stove. Then I can get the bread in." She ran over and knelt down before the old stove, and presently there was a great to-do with the brush and the little shovel and the old woolen cloths.

Mrs. Pepper sighed as she rolled up in a newspaper two coats that she had just finished. "I don't know what I should ever do without you, Polly," she said, looking over at her.

"Don't you, Mamsie?" cried Polly in great delight, and sitting back on her heels, she brought up a countenance with long black streaks running across it. "Don't you really, Mamsie?"

"No, I don't," said Mrs. Pepper, "and that is a fact. Mother wouldn't know what to do without you. But dear me, child, what a pair of black hands—and your face, Polly!" as she went into the bedroom to put on her bonnet.

Polly looked down at her hands. Then she burst out laughing. "I brushed back my hair," she said, "it tumbled into my eyes so," and she jumped up and ran to the cracked looking glass in the corner. "My! what a sight I am!"

"Let me see," cried Joel, rushing over. "Don't wash it off, Polly, let me see!"

David flung down the broom and tumbled after. "Let me see, too, Polly."

"I look just like that old dirty man who used to come

after rags," said Polly, turning around on them and holding up her hands.

"Oh, you do—you do!" howled Joel in huge delight, while Davie crowed and clapped his hands. "You do, just exactly like him, Polly!"

"Wait a minute," said Polly. She rushed out and came running back with Ben's old cap on her head and her arms in his coat. "Now wouldn't you think I was that old dirty man?" she said, stalking up and down the kitchen crying out, "Any rags, Mam?" and she swung the big potato bag at them.

"Oh, Polly," screamed Davie in a transport, "you are that old dirty man," while Joel marched after echoing, "Any rags, Mam?" and swinging an imaginary bag at every step he took.

Suddenly Polly stopped, tore off the cap and the coat. "Take back the potato bag into the Provision Room, Joel," she said, tossing it to him. "I forgot the stove, and the bread has got to go in. Oh, dear me!" She flew over to the sink, and presently back she came. "There now, I'm scrubbed clean, but I'll get all black again, I suppose," and she kneeled down again before the stove.

Mrs. Pepper came out of the bedroom and stopped a minute by the green door to smile at them all. Then she went out with her bundle to take to Mr. Atkins at the store; but first there was another errand of importance to attend to, so she turned off at the crossroad. The smile had dropped away from her folded lips, as she stepped swiftly along toward the Peters farm.

"Here she comes—here's Mis Pepper!" cried Matilda. "Do stop wringin' your hands, Ma. You ain't done nothin' else sence yesterday. Mis Pepper can't blame us."

"Oh, dear," mourned Mrs. Peters. " 'Twas th' quince sass that made all th' trouble."

" 'Twarn't th' quince sass at all," contradicted Matilda flatly. "Pa never said a word about it. Do stop—Mis Pepper's at th' door."

"*Rat-tat!*" went the old iron knocker. Matilda jumped, all her nerves askew, while Mrs. Peters sank down in the nearest chair.

"Oh, dear, there ain't time to get on a clean apurn." Matilda opened the big door—her tongue clapped up to the roof of her mouth, and she couldn't find a word to say.

"Is your father in?" asked Mrs. Pepper pleasantly. Then she looked into the scared face. "Don't feel badly—you couldn't help it," she said.

Matilda twisted her hands in her dirty apron. "We feel dreadful—Ma an' me," she said, and burst out crying.

"There—there," said Mrs. Pepper soothingly, trying to pat the nervous hands. "Don't, Matilda; your mother will hear you. Can I see your father?"

"He's in there." Matilda twitched out one hand from beneath the apron and pointed a shaking finger to the little room that old Mr. Peters called his office. Mrs. Pepper knocked at the door.

"You better go right in ef you want to see him," said Matilda in a loud whisper, "for he'll sneak out th' back door, ef he knows it's you." So Mrs. Pepper opened the door, and none too soon. Old Man Peters was crowding his long legs out of the big chair where he sat behind his desk, his eyes on the door leading out to the back yard.

"Oh, come in, Mis Pepper," he mumbled, his long face getting redder and redder. "Take a chair an' set."

"I do not wish to sit down, Mr. Peters," said Mrs. Pepper. "What I have to say will take but a few moments. I have come to see you about my boy."

"Yes—yes—" grunted the old man in a terrible alarm.

"Well, p'raps 'twas a mistake," he twitched the papers on his desk with nervous fingers, then finally ran them through his shock of grizzled hair. "I didn't mean to hurt th' boy none. But mebbe 'twas a mistake. You better set, Mis Pepper."

"It was more than a mistake, Mr. Peters," said Mrs. Pepper in a clear voice, and ignoring the invitation.

"Well—mebbe—mebbe," said the old man, wriggling around in his big chair. "See here now," he suddenly stopped and looked in a tremor into her black eyes, "I'll give you some money, an' that'll fix it up. How much do ye want?" he asked in an anguished tone.

"Money could never fix up a thing like this," said Mrs. Pepper. Her tone was quiet, but the black eyes blazed. Old Man Peters's hand fell in relief from the handle of his money drawer, but he slunk down in his chair.

"The only reparation you can make, Mr. Peters," Mrs. Pepper went on, "is to be very sure that you will never lay a hand again on a Badgertown child; not only upon my child, but upon any child. You understand that?"

"Ye—yes," mumbled the old man.

"And one more thing. That is, that you will treat your wife and Matilda as women should be treated."

"They're well enough off," declared Old Man Peters suddenly. Then he snarled out, "An' what bus'ness is it of yours, Mis Pepper, I'd like to know."

"Very well. If you don't promise this, I shall see that the injury to my boy is atoned for. I shall give the matter into the hands of the town authorities, Mr. Peters."

"Here—here—" screamed the old man, flinging out both hands as she moved off. "Stop, Mis Pepper! I didn't mean to say I wouldn't promise. Yes—yes—I do! Will you stop! I say I will!"

"And Badgertown will see that you keep that promise," said Mrs. Pepper. Then she opened the door. Matilda, who had a shaking eye at the keyhole, nearly fell over backward on the entry oilcloth.

"Oh, Mis Pepper," she gasped, seizing the strong arm. "Ma's takin' on somethin' awful in th' sittin' room."

"She won't do that long," said Mrs. Pepper grimly. "Come, Tildy."

"Oh, me—oh, my!" old Mrs. Peters was throwing herself from one side of the rickety sofa in the sitting room and moaning, with her fingers in her ears, when they came in.

"She's got th' high-strikes," declared Matilda with big eyes. "I must go up garret and git some feathers an' burn 'em right under her nose."

"Come back—no need for that, Matilda." Mrs. Pepper sat down on the sofa and drew the poor gray head into her arms. "There—there," she said, just as if one of the Five Little Peppers was cuddled within them. "You're going to see better times, Mrs. Peters. Your husband has promised to treat you and Matilda as women should be treated."

But Mrs. Peters not understanding, wailed on, burrowing deeper into the kind arms.

Tildy jumped to her feet. "Oh my soul an' body—did you make Pa say *that*?"

"Mr. Peters promised it," said Mrs. Pepper with a smile.

"Glory be!" Tildy set up a trot to the other end of the room, coming back to snap her fingers in glee. Then the joy went out of her face. "Pa never'll keep that promise in all the world," she gasped, drooping miserably.

"There is no doubt that the promise will be kept, Matilda," said Mrs. Pepper. "And if it isn't, why you just come to me." Then she laid Mrs. Peters's head back on the old sofa and went out and shut the door.

III

The Dark Cloud over the Little Brown House

"You don't say!" Old Man Beebe turned around on his little ladder where he was reaching down a pair of number six shoes for a customer. "Sho' now, I am beat, Mis Brown! Mebbe 'tain't true." He held the shoes aloft, the long strings dangling down.

"There ain't no morsel o' doubt about it," said Mrs. Brown decidedly. "I've jest come from the store, an' Mr. Atkins himself told me. I can't wait all day, Mr. Beebe; an' I said gaiters. I don't want no shoes."

"You said shoes," said Mr. Beebe. "However did I git up here, ef you hadn't asked for 'em."

"I don't know nothin' about th' workin' o' your mind, Mr. Beebe," said Mrs. Brown, "I said gaiters as plain as day —and do hurry!" She whipped the ends of her shawl impatiently around her gaunt figure.

"I d'no's I have any gaiters—that is—that'll fit you," said the little shoemaker, putting the "number sixes" into their box and slowly fitting on the cover. "P'raps I have a pair on the lower shelf." He got down laboriously from the ladder, put it in the corner, and began to rummage his stock.

"An' there's my bread waitin' to go in th' oven, an' I've got cake to bake for the sewin' s'ciety—do hurry, Mr. Beebe."

"I s'pose they've got to have rubber sides," mused Mr. Beebe, getting down on his knees to explore behind the chintz curtains that fell from the lowest shelf.

"Why, of course," said Mrs. Brown impatiently, "gaiters is gaiters, ain't they? An' I never saw a pair without them rubber sides to 'em, did you, Mr. Beebe?"

"I d'no's I did," said the little shoemaker, his head under the curtain. "Well, now here's a pair, I do believe," and he dragged out a box, whipped off the cover, and disclosed a pair with elastic sides. "Them's Congress gaiters," he said, "an' they look as if they'd fit like your skin."

"I'm sure I hope so," said Mrs. Brown, putting out her generous foot. "An' do hurry an' try 'em on, for mercy's sakes!"

"I'm hurryin' as fast as I can," said Mr. Beebe, coming over to the bench where the customers always sat for the shoes to be tried on, "but you've upset me so about that bad news. Sho' now!—to think that anythin' should happen to the Little Brown House folks."

"What's that—what's that, Pa?" Mrs. Beebe's head appeared in the doorway between the little shop and the sitting room. She had been frying doughnuts and she carried one in now on a blue plate, as she always did while they were nice and hot. "What's th' matter with th' Little Brown House folks? Oh, how do you do, Mis Brown?"

Mrs. Brown's nose wrinkled up appreciatively at sight of the doughnut.

"I hope nothin', Ma," said Mr. Beebe, not looking at the plate.

"You always have such luck with your doughnuts, Mis Beebe," said Mrs. Brown longingly.

"Well, what is it, anyway?" demanded Mrs. Beebe, setting down the plate on the counter that ran on one side of the little shop and coming up to the shoe bench. "What was you sayin', Pa, about th' Pepperses?"

"Polly's got the measles now."

"Good land o' Goshen!" exclaimed old Mrs. Beebe. Then she sat down on the other end of the bench and folded her plump hands.

"P'raps 'tain't true," he said, with trembling hands pulling on the gaiter.

"That's too tight," declared Mrs. Brown, wrenching her mind from the doughnuts and twisting her foot from one side to the other.

" 'Twon't be when th' rubber 'lastic has got stretched," said Mr. Beebe.

"Yes, an' then the 'lastic will be all wore out, an' bulge," said Mrs. Brown discontentedly. "Hain't you got another pair, Mr. Beebe?"

"Not your size," said the little shoemaker.

"Well, if Polly Pepper's got th' measles, I'm goin' right down to the Little Brown House," declared old Mrs. Beebe, getting up from the shoe bench. "I'll set out your dinner, Pa, the cold meat an' pie, and there's some hot soup on the stove. I'm goin' to stay an' help Mis Pepper," and she waddled out.

"Well, for mercy's sake, Mr. Beebe, try on th' other gaiter. I've got to git home some time today," said Mrs. Brown crossly, all hope of a doughnut coming her way now gone entirely.

The little shoemaker stood by the door of his shop

thoughtfully jingling the silver pieces in his hands, after his customer had gone out.

"To think o' Polly bein' took! Oh, dear, dear! I declare I forgot to give Ma some pink sticks to take to the children." He hurried out to the small entry, took down his coat and old cap and rammed his hands into his big pockets.

"Here they are, just as I saved 'em for Joel." Then he locked up his little shop and ambled down the cobblestones to overtake old Mrs. Beebe on her way to the Little Brown House.

But she got there first and opened the old green door without knocking. Mrs. Pepper was coming out of the bedroom with a bowl and a spoon in her hands. Her face was very white, but she tried to smile a welcome.

"Land alive!" exclaimed old Mrs. Beebe in a loud whisper. "Is Polly took?"

"Yes," said Mrs. Pepper.

"Well, I never!" Mrs. Beebe sank down in Mother Pepper's calico-covered chair. "That beats all—to think that Polly's took! Whatever'll you do *now!*"

"Take care," warned Mrs. Pepper, "she'll hear you," and she pointed to the bedroom.

"I'm whisperin'," said old Mrs. Beebe, holding her plump hands tightly together.

Mrs. Pepper hurried up to the loft to see how Ben was getting on.

And in came the little shoemaker, his round face quite red, he had hurried so.

"Is she bad?" The whisper was so much worse than that of old Mrs. Beebe, that she got out of the big chair and hurried over to him. "Pa, you mustn't—she'll hear you." She pointed to the bedroom and twitched his sleeve.

"I ain't a-talkin', I'm whisperin'," he said. "Is Polly bad,

Ma?" He pulled out his bandanna handkerchief and wiped his anxious face.

"Oh, I d'no," said Mrs. Beebe disconsolately. "Everythin's bad that Mis Pepper gits, deary me!"

"Well, I brought some pink sticks for Joel and Davie," said old Mr. Beebe, pulling out the paper from his pocket. "There, Ma," he laid them down on the table. "Where's th' boys?" he peered around the old kitchen.

"They're over to Deacon Blodgett's, I s'pose," said Mrs. Beebe. "Oh, dear me, they've got to work worse'n ever, now Ben's sick."

"Sho, now!" exclaimed the little shoemaker, dreadfully upset. "Where's Mis Pepper?"

"Up there," old Mrs. Beebe pointed to the loft stairs.

"I d'no what Mis Pepper is goin' to do now that Polly is took with th' measles," said Mr. Beebe in a loud whisper.

"Hush, Pa! You do speak dretful loud," as Mrs. Pepper came down the loft stairs.

"It's good of you to come, Mr. Beebe," she said, hurrying into the bedroom and closing the door.

"Mamsie," cried Polly, flying into the middle of the bed; the tears were racing down under the bandage that Dr. Fisher had tied over her eyes that morning. "Whatever will you do now that I've got 'em— Oh, Mamsie!" She threw her arms around Mother Pepper.

"Polly—Polly, child!" Mrs. Pepper held her close. "You mustn't cry. Don't you know what Dr. Fisher told you. There—there," she patted the brown hair as Polly snuggled up to her.

"I can't help it," said Polly, the tears tumbling over each other in their mad race down her cheeks. "I don't mind my eyes, if only I could help you. Oh, what will you do, Mamsie?"

"Oh, I will get along," said Mrs. Pepper in a cheerful voice. "And just think how good Joel is."

"It's good Joey hasn't got the measles," said Polly, trying to smile through her tears.

"Isn't it?" said Mrs. Pepper. "And Deacon Blodgett says he does splendidly working about the place. And Davie, too—oh, Polly, just think what a comfort those two boys are."

"I know it," said Polly, trying to speak cheerfully, "but I do wish I could help you sew on the coats," she said, and her face drooped further within Mother Pepper's arms.

"It's just because you have sewed so much that your eyes are bad." Mrs. Pepper couldn't repress the sigh.

"Mamsie, now don't you feel badly," Polly brought her head up suddenly. "Oh, I wish I could see your face—don't you, Mamsie?" She clutched her mother tightly, and the tears began to come again.

"Polly," said Mrs. Pepper, "now you and I have both got to be brave. It's not time for crying, and you must just be Mother's girl, and lie down and keep warm under the clothes. That's the very best way to help me."

"I'll try," said Polly, as Mrs. Pepper tucked her in under the old comforter.

But although old Mrs. Beebe was kind as could be, and Grandma Bascom hobbled over every now and then, and Parson Henderson and his wife helped in every imaginable way, a black cloud settled over the Little Brown House. And one day Badgertown heard the news: "Joel Pepper is took sick with th' measles, and he's awful bad."

"I don't believe it," said Mr. Atkins, turning off with the jug he was filling from the big barrel of molasses for a customer, "that boy can't be sick."

"Well, he is," declared the customer. "Look out! Th' 'lasses is all a-runnin' over th' floor!"

"Thunderation!" The storekeeper jumped back and picked his foot out of the sticky mess, while he thrust the jug under the bunghole. "Hold your tongue, Timothy Bliss! Joel Pepper was in here yist'day—no, that was David bringin' back th' coats Mis Pepper had sewed. 'Twas day before yist'day Joe came runnin' in, smart as a cricket. He warn't goin' to have no squeezles, he said, No, Sir!" Mr. Atkins turned off the spigot sharply and set the jug on the counter with a thud.

"He's got 'em now at any rate," said Mr. Bliss solemnly. "An' Mis Beebe says they wouldn't wonder ef he was goin' to die."

"*Die!*" roared the storekeeper. "Ain't you 'shamed, Timothy Bliss, to stand there sayin' sech stuff! Joel Pepper can't die." Yet Mr. Atkins gripped the counter with both hands, while everything in his store seemed to spin around.

"Mis Beebe said—standin' in th' door o' th' shoeshop as I come by," began Mr. Bliss, leaning up against the counter.

"Don't tell me no more," interrupted the storekeeper, waving both sticky hands excitedly. "It's scand'lous startin' such tales." Then he rushed over to the small door connecting with his house. "Ma—Ma," he screamed, "Joel Pepper's awful sick with the measles!"

"You don't say!" Mrs. Atkins came to the top of the stairs, her sweeping cap on her head and a dust brush in her hand. "Oh, me, Oh, my!" she mourned. "What will Mis Pepper do now, with both of her boys took sick?"

"Well, she's got Davie," said the storekeeper, determined to get some comfort, and hanging to the newel post.

"Davie's so little." Mrs. Atkins sat down on the upper

stair. "He'd help all he could, but he's so little," she repeated.

"David's awful smart," said Mr. Atkins.

"I know it; they're all smart, them Pepper children, but Joel's so up an' comin', you can't think of Davie somehow as takin' hold o' things. Seth Atkins, you've got 'lasses all over your trousers!"

She ran down the stairs and peered anxiously at her husband's legs.

The storekeeper twitched away. "That's Timothy Bliss' fault. He scaret me so about Joe," and he darted back into the store.

"I'm goin' to help Mamsie." David stood in the middle of the kitchen, twisting his hands together anxiously. "I'm getting to be real big now, Mrs. Beebe," and he stood on his tiptoes.

"Bless your heart!" exclaimed old Mrs. Beebe, making gruel on the old stove, "so you be, Davie."

"And pretty soon I'll be as big as—as Joel." Then he swallowed hard at the sound of Joel's name.

"So you will—so you will," said Mrs. Beebe. "An' you help your mother now, Davie boy."

"Do I?" cried Davie. A little pink spot came on each cheek, and he unclenched his hands, for he wasn't going to cry now.

"To be sure you do," declared Mrs. Beebe, bobbing her cap at him. "Your ma told me yest'day she depended on you."

"Did she?" David ran over to clutch her apron, the pink spots getting quite rosy. "Oh, I'm going to do just everything that Ben and Joel did—I am, Mrs. Beebe."

"Well, you look out, you don't work too hard, Davie"—

Mrs. Beebe stopped stirring a minute and regarded him anxiously—"that would worry your ma most dretful. There that's done." She swished the spoon about a few times, then poured the gruel into a bowl. "Now, then, I'll give it to Ben."

"Oh, let me," cried Davie, putting up both hands eagerly.

"You're too tired—you've ben a-runnin' all th' mornin'," began Mrs. Beebe, yet her stout legs ached badly.

"I'm not tired," cried Davie, and in a minute he had the bowl and was going carefully up the loft stairs.

"Now that blessed child is just like the rest o' th' children," mused old Mrs. Beebe, sinking down in a chair. "Davie's quiet, but he get's there all the same."

And Davie's little legs "got there all the same" through the dark days when Joel went deeper and deeper into the gloom. And the Little Brown House people held their breath in very dread of the coming hours. And good Dr. Fisher lay awake every night after the day's hard work, going over and over in his troubled mind how he might save Mrs. Pepper's boy.

"Oh, dear me!" a voice broke in upon the woodshed where Davie sat on the chopping block. His legs ached dreadfully, but he wasn't thinking of them. He was awfully afraid he was going to cry after all, and he twisted up his small cheeks, and held his hands together oh, oh, so tightly!

"Just as I expected," Miss Jerusha Henderson put her head in, "all this talk about the Pepper children workin' to help their mother is just rubbish," she sniffed and came up to the chopping block; "there you set, you lazy boy, you."

"I'm not a lazy boy," said David, getting off from the chopping block. "Mamsie told me there wasn't anything to do now." His little cheeks burned like fire.

"Anything to do!" Miss Jerusha raised her long fingers

and waved them about. "Did I ever—and look at all this messy place! Why ain't you choppin' wood I sh'd like to know?"

"Mamsie told me not to do anything till she called me." His head ached dreadfully, and he wanted to run, but he stood his ground.

"If ever I saw a woman who spoiled her children, it's your ma," said Miss Jerusha, sniffing again. "It's no wonder she has trouble."

David swallowed hard, then he looked up into her snappy little black eyes. "I wish you'd go away," he said quietly.

"Of all the impertinent boys!" exclaimed the parson's sister, an angry flush spreading over her gaunt face. "Well, I'm not going, I can tell you that. And I shall come every day and do my duty by you, David Pepper."

"No," said David, "you mustn't come any more."

"And I am going to speak to your ma now and tell her what a naughty boy you are." Miss Jerusha picked up her gingham gown and went off on angry feet out of the woodshed.

David ran past her and up to the door of the Little Brown House. When she got there he was holding the latch with both hands.

"You get off that doorstep!" cried Miss Jerusha, now in a towering passion, and seizing his little calico blouse, "I declare I just ache to give you a whipping!" She raised one long hand threateningly. "You don't get any with that silly mother of yours. Get off that doorstep, I say! It's my duty to speak to your ma."

"You can't," said Davie stoutly, "because you can't get in." He gripped the latch tighter, and his blue eyes flashed just like Mother Pepper's black ones.

"Can't, hey?" Miss Jerusha's hard hand was laid not very

gently on David's little ones holding the old latch. Her other was raised threateningly. "Let go of that latch, or I'll box your ears."

Davie clung tighter than ever to the latch. Down came Miss Jerusha's hand on his small ear. An angry red spot was on her cheek, and she struck again.

"What's this—what's this?" Dr. Fisher came briskly up the path. The parson's sister turned suddenly, her hand falling to her side.

"This boy has been very naughty," she said, the blood rushing over her gaunt cheeks.

Dr. Fisher set his big spectacles straight, and regarded her keenly.

"He has sassed me by holding this door, an' I'm goin' in to see his ma."

"Davie's just right," said the little doctor. He turned to give an approving smile to him still clinging to the old latch.

"*Jest right!*" screamed Miss Jerusha, in a towering passion. "Do you know who I be? I'm Parson Henderson's sister."

"Yes, I know," said Dr. Fisher, "and I'm dreadfully sorry for the parson. I wish I could help him. But as for David here, he's got my permission to keep out anybody he wants to. Mrs. Pepper isn't to be worried by visitors."

"I shall report you to the parson," said Miss Jerusha, getting off from the flat stone.

"Yes, do," said Dr. Fisher, as she stalked down the path. Then he went into the Little Brown House to battle for Joel's life.

IV

Sunlight Through the Cloud

DEACON BLODGETT exclaimed, " 'Tain't no use, I can't set myself to work on nothin'," and then leaned helplessly against the barn door.

Mrs. Blodgett sighed. She was far beyond words. At last she threw her apron over her head. When she did that, the Deacon knew she was pretty far gone.

"Don't, Ma," he begged, "take on so. Hem!" He swallowed hard and smote one big hand across the other. " 'Twouldn't be so bad ef I c'd jest see David a-runnin' in to pile wood. Land! how smart that boy works to try to take Joel's place!"

"Don't speak of Joel, Pa," said Mrs. Blodgett in a muffled voice. "Mercy me, ef he sh'd die!"

"Joel ain't a-goin' to die," declared Deacon Blodgett stoutly, "don't you think it, Ma."

"I d'no," Mrs. Blodgett shook her head till the apron flapped dismally. "No mortal man c'd do more'n Dr. Fisher. Do look down th' road, Pa, an' see ef his gig is comin'."

"Dr. Fisher won't leave the Little Brown House today till

Joel's better," declared the Deacon, not moving; but his eyes roved anxiously up and down the thoroughfare.

"I wish you'd go over to Mis Pepper's, an' find out how Joel is," Mrs. Blodgett's voice came out in a thin little quaver from behind the apron.

The Deacon braced up firmer yet against the barn door. Then he said, "You better go yourself, Mother."

"Mercy!" ejaculated his wife with a shiver, "I'm about sick as 'tis now, I couldn't never face Mis Pepper— Oh, dear me!"

"Neither can I—an' all is, I'm goin' to work." Deacon Blodgett brought himself suddenly away from the barn door and strode off.

"Where you goin', Pa?" Down fell Mrs. Blodgett's apron from her head.

"Down to th' east paster," said the Deacon, not turning his head. "I can't stand still no longer an' think o' nothin' but that boy."

"Well, I ain't a-goin' to stay to home," declared Mrs. Blodgett. "Nobody to talk to but Mary Ann, an' she keeps harpin' on the Pepperses. I'll go down an' see Grandma Bascom."

So she tied on her bonnet with trembling fingers and hurried off. When she left the main road and struck the little lane that led down to Grandma's house, she stopped abruptly. "Oh, dear me! that's almost as bad as to go to Mis Pepper's, for Mis Bascom'll take on somethin' dreadful. My! what's that in th' bushes!"

A little crackling noise struck her ears, and one or two small branches stirred in the shrubbery alongside the road. There wasn't any wind to speak of, and Mrs. Blodgett paused in fright, her fingers on her lips; but being no coward, she marched up and shook the nearest bush.

"We don't want no tramps in Badgertown," she began. Then she burst out, "Why, *David Pepper!*"

There on the ground, his face grubbing into the grass, lay David squirming back and forth, his little hands clenched.

"You poor little creeter, you!" Mrs. Blodgett got down on the ground beside him and fairly gathered him up to her ample bosom. "You couldn't cry in the Little Brown House, an' so you've come out here. Poor lamb!"

"*Joel!*" 'Twas all that Davie was capable of.

"There—there—now you jest stop!" Mrs Blodgett spoke sharply, she was so scared for the sobs were shaking David from top to toe; but to stop was beyond him, so she laid him down on the grass.

"Now I'm jest goin' to your house an' see how things is, Davie. Then I'll come back an' tell you." She got up with difficulty and shook her calico gown free from the dirt and mold.

"Don't—don't!" screamed David, sitting up. "Oh, Mrs. Blodgett, *don't!*"

"Yes, I'm goin', Davie, an' you better come along of me." She held out her hand. "Your ma would want you to." "'Tain't half so bad as to let him stay here an' be scared to death in them bushes," she reflected.

"Would Mamsie want me to?" asked Davie, blinking at her through the tears that ran down his cheeks.

"She certainly would," declared Mrs. Blodgett. "Oh, my!" she cried, pricking up her ears. "Well, you wait here a minute. I'll come back for you."

She darted down the road, if such locomotion as she set up could be called darting, and presently she saw just ahead Dr. Fisher's old gig.

"Wait!" she tried to scream, but her tongue flapped up to the roof of her mouth and stuck there, as she panted on.

A farmer's boy in an old wagon coming around the corner thrust his fingers in his mouth and gave such a whistle that the little doctor thrust out his head.

"Lady wants you—she's a-runnin' fit to split," said the boy, pointing to the Deacon's wife pounding the dust up dreadfully at every step.

Dr. Fisher pulled up the old horse and hopped out of the gig.

"Good gracious, is that you, Mrs. Blodgett!" he exclaimed, hurrying to meet her.

The Deacon's wife was beyond speech, only being able to puff, her hand at her side and her face very red. So the little doctor began the conversation.

"Do you know where David Pepper is?" he asked anxiously.

That made Mrs. Blodgett find her tongue. "He's in them bushes," she said, pointing a shaking finger back down the road.

"Get in—get right in," said Dr. Fisher joyfully, taking hold of her fat arm and hurrying her to the gig, "and we'll get Davie—his mother's awfully worried about him."

Mrs. Blodgett had no chance to speak further until the gig was well under way for David's bush. "He don't look as ef Joel was worse," she said to herself, peering into the little doctor's face, "but I'm mortal afraid to ask."

"And now that Joel is going to get well," said Dr. Fisher, "why, we must get David home to his mother."

"*Joel goin' to git well,*" screamed Mrs. Blodgett, nipping his arm and turning her red face toward him.

"Yes, indeed!" declared the little doctor. "Praise God— Joel is saved to us all!" His face was very grave, but there was a light in the eyes back of the big spectacles that made the Deacon's wife say brokenly, "Bless th' Lord!"

"You may well say that," said Dr. Fisher brokenly.

"An' you too—I say bless you!" cried the Deacon's wife heartily, "for I guess th' Lord Himself can't do much ef folks won't help, too. Well, here's David in that bush there."

Dr. Fisher pulled up the old horse sharply, tossed the reins over the dashboard, and leaped out over the wheel.

"Hulloa, David!" he cried, pushing back the branches. "Well—well!"

Davie shivered and shrank back further under the bush.

"Oh, Joey is going to get well," said the little doctor cheerily, poking his big spectacles in under the branches.

David sprang up and threw his arms convulsively around the little doctor's neck.

"There—there—good gracious, you hug worse'n a bear, Dave," cried Dr. Fisher, bundling him up in his arms. "Now then, hop in with you!" He deposited him on the old leather seat and jumped into the gig beside him. "We must get you home to your mother before you can say Jack Robinson!"

If David's legs had a hard time of it when Joel was so sick, it was nothing to the way they had to run now that the dark cloud had passed over the Little Brown House.

Up and down the loft stairs where Joel tossed impatiently on the shakedown, Davie toiled to suit Joel's demands, who wanted something every minute. At last Mrs. Pepper interfered. "You musn't, Joey," she said. "Davie will be worn out."

"I've been sick," declared Joel, with an important air, "and Dave likes to get things."

"Yes, I do," said Davie eagerly, and lifting a pale face. "Do let me, Mamsie."

"There, you see," said Joel triumphantly.

"No," said Mother Pepper, "you mustn't send him over the stairs so much, Joey. He's very tired."

"I'm not much tired," said David, wishing that Mamsie wouldn't keep him from waiting on Joel.

"Yes, you are, Davie child. You've been Mother's boy all these weeks, and worked so hard."

A pink flush crept all over David's pale little face. He folded his hands and stood quite still.

"I'm Mother's boy, too," declared Joel, "ain't I, Mamsie?" He rolled over in the shakedown and fastened his black eyes on her.

"Indeed you are," declared Mrs. Pepper warmly, "both of you. But, Joel, I want you to remember how hard Davie has worked all the time that Ben and you have been sick. You must never forget that, Joey."

"I won't forget," said Joel, "and I want to get up." With that he gave his legs a fling and ran his toes out of bed.

"Oh, Joel," cried Mother Pepper in alarm, "you mustn't do that. It is the very worst thing that could happen to a boy with the measles—to get his feet cold." And she tucked him in again snug and tight.

"My toes are hot," said Joel, wriggling worse than ever and making the old comforter bulge up at the side.

"I'll sit on it, Mamsie, and hold it down," said Davie, getting on the edge of the bed. "There."

"Ow! No, you don't," declared Joel, bouncing up so suddenly that Davie slid off to the floor in a little heap.

"Joel—Joel!" reproved Mother Pepper.

"Well, he was sitting all over my toes," declared Joel, throwing his legs about, so that Mother Pepper had to tuck him all up again.

"Can't you pin him in, Mamsie?" asked Davie, picking

himself up to hover over the bed. "I will get your big shawl pin," and he started for the stairs.

"Hoh! I ain't going to be pinned in bed," cried Joel in a dudgeon. "Mamsie, make him come back," he whimpered. "Don't let him get the pin, I'll be good."

"See that you are then, Joel," said Mrs. Pepper. "Come back, Davie," as he was halfway over the stairs. "Joel is going to be a good boy, and keep his feet in bed."

"Oh, dear," grumbled Joel, flouncing all over the bed as David ran back, "I want Polly to come up and tell me a story."

"Polly can't come now," said Mrs. Pepper. There was a little white line around her mouth; she had her back to the bed, so that Joel could not see her face.

"She never comes," grumbled Joel. "Oh, I'm so hot. Why can't she come, Mamsie?"

"Can't I tell a story?" said David, coming close. "I will, Joey."

"Phoh!" Joel bent his black eyes on him. "You can't tell a story, Dave Pepper."

"Now I think Davie could tell a story very nicely," said Mother Pepper with a smile for David.

"I can try," said Davie, his heart beating dreadfully at the mere thought. But something had to be done to keep Joel from finding out that Polly's eyes were so bad.

"All right," said Joel ungraciously, "but I know it won't be good for anything."

"Now that's very nice of you, Davie, and I know it will be a good story, Joel." Mrs. Pepper gave a final tuck-in to the old comforter and went quickly downstairs.

"Get up on the bed, Dave," said Joel, beginning to feel better about the story, since Mamsie thought it would be a good one. So David hopped on the foot of the shakedown, and folded his hands, and wonder how in the world he was ever going to begin.

"Well, begin," said Joel impatiently.

"Well once," said David, "there was—"

"Yes," said Joel, "go on."

"There was—"

"You said that before."

"I know it. Well, there was—"

"Stop saying there was," cried Joel crossly.

"But there really was," insisted David, feeling sure that in another moment he should certainly jump off from the bed and fly over the stairs.

"Well, go on. Was what?" roared Joel, flinging back the comforter.

"Oh, you mustn't do that," cried David, sliding along on the bed, still feeling that he would rather do the tucking up than to tackle the story. "Mamsie said you must keep the clothes up," and he pulled the comforter up around Joel's neck.

"Go away," cried Joel, "and you can't tell a story any more than—than—an old hopper toad."

"I'm not a hopper toad," cried David, a little pink flush coming over his face.

"Yes, you are, Dave Pepper, a bad old hopper toad," insisted Joel vindictively, "and you don't know any story, you old hopper toad, you!"

David's face worked dreadfully. "I ain't—and I won't tell you any story." He got off from the bed and marched to the stairs.

"Oh, you must," cried Joel in alarm. A bad story was better than none. "You promised, and you've got to, or I'll call Mamsie, and tell her." He tossed off the old comforter again.

"Don't call Mamsie," cried Davie, hurrying back.

"All right," said Joel. Then he snuggled down in the bed and drew the long-suffering bedclothes up so that only his ears were sticking out. "Go on."

"Well," said David, climbing on the foot of the bed again and beginning very slowly, "Once there was—"

"Don't say that again," commanded Joel, sticking up his face from the folds of the comforter.

"A boy," said David hurriedly.

"How big was he?" asked Joel with faint interest. But it was just as well to get the age settled on in the beginning.

"Oh, about as big as—" David hesitated.

"Have him as big as me," said Joel, "and his arms as big," he thrust out one, "and his legs just as exactly as big," and he stuck out his foot.

"Oh, get back, Joe," cried David, frantically pushing up the bedclothes.

"Well, go on," said Joel, huddling down again.

"And this boy was going along one day—"

"What was the boy's name?" asked Joel suddenly.

"I don't know," said David helplessly.

"Don't know," Joel gave another kick to the clothes, and snorted, "Hoh!—you're a great one, Dave Pepper, to tell a story about a boy and not know his name."

"Well, it was—" David floundered helplessly, "Peter," he brought out finally.

"All right," said Joel, quite satisfied. "Now go on."

"Well, one day, he was going to school."

"Oh, don't have him go to school," whined Joel, dreadfully disappointed that a boy with such a satisfying name as Peter should waste time over books. "Make him going to shoot something—go—bang!" Joel threw up his arms, and screwed up one eye over an imaginary gun.

"All right, I will," said David accommodatingly. "Well
—but you must put in your arms, Joel."

"Go on," said Joel, huddling back in bed again, "go on,
Dave."

"Well, so Peter was going to school, and—"

"No—no," interrupted Joel, "he was going out to shoot
something; you said so, Dave."

"So I did," said Davie. "Well, Peter was going out to
shoot something, and—"

"What was he going to shoot?" demanded Joel.

"I don't know," said Davie helplessly.

"Oh, dear," grumbled Joel, "you don't know any story,
and you won't let Peter do anything," and he flounced all
over the bed.

"Oh, I will—I will," cried Davie in great distress. "I'll
let Peter shoot anything you want—I will truly, Joel."

"I'd rather have a bear," said Joel, stopping his tossing
about; "no, two bears. Make it two bears, Dave," he cried,
very much excited.

"I will," said David, thinking it just as easy to deal with
two bears, as long as he didn't know in the least what to do
with one. "Well, Peter was going to school—I mean out to
shoot something, and he went down the road—"

"With his gun over his shoulder," interrupted Joel.

"Yes, with his gun over his shoulder, and—and then he
turned down the corner."

"Don't have any corner," said Joel, "he went right
straight into the woods, *slap bang!*"

"Oh, yes," said David, "he went into the woods, and—"

"And have the bear—no, the two bears, come right now
this very minute."

"Yes," said David, "I will. Well, Peter went into the
woods, and he saw a big tree, and—"

"Ow! Don't have any tree," howled Joel. "Make a big hole for the bears to live in."

"I won't have any tree," said David.

"Peter heard an awful noise," and Joel growled fiercely, "and all of a sudden—gee whiz! and Peter looked up at a big pile of stones—no, let's have it a cave, an awful big cave."

"Yes, let's," said David, leaning forward in great delight from his post on the foot of the bed.

"Oh, such a big noise!" and Joel gave another growl, so much worse than the first that Davie gave a little scream, and a delightful shiver ran up and down his small back as Joel showed all his little white teeth, "and Peter put up his gun, for the two bears were looking out of the cave just like this—" Joel's black eyes were simply dreadful, they were so big, and he bounced up to sit in the middle of the bed.

"Oh, Joey," exclaimed David in great distress, "do lie down. Mamsie won't like it—oh, Joey!"

"Oh, dear!" Joel tumbled back. "I can't shoot the bears lying down."

"Well, you've got to," said Davie, tucking him up again, "for Mamsie would feel dreadfully to have you sit up. Now go on about the bears."

"Well, the two bears—no, one bear, jumped out of the cave first, and Peter put up his gun, and *Bang!* and over went the bear, and—"

"Oh, Joey!" cried Davie, in his post again on the foot of the shakedown, his blue eyes aflame, "did Peter kill the bear?"

"Yes, of course," said Joel, "just as dead as dead could be, and the other one, too—oh, no," he cried suddenly, "I'm going to have the other bear chew Peter."

"Oh, no, Joel," exclaimed David in horror. It was bad

enough for a boy to be kept from school and turned into the woods, without being chewed up by a bear. "Don't let him, Joe," he begged, clasping his hands in great distress.

"Well, he won't chew him *all* up," said Joel unwillingly, "only his legs and—"

"Oh, don't let the bear chew Peter's legs," cried David, leaning over close to Joel's face; "then Peter can't run away."

"I'm not going to have Peter run away," declared Joel, bobbing his black head decidedly. "Oh, yes, I will, too," he cried joyfully, clapping his hands. "I'll have the bear chew him a little on one leg, and then when Peter runs, the bear can chase him, and chew him on the other, and—"

"Joel," exclaimed David, with very red cheeks, "I think that bear is a bad old bear, and I don't like him."

"And then he can chew Peter all up, every teenty speck," cried Joel, with sparkling eyes. "Yes sir!" smacking his lips.

David tumbled quickly off from the bed and made for the stairs. "I'm not going to stay here if you have Peter chewed up," he declared, his blue eyes flashing.

"Dave, don't go." Up went Joel's head from the pillow, "I won't let him be chewed up. You can have that bear for your own. Don't go, Dave."

"Can I have him for my very own?" asked David, drawing near the bed.

"Yes, you may," promised Joel, swallowing hard, "if you'll come back."

"I shan't let Peter be chewed up," said Davie, clambering on to his old place on the bed once more, "and I shan't have him shoot the bear either."

"What will you do?" cried Joel in great astonishment.

"I'm going to have the bear go right into his hole again;

and Peter is going to school," said David with great decision.

"Oh, dear me!" Joel rolled over in terrible disappointment.

"He's my bear," said David, "you gave him to me, and—"

"Well, Peter isn't yours," said Joel, interrupting. "I'm going to have Peter, so there!"

"You may have the bear, and I'll take Peter," said David eagerly.

"You may. I don't want Peter—you won't let him do anything," said Joel. "I'd a great deal rather have the bear," he brought up in great satisfaction.

"Well, how nice that is, Davie, for you to tell Joel a story." Mother Pepper coming up the stairs to the loft, beamed approvingly at him.

David's cheeks got very hot. "I didn't tell the story," he said, and his face fell.

"He had Peter," said Joel quickly.

"Joel had two bears, and he told all about 'em," said David. "I didn't tell any story," he said again in a sorry little voice.

"And—and—he told about Peter, and he's going to school," Joel brought up with a wry face.

"Well, now," said Mother Pepper, "I think that must have been a very good story, and how nice that you two boys could tell it together."

V

On the Maybury Road

PHRONSIE crept up to the woodpile and peered around it. "Are you sick, Davie?" she asked in a soft little voice.

Davie jumped up, tossing the soft waves of light hair from his forehead. "I'm not sick a bit," he said.

"What makes you cry then?" persisted Phronsie, picking up her pink calico dress to clamber over the wood.

Davie turned his back and wiped his hot cheeks.

"I see some tears," said Phronsie in a distressed little voice; and stumbling on over the wood, a big stick slipped down against her toes.

David whirled around. "Don't come!" he screamed, making frantic dives over the woodpile. Away went two or three sticks, carrying Phronsie with them.

It was all done in a minute, and he had her out from under them. When he saw the blood on her little arm, his cheeks went very white and his legs wobbled.

"I've got to get Mamsie," he said, and rushed for the kitchen door.

"I'm going to get Mamsie," wailed Phronsie after him.

David lent speed to his feet and burst into the old kitchen were Polly was brushing up the floor.

"Phronsie's hurt!" he screamed. "Do come, Polly. I've spilled wood all over her." With that he rushed into the bedroom. "Mamsie—why where—"

Polly dropped the broom and flew out of doors, Davie at her heels.

"I can't find Mamsie," he panted.

"No, she's gone to Mrs. Blodgett's," Polly threw over her shoulder as she ran on. "Where *is* Phronsie? Oh, Davie, where is she?"

"By the woodpile," gasped David flying back of the shed.

But when they both got there, Phronsie was nowhere to be seen. To find Mamsie was her one thought, and since she knew that Mother Pepper was helping Mrs. Blodgett, why of course the hurt arm must get there as soon as possible. So she wiped up her tears on her small pink apron and trudged on past the lane that led to Grandma Bascom's and into the highroad.

Polly and David pulled the wood about with frantic hands, Davie saying all the while, "She *was* here. Oh, Polly, she was."

"Now, David," Polly seized his arm, "you must stop saying that for she can't be under here. See," she pointed to the sticks of wood sprawling about.

"But she *was* here," declared David, pawing wildly in and out among the sticks.

Polly darted off into the shed and hunted in each corner, calling Phronsie at every step. Then she ran out to comfort David, and to keep up the search.

"I declare to goodness, John, ef here ain't a little girl on th' road!"

A woman in an old high farm wagon twitched her husband's arm. "Do stop an' take her in. My sakes! ain't she a mite, though!" pushing back her big sunbonnet in order to see the better.

But before the old white horse lumbered up to the mite, down went Phronsie in a small heap in the middle of the dusty road.

"John—John!" screamed his wife. "Stop! You're a-runnin' over her!"

"Land o' Goshen! ain't I stoppin'?" roared her husband at her. The old horse almost sat down on his tired haunches at the sudden twitch on the reins. Then the farmer leaned forward and stared ahead down the road.

"Ef you ain't goin' to git out an' pick up that child, I am, John Brown. Sech a mortal slow man I never see," snorted his wife scornfully.

"An' sech a flutterbudget as you be, no man ever saw," Mr. Brown found time to say as he got slowly down over the wheel.

"Somebody's got to flutterbudget in this world," said his wife after him, as he walked slowly over to the small pink heap, "or everybody'd go to sleep. Bring her to me, John. Oh, do hurry! Bring her to me!"

"I want Mamsie," said Phronsie, as Mr. Brown leaned over her.

"Hey?" said the farmer, bringing his rough face with its stubby beard close to her little one.

"I'm going to my Mamsie," said Phronsie, her brown eyes searching his face, "and my foots are tired." With that she put up her arms.

"I'll be blowed!" exclaimed Mr. Brown. Then he saw the little bloodstained arm and he started back.

"Take me," said Phronsie, as she clutched his shaggy coat, "please, to my Mamsie."

"Where'd you git hurt?" asked Mr. Brown, with no eyes

for anything but the small arm with its bloody streak.

Phronsie looked down and surveyed it gravely. "My Mamsie will make it well," she said confidently.

"John—John!" screamed his wife, from the high wagon, "are you goin' to stay all day with that child in th' middle of the road, or do you want me to come an' look after her?"

"You stay where you be, Nancy," said Mr. Brown. "I don't know no more'n th' last one," this to Phronsie, "where 'tis you want to go to. But I'll take you there all th' same. Now, says I, hold tight, little un.""

"I will," said Phronsie in a satisfied little voice, putting her arms around his neck. So he bundled her up in his great arms and marched to the high wagon.

"Give her to me," cried his wife, hungrily extending her hands.

"I wouldn't ef I didn't have to drive," said Mr. Brown, as he clumsily set Phronsie on the broad lap. "She's hurt her arm. Be careful, Mother," as he got into the wagon and began to drive off.

"My soul an' body!" exclaimed Mrs. Brown, pausing in the hugging process now set up, to regard the little bloody arm. "Oh, how'd you get that?"

"I'm going to my Mamsie," announced Phronsie joyfully, and ignoring the injured arm. Then she laughed, showing all her little teeth, and snuggled against Mrs. Brown's big shawl.

"Ain't she too cunnin' for anythin'!" exclaimed Mrs. Brown. "Did you ever see th' like? But how'd you git hurt?" she demanded, turning to Phronsie again.

"It was the wood," said Phronsie, gravely regarding her arm again. "And I'm going to Mamsie."

"She keeps a-sayin' that," said Mr. Brown. "Now, how in thunder will we know where to take her?"

"Don't swear," said his wife.

"'Thunder' ain't swearin'," retorted Mr. Brown with a virtuous air. "I c'd say lots worse things."

"Well, git out and say 'em in th' road, then," advised his wife, "an' not before this child. Where'd you say you was a-goin'?" She bent her large face over the small one snuggled against her ample bosom.

"To my Mamsie," said Phronsie, so glad that at last she was understood.

The wrinkles in Farmer Brown's face ran clear down to his stubby beard, as he slapped one hard hand on his knee.

"Oh, yes—yes," said his wife, nodding her big sunbonnet.

"Don't pretend you understand her, Mother," Mr. Brown turned to his wife, "for you don't—neither of us do, no more'n th' dead."

"You let me be, John," said Mrs. Brown, "an' I'll attend to this child."

Farmer Brown whistled and looked off up to the clouds; perhaps something might come down to illuminate the situation.

"Now, where is Mum—Mam—whatever you said?" began Mrs. Brown, patting Phronsie's yellow hair.

"Off there." Phronsie pointed a small finger off into space.

"I see," said Mrs. Brown, nodding her sunbonnet again. The puckers were beginning to come in her face. Mr. Brown, taking his gaze off from the clouds, looked at her and grinned.

"Well, now let's see," said Mrs. Brown reflectively, and with a cold shoulder for the farmer, "Mamsie—"

"Yes." Phronsie gave another little laugh and wriggled her feet. It was so lovely that they understood her; and she was really on the way to her Mamsie.

"Let's see—now what road did you say you want to go to git to this—Mamsie?" began the farmer's wife, smiling encouragingly at her.

"Why, don't you know?" Phronsie lifted her head suddenly to gaze into Mrs. Brown's face. "Off there." Again she pointed to space.

"You keep still." Mrs. Brown thrust her elbow into the farmer's side, as she saw his mouth open. "You're more care than th' child. I'll find out—you keep still!"

"*Hem!*" said Mr. Brown loudly.

"And please have us get to Mamsie soon," begged Phronsie, beginning to look worried.

"Yes—yes," Mrs. Brown promised quickly. "Well, now let's see—how does Mamsie look?" she began.

"Why, she's my Mamsie, and—"

"*She?*" screamed the farmer's wife. "Oh, my soul an' body! I thought 'twas a house."

"Thunder!" ejaculated Mr. Brown. "Now we're in a fix, ef it's a woman. Th' Lord knows how we'll ever find her."

"Where'd you come from?" Mrs. Brown now found it impossible to keep the anxiety from running all up and down her big face. Phronsie put up her trembling little lips and pointed off, still into space.

"John," his wife burst out, "we are in a fix, an' that's th' solemn truth."

The farmer took off his old cap and scratched his head. "Well, anyway, we've got th' little gal, an' you've always wanted one, Nancy."

"Ef we can only keep her." Mrs. Brown hugged Phronsie hungrily to her breast. "Oh, my little lamb!"

"I want my Mamsie!" said Phronsie, nearly smothered. "*Please* take me to my Mamsie!" and she struggled to get free.

"Don't you want to go to a nice house?" began the farmer's wife in a wheedling way, as she set her upon her knees.

"There—there." Mr. Brown whipped out a big red handkerchief and wiped off the tears from the little face. "Ma, she's a-cryin'," he announced in an awful voice.

"There are chickens," said Mrs. Brown desperately, "and—"

"Are there little chickies?" asked Phronsie, as Mr. Brown gave her face another dab with the big handkerchief.

"Yes—yes, awful little ones," cried Mrs. Brown, "just as little as anythin', an' yellow an' white an' fluffy."

Phronsie clapped her hands and smiled between her tears.

"An' there's pigs, little ones," broke in the farmer, to hold all advantage gained, "an' you can scratch their backs."

Phronsie tore off her thoughts from the little chickens, yellow and white and fluffy, to regard the farmer. "Ooh! I want to see the little pigs," she cried, leaning over to look into Mr. Brown's face, "and I'm going to scratch their backs right off."

"So you shall—so you shall," he cried, "when you get to my house."

Phronsie's lip fell suddenly, and she flew back to Mrs. Brown's arms. "I want to go to the Little Brown House," she wailed, casting herself up against the kind breast.

"John, can't you let well enough alone?" scolded his wife. "She was took with the chickens. There, there, child, don't cry."

"She liked my pigs best," said the farmer sullenly. "G'long there!" slapping the leather reins down smartly on the back of the old white horse.

"I want to go to the Little Brown House," Phronsie wailed steadily on.

"Well, that's where you're goin'," said the farmer. He turned suddenly. "That's jest where we're a-takin' you to, the Brown house."

"Are you?" cried Phronsie, her wails stopping suddenly.

"Sure," said Mr. Brown decidedly. "Now, Ma, we'll take her home with us. We'll inquire all along th' road ef anybody knows who she is," he said in a low voice over Phronsie's head. "She'll be all right when she sees them pigs an' chickens."

"An' ef we can't find where she b'longs, why, we'll adopt her, an' she'll be ours," finished his wife, all in a tremble. "Oh, you sweet lamb, you!" She kissed Phronsie's yellow head.

Phronsie, quite contented now that she was on the way to the Little Brown House where Polly was and Mamsie would soon come, presently began to hum in a happy little voice, and the old white horse and big high wagon went jogging on over a short crossroad leading to Maybury, where the farmer and his good wife lived.

Meantime, Polly and Davie were having a perfectly dreadful time searching everywhere, even turning an old barrel, afraid that Phronsie had pulled it over on herself, and scouring every inch of the ground around the Little Brown House. Then Davie dashed off at top speed, down over the lane leading to Grandma Bascom's, sure of finding Phronsie there.

But Grandma, feeding her hens from a tin pan of potato and apple parings, shook her cap hard when Davie stood on his tiptoes and screamed into her ear all about Phronsie.

"Oh, the pretty creeter!" she mourned, and the pan in her hands shook so that it fell to the ground, and the hens clattered around and scratched and fought till every bit of the potato and apple skins was gobbled up.

Davie rushed off from the tangle of hens about Grandma's feet, with only one thought—to get to Deacon Blodgett's as fast as he could. And flying down the lane, he ran into the main road, just after the old white horse and big high wagon had turned the corner leading to Maybury, carrying Phronsie off to the Brown house.

"Whoa—there—Great Saint Peter!" shouted somebody at him. Davie was so blind with the drops of perspiration running down his face that he couldn't see, and besides, by that time his small legs were so used to running that they kept on, even after the young man in the top buggy had pulled up in astonishment.

"Ain't you ever goin' to stop?" roared the young man, leaning out of the buggy and staring at him.

"I can't," panted Davie, pausing a moment.

"What's th' matter? Goin' for th' doctor?"

"I'm goin' for Mamsie," said Davie, rushing on.

"Hold on! Who you're goin' for?" roared the young man.

"Mamsie," panted Davie, whirling around.

"I d'no what in th' blazes that is," the young man took off his cap and scratched his head. "Well, what are you goin' for, lickety-split like that! Come here, you boy!"

Davie came slowly up to the side of the buggy. Somehow a note of hope began to sing in his small heart that maybe the young man might help.

"I let my sister get wood spilled all over her," he said, his face working dreadfully, "and she's lost, an' I'm going to Mamsie."

"I can't make head nor tail of it at all," said the young man. Then he put on his cap, since scratching his head did no good. "Well, your sister's lost, you say?"

"Yes," said Davie, hanging to the wheel. "Oh, have you seen her, Mr. Man? She had on a pink dress—"

"Hey? Oh, thunder an' lightnin'!" he slapped his knee with a red hand, "was she a little gal?"

"Yes—yes," cried Davie, with wide blue eyes. "Oh, *have* you seen her, Mr. Man?"

"I think likely," said the young man, bending over till his face nearly touched Davie's hot cheek, "an' then again, mebbe I hain't. I've seen a little gal in a pink dress, but she may not be your sister. How big was she?"

Davie released his clutch on the wheel to bend down and measure where Phronsie's head would come if she stood there in the road before him, the young man leaning out to critically watch the proceeding.

"I b'lieve as sure as shootin' that's th' little gal." Then he whistled and slapped his knee again.

"Oh, Mr. Man, help me to find her!" Davie grasped the wheel once more and held on for dear life.

"Well, I can't as long as you hang on to that 'ere wheel," said the young man. "Now you hop in, and I'll catch up with that young one in three shakes of a lamb's tail."

Over the wheel went Davie, to sink down in a small heap on the old leather seat.

"Yes, sir—ee!" declared the young man again. "I seen her in Mis Brown's lap as sure as shootin'. It's lucky she's fell in such good hands. Well, I'll catch up with that old white plug of a horse. G'lang!" He whipped up, passing the turn in the road where Phronsie was being carried off in the high wagon on the "short cut" to the Brown house in Maybury.

VI

Back to Mamsie

"TH' BEEF's biled 'mos' to nothin'," said Mrs. Brown, sticking a long iron fork into the pot of corned beef, surrounded by bubbling heaps of cabbage. She had thrown off her sunbonnet on the old sofa in the sitting room, and hurried into the bedroom where she had deposited Phronsie, fast asleep, on the gay patched bedquilt.

"There, you sweet lamb, you!" Then she hurried out to see about the belated dinner.

"John," she called, as she ran out to the barn, "come, dinner's ready."

Farmer Brown turned as he was leading the old white horse to his stall. "Is she awake?" pointing with his thumb to the house.

"No," Mrs. Brown sped back to the kitchen.

"What'll we do with that little gal?" the farmer's face puckered all up with dismay as he reflected: "Nobody on th' road knows th' fust thing about her, an' I s'pose her ma's cryin' her eyes out." He slouched up to the kitchen door.

"I thought you was never comin'." His wife set the big blue platter with the corned beef and its generous fringe of cabbage on the table; then down went the dish of potatoes and the loaf of bread. "Th' beef's all biled to pieces," she said, getting into her chair.

"What beats me," said Mr. Brown, sitting down heavily and taking up the horn-handled carving knife and fork, "is, what are we to do with her." He pointed with carving knife to the bedroom.

"I d'no," said his wife; "do help out that beef. It's all biled to death," passing her plate.

"It will eat just as good," said the farmer, cutting off a scraggy strip and dishing up a generous spoonful of cabbage to go with it to the waiting plate. "Well, Nancy, I'm beat to know what we're goin' to do with her."

"Do stop talkin' about her," cried his wife. "She's asleep now. And I'm as nervous as a witch."

"I s'pose we might as well eat," said the farmer, helping himself liberally. "Mebbe we can decide what to do better after we have eat."

"I can't think why I didn't set that pot clear back on the stove," said Mrs. Brown in vexation. "I might 'a' known 'twould bile too fast when we went to Badgertown. I didn't s'pose we'd be gone so long."

"Well, ef we'd got home sooner we wouldn't 'a' come up with the little gal," observed the farmer philosophically, while his portion of beef and cabbage was going rapidly to its last resting place.

"What good will it do that we found her?" said his wife discontentedly. "We've got to give her up."

"Well, I s'pose so," said Mr. Brown slowly. "Hem! Ain't I ever goin' to have no tea?" he asked in an injured voice, looking hard across at his wife.

"Oh, mercy!" Mrs. Brown hopped out of her chair. "I don't wonder that I forgot th' teapot. Th' Angel Gabriel couldn't never remember anythin' on sech a mornin' as

we've had!" She whipped her husband's big blue cup off
from the dresser, bringing it back full and steaming hot.

"I guess th' Angel Gabriel hain't ever had much to do
with tea," said Mr. Brown, putting in a good spoonful of
brown sugar and all the cream that would get safely into
the cup. "He's got enough to do a-blowin' that horn o' his'n.
Well, don't worry, Ma. Do set down an' take it easy. Th'
little gal hain't got to go yet."

"But we've got to start after dinner about it." Mrs. Brown
played nervously with her knife and fork. Then she threw
them down on her plate, jumped up, and turned her back
on the farmer, dinner and all.

"My soul an' body!" cried Mr. Brown, his knife halfway
to his mouth. He stopped to stare aghast at her. "You hain't
never acted like this, Nancy."

"Well, I hain't never had nothin' like this to set me
goin'," said Nancy, her voice trembling. "To think that
child should 'a' sprung up today, an' I've always wanted a
little gal—"

Farmer Brown shook all over. Down fell the knife to the
kitchen floor. He glared all around the big kitchen as if
somehow that were to blame. Then he cleared his throat
two or three times. "P'raps they'll let us keep her, Nancy,"
he managed to get out at last.

But Nancy, sobbing in her apron, was beyond the sound
of comfort.

"You know as well as you set in that chair that they
won't," she sobbed. "Oh, dear, why did we find her—and
I want a little gal so!"

"*Hush!*—somebody's comin'," warned the farmer. Round
the corner of the house came two figures, and pretty soon
"*Rap—Rap!*" on the old door.

"Set down, Nancy," cried her husband; "for goodness

sake, all Maybury will think you an' me's ben quarreling!"

"They couldn't think that, John," cried Mrs. Brown in dismay, and hurried back to the dinner table.

"When they see you a-cryin', you can't tell what they'd think," said the farmer grimly, and taking his time about opening the door.

"I ain't cryin'," said his wife, wiping all traces of the tears from her large face, and sitting very straight in her chair, as she got her company face on.

"Oh!" Mr. Brown flung wide the big door. "How do, Hubbard." Then his eye fell on a very small boy with big blue eyes, who was crowding up anxiously, and, not waiting to be invited, was already in the kitchen and staring around.

"You must 'xcuse him," said young Hubbard, "he's lost his sister."

The farmer's wife jumped out of her chair and seized the boy's arm. "Don't look so; she's all safe here."

"I must take her to Mamsie," said Davie, lifting his white face.

"Yes—yes," said Mrs. Brown, while the old farmer and the young one stood by silently. "You come in here, an' see for yourself how safe she is."

Davie rushed into the bedroom and gave one bound over to the big bed. Phronsie was just getting up to the middle of it, and wiping her eyes. When she saw Davie she gave a little crow of delight. "I'm going to Mamsie," she announced, as she threw her arms around him.

"Yes," said Davie, staggering off with her to the kitchen.

"You're goin' to have your dinner first," said the farmer's wife in alarm. "Gracious me—th' very idea of goin' without a bite," she added, bustling about for more dishes.

"We can't," said Davie, struggling along to the door. "I must get her to Mamsie."

"Young man," roared Farmer Brown at him. "You set down to that table. Now, Ma, dish up some hot meat an' taters."

"And a glass of milk," said Mrs. Brown, hurrying into the pantry.

"I want some milk," cried Phronsie, hungrily stretching out her arms. So before David hardly knew how, there she was sitting on the big family Bible that Mr. Brown placed on one of the chairs before the dinner table. When she saw it was really and truly milk with a frothy top, she was quite overcome and sat looking at it.

"Drink it, little gal," said Farmer Brown, with a hand on her yellow hair.

Phronsie laughed a pleased little gurgle, and set her small teeth on the edge of the mug, drinking as fast as she could.

"Hulloa—hold up a bit," said the farmer, with a big hand on her arm. Phronsie's brown eyes over the cup edge turned on him inquiringly. "Go slower, little gal." Mr. Brown took the mug and set it on the table. "Th' milk will wait for you."

"It is nice," said Phronsie, beaming delightedly at him.

"So 'tis," said the farmer, wiping off the milk streaks from her face. "An' you shall have th' rest by an' by."

"Shall I?" asked Phronsie, looking at the mug affectionately.

"Sure," declared Mr. Brown.

Meantime the farmer's wife was having a perfectly dreadful time with David, who stood impatiently off by the door, his hand on the latch.

"For mercy's sakes!" she exclaimed, "do you set down an' eat dinner, Jed," to the young farmer, "an' p'raps th' boy will listen to reason an' eat some too."

"Now see here, young man," Farmer Brown stalked over

to David, as Jed Hubbard, nothing loath, slipped into his chair to tackle the corned beef and cabbage, "how d'ye s'pose you're goin' to git that little gal to your ma—hey?"

"I'm going to carry her," said David, "and we must go." He turned a pleading face up to the farmer.

"You carry her?" repeated the farmer. "Hoh! Hoh!" he threw back his head and laughed.

"Don't laugh at him, Pa," begged Mrs. Brown, piling on more food to Farmer Hubbard's plate; "he's awful distressed," as Davie begged, "Do let us go—Mamsie will—"

"You're a-goin'," Mr. Brown interrupted. "I shall take you an' th' leetle gal in th' wagon as soon as you've et."

"Will you really take us to Mamsie?" cried Davie, the color coming quickly into his white cheeks.

"Sure," promised the farmer heartily, as David flew into the chair that Mrs. Brown had dragged up to the table.

"Now get him a good plateful, Ma," said the farmer, getting into his own chair. "Land—I hain't worked so hard for many a day—whew!"

But although David had a "good plateful" before him, it was impossible for him to eat to the satisfaction of the good people, as he turned anxious eyes upon Farmer Brown and then to the door.

"I don't b'lieve he'll swaller enough to keep a crow alive," said Mrs. Brown in dismay. "Pa, wouldn't it be best to do up some vittles in a paper, an' he can eat on the way."

"I've come to the conclusion it would," said her husband grimly.

"An' I'll put in some cookies for th' little gal," said his wife, darting into the pantry to the big stone jar.

"An' I'll harness up," said Mr. Brown, going to the big door.

The young farmer looked up from his dinner. "You better take my horse, Mr. Brown," he said.

"Kin you spare her?"

"Yes—an' take th' buggy too. You can have it all as easy as anything. You an' me are such close neighbors, I can come over an' git it tonight."

"Now that's real kind," said Farmer Brown, going out.

"Th' buggy?" repeated Mrs. Brown, coming out of the pantry with the bundle of cookies. "Well, I'm goin', too, Jed. I don't b'lieve there's room for us all to set comfortable."

Jedediah looked her all over. " 'Twill be a close fit, maybe, but the wagon's so heavy. Must you go, Mis Brown?"

"Jedediah Hubbard," Mrs. Brown set down the cookies on the table and looked at him hard. "I ain't a-goin' to give up that little gal a minute sooner'n I've got to," she said decidedly. "An' I'm goin' to see her ma."

"All right, Mrs. Brown," and Jedediah returned to his dinner.

But when the starting off arrived, there was a pretty bad time—Farmer Brown protesting there wasn't "enough room to squeeze a cat in." Mrs. Brown ended the matter by saying "There ain't goin' to be no cat," and getting in she established herself, Phronsie on her lap, on one half of the leather seat of the top buggy.

"Where's the boy goin' to set?" demanded her husband, looking at her.

"I d'no about that," said his wife, wrapping her shawl carefully around Phronsie. "Yes, you can carry the cookies, child. Menfolks must look out for themselves," she said coolly.

"It's all very well for you to set there an' tell me that," said Farmer Brown in a disgruntled way as he got in over the wheel, "but then, you're a woman."

"Yes, I'm a woman," said Mrs. Brown composedly. "Oh, th' boy can set on a stool in front. Jed, just bring out that little cricket from th' settin' room, will you?"

David, with the paper bag containing slices of corned beef between pieces of bread, not caring where he sat so long as he was on the way with Phronsie to Mamsie, settled down on the cricket that young Mr. Hubbard brought. Then he looked up into the young farmer's face. "Goodby," he said, "and thank you for bringing me here."

"Oh, good-by, youngster," said Jedediah, wringing a hand that tingled most of the way home. "Well, I hope to run across you again some time. If you ever lose your sister, you just call on me."

"We aren't ever going to lose Phronsie," declared David, bobbing his head solemnly, as the top buggy and the young farmer's horse moved off.

Mrs. Brown didn't utter a word all the way to Badgertown except "How d'ye s'pose Jedediah ever found that we had the little gal?"

"Let Jed Hubbard alone for findin' out anythin'," said Farmer Brown. He was so occupied in gazing at Phronsie, carefully eating around the edge of each cooky before enjoying the whole of it, that the smart young horse went pretty much as he pleased. Finally Mr. Brown looked down at Davie on his cricket.

"Ain't you ever goin' to eat your dinner, young man?" he said. "Ef you don't we'll turn an' go back again," he added severely.

"Oh, I will—I will," cried Davie, who had forgotten all about his dinner in his efforts to measure the distance being overcome on the way home to Mamsie. And he unrolled the paper bundle.

When it was all exposed to view, the corned beef smelt so good that he set his teeth in it, and gave a sigh of delight.

Farmer Brown winked across to his wife over Davie's head and presently the bread, and even a cold potato well sprinkled with salt, disappeared, and only the empty paper lay in Davie's lap.

"Throw it out in th' road," said Farmer Brown, well satisfied that the dinner was at last where it should be.

"Oh, no, no," said David, holding the paper fast.

" 'Tain't no good—throw it out, boy."

"Mamsie wouldn't like me to throw papers in the road. It scares horses."

"Sho—now!" Farmer Brown pushed up his cap and scratched his head. "I guess your ma's all right," at last he said.

When the Little Brown House popped into view, David flew around on his cricket excitedly. "There 'tis!"

"I see it," said Farmer Brown. "Set still—we'll be there in a minute."

"It's my Little Brown House," cried Phronsie, trying to slip out from Mrs. Brown's lap.

"Oh, you lamb—do wait. Little gal, we'll take you there in a minute. Set still, child."

"And I see Mamsie—oh, I want my Mamsie!" cried Phronsie, struggling worse than ever, her little legs flying in her efforts to be free.

David stood straight, his head knocking the buggy top. "Polly, we're coming!" he shouted.

"Hold on—don't you jump!" roared the farmer, catching his jacket, as Polly dashed up to the buggy and ran along by its side, the brown waves of hair flying over her face.

"Mamsie!" called Phronsie, leaning as far as she could from Mrs. Brown's lap, "see my arm," as Mrs. Pepper drew near, and she held it up with its bandage soaked in opodeldoc that the farmer's wife had tied on.

"*Whoa!*" Farmer Brown brought the Hubbard horse up with a smart jerk. "You might as well git out here," he said, "for I'll never keep you two in this buggy till we git to th' house."

"I never can thank you," Mother Pepper was saying, as the farmer's wife got heavily out of the buggy, "for all your goodness."

Mrs. Brown's mouth worked and she tried to speak. "I wish—" she looked off to the Little Brown House, but she couldn't finish what she had been composing all the way along—"you'd let me have this little gal for a while, anyway; you've got so many children; and I haven't got one." So she only kept on wobbling her lips and twisting her hands.

"*Hem!*" Farmer Brown cleared his throat. "I'll come over an' git them two," pointing a rugged forefinger in the direction of Davie and Phronsie, "ef you'll let 'em come over an' pass th' day with us some time."

"He's got chickies," said Phronsie, raising her head from Mrs. Pepper's arms.

"And pigs," said Farmer Brown, "little uns—don't you forgit them."

"And dear sweet little pigs—oh, Mamsie, and I am going to scratch their backs."

"An'," Farmer Brown whirled around on David, "this young man's comin', sure! He's a right smart boy, an' I've took a fancy to him."

"They shall go," said Mrs. Pepper with a bright smile. "And Phronsie will never forget you, dear Mrs.—"

"Brown," said the farmer promptly, seeing his wife couldn't speak.

"No, she will never forget you, dear Mrs. Brown." Mother Pepper got hold of the big hand, twisting its mate.

The farmer's wife clutched it. "You see, I always wanted a little gal," she whispered close to Mrs. Pepper's ear.

Then Mother Pepper did a thing the children had never seen before. She leaned forward and kissed the large face.

"We must be goin'," declared Farmer Brown, whipping out his big red handkerchief to blow his nose loudly. "*Hem!* Come, Ma."

"Did Mamsie cry when we didn't come home?" asked David anxiously, as they all filed off toward the Little Brown House.

"No. Oh, I'm so sorry you worried, Davie," cried Polly. "You see I ran down to Deacon Blodgett's to tell Mamsie, and Mr. Atkins saw me go by, and he called out that a Mr. Hubbard had you in that very buggy you came home in."

"Yes, he did," said David.

"And he said he knew you were going after Phronsie."

"Yes, we did," said David.

"And then he told us that a man in the store said that some folks over at Maybury—real good folks, had Phronsie in their wagon, and—"

"Yes," said David, "they did."

"So we knew everything was all right," Polly ran on gaily, "and Mamsie said all we had to do was to wait patiently, and not stir Ben and Joel up where they were at work in Deacon Blodgett's south meadow, so—"

"Polly," cried Davie excitedly, as they ran into the Little Brown House, "I like that big Mr. Brown very much indeed."

VII

"Good-by, Children"

"I MUSTN'T cry again," said David to himself the next morning. He stopped a minute picking up the chips, before he threw them into the old basket. "Maybe I'll get to school some time and learn things."

Then he threw the chips into the basket until it was full enough to empty into the wood box behind the old stove in the kitchen.

"Mamsie," cried Joel, rushing in at dinnertime, " 'twasn't any fun piling wood at Deacon Blodgett's without Dave."

"Davie can't pile wood today, Joel," said Mrs. Pepper, "he had such a hard time yesterday going after Phronsie." She glanced over at him affectionately as she went into the pantry for the cold potatoes to fry.

David began eagerly, "Oh, Mamsie—" then he stopped when he saw her face.

"Oh, dear," grumbled Joel. "It's awful hard work piling wood without Dave. Isn't dinner ready?" he asked impatiently.

"It will be in a few minutes," said Mrs. Pepper, slicing

the potatoes over by the table. "See, Joey, I'm going to give you fried potatoes today."

"Oh, goody!" exclaimed Joel, rushing over to the table and smacking his lips. "See, Dave, fried potatoes!"

David tried to smile as he turned off.

"And I shall fry them brown," said Mrs. Pepper, cutting the last potato into thin strips.

"She's going to fry 'em brown," announced Joel in great excitement, and running over to pull David's jacket, "real crispy brown, so they'll crack in your teeth. Won't you, Mamsie—really crispy, cracksy brown," deserting David to rush over to the table again.

"Yes," said Mrs. Pepper, smiling at him, as she went over to the stove to set on the frying pan. "Where's Ben? It's time that he was here."

"I forgot," said Joel, a flush spreading over his round cheeks. "Deacon Blodgett said Ben wouldn't come home."

Mother Pepper paused with the frying pan in her hand. "Did Deacon Blodgett say why?"

"They're going to take something to eat in a basket," said Joel, beginning to look very injured, "and they wouldn't take me. They told me to run home and tell you."

"Oh, Joey, and you forgot a message," said Mrs. Pepper reprovingly.

"I didn't mean to," said Joel, hanging his head.

"Didn't mean to doesn't excuse such a thing," said Mrs. Pepper. Then she set the frying pan at the back of the stove and stood quite still.

"Mamsie—I didn't," cried Joel, running over to hide his head in her gown, "I truly didn't," he howled.

"No, he didn't mean to," echoed David, drawing near in great distress.

"I know, Davie," said Mrs. Pepper, stroking Joel's stubby

black hair as he burrowed in her gown, "but it is a very bad thing to forget a message."

"I won't ever do it again," whimpered Joel, his brown hands holding fast to her gown.

"I hope not, Joel." Then she glanced over at the thin slices in the dish on the table. "Ben does like fried potatoes so much! That's the reason I was going to have them today."

"He can have mine," said Joel, twitching his head away from Mother Pepper's gown, and not looking at the potato dish, for his mouth watered dreadfully.

"And give him mine," said Davie, hurrying over to Mrs. Pepper.

"No, children, there is enough for all, and I will fry some for Ben at another time. Run down and see if Polly and Phronsie are coming from the store."

"Oh, dear, my legs are tired," said Joel crossly, and tumbling on the kitchen floor, he waved them in the air.

"I'll go—I'll go," said Davie, running to get his cap.

"No," said Mother Pepper. "You are not to go, Davie."

"Dave wants to go," said Joel, rolling over to look at her with his black eyes.

"Davie is very tired since yesterday," said Mrs. Pepper. "Get up, Joel, and go to the gate at once."

"Polly's always late," grumbled Joel, getting up to his feet.

"Polly is never late," said David stoutly. "She's always and ever here," and his face got very red.

"There—there, boys," said Mrs. Pepper. "Run along, Joel."

"Mamsie," David ran over to her as the big green door banged, "I'm not tired. Please let me help about things."

"You must be tired, Davie," Mrs. Pepper beamed affectionately at him, "and it won't do for you to run your legs off for I depend so much on you."

David looked down at his legs. Then he straightened up. "Do you really depend on me, Mamsie?" and the color ran all over his little cheeks.

"Indeed I do," said Mother Pepper heartily. Then she glanced up at the clock. "Polly and Phronsie ought to be here."

"They're coming," shouted Davie gleefully, and rushing to the big green door, he swung it wide. In jumped Joel, swinging the molasses jug, and after him Polly and Phronsie.

"Whoop!" screamed Joel, "isn't dinner ready? We're going to have fried potatoes," he announced to Polly.

"Fried potatoes!" exclaimed Polly in astonishment. Then she ran over to the old stove. "Oh, Mamsie, *fried potatoes!*" wrinkling up her nose at the sizzling in the old frying pan.

"I like it," said Phronsie, clutching a little paper bag; "let me smell it, Polly, do!" standing on her tiptoes.

"I thought Ben was coming home to dinner, and he does so like fried potatoes," said Mrs. Pepper in a low voice, as she turned the slices.

"Isn't Ben coming to dinner?" asked Polly.

"No—hush, Polly!" with a glance over at Joel, coming out from the pantry where he had put the molasses jug. "Ben's gone somewhere with Deacon Blodgett. Now hurry and get on Phronsie's eating apron."

"Joel was awfully good—he took the molasses jug from me," said Polly, tying on Phronsie's checked eating apron.

"I'm glad he thought to do it," said Mother Pepper with a smile. "Now sit down, children, the potatoes are done."

"And Mr. Atkins gave Phronsie a whole lot of pepper-mints," said Polly, when the meal was half over and the plates were scraped clean from all trace of potato slices.

"Yes, he did," said Phronsie, bobbing her yellow head, and taking off her gaze from the dish where the delightfully brown crackly things had been. When she had been obliged to relinquish her little paper bag, after the eating apron was on, she had insisted that it should be kept in her lap. So now she patted it lovingly.

"Oo! Peppermints!" screamed Joel. "Let's see, Phronsie," and he hopped out of his seat.

"No, no, Joey," reproved Mother Pepper.

"She said peppermints," said Joel, slipping into his chair.

"I will give you some," said Phronsie, with another little pat on the paper bag, "and Davie too," beaming across the table at him.

"Oh, now—give 'em now," cried Joel, thrusting out his hand, his black eyes sparkling.

But Mother Pepper said "No," again; that they must all wait till after dinner, and the dishes were washed up and the floor swept. Then if Phronsie wanted to divide her peppermints, why, that would be the best time of all.

So there was a merry bustle to see who would get through the part of the work that belonged to each one. And there was so much fun and laughter that anyone peering in at the Little Brown House would really have supposed that play was going on. At last it was all done, and Mamsie, over in the corner sewing on one of the coats that Polly had brought home in the bundle, declared that everything was very nice, and that she couldn't have done it any better herself.

"Now the peppermints," cried Joel, running away from the sink where he had been scrubbing his hands and polishing them on the big roller towel. "Now, oh, goody!" He ran over to Phronsie, still clinging to her paper bag.

"Let's all sit down on the floor," proposed Polly. So down the whole four of them got in a ring, each one drawing a long breath of anticipation.

"I'm going to give Mamsie one first," announced Phronsie, slowly beginning to open the paper bag.

"Let's see how many you've got, Phronsie," said Joel, putting out an impatient hand.

"Don't, Joey," said Polly, seizing his hand. "Let Phronsie open her own bag."

"I'll open my bag," hummed Phronsie, suiting the action to the word. Then she drew out a peppermint drop, a pink one.

"She's so slow," said Joel impatiently. "Turn up the bag, do, Phronsie."

"Let her do it her own way, Joey," said Polly. "They are her peppermints and we must all wait."

"Oh, dear!" groaned Joel, holding his hands tightly together, his black eyes on the peppermint drops.

It took some time in this slow way for Phronsie to get them all out. She hummed in a soft little voice as she drew them forth, one by one, and laid them in Polly's lap. There were nine—five white ones, and four pink ones.

"Aren't there any more?" cried Joel. "Let me shake the bag—maybe there's another one."

But all the vigorous shaking that Joel administered couldn't produce another peppermint drop.

"I shall give Mamsie this one," said Phronsie, picking up one of the pink drops and running over to Mrs. Pepper's chair. "Please open your mouth, Mamsie."

And the pink peppermint being dropped into Mother Pepper's mouth, Phronsie ran back in great satisfaction.

"Now me," cried Joel, sitting back on his heels and holding out his hands.

"Oh, Joey, Ben ought to have one saved for him," said Polly reprovingly.

"I shall give Bensie this one," said Phronsie, patting another pink drop.

"Ben wouldn't care," began Joel. Then he stopped, seeing Polly's brown eyes.

"That's fine," said Polly, smiling at Phronsie. "Now I'm going to put this peppermint drop up on the table, and you shall give it to Ben when he comes in."

"I shall give it to Bensie when he comes in," hummed Phronsie. "And this one is for you." She held up the third pink peppermint to Polly's mouth.

"Oh, no, child," said Polly, shaking her head. "You must save those other two for yourself, you know."

"Then there won't be any pink peppermints," broke in Joel, awfully disappointed, "and I wanted one."

"But Phronsie must save some for herself," said Polly. "She just loves pink candy."

"I will give you a pink one, Joey," said Phronsie, beginning to look worried as she saw his face.

"No, Joel, you oughtn't to," said Polly.

"But I don't want an old white one," grumbled Joel; "mean old white one."

"Then you'd better not take any," said Polly coolly. "No, Phronsie, you must keep those two pink ones. Mr. Atkins would want you to."

"Would Mr. Atkins want me to?" asked Phronsie doubtfully.

"Yes, of course," said Polly decidedly. "Now, Davie, it's your turn, as Joel doesn't want any."

"Oh, I do—I do!" screamed Joel. "I do want a peppermint, Polly Pepper."

"All right, then give Joel a white one, Phronsie, and then

one to Davie. There, now isn't that too splendid for anything!" as the two boys began at once to crunch their peppermints.

David suddenly stopped. "You haven't any, Polly."

"Oh, Phronsie is going to put a white one in my mouth," said Polly gaily, and opening her mouth very wide.

"I'm going to put one in your mouth, Polly," laughed Phronsie. So Polly bent her head down, and in went a white peppermint drop.

"Now says I—in goes one in your own mouth, Phronsie, —a pink one," and in it went.

There was such a crunching of peppermint drops going on that no one heard the big green door open, until Mrs. Pepper said, "Why, how do you do?" Then they all whirled around. There was Mr. Tisbett, the stage driver, whip in hand.

Immediately he was surrounded by all the four children, Joel howling, "Oh, I know you've come to take us in the stagecoach," and trying to get the whip.

"No, I hain't, not this time. You let my whip be, Joel," and in the midst of the clamor, he marched over to Mrs. Pepper. "I've come for you, ma'am."

"For me?" exclaimed Mrs. Pepper.

"Yes'm. Ef you don't stop, Joel Pepper, scrougin' for my whip, I'll—" Mr. Tisbett didn't finish, but he looked so very fierce that they all fell back.

"Hoh!" exclaimed Joel, "I ain't afraid of him," and he swarmed all over the big stage driver. "I'm going on the stage. Let me sit up in front with you, Mr. Tisbett," he begged.

"Yes'm," Mr. Tisbett tucked the big whip under his arm and turned his twinkling eyes toward Mrs. Pepper. "Old Miss Babbitt has broke her hip, and—"

"Oh, dear me!" exclaimed Mrs. Pepper, dropping her work to her lap.

"Fact; fell down th' cellar stairs; stepped on th' cat, an' away she went."

"Did she kill the cat?" cried Joel, tearing off his attention from the whip.

"Land o' Goshen! You can't kill a cat," declared the stage driver; "never heard o' such a thing in all my born days. Well, she set up a screechin' for you, Mis Pepper." He whirled around again to Mother Pepper's chair.

A look of dismay spread over Mother Pepper's face.

"She's in an awful bad fix," said Mr. Tisbett solemnly, "an' there ain't a neighbor that'll go nigh her. An' she keeps a-screamin' for you," and Mr. Tisbett leaned against the table.

"Polly, child, come here." Mrs. Pepper was already folding up her work.

"What is it, Mamsie?" as the group made way for her, the stage driver regarding them all with a relieved air as if responsibility of the whole affair was now off his mind.

"Do you think that you could get along without Mother for a little while?"

"For overnight?" asked Polly, in an awe-struck tone.

"Yes—can you do it, Polly? Poor old Miss Babbitt needs me; but I won't go if you can't manage without me." She rested her black eyes on Polly's flushed cheeks.

"You've never been away all night," began Polly, her cheeks going very white.

"I know it," said Mrs. Pepper, a little white line coming around her mouth. "It hasn't been necessary before. But now, it seems as if the poor old woman needs me. And you're a big girl, Polly, and then there's Ben to help you. Well, what do you say, child?"

"She's an awful cross old woman," said Polly grudgingly, not being able to look into her mother's face.

"That doesn't make any difference," said Mrs. Pepper. "She needs me."

Polly drew her shoe back and forth across the floor, still not looking into her mother's face.

"It shall be as you say, Polly," said Mrs. Pepper quietly. Meantime the stage driver had drawn off into a corner, the three children surrounding him.

"Oh dear me!" began Polly, with a long breath and twisting her hands; then she burst out, "Mamsie, I'm awfully wicked—but I don't want you to go."

"Very well," said Mrs. Pepper, "then I will tell Mr. Tisbett that I cannot go," and she began to get out of her chair.

"But supposing," said Polly, with a little gasp, seizing her mother's arm, "nobody had come to help you when my eyes were bad?"

"Yes, just supposing," said Mother Pepper, sitting quite still.

"And now it's worse, for she's an old, old woman."

"Yes, Polly."

"Then," said Polly, feeling sure she was going to cry, "I think you ought to go, Mamsie. Oh, dear!"

"Are you quite sure, Polly child?"

"Yes-es—yes, Mamsie!" and Polly swallowed her sob. When she found that she could do that, she threw her arms around Mrs. Pepper's neck. "Oh, Mamsie, I do want you to go—really and truly, I do, Mamsie—and I'll take care of the children."

"I know you will, Polly. Now that's my brave girl," and Mother Pepper gathered her up in her arms and held her close.

"And I'll pack the bag," said Polly, running off on happy feet to drag out the old carpetbag from the closet in the bedroom.

And pretty soon the kitchen was in a great bustle, the children getting in each other's way to help Mrs. Pepper off. And Mr. Tisbett kept saying, "Well, I never!" and slapping the big whip against his knees, making Joel drop whatever he was doing to run over at the enchanting sound. And Phronsie had to tie on Mamsie's bonnet—and everyone hurried to help her into the stage.

"Good-by," said Mother Pepper, as all four tried to get on the step for a last kiss. "Be good, children, and obey Polly!"

"I'm going to be good," declared Joel stoutly.

"I'll try," said David.

"Let me tie your bonnet again," said Phronsie, with pleading hands.

"Oh, Phronsie, you can't tie it again," said Polly. "Mr. Tisbett has got to go," as the stage driver up on the box was cracking his whip impatiently. "You can kiss Mamsie once more."

"I can kiss my Mamsie again," said Phronsie, as Polly held her up.

"Good-by, children," said Mrs. Pepper to them all, as the big stage lumbered off. But her last smile was for Polly.

VIII

"Old Father Dubbin"

THE four little Peppers went in and shut the big green door.

"I want my Mamsie." Phronsie stood still in the middle of the kitchen floor.

"So do I," howled Joel.

Davie began, but stopped at sight of Polly's face.

"Now see here," cried Polly, running over to throw her arms around Phronsie, "we must all be good. We promised Mamsie, you know."

"I want her back," cried Joel in a loud voice, as Phronsie wailed steadily on.

"How would you like to play 'Old Father Dubbin'?" cried Polly in a shaking voice. "Wouldn't that be just too fine for anything!"

"Can we really?" cried Joel, his shouts breaking off suddenly.

"Yes," said Polly. "Now, pet, we are going to play 'Old Father Dubbin.' Don't you want to, Phronsie?"

Phronsie showed her little white teeth in a merry gurgle. "I do want to play it ever so much, Polly," she said, smiling through her tears.

"Hurrah! Hurrah!" screamed Joel, hopping about. "Come on, Dave, we're going to play 'Old Father Dubbin!' We haven't played it forever and ever so long," he added in an injured tone.

"Of course not," said Polly, bustling about. "Now, boys, come and help me get ready."

No need to tell them this, as they scampered after her.

"Old Father Dubbin" was saved, since Polly made up the game, for very special occasions like the present when it was absolutely necessary for the children to be diverted. So now the kitchen rang with the noise, and they all spun around till tired out, for of course the one idea was to keep everybody from a chance to cry.

At last Polly looked up at the old clock. "Oh, my goodness!" she exclaimed, brushing her brown hair out of her eyes. "We've got to stop. We can't play all the time. Dear me! I haven't got a bit of breath left."

"I have," declared Joel, "and we haven't played more'n half of all the time. Don't stop, Polly—don't stop!" He came whirling up to her.

"Don't stop," echoed Phronsie, dancing up. "I want 'Old Father Dubbin' some more."

"I very much wish," said Davie with red cheeks, "we could play it again, Polly."

"No," said Polly decidedly, "it's five o'clock, and we must all set to work now. Besides, Ben will get home soon."

"Oh, dear!" grumbled Joel. "What'll we work on, Polly?"

"Well," said Polly, "you and Davie can go and chop some kindlings for tomorrow morning."

"We're always chopping kindlings," said Joel peevishly.

"Of course," said Polly, in a cheery voice, "because we're always wanting them. Now go along, boys. I must sweep up, for we've made such a dust playing 'Old Father Dubbin,' " and she dashed off after the broom.

"And I'm going to sweep up, too," cried Phronsie, running over to the corner where her little broom was kept behind the wood box.

"Come on, Dave, we've got to chop those old kindlings," said Joel gloomily, going over to the door.

"I'm going to bring in a lot," said Davie, spreading his arms wide.

"I'm going to bring in enough for two hundred—no, five hundred mornings," declared Joel, as they ran out to the woodshed.

"Now, Phronsie," said Polly, when the sweeping up was all done and the chairs placed back neatly against the wall, "I think you and I better set the supper table. Ben will be here soon, you know." She gave a long sigh and gazed out of the window. Oh, if Ben would only hurry and come! It was getting dark, and the hardest hour of all the day to have Mamsie away was drawing near.

"Bensie will be here soon," hummed Phronsie, running over to help Polly lay the tablecloth.

"Yes," said Polly. "Now, that's a good girl, Phronsie. You see—"

"I've got the most," cried Joel, staggering in at the doorway, his arms full of all sorts and sizes of sticks. "Whickets! See me, Polly!"

"Oh, Joey, I don't want to see you when you say such words," said Polly reprovingly.

"I won't say 'em any more. Now look—look!" Joel swelled up in front of her, and brandished his armful.

"Oh, my!" exclaimed Polly, "what a nice lot! And Davie, too! Dear me, how you two boys do help!"

"I haven't got so much," said David, drawing slowly near with both arms around his kindlings.

"His sticks are better than mine," said Joel critically, as the boys stood before Polly.

"Yes," said Polly, her head on one side to view them the better. "I believe they are, Joel. Well, it's a nice lot altogether, anyway. Now put them all in the wood box."

"Now what shall we do?" asked Joel, fidgeting about, the kindlings all dumped in the wood box, and going over to Mother Pepper's big calico-covered chair, his round face very sober.

"I believe," said Polly meditatively, "we'd better light the candle—it's growing dark."

"Why, Polly Pepper! Light the candle!" exclaimed Joel. "Mamsie wouldn't light it so early."

Phronsie stopped suddenly in putting her blue and white plate on the table. "I want my Mamsie," she said soberly. Then she sat down in a little bunch on the floor and put her head in her lap.

"Oh, dear me!" cried Polly in dismay. Would Ben ever come! "I wonder if you don't all want me to tell you a story."

"Oh!" screamed Joel and David together, "we do—we do!" running over to her.

"Well, I can't tell a story while Phronsie is crying," said Polly, at her wit's end what to do next.

"Phronsie—stop crying!" Joel rushed over and shook her pink calico sleeve. "Polly can't tell a story while you're crying. She won't stop," he announced wrathfully.

For Phronsie kept on in a smothered little voice, "I want my Mamsie."

"Phronsie," Davie kneeled down on the kitchen floor beside her. "Please stop. Polly wants to tell a story. You'll make Polly sick if you don't stop crying."

Up came Phronsie's yellow head, and she wiped off the tears with one fat little hand. "Do I make you sick, Polly?" she asked, in a tone of deep concern.

"Yes, I think I shall be," said Polly gravely, "if you don't stop crying."

"Then I will stop," said Phronsie brokenly. "I don't want you to be sick, Polly. Please don't be."

"Now if ever there was a good child, it's you, Phronsie," cried Polly, seizing her to smother the little face with kisses. "Well, come on, boys, we must sit around the fireplace, and I'll tell you a story."

"There isn't any fireplace," said Joel, as Polly led the way over to the stove.

"Well, I'm going to pretend there is," said Polly, getting down on the floor in front of the stove, "and a splendid fire, too. My! don't you hear the logs crackle, and isn't this blaze perfectly beautiful!" and she spread out both hands.

"You're always pretending there are things that ain't there," grumbled Joel.

"Of course," said Polly gaily, "that's the way to have them."

"I think the blaze is beautiful, too," declared Davie, throwing himself down by her side and spreading his hands.

"Well, I guess I'm going to have some of the blaze," said Joel, in an injured tone, and he crowded in between Polly and David.

"Well now, Phronsie, put your head in my lap," said Polly. But she turned a cold shoulder to Joel.

Joel fidgeted about. "Dave, you can sit next to Polly."

"That's right," Polly flashed him a smile over Phronsie's yellow head.

"You may have the place," said Davie, trying not to want it very much.

"I'll tell you what," said Polly, "how would it do for each of you to have the place half of the time, and I'll tell you when to change?"

A smile ran over David's face.

"All right," said Joel, folding his little brown hands. "Now begin."

"Well, now, I'm going to tell you about—" said Polly.

"Oh, the circus story!" shouted Joel wildly. "Do tell about the circus story, Polly."

"Do you want the circus story, Davie?" asked Polly.

"Say yes, Dave. Do say yes," said Joel, nudging him.

"Yes, I do," said Davie in great satisfaction.

"And you'd like to hear about all the animals, Phronsie, wouldn't you?" asked Polly, bending over the yellow head in her lap.

"Polly," asked Phronsie, lifting her head in great excitement, "is that about the dear, sweet little monkey?"

"Yes, Pet," said Polly, "it is."

"Then," said Phronsie, clapping her hands, "I should like to hear about it very much indeed. Please begin right straight off, Polly," and she laid her head down in Polly's lap again.

"Well, you see," began Polly—would Ben never come!

"Don't say 'you see,'" interrupted Joel impatiently; "do tell about the animals, and have a bear—no, two bears—"

"You're always having a bear," said Polly, with a little laugh. "Well, there were lots of bears in this circus I am going to tell you of."

"How many?" demanded Joel.

"Oh, fifty," said Polly recklessly.

"Whickets!" cried Joel in amazement.

"Now, Joel, I can't tell any story if you're going to say such naughty words."

"I won't—I won't," cried Joel in alarm at losing the story. "Were there really fifty bears, Polly?"

"Yes," said Polly, bobbing her brown head. "And the

circus man said he was thinking of buying two more."

"Oh, dear me!" cried Joel, quite overcome and snuggling down against her arm. "Well, go on."

"Well, there was a hip-hip-pot-amus," Polly finally brought the whole out with great pride.

"Yes, yes," said Joel.

David clasped his hands in silent rapture, and kept his gaze on the black stove that was a crackling fire on the hearth.

"And a rho-do-den-dron," added Polly, "and—"

"What's a rho-rho-do—what you said?" interrupted Joel, his head bobbing up again.

"Oh, a great big creature," said Polly.

"How big?" demanded Joel.

"Oh, my goodness—I can't ever tell how big he was," said Polly.

"I want to know how big he was," grumbled Joel. "So big?" he spread his arms wide.

"Oh, dear me!" cried Polly, with a little laugh. "Why, that isn't anywhere near as big, Joey Pepper, and he splashed into the water, and—"

"Where did he splash into the water?" cried Joel. "Say, Polly, where did he?"

"Why, there was a pond next to the circus tent," said Polly, going on wildly, her gaze on the window to see when Ben came around the corner of the Little Brown House.

"As big as the pond over at Cherryville?" demanded Joel.

"Yes, just as big as that," said Polly, willing to make it any size.

"Dave," cried Joel, poking his face over David's shoulder, "it was just like that great big pond over at Cherryville. Only Mr. Tisbett wouldn't let us go near it," he said resentfully; "he wouldn't, Polly, when he took us over on the stage. Well, go on," and he threw himself back against Polly once more. "Make him splash, and splash, that great big thing. What was his name, Polly?"

"Rho-do-rho-do-den-dron," said Polly, wishing she never had seen the picture in the animal book on Mrs. Blodgett's center table. "Well, now, it's time for you and Davie to change places, Joel. Why!"

"Hulloa! So you've got a rhododendron, Polly."

"Oh, Ben!" every one of the children jumped to their feet.

"We've been playing 'Old Father Dubbin,' " announced Davie.

Ben choked off what he was going to ask, "Where's Mamsie?" If "Old Father Dubbin" had been played, something pretty bad must have happened, for Polly to rescue the Little Brown House from gloom with that game. "Well, now," he said, "I suppose we've got to have that story finished."

"Yes, yes, we have," howled Joel, dancing about. "Go on, Polly, do," and he flopped down in front of the stove and thrust out his hands. "There's a big fire on the hearth," he said to Ben.

"And hear the logs crackle," said Davie, sitting down by his side and spreading his hands, too.

"Oh, I see," said Ben gravely. "Now come on, Phronsie, and we'll hear the rest about that wonderful rhinoceros," and he sat down, pulling her into his lap.

"No, no, that wasn't his name," contradicted Joel, " 'twas —oh, what was it, Polly?" and he wrinkled up his face.

" 'Twas what Ben said," Polly hung her head.

"Your name is prettier than mine, anyway, Polly," said Ben. "Well, now, let's hear the rest of the story."

So Polly, quite happy now that Ben was actually there,

ran her arm in his, and launched into such a merry account of what that rhinoceros was capable of that even Joel was satisfied and David wasn't conscious of breathing.

A gentle pull brought Polly to suddenly. "Tell about my dear, sweet little monkey, do, Polly," begged Phronsie.

"To be sure—how could I forget you?" cried Polly remorsefully.

"Oh, I don't want a monkey," screamed Joel. "We can have him any day. Do go on about that—that—"

"See here, Joe," Ben gave him a small pat on his back, "it's time to rest that rhinoceros. He's awfully big, and he gets tired easily."

"Well, then, go on about the monkey," cried Joel.

"I'm going to have my dear, sweet monkey now," whispered Phronsie in Ben's ear.

"Yes, I know," Ben whispered back. "Well, go on, Polly."

So the monkey went through all the antics that belonged to one, and a good many more that hadn't anything to do with a monkey at all.

At last Ben looked up at the old clock. "Whew! Well, Polly Pepper, I should say it was time for supper!"

At that they all jumped up, and in the scuffle to get to the table first, Polly drew Ben aside. "Mamsie's gone to old Miss Babbitt's," she whispered. "Mr. Tisbett came for her. Miss Babbitt has broken her hip."

"Whew!" said Ben again.

"And how shall ever we get the children to bed," said Polly, in a distressed little voice, "without Mamsie?"

Ben looked all around the old kitchen with a sober face. "Same's you've done all the afternoon—keep 'em busy."

"We can't play 'Old Father Dubbin' again," said Polly. "We must save that for next time when things are bad."

"That's so," said Ben. "Then it must be blindman's buff, or puss in the corner, I suppose."

"What are you whispering about?" cried Joel, coming up curiously. "You're always getting off into a corner and whispering things."

"Well, that's because we can't talk unless we do get into a corner. You're always poking around so, Joe," said Ben. "Come on now, all hands to supper!"

He swung Phronsie up to his shoulder and then into the chair that he had made high enough for her by nailing a board across two strips of wood. "Now says I, here you go, Puss!"

They were all so tired when they got through with blindman's buff, the supper dishes first being well out of the way, that Phronsie, who wanted to be "Puss," fell asleep on the little cricket before they could get her into the corner. So Polly bundled her off to the trundle bed and tucked her up with a kiss.

"Now the worst is over," she said, coming out of the bedroom, to Ben.

"And you two boys—it's time you were off," said Ben, pointing to the loft, "or you'll tumble asleep like Phronsie."

"I'm not sleepy," said Joel, digging his knuckles into his black eyes and trying to keep awake.

"I am," said Davie, "and my legs are tired." And he stumbled off to the loft stairs.

"Hoh!" exclaimed Joel, following slowly, "I ain't sleepy a single bit. And Polly and you are going to talk over secrets after we're gone," and he turned halfway up the loft stairs to show an injured face.

"Well, you wouldn't hear any secrets if you stayed," declared Ben coolly, "so you might as well take yourself off, Joe."

IX

The Old Book Box

MRS. PARSON HENDERSON for once left her breakfast dishes unwashed.

"It's no use—I must get over to the Little Brown House at once." She took down her sunbonnet from its nail in the entry and stopped to put her head in the study doorway.

"You'll be surprised to see the kitchen if you go out there," she said, "and the morning work not done."

"Jerusha isn't here, so no matter," said the parson, looking up from next Sunday's sermon with a smile.

"I can't keep away from those poor Pepper children, since you heard down at the store that their mother was away last night at Miss Babbitt's."

"Mehitable, I'm glad enough that you're going over to see Polly. I thought it would be as much as my life was worth to suggest it till those breakfast dishes were washed." He laughed now like a boy.

"There are some things more important than breakfast dishes," observed his wife grimly. Then she hurried off, cross-lots, to the Little Brown House.

Nobody was in the old kitchen; that she saw through the

window. So she hurried around the house and there under the scraggy apple tree was Polly before the big tub on its bench, scrubbing away on a pile of clothes and trying to sing, but it was a quavering little voice that the parson's wife heard.

"Go and get your little tub, Phronsie," said Polly, breaking off from the poor little song, "and wash Seraphina's clothes."

"I want my Mamsie." Phronsie, a picture of woe, stood quite still under a sheltering branch of the old apple tree.

"Oh, Phronsie," said Polly, trying to speak gaily, "just think of Seraphina, poor dear, wanting her clothes washed. Only think, Phronsie!"

"I want my Mamsie," said Phronsie, not offering to stir. Her lips trembled and Polly knew in another moment that the tears would come in a torrent, so she flung her hands clear of the soapsuds and started to run over to her. Instead she plunged into the parson's wife just making up her mind to come around the corner into full view.

"Oh, dear!" gasped Polly in dismay, her soapy hands flying up against the clean blue print dress.

"Never mind," said Mrs. Henderson, "soap never hurt any calico dress," seizing the wet hands. "Oh, my!" and she hurried over to Phronsie, too scared at Polly's plunge to cry.

"Well—well." Then as Polly ran to get a dry cloth to wipe off the front of the clean print dress, the parson's wife sat down on one of the big stones that Ben and the other boys had brought into "the orchard" to play tea party with whenever the much-prized hours from work would allow.

Phronsie came slowly to her. "I want my Mamsie," she said, patting Mrs. Henderson's gown to attract attention. "I want her very much indeed, I do."

"Yes, I know." Then the parson's wife lifted her on her lap. "So does Polly want Mamsie—and Davie. Where is Davie?"

Phronsie pointed a small finger up to the branches of the apple tree.

"Oh, Davie, are you there?" Mrs. Henderson cocked up one eye. There sat Davie huddled up in a crotch of the tree, his head in his hands. "Dear me. I thought it was a big bird!"

"Davie is a big bird," echoed Phronsie, smiling through the tears that were just ready to roll down.

"Isn't he," said the parson's wife with a little laugh. "Well, now, come down, big bird."

"Come down, big bird," cried Phronsie, clapping her hands and hopping up and down, as Polly ran out with the clean cloth.

"Now that is as good as ever," declared Mrs. Henderson, as Polly wiped off all trace of the soapsuds. "Well, here comes Davie," as he slid slowly down from branch to branch.

"That's a good boy, Davie," said Polly approvingly, the sparkle coming back to the brown eyes.

"Isn't he?" said Mrs. Henderson. "Well, now, Davie, I wonder if you won't come over to the parsonage and help me this morning?"

"Can I help you?" asked Davie, raising his swollen eyes to her.

"Yes, indeed; ever so much," declared Mrs. Henderson quickly. "I've some work to have done in setting up my attic, and you can help me."

"Then I'll come," said Davie, with a long breath of satisfaction.

"Now that's good," said the parson's wife.

"I want to go, too," said Phronsie, laying hold of Mrs. Henderson's gown.

"Oh, no," said the parson's wife, "you must stay and help Polly. Poor Polly—see how busy she is!" pointing over to the washtub where Polly was splashing away for dear life.

Phronsie's hand dropped from Mrs. Henderson's gown. She ran over unsteadily to the big tub on its bench. "I'm going to help you, Polly," she said, standing on her tiptoes.

"So you shall," said Polly, flashing over a bright smile to the parson's wife. "Run and get your little tub, and see if you can get Seraphina's clothes washed as quickly as these," she doused one of the boy's little calico jackets up and down in the suds.

"But I want to help on these things," said Phronsie, patting the big tub with a disappointed little hand. "Please, Polly, let me."

"No," said Polly decidedly, "there isn't room for more than one here. Besides Mamsie wouldn't like it."

"Wouldn't Mamsie like it for me to help in the big tub?" asked Phronsie.

"No, she wouldn't," said Polly decidedly.

Phronsie slowly let her hand drop to her side. "Would Mamsie want me to wash dolly's clothes?" she asked, her brown eyes fastened on Polly's face.

"Yes, indeed, she certainly would," declared Polly decidedly. "There now, that's clean, until Joey gets it dirty again," and she wrung out the little calico blouse.

"Then I shall wash my dolly's clothes," declared Phronsie, marching off to the woodshed where her little tub was kept.

"And you come with me, David," said Mrs. Henderson,

"for I must get to work in my attic. Polly, don't worry, child—we'll find some way to get your mother back here," she whispered on the way out of the yard. And taking David's hand, the parson's wife went swiftly home, hoping at every step that no parishioner had caught sight of those unwashed breakfast dishes.

"I'm going to wipe them dry," said David, as she poured the boiling water into the dishpan. "May I, Mrs. Henderson?"

"You certainly may," said the parson's wife, setting the big iron teakettle back on the stove. "Now that's a good boy, Davie Pepper. Get a clean towel in the table drawer."

So Davie ran over and fished out a clean towel, and the dishes were soon done and piled on the dresser. And none too soon! Here came around the corner of the parsonage Miss Keturah Sims to borrow a colander to strain blackberries in.

"I've got to make jell this mornin'," she announced, coming in without the formality of knocking, "an' my colander's bust." Her sharp black eyes, the sharpest pair in all Badgertown for finding out things, as the parson's wife knew quite well, roved all over the kitchen.

"You shall have it," cried Mrs. Henderson, running into the pantry on happy feet. "Oh, Davie Pepper," she cried, as the door closed on Miss Sims, "you don't know how you've helped me!" She stopped to drop a kiss on the soft light hair.

"Have I?" cried David, very much pleased. "Have I helped you, Mrs. Henderson?"

"Indeed you have!" she declared. Then she stopped in the middle of the kitchen. "I remember what your mother once said."

David drew near, holding his breath. To hear what

Mamsie said was always a treat not to be lightly put one
side.

"She said," repeated Mrs. Henderson, "that if anyone
felt bad about anything, the best way was to get up and do
something for somebody. And so you stopped crying and
worrying Polly and came over here. And you don't know,
David Pepper, how you've helped me! Well, we must get
up into the attic." She hurried over to the broom closet.
"Get the dustpan, David, behind the stove."

"I will," cried David, clattering after it.

"And the little brush."

"Yes—I will."

"And the dustcloth, hanging on the back entry nail,"
Mrs. Henderson's voice trailed down the attic stairs. And
Davie, gathering up the various things, hurried up after her.

"Dear me, how hot it is!" exclaimed the parson's wife,
hurrying over to open the window at the end.

"I'll open it," cried David, depositing his armful so hastily
that down the stairs rattled the little brush and the dustpan,
and only the dustcloth remained.

"No, no, Davie, I must open it," said Mrs. Henderson,
suiting the action to the word. "And remember, dear," as
he brought back the truant articles, "you must wait patiently
till I tell you what to do."

"I'm so sorry," said David penitently, still holding the
runaway broom and dustpan.

"I know, dear—and next time, remember to wait until
I tell you what I want you to do. Well, the first thing, now
that the window is open, and we have some fresh air to work
by, is to get these trunks and boxes out from this corner."
She was over there by this time and down on her knees
under the eaves.

"I'll pull 'em out," began Davie, then he stopped and looked at her, "if you want me to."

"That's a good boy," Mrs. Henderson turned and looked at him. "You've no idea what a comfort it is, David Pepper, to have anyone who wants to help, wait till he's told what to do! Well, you mustn't even attempt to pull these trunks and boxes about. We will each take hold of a handle, then it will be easy to shove them out." She got up suddenly. *Rap!* went her head against a low-lying beam.

David stared at her in dismay. "Oh, dear!" he exclaimed, quite aghast.

"Yes, that did hurt," said the parson's wife, feeling of her head, "and it was all because I was in too big a hurry. Now I'm going downstairs to bathe it, and you may—" She hesitated and looked about. "Why, there is that little box of books, David. You may take them out and dust them, for somebody has left the cover off. There it is now, behind that table." She pointed to an ancestral piece of furniture with one leg missing. "Take your dustcloth, child, and begin, then pile the books neatly in the box, and set the cover on," and she went swiftly down the stairs.

David ran over and picked up the dustcloth where he had thrown it on the floor. *Books!*—to think there were books in that box! His small fingers tingled to begin, and he threw himself down on the floor beside the box, and peered in. There were green books, and red ones, and very dull gray and black ones, all more or less dilapidated.

He drew a long breath, his blue eyes widening as his hands clutched the sides of the box. "I better take 'em all out first," he said to himself, and lifting the upper layer very carefully, he laid them down, one by one, on the floor beside him. A red-covered book, the back of the binding almost in tatters, slipped from his fingers and fell to the attic floor.

"Oh, dear me!" he was going to exclaim, when his gaze fell upon the pages before him. There was a big picture on one side and a whole lot of reading on the other page.

David leaned over to stare at the picture. Then he rested his elbows on the attic floor and stared harder than ever. The picture showed a boy seated before a desk, bent over a slate, on which he was writing, and opposite to him the book said, "I must get my lesson for tomorrow," in great big letters.

David knew very well what these big letters said, for Mother Pepper had often told Polly to lay down her work when she was trying to help Mamsie on the coats for Mr. Atkins, telling her, "You have sewed enough, Polly child. Now get the big Bible from the bedroom, and read aloud. And then you can teach the children, Polly," she would always add.

So Davie had picked up everything he possibly could about any big letters that were likely to come his way.

"The boy is going to school," said David, unable to tear his eyes from the picture, "and he's going to learn a lesson. Oh, dear, I wonder when I shall ever go to school! And he's got a slate and pencil."

At that David was so lost at the idea of any boy being rich enough to own a slate and pencil that he sat perfectly still, and a big spider hurried out of her web and ran along the eaves, to stare down at him. Finally seeing that he didn't stir, she slipped down swiftly on her gossamer thread and landed right in the middle of the book with the dilapidated red binding. This woke David up. And of course Mrs. Spider then ran for her life.

"I'm going to see if there are other boys with slates and

pencils," said David, turning the leaves. There lay the dust-cloth beside him, but he never thought of that. And as he couldn't read very much, but had to study each letter carefully, he didn't get on very fast, especially as there was a picture on every other page. And of course he must see what the big letters opposite said it was all about.

The first thing he knew there were some steps coming up the attic stairs.

David's head came up suddenly and the old book slipped away from his grasp.

"My mother says you are to come down to dinner," said Peletiah, coming slowly up.

David stared at him. Then his little face got hot all over.

"My mother says you are to come down to dinner," said the parson's son.

"I—I can't," said David miserably, and his head hung down.

"My mother says you are to come down to dinner," Peletiah said, exactly as if giving the message for the first time.

"No, no," said David, unable to see anything but the idle dustcloth lying on the floor.

"My mother says—" began the parson's son, not moving from his tracks.

"Da—vid!" called a voice over the attic stairs, "come, child, to dinner. You must be hungry, working so hard."

David crouched down by the side of the box. "I haven't worked," he said, "and I can't have any dinner."

"My mother says—"

"Yes, come, child," called the voice over the attic stairs, "and, Peletiah, you must come down, too." Peletiah, considering the last command to come to dinner much more to his taste and more binding than the message he was sent up to the attic to deliver, shut his mouth as he was just going to begin on his message once more, and went down the stairs.

David looked wildly around as he was left alone, with no one but the big spider now in her home web once more. To get to the Little Brown House and to Polly was now his only thought! He would be carrying disgrace there—but he must go. Then jumping to his feet, he ran as fast as he could down the attic stairs to the back entry. The knives and forks were going pretty fast as he dashed past the dining room. Oh, how jolly it all sounded, and a most enticing smell of all things good was in the air, as he dashed past and out into the parsonage yard.

"What's that?" asked Parson Henderson, and he laid down the big carving knife and fork just as Mrs. Henderson was saying, "I wonder why Davie Pepper doesn't come down to dinner. I've neglected the poor child, for when Mrs. Jones came to see me about the Sewing Society, I couldn't get back to the attic."

Peletiah got out of his chair and went to the window, followed by Ezekiel. "There's David Pepper," he said, pointing with a slow finger to a small boy running blindly on across the parsonage yard.

X

Mary Pote Helps

DAVID rushed into the old kitchen in a whirlwind of distress. There was no one there, and stumbling over to Mamsie's big calico-covered chair, he flung himself down and buried his head on the cushion.

"Now, Phronsie," said Polly, running in, "you've been such a good girl, I'm going to give you a piece of that gingerbread dear Mrs. Beebe gave us the other day. Shut the door, child."

Phronsie obediently pushed the big green door to, and pattered after Polly.

"You see," said Polly, running her head into the old corner cupboard, "Ben and Joel will have a good dinner at Deacon Blodgett's, and Davie is at the parsonage—I'm so glad he was such a good boy to help Mrs. Henderson."

"Ugh!" came a noise from the corner over by Mrs. Pepper's big chair.

"What was that?" cried Polly, pulling her head out of the cupboard. "Don't be afraid, child," as Phronsie huddled up to her.

"But I am, Polly," said Phronsie snuggling up closer than ever, "very much afraid."

"Mamsie said we weren't to be afraid at things, but to see what they were, so I'm going to." Polly ran across the old kitchen, Phronsie hanging to her.

"*Why, David Pepper!*" cried Polly, nearly tumbling over him as she ran around Mother Pepper's big chair. Then she turned very white.

"What is it, Davie? Oh, where are you hurt?" she asked, while Phronsie with a little wail, threw her arms around him, too.

"I'm not hurt," sobbed David. "Oh, dear, dear!"

"*Not hurt!*" gasped Polly, hanging to the chair.

"I've been a bad boy," cried David in a spasm of grief, and holding to the old cushion with desperate little hands.

"Oh, never, Davie," exclaimed Polly, "you couldn't be ever in all this world. Why, you are our Davie."

At this Davie's despair was greater than ever, and he burrowed his face deeper in the old chair.

"You see, Davie," Polly ran on, "Mamsie trusts you, so you couldn't be bad." Phronsie meanwhile had sunk to the floor, and was silently gazing at the misery, lost to everything else. "No, you couldn't be bad, because Mamsie trusts you so," she repeated.

This was so much worse that David began to scream, and without any more words, Polly lifted him up and sitting down in Mamsie's chair, she held him tightly in her lap.

"Now, David Pepper," she said sternly, "you've just got to tell me what you've done."

"I—I—can't," David hid his wet little face on her shoulder.

"Mamsie tells us not to say 'can't,' " said Polly decidedly. "Begin and tell me."

"She—told—me—" began David in a shaking voice.

"Mrs. Henderson?"

David bobbed his head.

"Go on."

"She—told—me—to—"

"Yes."

"To dust—the—books—and—"

"Well, go on."

"And I didn't—oh, dear!"

"And you disobeyed dear Mrs. Henderson! Oh, David Pepper, how could you!" Polly turned very white again, and cold little shivers ran up and down her back. To think that the parsonage people should ever have one of the Pepper children disobey them!

When Polly said, "David Pepper, how could you!" it wasn't to be lightly borne. So now David raised such a despairing little face that Polly hastened to say, "Well, you must tell me all about it."

"There was a boy in the book—"

"What boy?" said Polly, very much puzzled.

"I was going to dust him, and the other books."

"Oh, you mean you were going to dust the books," said Polly, beginning to see a little light.

"Yes," said David, trying to keep back the sobs.

"Well, stop crying and tell me all about it—every single thing." Polly gathered him up more closely. "Now then, Davie, you began to dust the boy."

"No, I didn't," said Davie in a fresh anguish. "I didn't dust him a bit; not once, Polly—oh, dear!"

"Why?" asked Polly.

"He had a slate and pencil, and—and—he was going to school," said Davie in another outburst of grief.

"Oh, I see," said Polly with more light, "and you wanted to read about him?"

"Yes, I did," said Davie, "it told all about him."

"Well, why didn't you dust the books just as Mrs. Henderson told you? It didn't take long, I'm sure, to find out about that boy."

"I wanted to see if other boys were going to school, and had slates and pencils—oh, dear!" he sobbed.

"Well, now I guess I know all about it," said Polly. "Phronsie, you must stop crying," for Phronsie was softly wailing on the floor in front of Mamsie's old chair. "You forgot about dusting the books, Davie?"

"Yes, I did," said Davie. "Oh, dear!" and he burrowed further than ever in her arms.

"Well, that was bad," said Polly, "when she told you to do it. But it's worse to cry about it now—because crying doesn't help it any. Well, now, is there anything else to tell me?"

"Peletiah came up in the attic and told me to come down to dinner. And Mrs. Henderson called me and—"

"And you didn't go?" cried Polly in astonishment.

"No, I couldn't have any dinner, I'd been bad—and I ran home."

"Oh, dear—dear!" exclaimed Polly in great distress. To have one of the children lacking in politeness was a terrible thing, and here was a blow that quite unnerved her. When David saw that, he was quite overcome, and he cried on steadily.

"Something must be done," thought Polly. "Oh, dear, if Mamsie were only here."

"David," she said, "you must go straight back to the parsonage and beg Mrs. Henderson to forgive you."

David shrank into a little heap. "Oh, I can't do that, Polly; she'll make me stay to dinner."

"That would never do," said Polly.

So she hopped out of the big chair and set him on his

feet. "I'll get you something to eat, and then you can tell her you have been to dinner if she asks you." And presently David was seated before the old table, and eating, as well as he could for his tears, a cold potato well sprinkled with salt and a generous slice of brown bread.

But he didn't get to the parsonage after all, for just as he was swallowing the last mouthful, in walked the parson's wife.

"I want you to come over tomorrow, Davie," she said, just as if nothing in the world a bit unpleasant had happened, "and you and I will work in the attic."

"Dear Mrs. Henderson, Davie has something he wants to say to you," Polly began in a trembling voice.

David got out of his chair and went over on unsteady feet to her.

"I didn't mean to be bad," he said, his poor swollen little face working dreadfully.

"I know, dear," said the parson's wife, bending over him sympathetically and stroking the soft, wavy hair with a kind hand.

"But it was bad," said Polly, "for him to forget, and not obey you."

"Yes," said Mrs. Henderson.

"And I'm sorry," said Davie, his hands twisting together.

"And you'll come tomorrow, and help me, and that will show that you are sorry," said the parson's wife.

"I'll go tomorrow," said David, with a crooked little smile.

"And Peletiah and Ezekiel are going away to their grandmother's again tomorrow," said Mrs. Henderson, "just as they did today. So, you see, I shall need you very much, Davie."

"Now, how in the world can I find anyone to take Mrs.

Pepper's place nursing Miss Babbitt?" The parson's wife puckered up her forehead all the way down the road with anxious thought. "If here doesn't come Dr. Fisher!" as the old gig swung into view at the turn of the road.

Dr. Fisher pulled up suddenly. But she didn't wait for the old horse to stop. "Dr. Fisher," she began, hurrying up to the side of the gig, "can't we find someone to take Mrs. Pepper's place over at Miss Babbitt's?"

Dr. Fisher looked out at her gloomily. "I'd give a good deal if we could," he said. "That idiot of a Bunce woman— she was there when Miss Babbitt fell down the cellar stairs, and she began to scream for Mrs. Pepper. And she rushed out—the Bunce woman—and caught Mr. Tisbett going by on the stage, and sent him for Mrs. Pepper. And now Mrs. Pepper won't desert Miss Babbitt." He switched the whip gloomily from side to side, his face getting more and more sober every moment.

"But she must desert Miss Babbitt," declared the parson's wife frantically.

"You know Mrs. Pepper will never desert anyone in trouble." The little doctor slapped the whip into its socket and glared at her through his big horn spectacles.

"There's Polly doing her best to keep things together," cried Mrs. Henderson. " 'Twould go to your heart, Dr. Fisher, to see her!"

"It's gone to my heart a good many times," said the little doctor, relapsing into gloom again, "to see her. But what can we do? There isn't a woman fit to take care of Miss Babbitt, who'd be willing to go."

"There's Mary Pote," said the parson's wife suddenly with a brightening face.

"Mary Pote?—well, Miss Parrott owns her, soul and

body." Dr. Fisher set his big spectacles straighter on his nose and glared at the parson's wife worse than ever.

" 'Twouldn't do any harm to try," said Mrs. Henderson. "Maybe Miss Parrott would let her go."

The little doctor sniffed scornfully. "Well, will you try?"

Mrs. Henderson looked off to the distant fields, an awful feeling at her heart. Then she swallowed hard. "Yes, I will," she said, "if I can get over to Miss Parrott's."

"No trouble about *that*," cried little Dr. Fisher joyfully. "Hop right in, Mrs. Henderson," and before her resolution had time to cool, there she was in the doctor's gig and well along on the way to the estate of the aristocratic Miss Parrott.

When the gig turned into the handsome stone gateway, the parson's wife had all she could do to keep from jumping out over the wheel. Suppose she should anger the only rich parishioner of her husband's! But she was there on the big stone steps, and the butler was opening the heavy oaken door. There was nothing to do but to go in, Dr. Fisher driving off to call for her later. And presently she was ushered into the long drawing room, with its rich carpeting, its ancestral furniture and portraits, all shrouded in the gloom of an apartment little used, and left to her wildly beating heart for the only sound to entertain her.

And there presently broke in the rustle of a stiff black silk gown advancing toward her, and in the gloom she saw the tall and haughty figure of the rich Miss Parrott.

How she told her story, she never could remember, but it was all out at last. And Miss Parrott sat erect, without uttering a word until the parson's wife thought as she told her husband that night, "I should go through the floor."

At last Miss Parrott broke the silence. "It's those Little Brown House people you want to help?"

"Yes," said Mrs. Henderson, unable to get out another word.

"And you want me to let Mary Pote go to take care of Miss Babbitt?"

"Yes," said the parson's wife faintly, "at least till they can get Miss Babbitt's niece to come."

"*Um*—" There wasn't another sound in the room except the wild beating of Mrs. Henderson's heart, until Miss Parrott got her long figure out of the high-backed chair, and the stiff black silk gown rustled over to the bell cord.

"Send Mary Pote to me," said Miss Parrott to the stiff old butler who appeared.

And again there was silence in the long gloomy drawing room. Mrs. Henderson couldn't tell, for the life of her, whether or no she had harmed her husband's interests, perhaps driven him from Badgertown parish. At last in came Mary Pote, a round, roly-poly person, half seamstress, half dressmaker, solely devoted to the spinster's interests, who lived in a small cottage on the Parrott estate. Whoever thought of asking for Mary Pote's services!

"Mary Pote," said Miss Parrott, "you may get your bonnet, and pack your bag. You are to go to take care of some tiresome old person who had nothing better to do than to fall down the cellar stairs and break her hip."

"But I was making over your black batiste, Miss Parrott," began Mary Pote with the privilege of an old servant.

"When I want my black batiste finished, I will tell you so, Mary Pote. Do as I bid you. Oh, one thing more. You are going so that a Mrs. Pepper—she's the mother of some children living in a poor old brown house in Badgertown—"

"I know them," said Mary Pote, turning back.

"Don't interrupt me—well, their mother has gone to take care of that odious old Miss Babbitt, and you are to take her place."

"Now I'm glad enough to go," cried Mary Pote joyfully, "for that Mrs. Pepper of all folks is the best woman, and—"

"There, there," said Miss Parrott, waving her off with long fingers on which ancestral rings shone. "Get along, Mary Pote, and do as I say. One thing more—tell Simmons to get the brougham ready and drive Mrs. Henderson and you down there."

The parson's wife got out of her chair. "Dr. Fisher brought me, and he will take me back," she said.

Miss Parrott waved her back with the long fingers.

"I know nothing about how you got here," she said; "it doesn't interest me in the least. I am taking charge of the case now, and not Dr. Fisher, nor anybody else."

XI

"I'd Try to Learn"

"Now, David, it's your turn." Mr. Atkins leaned both hands on the counter. "What did you want?"

"Three pounds of Indian meal, if you please."

"That's easy got, an' it's fresh an' sweet." The storekeeper went over to the big box in the corner. "Thought I never should get round to wait on you. Beats all how some women trade. That Miss Pride 'ud finger everything in the place, an' finally buy a lemon. Well, here you be!" He twisted up the paper bag with an extra twirl and handed it over the counter. "Well now, how's things over to the Little Brown House?"

David reached up with a shaking hand for the paper bag.

Mr. Atkins picked up the knife and cut off a snip from the big yellow cheese, and began to chew it. "He's too little," he said to himself; "no, I've got to find some other way to help 'em. *Hem!* well—" and he cut off another snip, "I s'pose Polly finds it pretty easy to keep the Little Brown House goin' these days, don't she?"

David's face turned quite white. If he could only forget how he had run out that very morning to get the kindlings behind the woodpile, and Ben and Polly were talking!

"It's every bit," said Ben, turning his old leather purse upside down, "ten cents, Polly."

"Oh, dear—dear! What shall we do, Ben? The potatoes are 'most gone and everything is so much worse!"

"Don't feel so bad, Polly. Things will get better, I guess," said Ben.

And then Davie, peering around the woodpile, saw him pat Polly's shoulder.

"Ben," said Polly, and she threw her arms around his neck, "we must think up some more ways to help Mamsie. We must, Ben."

Ben held Polly closely, but he said nothing, for he couldn't for his life think of a word of comfort, and his face worked dreadfully.

"Oh, dear me!" cried Polly in dismay when she saw that. "Don't look so, Ben. And you mustn't feel bad."

"Polly," said Ben, drawing a long breath, "we'll both think hard, and meantime, you and I mustn't stop our work. We ought to be at it this very minute."

"That's so," said Polly, breaking away from him, "and Mamsie told me to send Davie down to the store for some Indian meal."

At that Davie ducked behind the woodpile, and then ran after Polly into the Little Brown House. And now here he was in all his misery, standing before the counter, with Mr. Atkins asking this dreadful question!

"Hem!" said the storekeeper again. Seeing Davie's face, he couldn't keep eating cheese all day, so he threw down the knife, and before he knew it, he was saying, "How would you like to come here an' help me keep store a little while every now and then?"

Davie's blue eyes flew open at their widest, and he had all he could do to hang to the paper bag of Indian meal.

"You could set here an' watch things," Mr. Atkins ran on, surprised to find how very much he needed a small boy for that very thing, that hadn't occurred to him before. "An' then when I want to go to dinner, I'd admire to have th' store kep' open." At last he stopped suddenly. "What d'ye say, Davie?"

Davie found his voice after swallowing very hard.

"Could I really help you, Mr. Atkins?" he burst out, standing on his tiptoes, the very idea making him quite tall.

"Sure!" declared the storekeeper, slapping his thigh. "Beats all why I didn't think of it before. Well, what d'ye say, David?"

The color rushed all over David's face till it became rosy red. "Oh, Mr. Atkins," and he dropped the bag, "can I come here and help keep the store?" and he clasped his hands.

"That's what I been a-sayin' to you," cried the storekeeper, his pale green eyes sparkling.

"Can I really?"

"Sure as shootin'—I'd like it first rate. You'd be an awful help. You see, you could find out what folks wanted, an' come an' call me when I'm in th' house." Mr. Atkins pointed his big thumb over to the door that shut off the place where he ate and slept.

"Yes," cried Davie eagerly, "I could, Mr. Atkins."

"An' then you—you could hand me th' string when I wanted to tie up th' bundles."

"Yes, I could."

"An' then," said Mr. Atkins, casting about in his mind for the other things that now loomed up as most important in which he was to be helped, "why, then, you could hand me th' paper."

"Yes," said Davie, "an' couldn't I sometimes tie up bundles, Mr. Atkins?" he asked anxiously.

"I shouldn't wonder if you could," cried Mr. Atkins; "you're so smart, Davie Pepper, you'd learn real easy," and he slapped his thigh again.

"I'd try to learn," cried David in a glow, "and then I could help you, couldn't I, Mr. Atkins, keep store when I could tie up bundles?"

"You'd help me splendid before you learn to tie up bundles," declared Mr. Atkins just as excited, "just bein' here an' waitin' on me."

"And I'm going to learn to tie up bundles," cried David in a transport. Then he looked down at the paper bag of Indian meal at his feet, and he hung his head. "I'm so sorry," he faltered. Oh, now Mr. Atkins wouldn't want him, of course. A boy who dropped bundles all over the place wasn't to be trusted; and this splendid chance to help Mamsie was gone.

" 'Tain't such a dreadful thing to do," observed the storekeeper, leaning his long figure over the counter to take note of the trouble. "I dropped bundles when I was a boy, Davie."

"Did you?" said David, greatly relieved that a boy who grew up to be such a smart man as the village storekeeper did such a thing; and he picked up the paper bag with hope once more springing in his heart.

"Sure!" declared Mr. Atkins, "I was a great deal bigger than you be."

"How much bigger, Mr. Atkins?" asked David, clutching his bag.

"Oh, I guess 'most a foot taller," said Mr. Atkins, scratching his head, "an' once I dropped a 'lasses jug."

"Oh, Mr. Atkins!" exclaimed David, quite overwhelmed.

"Yes, I did," said the storekeeper, delighted to see the comfort this revelation gave. "An' 'twas in th' dusty road. Just think of that, David Pepper!"

"Can I help fill molasses jugs when people want them?" asked Davie suddenly. If that could ever be allowed, his happiness would be complete indeed.

Mr. Atkins whirled around. "Well—p'raps," he began slowly. Then he saw David's face. "Now I shouldn't wonder ef you could before long learn to fill them jugs. An' that would be a most dreadful help, David, for it's slow work as stock still, I tell you. Now run along an' ask your ma ef you can come an' help me in th' store a little now and then. You never must go into anythin', you know, without askin' her."

"An' ef ever I see a boy run," reported Mr. Atkins that day at dinner to his wife, " 'twas Davie Pepper, Ma; when I said that, his legs jest twinkled." And the storekeeper sat back in his chair to laugh. He even forgot to ask for a second helping of pie.

"Mamsie!" Davie sprang into the Little Brown House, swinging his bag of Indian meal, nearly upsetting Phronsie coming to meet him, Seraphina upside down in her arms.

"Goodness me, Davie!" exclaimed Polly, coming out of the Provision Room, the tin pail of bread in her hand, "what *is* the matter?"

"Where's Mamsie?" cried Davie, his blue eyes shining, and turning a very red face on her.

"She's gone to Grandma Bascom's," said Polly, dropping the pail to seize his little calico blouse, "and do give me that bag, Davie."

Davie gave up the bag and tore himself away from Polly's hold. "I must ask Mamsie," he shouted, running to the door.

"My senses!" cried Polly, "what *is* the matter?" She wanted to rub her eyes to see if it really was Davie who stood before her. "Wait! Mamsie's coming home in a few minutes. Why, here she is now!" glancing out of the window.

David sprang out. "Oh, Mamsie," he precipitated himself upon Mother Pepper halfway up the path. "He wants me to help him, and I'm going to learn to tie up bundles, and he said he thought some time I could fill molasses jugs, if you'd say yes. Can't I, Mamsie?"

"Dear me!" Mrs. Pepper held him by both little shoulders. "What is it all about, Davie? No, no, don't try to speak now," she added, seeing his face. "Come in and tell Mother."

And pretty soon, over by her big old calico-covered rocker, the story got out, Polly hanging over them both, and Phronsie, who had dropped Seraphina on the way, leaning, perfectly absorbed, against Mother Pepper's knee.

"To think of my boy being wanted to help Mr. Atkins!" cried Mrs. Pepper with shining eyes. "Oh, Davie!"

"Can I—can I?" cried David, feeling as if he couldn't wait another minute for the "yes" that all his hopes were hanging upon.

"Can you? Yes, yes, Davie." Mrs. Pepper gathered him up into her lap. "Oh, what a help you'll be to Mother, if you are a good boy and learn to do everything in the store that Mr. Atkins tells you!"

Polly ran down the road a good piece to meet Ben when he came home from Deacon Blodgett's. Joel had scampered on ahead. "Where are you going?" he had screamed as Polly flew past.

"Going to walk home with Ben," she had shouted, flying along.

"My goodness, Polly," cried Ben, as she rushed up to him, "is the house afire?"

"Mercy no!" Polly gasped for breath. "You can't think," she panted.

"Hold on!" Ben pounded her on the back. "You're going like a steam engine, Polly."

"Well, I feel like a steam engine," said Polly, with another gasp. "Oh, Ben, you—can't ever guess—what's happened."

"Come on over here." Ben dragged her off to the stone wall. "There now, tell me all about it."

"Well, in the first place," said Polly, sitting down on the wall, Ben by her side, and drawing a long breath, "I don't ever mean to be so bad as I was this morning, Ben."

She folded her hands in her lap and a sorrowful little look came into her brown eyes.

"You weren't bad," contradicted Ben stoutly. "And anyway, if you were, I was worse."

"Oh, no, Ben," said Polly quickly. "You are never as bad as I am, and you always see something better ahead."

"Indeed I don't, Polly," declared Ben, "you're the one to pretend that things are good, and you have such splendid plans. I never can think of anything. Well, anyway, tell what's happened at home."

"Ben," said Polly, suddenly lifting her face, the color rushing all over it, "just when the potatoes are all gone, and there isn't much bread in the pail, what do you think—you can't guess, so I'll tell you. Mr. Atkins has asked David to come now and then to help him in his store."

"Not our Davie!" exclaimed Ben, nearly tumbling off the stone wall; "why, he's too little. You must be dreaming, Polly."

"Indeed I'm not dreaming," declared Polly indignantly. "And Davie wouldn't ever say things that aren't so. You know that, Ben Pepper."

"Yes, I know," said Ben—but he looked very puzzled.

"And anyway, even if we don't understand it," said Polly wisely, "why it's so. And just think what a help to Mamsie. And it's come when I was so bad this very morning."

"You weren't bad," declared Ben again. And there they had it all over again.

"But you will be—we shall both be," he wound up with a laugh, "if we sit here on this stone wall much longer."

"That's so," said Polly, with a little laugh, and hopping off from the wall, they both ran off, hand in hand, down the road to the Little Brown House.

When they got there everything was in a truly dreadful state. There lay Joel, face down on the floor, crying as if his heart would break. "I want to go to help in the store," he screamed over and over, till nobody else had a chance to be heard. David was hanging over him in the greatest distress, saying, "I won't go, Joey—you may go, Joey."

Mrs. Pepper shook her head, and said quietly, "Oh, yes, Davie, you must go; you have promised Mr. Atkins."

"I want to tie up bundles," screamed Joel, kicking his heels on the floor. "Oh, dear—dear—boo—hoo—hoo!"

"Perhaps," Davie ran over to Mother Pepper's chair, "Mr. Atkins would let Joey come and help him instead of me," he said.

"No, Davie," said Mother Pepper, shaking her head worse than ever, "Mr. Atkins asked you, and you have promised. Always remember a promise once given must be kept," and she patted his flushed cheek. "Joel, come here!" It was impossible for Joel to stay on the floor kicking his heels and screaming when Mamsie spoke in that tone, so he got up and drew slowly near to her, digging his knuckles into his streaming eyes.

"Davie couldn't ask Mr. Atkins to let you take his place, even if he hadn't promised, for you are so much bigger than Davie, that he isn't strong enough to help Ben pile wood as you do. Why, you are my big boy, Joey!" She patted his stubby black hair affectionately.

"So I am," said Joel, as if a wholly new idea had struck him, and wiping off the last tear on the back of his little brown hand. "You see, I couldn't go, Dave, instead of you, to help Mr. Atkins in the store, for I am so much bigger than you, and I've got to pile wood and help Mamsie."

Davie drew a long breath of relief.

"So you have," he said. Then he laughed gleefully.

"And I'm so hungry," announced Joel, the matter all settled now comfortably. "Oh, dear, isn't dinner ready?"

"Yes," said Polly, running over to the stove, "and we've got mush today—Indian meal mush—just think. Do get the molasses pitcher, Ben!"

"No, let me," begged Davie, all aglow with the delightful visions of molasses jugs being filled by his hands from the big barrel in Mr. Atkins's store.

"So you may, Davie," said Polly, putting the big dish of mush on the table.

XII

Hop-O'-My-Thumb

"Now, David, ef you warn't here," said Mr. Atkins, "I couldn't go off this morning."

"Couldn't you, Mr. Atkins?" said David happily, over in the corner dusting the cans of peas and beans piled on the shelves, and he whirled around, the dustcloth in his hand.

"No, never in all this world," the storekeeper smote his hands together smartly. "Now you see, Davie, what a help you be to me."

"I'm so glad I'm a help to you, Mr. Atkins," cried Davie, the color all over his face, and his heart going like a trip hammer.

"I've got to go over to Simon Beeton's farm to see about them potatoes," said Mr. Atkins, "for he'd cheat me out of my eyeteeth ef I bought 'em without seein'. An' now I can leave so easy in my mind, Davie, seein' you are here."

Davie's bosom swelled, and he stood quite still. Oh, how glad Mamsie will be! And how good it was that Mr. Atkins's eyeteeth were now not in any danger.

"An' you can take th' orders, David," said Mr. Atkins,

hurrying over to the counter to pick up the slate. "You can write so nice an' plain now, that I'll know all what folks want when I get back."

David longed to ask, "Can't I give 'em the things they want?" But Mother Pepper had told him the first morning that he went to the grocery store not to ask Mr. Atkins if he might do anything, but to wait to be told.

"An' sometime—maybe the next time I go tradin', you may wait on th' customers," said Mr. Atkins encouragingly, "so you must learn all you can, David."

David smothered a sigh, but he stood quite tall. "I'll do everything I can, Mr. Atkins," he said.

"That's right, an' ef anythin' extry comes up, you run into th' house for Mis Atkins."

"Yes, I will," promised David, feeling sure that he would understand if he gave his whole mind to it.

"Well, I must be off," cried the storekeeper with an eye to the old clock on the shelf above the cans of peas and beans, and the door slammed as he hurried into the house.

David stood still to draw a long breath and look around. He was actually left in charge of Mr. Atkins's store!

For just one minute he couldn't believe it, then the joyful truth rushed over him. He wanted to run over and practice writing on the slate just as he had been doing every day when there wasn't anything that Mr. Atkins set as a task. But now today it was different.

"You dust down them shelves, Davie," the storekeeper had said that very morning, "they look mortal bad, an' old Mis Shaw kept starin' 'em all over yest'day, an' she looked 'shif'less,' though she didn't say it, all th' time she was in the store. An' I'm afraid she'll think everythin's dusty, jest because I hain't had no time to move them pesky cans."

So as dusting the shelves was the task set for him now,

why he must keep at it. And David turned his back on the beloved slate lying on the counter with the slate pencil dangling off by its string.

"If I could only have a slate all my own," said David to himself, as he began again on the lower shelf, patiently chasing every bit of dust from it, and moving each tin can carefully to one side. "Perhaps I will, some time." He had finished that shelf and looked up to the next one. "I must get the stepladder," he said, "for Mr. Atkins told me to dust 'em all."

And presently he was mounted up there, dustcloth in hand, when a voice back of him called, "Hello—Hello, there!"

David whirled around on his stepladder.

"Where's Mr. Atkins?" cried a farmer, whip in hand, advancing into the store.

"He's gone to buy potatoes," said David.

"Well, who's in charge o' th' store?" demanded the man.

"Mr. Atkins told me to put down on the slate what people asked for," said David. He wanted dreadfully to say that he was in charge of the store, but Mr. Atkins hadn't said that.

"Oh—ho!" roared the farmer, throwing back his head to laugh. "Well, that *is* a good one—a little hop-o'-my-thumb like you. Ho! Ho!" David's cheeks got very hot, and his small legs trembled under him, as he got down from the stepladder, laying his dustcloth on the top step, and went over to the counter.

"Mr. Atkins told me to write down what the folks wanted," he repeated, picking up the slate.

The farmer stopped laughing and drew up to the counter, looking at him curiously.

"You tell Atkins I've got apples as good as th' next one, an' I want he should give me some money for 'em."

David drew the slate pencil up into his fingers. Oh, dear—what was he to write! This wasn't anything to do with orders; but the farmer's cold eyes were on him, and he was just getting ready to laugh again, so something must be done.

"What is your name?" he asked, raising his blue eyes.

"Jones—Simeon Jones," said the farmer, his big mouth twitching under his heavy beard, as he looked down at the small figure.

David began with a beating heart; but as he went on he forgot all about the farmer, thinking only of Mamsie. He mustn't break down, for if he did, he would get no more chance to keep store for Mr. Atkins.

"Let's see what you've ben writin'," Mr. Jones slouched over the slate as Davie laid it on the counter. "Thunder, that ain't th' way to put it."

"You said you wanted some money," said Davie, standing his ground, but his legs trembled all the same.

Mr. Simeon Jones held up the slate and squinted at the crooked letters, having hard work to keep from running into each other. "Mr. Jones wants you to give him sum munny for his appuls."

"I ain't a-beggin'," he said, "an' besides, he hain't bought th' apples yet. I want him to buy 'em an' pay me cash down." He slapped the counter with his heavy whip, then tucked it under his arm.

David reached over and got the little sponge that had wandered off by itself, the storekeeper declaring it got in the way when it dangled on the string alongside the slate pencil. Then he rubbed out everything but "Mr. Jones," and began again, the big farmer leaning against the counter to watch the work go on.

"Mr. Jones wants munny for his appuls."

"No—no," roared Mr. Simeon Jones in such a tone that David, clinging to the slate pencil, jumped in dismay. "I tell you he hain't bought 'em yit. Here, give me that ere slate an' I'll write it myself."

"No—no," said David, clutching slate and pencil and all, and backing off to the end of the counter. "Mr. Atkins said I was to write it." He was in mortal terror that the farmer's big hand, now raised, would seize his last chance of ever being put in trust again in the store.

But Mr. Simeon Jones, not really being armed and equipped for much writing, either on a slate or on anything else, decided that he didn't care to undertake any job along that line; so his big hand dropped.

"Well, you write it as I tell you," he commanded gruffly, "or you won't get no jobs in this store, when I tell Atkins."

Which being exactly what David was terrified about, he began once more: "Mr. Jones wants you to bi his appuls—and—"

"Pay him cash," shouted the farmer over David's shoulder.

"Pay him Kash," finished David, the pencil trembling in fear of more messages to follow.

"That will do," said Mr. Jones, quite mollified; "it'll clinch the business." Then he drew off and looked at David tucking the slate in its place on the counter. "Say—did you mind when I laughed at you?"

David wanted dreadfully to stand up like a man and say "No," but Mother Pepper had said, "always tell the truth."

"Yes," he said slowly, "I did."

"Thunderation!" exploded the farmer, and a dull red crept up into his swarthy cheek; one of his big hands went into his pocket. "There, I ain't a-goin' to laugh at you no more," and he held out a coin. "You're a real smart boy ef you ain't any bigger'n a pint o' cider. There's a dime for ye."

David jumped back as if shot, and put his hands behind him.

"Take it," urged Mr. Simeon Jones, pushing the dime nearer.

"Mamsie wouldn't like it," was all that Davie could manage to say.

"Mamsie—who's him?" demanded the farmer.

"She's our mother," said Davie, keeping his hands behind him.

"Saltpeter!" ejaculated Mr. Simeon Jones. "Well, then, I s'pose you can't take this 'ere dime, ef she wouldn't like it, eh?"

"No," said David, quite happy that he was at last understood.

"Well, I shall tell Atkins you've done fust rate," said the farmer, slouching to the door. Then he went out with another curious look at David, got into his big wagon, and drove off.

Davie went back to the stepladder, climbed up, and wiped all the shelves. He wanted to sing, but that wasn't the way, he was quite sure, to keep a grocery store. So he shut his lips tightly together, but his blue eyes shone as the dustcloth went busily on its way into all the corners. At last it was all done, and every one of the tin cans of peas and beans in neat rows were in their places. Then he got down from the stepladder and gazed at them all in great delight.

"Now I can practice my writing on the slate," he cried joyfully. And scampering over to a barrel of sugar standing by the counter, he got on it, slate in hand, and fell to laboriously forming all the best letters that Polly had showed him how to make.

"I must be careful not to rub out 'Mr. Jones,'" he said. So he laid a paper lying on the counter ready for a bundle to be tied up, between the farmer's message and his knees, and presently he was lost to all but the blissful prospect of some time being able to write things as beautifully as Polly herself.

The first thing he knew the door to the grocery store was slowly opened, and Davie lifted his head.

A young man stepped softly in. He wasn't the kind that was seen around Badgertown, and Davie didn't like his looks in the least.

"Well, old man," said the newcomer, drawing nearer to David's barrel and looking him all over with a pair of evil eyes, "where's the boss?"

"I don't know what you mean," said David.

"Why, the boss who runs this store," the young man flirted a pair of long and grimy fingers comprehensively.

"He isn't here," said David, not taking his blue eyes from the face that now he liked less than ever.

"And he's left you to take charge of the shebang?"

"I don't know what that is," said David.

"The store—the store," the visitor cried impatiently, and threw his dirty fingers about more recklessly than ever. Then he snapped them in David's face.

"He told me to write things that folks asked for on the slate," said David.

The young man broke into a laugh as much more unpleasant than that of Mr. Simeon Jones as could be imagined. Then he broke off suddenly to listen. "Somebody might be passing," he muttered. "See here, old man, there wasn't any need for you to tell me about your boss. I saw him drive away and I was coming in then to pay you a call; thought you might be lonesome," and he chuckled under his breath; "then that other old party hove along, so I couldn't get here till now. Look here!" It was impossible for Davie to obey this command any better, for he had never taken his blue eyes from the face, now just above him, as he sat on the barrel, slate in hand.

"I ain't going to have any fooling," the young man was saying between his teeth, and he raised one hand threateningly. "I'll tell you that to begin with—I've come here for money. You can't help yourself, for the boss is away."

He put both dirty hands on the counter and vaulting over it, twitched open the drawer to rummage in the till.

Davie sprang down from his barrel. "You mustn't do that," he screamed, "that's Mr. Atkins's money."

"You shut your gab." The young man, one fist full of silver pieces and pennies, raised his head, his wicked eyes sparkling in anger.

"You mustn't take it! It's Mr. Atkins's money!" David, his heart going like everything, beat on the counter with one small hand. Oh, if some customer would only come in!

"See here—you'll get the worst beating you ever had," declared the young man, "if you don't hold your tongue." He hissed out the last words and bent over the till again.

David, in mortal terror that whatever he did, he couldn't keep Mr. Atkins's money from being carried off, cast another imploring glance at the door for a possible customer. No one was in sight, Badgertown street in front of the store being free from all pedestrians, and there wasn't a wagon to be seen. Then Mr. Atkins's words flashed upon him, "If anythin' extry comes up, you run into the house for Mis Atkins."

This was certainly "somethin' extry," and it was quite time to run into the house and call Mrs. Atkins. He made one leap for the little door that shut off the storekeeper's home, and the first thing he knew, he was seized violently from behind and thrown in a heap to the floor.

David could not hear the words—he only knew that the awful eyes were glaring at him, and he shut his own so that he could not see, as the young man hissed out something. At last he made out, "No, you don't, my fine sir. I'll attend to you before I go." Then he was dragged off to a corner, thrown behind some bags of oats, and tied fast to a rope hanging from the neck of one. "I guess you won't run much with one of them bags at your heels," and the young man surveyed his work with a grin.

"Da—vid!" rang out the voice of Mrs. Atkins. "Where are you?"

The young man on his way back to the till started and pricked up his ears.

"Oh—she'll be killed!" David screamed. "Don't come in!" The little door was flung wide, and Mrs. Atkins, all in a hurry as dinner was waiting, got herself into the store just in time to see a tall figure flying past and out into Badgertown street.

"My sakes!" she ejaculated. Then she gave a wild look around. "David, where be ye?"

"Here," said David, behind the bags of oats. "Oh, Mrs. Atkins, did he take any?"

"For th' land sakes—David Pepper!" The storekeeper's wife knelt down by his side. When she saw the rope she was quite overcome, and she fumbled helplessly at the knots.

"Did he—did he?" implored Davie in great distress, "take any of Mr. Atkins's money?"

"Money?" Mrs. Atkins hopped to her feet in great alarm and scuttled over to get behind the counter. "My soul an' body!" she exclaimed, pawing among the loose dimes and nickels and pennies dropped by the young man when he sprang for David.

"Did he?" implored Davie. "Oh, do tell me, Mrs. Atkins —did he take any money?"

"It looks as if he'd ben interrupted." The storekeeper's wife drew a long sigh of relief as she settled the coins back into the till and slammed to the drawer. "I don't b'lieve he got a single cent, David Pepper," she said, coming back to him.

"Oh, I'm so glad," said Davie.

"An' now I'll untie you," she said, getting down on her knees. "My gracious!" and she shook with fright, "sech a risk as you've run!"

"I'm so glad he didn't get any money," breathed Davie blissfully.

"An' you've saved it," Mrs. Atkins, getting the last knot out, threw the end of the ropes off, "just think of that, David Pepper!"

David's blue eyes shone. "I wish I could have kept him," he said, as he got up to his feet.

"Land!—don't say that—you've done splendid!" said Mrs. Atkins, and she shivered as she got up.

XIII

"Don't Hurt Him"

Mrs. Atkins ran to the door. "Beats all how a man ain't never on hand when he's wanted," she exclaimed in vexation, peering up and down the street.

"Well, now, ef here ain't Mr. Jones heavin' along," she cried joyfully, and picking up her calico gown, she sped over the step, bawling out, "Do stop—Mr. Jones!"

"What's th' matter, Mis Atkins?" asked the farmer leisurely driving up.

"I'll tell you, only do get out," she cried excitedly.

"Hain't nothin' happened to that little feller, has they?" the farmer pointed his thumb in great concern toward the store.

"No—no—but ef it hadn't ben for Davie, Mr. Atkins would 'a' ben robbed," declared Mrs. Atkins; then she thrust her head back into the store, "Davie, come here, an' tell us all about it. We must catch th' man, or he'll try it again, like enough."

"Sho!" exclaimed Farmer Jones, as Davie ran out to the step. Then he whistled, "Whew! Hop-o'-my-thumb," he was going to say. But remembering how the small boy hadn't liked that, nor the laugh, he whistled again, as he got slowly out of the wagon.

"Tell it, Davie," Mrs. Atkins kept saying, "just exactly how it all happened." And then a small knot of farmers drew near, so there was quite a little crowd.

As Davie forgot to say much about himself, Mrs. Atkins and Farmer Jones were obliged to prod him with questions. At last the story was pieced out.

"We must catch the fellow," exclaimed one farmer, "else he'll be trying the same game again."

"Like enough we'll be murdered in our beds," said a woman, pushing her way into the center of things, "an' 'twon't be safe to live in Badgertown."

And a thin voice on the fringe of the crowd piped out, "I warrant it's the same man that stopped to my house this mornin' for somethin' to eat."

"What did he look like, Grandsir Tibbs?" cried two or three.

"I dunno no more'n th' dead," said Grandsir querulously. His voice shook worse than ever, under the excitement of the thing. "His cap was drawed over his face—I shet th' door on him."

"Well, we've got to catch th' feller," declared a stalwart farmer, "an' this boy," laying his hand on David's small shoulder, "is th' only one who knows what th' tramp looks like. Come on, youngster," and before he knew what was going to happen, Davie was lifted up and dumped into a wagon, the owner jumping in and gathering up the reins.

"Stop!" cried the storekeeper's wife, when she saw this, trying to break through the crowd.

"Catch th' feller—come on—" the cry was taken up, and the other farmers in the wagons drove off after the one carrying Davie, Mrs. Atkins running along as far as her breath would permit, crying, "Stop—you mustn't—take th' boy! He's David Pepper," and sometimes she said, "He's Mis Pepper's boy." But no matter how she screamed it, the wagons rolled on, and at last she sank down by the roadside.

"He'd take to th' woods mos' likely," said the farmer who had David as a companion and thus was the leader, pointing off with his whip as he stood up in the wagon and looked back at the procession.

"Yes—yes," they called back. So to the woods they whipped up.

When they drew up to a thick grove of pines skirting Badgertown, they all tumbled out of the wagons and peered cautiously in.

"One of us must set out here with th' boy—we ain't a-goin' to drag him in."

"I'll set," offered one man, coming up to Davie's wagon.

"Yes, I know you'd offer," said the farmer to whom that vehicle belonged, "but all th' same, you ain't a-goin' to have that easy part. Simeon Jones—you come an' take keer o' this boy, will you, till we fetch out th' feller?"

"All right," said Farmer Jones, driving up. "Come, git in here;" he again came perilously near to saying "hop-o'-my-thumb," but he coughed and just saved himself.

David, being in that position where there was nothing to do but to obey, jumped out of his wagon and into that of Farmer Jones, who received him gladly.

"Sho now!" began Mr. Jones, clearing his throat, "th' tramp robbed Mr. Atkins—eh?"

"He didn't get any money," said David, folding his small hands.

"That's good!" cried Farmer Jones, slapping his leg. "Well, I 'spect you kept him from it," he said, looking down admiringly at the little figure on the other half of the old leather seat. "Gosh! You ain't bigger'n a half a pint o' cider, but I b'lieve you did it—eh?"

David fought shy of this question and said nothing. But it was no use. By little and little, Farmer Jones, being a man who, to put it into his own words, "stuck to a thing like an old dog to a bone," wormed the story out of David, helplessly miserable at being obliged to tell it.

Suddenly the body of Badgertown citizens trooped out from the woods. In the midst of them was the young man with the evil eyes, who had visited Mr. Atkins's store.

Everybody was shouting in chorus, and Farmer Jones clapped Davie's shoulder with a glad hand. "Say, youngster, that's th' feller, ain't it?"

David drew a long breath. But Mamsie, having often said, "Tell the truth," he said, "Yes." And one of the young farmers, finding the capture a trifle dull, crowded roughly up against the prisoner. This was the signal for the others, who began to wreak a little of the vengeance to come upon their man.

David stood straight up in the wagon. "Don't hurt him," he begged.

The young man with the evil eyes turned them upon Davie; but he said nothing.

"Easy there," commanded Farmer Jones.

"We don't want such fellers comin' to Badgertown," said the first young farmer. "Come on, boys, we must give him a hustle before we fetch him to Cherryville jail."

"You mustn't hurt him," said Davie in a loud voice. His cheeks were very red, and his blue eyes flashed.

"What this boy says, goes," cried Farmer Jones sharply. "D'ye understand?"

They did, Simeon Jones being a person to be reckoned with. And pretty soon the young man who had visited

Mr. Atkins's store had his hands neatly tied together with a piece of rope, and he found himself in a wagon, the horse being turned to the road leading to Cherryville jail.

"You tell that boy," he nodded his head over toward David, "that 'tain't his fault that I'm took, an' I'm obliged to him for trying to save me."

But David burst into tears and flung himself down on the floor of the wagon.

"I've got to hurry back and lock up th' store," Mrs. Atkins was saying about this time, getting up from the roadside, "an' then I must get over to Mis Pepper's an' tell her all about it. Goodness me—how'll I ever do it?"

But Mother Pepper had the news before the storekeeper's wife reached the Little Brown House, for Davie was there. Farmer Simeon Jones, aghast at the flood of tears, had hurried him home as fast as the old horse could go.

"Your ma'll say you done right," he kept repeating over and over. "Don't you be afcard. An' th' man ain't goin' to be hurt. An' they give real good meals, I've heard say, over to Cherryville jail."

But all this was no comfort to David, and he wailed steadily on.

"Well, I'm blest ef I ain't glad to see that 'ere Little Brown House," declared Mr. Jones, very spry at getting out as the old horse stopped at the gate. David, half blinded by his tears, stumbled out and up to the big green door. Mother Pepper opened it. "I couldn't help it, Mamsie," he cried, huddling into her arms.

"I'll tell ye, Marm," said Farmer Jones, looking into her black eyes, "fust go-off, so's you needn't to worry. This boy o' yourn has done just fine."

"I couldn't help it, Mamsie," Davie kept saying.

"There—there—Davie—" Mother Pepper held him

closely, while one hand patted his soft light hair; then she looked up inquiringly.

"Simeon Jones is my name, Marm," said the farmer. "Might I come in—it's kinder a long story."

"Yes, indeed," and once in the old kitchen, the farmer's tongue took up the tale and ran it off glibly. And just at the very end in hurried the storekeeper's wife.

"Now, Davie," said Mother Pepper, when at last it was all out, "you did just right." How her black eyes shone! And she kissed his hot cheek.

"But the poor man—he's in jail," moaned David.

"That had to be," said Mrs. Pepper firmly. "Don't you see, child, if he were allowed to go free, Badgertown people wouldn't be safe from robbers."

"Mamsie, I don't believe he's going to steal any more," said David, wiping up, the comfort settling down into his heart, since Mamsie had said it had to be.

"We will hope not," said Mother Pepper, with another kiss.

"Hoh!" Joel rushed in, his black eyes ablaze and his cheeks as red as could be. He had heard the story at Deacon Blodgett's, for all Badgertown was afire with it. "If I'd been there, I'd 'a' smashed that old burglar." He doubled up his small fists and swung them in the air.

"Joel—Joel—" said Mrs. Pepper reprovingly.

"Ha! Ha!" laughed Farmer Jones, slapping his thigh.

Joel rushed up to him. "Well, I would," he cried. "You needn't laugh, you, Mr. Man."

"Joel, come here." When Mother Pepper spoke in that tone there could be no delay. So up to her chair he marched, yet he had a backward eye on that old farmer who sat in that chair laughing at him.

"You're pretty smart, Joel," said the storekeeper's wife, "but Davie did the best after all."

"But I could 'a' smashed him," declared Joel, transferring his attention to her, "if I'd only been there. Why ain't I ever there when a burglar comes," he cried in anguish. "Why ain't I, Mamsie?"

"Well, I must be a-goin'," said Farmer Jones, getting out of his chair. "You've got two smart likely boys, Mis Pepper, but the little un is the most to my taste. Ef you're goin' home, Mis Atkins, I'll take you back."

"I'm obliged enough, I can tell you," said Mrs. Atkins, "for I hain't run an' ben scared to death in a long spell like I've ben today. Good-by, David. You've took care of our store every bit as good as a man."

Davie kept in the Little Brown House for days after that; nothing could persuade him to venture on Badgertown streets, where the folks were likely to waylay him, and want to know all about his adventure in Mr. Atkins's store. And when anyone came to the Little Brown House, as many did, to hear all about it, Davie would run out and hide behind the woodpile until they had gone.

"You can't do that all the time, Davie," said Polly one day, finding him there. "I'm going down to Mr. Beebe to get him to mend Mamsie's shoes, and you come with me."

"Oh, I can't, Polly," said Davie, shrinking back; yet his blue eyes were full of longing.

"Nonsense!" exclaimed Polly gaily. "Come along, I'll race you to the gate."

That was beyond Davie's resistance. To race Polly was the children's great delight. So off they ran, and as luck would have it, David got to the gate first.

"That's fine!" declared Polly, tossing back her hair from

her rosy cheeks. "Well, now, come on for another spin."

They had almost reached Mr. Beebe's little shop when an old lady coming out of a shop opposite beckoned violently with her black satin parasol. The long fringe waved back and forth as she shook the parasol with an air of command.

"It is Miss Parrott," said Polly in an awe-struck voice. "You go in to Mr. Beebe's shop and I'll run across to her."

Davie, quite glad to escape and especially into dear Mr. Beebe's shoeshop, hurried over the cobblestones, while Polly flew across the street. His foot was on the step when a voice said: "Bring the boy—he's the one I want to see."

"You will have to come, Davie," said Polly, hurrying back.

"Oh, I can't," said Davie, crowding up against the shoeshop door. "Don't make me, Polly." He turned a distressed little face as she hurried up.

"Yes, you must," said Polly. "Mamsie would say so."

"Would Mamsie say so?" cried Davie, hanging to the big knocker. "Would she really, Polly?"

"Yes," said Polly, "she would. Come on, Davie," and she held out her hand. So together they went across the narrow little street, David hanging back on lagging footsteps.

Miss Parrott's big coach was around the corner. There she stood now, waiting for them.

"I want to hear all about what happened in Mr. Atkins's store," she said, "and I am going to take you two children to drive, and then, David, you can tell me the story on the way."

"Oh, Miss Parrott," cried Polly, dismayed at Davie's frantic clutch on her hand, "I have to take Mamsie's shoes for Mr. Beebe to mend." Yet her eyes sparkled at the very thought of riding in that Parrott grand coach!

"Run across then with them," said Miss Parrott. "Come, David, you and I will get into the carriage, and Polly will join us."

"I'll take the shoes over to Mr. Beebe," cried Davie frantically, and he reached for Polly's bundle.

"No, David," said Miss Parrott, "Polly must do it. You come with me." And there he was, his little hand in hers, on the way to the coach waiting around the corner, and Polly flying across the street to the little shoeshop just as frantic to get back to him.

"Now, then, we can be quite comfortable," said Miss Parrott, having them all settled in the big stately old coach, the order to drive given to the coachman, who matched up in dignity to the coach and the Parrott estate, "and you shall give me the whole story. Begin at the beginning, David."

XIV

In the Parrott Playroom

MISS PARROTT looked the two children over carefully. Then her glance rested on David. He sat tucked up in the corner of the green leather seat, as far away from the keen dark eyes as he could get, his hand tightly clasped in Polly's.

"Now then," said Miss Parrott, the investigation being over, "you must tell me everything about it. I was unable to get a satisfactory account at Atkins's store."

Davie gave a sob and ducked farther back into his corner. This was so much worse than being waylaid for a recital of his adventure by the ordinary run of Badgertown citizens that he couldn't conceal his dismay. To think of being fastened up in the Parrott coach and made to tell of what was now a perfectly hateful thing, since he was to be petted and praised for his part in it, made him sob again; and he flung himself up against Polly and hid his burning face on her shoulder.

"Oh, Miss Parrott," Polly broke out, "Davie cannot bear to talk about it. He only did what he ought to." She forgot that she was talking to the aristocratic lady, whose comings and goings in this same stately coach to the little church on Badgertown green were eagerly watched for of a Sunday. She raised her brown eyes pleadingly.

132

"That is where you are very wrong to encourage your little brother in refusing to answer my questions. And I must insist on knowing all about what happened." The tall aristocratic figure on the seat opposite loomed up so forbiddingly that Polly had all she could do to keep from joining in Davie's distress. But this would never do. Besides, Miss Parrott was saying, "I am sure your mother, whom I have heard brings you children up most excellently, would wish your little brother to answer my questions."

"Davie," said Polly desperately, bending her head down to his ear, "you must sit up and tell Miss Parrott about it. Mamsie would want you to."

She had to say it over three times, "Mamsie would want you to," for instead of sitting up, Davie burrowed deeper against her shoulder. At last her tone was so decided that anything being more desirable than to lose Polly's approval, David somehow got up into a sitting posture; and before he quite knew what he was going to say, there he was doing his best to let Miss Parrott understand just what happened in Mr. Atkins's store. He must please Mamsie.

And to his great surprise and relief, Miss Parrott never said one word of praise for anything that he did, and as for petting him, she still sat bolt upright at the conclusion of the tale, and only said, "Thank you for telling me."

David drew himself up and began to enjoy himself. As for Polly, her brown eyes danced and the color came back in her cheeks.

"I am going to take you home with me," said Miss Parrott suddenly.

"Oh," cried Polly, wrenched away from the bliss of actually driving in the Parrott coach, "we can't go. Mamsie doesn't know where we are, and we ought to go home now."

"I suppose," said Miss Parrott reflectively, "that I ought

to drive around and ask your mother." But she bit her lip, being accustomed to do all things as she chose without leave or license from anybody. Still a woman should be asked about the movements of her own children. So she gave the order to the old coachman, and the horses were soon turned in the direction of the Little Brown House.

Davie forgot himself and sprang out without a word of thanks, and rushed up to the old green door.

"Oh, do forgive him, Miss Parrott," begged Polly in distress, "he didn't mean to be rude."

For answer Miss Parrott only said, "Will you ask your mother to come out here?" But she smiled, so Polly knew that things weren't so very bad, and she ran up the path, greatly relieved.

And presently Mrs. Pepper came out with Polly, and to the great astonishment, said, "Yes, the children could go," and "Run in, and put a clean blouse on, Davie."

"The boy looks well enough," said Miss Parrott decidedly. "I'm sure you keep your children always clean, Mrs. Pepper—everybody says so."

But Mrs. Pepper only smiled, and Polly ran into the house to get Davie ready. For when Mamsie said a thing, she always meant it, and pretty soon out they came, Davie quite fresh in another calico blouse and not entirely at rest in his mind as to the visit at the Parrott estate.

When they drove up with a flourish before the big front door with carved stone lions on either side, Davie held Polly's hand closely, and surveyed everything with wide blue eyes.

The butler, a dignitary resplendent enough in the children's eyes to be the owner of many estates, came down the wide hall. Miss Parrott gave him instructions concerning her guests, whom he viewed with cold unconcern.

"Now, then, children," she said, "I'm going to take you into the garden and leave you there. You will be called when luncheon is served," and turning off from the big hall to a narrow passage, they came to a green lattice door.

Miss Parrott opened this. "Oh!" cried Polly, clasping her hands in delight. And Davie forgot his fright and gave a little squeal.

"It's so perfectly beautiful!" exclaimed Polly.

An old-fashioned garden, bright with hollyhocks and all sorts of dear, homely flowers, a little square plot in the center, around which were stone seats, burst upon their view. All off in the distance were terraces and lawns, with all manner of splendid trees, and pleasant paths intersecting.

Miss Parrott's long gaunt face drew up into a pleasant smile that seemed to say, "Good-by to your wrinkles."

"Now run along, children, and enjoy yourselves," she said. "You will be called when luncheon is ready. Be sure that you come in at once."

"Polly," said Davie in an awe-struck voice, "do you suppose the lady can come in here every time she wants to?"

"Of course," said Polly, longing to hop up and down, but perhaps someone would see her and it wouldn't be considered proper. "Why she lives here, Davie."

Davie drew a long breath. To live in this beautiful place and come out in this wonderful garden! He drew a long breath and stood quite still beside the green lattice door.

"Let's go and sit down on one of those little stone seats," said Polly.

So the children walked quite properly over and sat down on one of the seats in the little green square.

"Polly," said Davie, "I very much wish that we could go over under those trees," pointing to a bit of greensward where the noonday sun was making cool shadows.

"Why, we can," said Polly. "Miss Parrott said we could run about and enjoy it all." She got off from the little stone seat and held out her hand.

"Oh, Polly, can we really run?" cried Davie in great excitement.

"Yes, indeed," cried Polly, finding her courage in David's happiness. "Come on, I'll race you to that big pine tree."

"Now what does Miss Parrott want with the likes of them poor children," exclaimed a scornful housemaid, peering out of the green lattice door.

"Hevin knows!" cried the butler, raising both hands, "and they are actually to stay to luncheon."

Upstairs under the gambrel roof overrun with sweetbrier, Miss Parrott was sitting by her window, listening to the childish peals of laughter, as Polly and David played hide-and-seek between the ancestral trees.

"I haven't felt so happy here," placing her hand on her heart, "since Sister and I played there."

The butler flung open the green lattice door, and said harshly, "Come in to luncheon," and started to find Miss Parrott just behind him.

"That is scarcely the way to summon my guests," she said.

"Beg pardon, ma'am," said the butler obsequiously.

"I want you to go out and treat them as you would any other of my friends," said Miss Parrott.

And the butler with a sullen face, but a back that expressed nothing but complete submission, stalked down the garden path to the big trees whence the happy sounds proceeded. And the scornful housemaid confided it all to the equally disdainful cook, who said never in her twenty-five years of service on the Parrott estate had she seen such goings on.

When the three were seated around the luncheon table in the handsome dining room, Davie was quite over-whelmed at the array of silver and glass that shone upon the polished mahogany table. And Polly turned pale and only hoped they should neither of them do anything to disgrace Mamsie.

But although they didn't know what to do with all the knives and forks, Miss Parrott never appeared to notice. Polly, who hadn't been able to forget the disdainful butler, saw him back of Davie's chair scornfully survey the efforts to carry the food up nicely to the small mouth and the color flew over her cheek. Then Miss Parrott said to him, "I shan't require you any more. Bring me the bell—and I will ring if I need you."

And the butler quite humble once more, brought the little silver bell from the massive sideboard heavy with an-cestral plate, and went out of the room, his head lowered by several inches. Polly's hot flush died down on her cheek, and things began to get comfortable.

"Now," said Miss Parrott, when luncheon was over, "I am going to show you some things that I played with when I was a little girl." She had a faint pink color on her sallow face, and she smiled as if quite content. But still she didn't know what to do with her guests to make them happy.

David wanted to ask, "Were you ever a little girl?" as he looked the long, angular figure up and down, but he kept quite still.

"Oh, would you really?" cried Polly in delight.

"Yes," said Miss Parrott, greatly pleased, "would you really like to see them?"

"Oh, we would—we would!" declared Polly.

"Come this way then," and out into the big wide hall, and over a broad and winding staircase dim with the shaded light of a tall Colonial window, they went, then down a narrow passage, at the end of which were two cunning little steps.

"Here was our playroom—Sister's and mine," said Miss Parrott, pausing at a door, and taking a key from her black silk bag, she fitted it in the lock. And presently there they all three were in a long, low-ceilinged room. It had shelves on two sides filled with books and games and dolls—and there was a small table in the center, and little chairs scattered about.

Miss Parrott turned her back on it suddenly and made as if she were going out. But she faced the children in a minute and smiled, and again she put her hand to her heart.

"Now you can each pick out something, and I will tell you about it," she said, seating herself on an old-fashioned broad sofa.

Polly stood quite still before her with shining eyes. "Can we really touch the things?" she asked.

"Yes, all you like," and Miss Parrott actually laughed.

"Davie," Polly ran up to him, "we can choose something and take it to her and she will tell us about it," she said. Then she ran off to the corner where the dolls sat up in all their faded and old-fashioned glory.

David went over to one of the bookshelves. At first he only gazed; then he put a timid finger on one and another. At last he selected a worn old reader whose pages were interspersed with pictures, and holding it closely, he marched up with it to Miss Parrott's sofa, just as Polly came flying up with a big rag doll in a little checked silk gown, a quaint neckerchief, and a big mobcap.

"I will tell you about yours first," said Miss Parrott, taking the doll. Then she laughed, "Well, you see Sister and I both had the promise of a new doll. We were to own it together, because that was the way we had everything," and she waved her hand around the playroom. "Well, our mother had given the order to have it made and dressed, and its face was to be painted by a real artist. Oh, you can't think how we watched for that doll. We were quite impatient for its arrival. The lady who was to dress it kept sending word that she had been detained from doing the work, but that it was to be quite fine. We were letting our imaginations run riot with all sorts of splendid ideas on just how that doll was to look. Sister decided it would be dressed in a pink satin gown with a little pink cap, but I hoped it would be all in blue. Well, we used to watch at the window, a part of every day for the big box containing that precious doll.

"At last one day Sister was at the window, and she screamed 'Judith—Judith!' "

Davie forgot his awe, to burst out, "Was that your name?"

"Yes, dear," said Miss Parrott, very much pleased that he had found his tongue. "I was named for my grandmother."

"Oh," said David.

"And Sarah was my sister's name; she was named for our mother."

"Oh," said David again.

"Well, we ran after the big box as it was carried into the sitting room, and Mother had one of the maids cut the heavy cord and then Sister and I were each to lift one end of the cover and take it off. You can't imagine, children, what that moment, so long waited for, was to us!"

Polly and Davie each side of Miss Parrott, the big rag doll on her lap, didn't dare to breathe, so afraid they should miss something of this great moment.

"We lifted the tissue paper with trembling fingers, and

there lay this doll," Miss Parrott lifted it, "and we had watched every day for a pink or a blue satin one!"

Polly broke the silence first. "Oh, I think this one was the nicest to play with."

"So it was, child, but we were silly little girls, and we had set our hearts on quite another kind of doll. Well, what do you think we did? I am quite ashamed to tell you, but you shall have the whole story. We threw ourselves down on the floor, our arms around each other, and declared we didn't want that doll."

"Oh, dear!" exclaimed Polly.

"And so our mother said 'Very well,' and she had the tissue paper all put back over the doll, the cover put on, and the box tied up. And then it was taken away and put up on a shelf over the linen press."

"Oh, dear!" breathed Polly again.

"And that doll stayed up there all one year, and we never said we were sorry, and asked for her. And one day an awkward servant in cleaning that shelf, knocked the box off, and then he became frightened, so he opened it to see if he'd broken anything. And somebody calling him, he left the box on the floor, and a little dog we had, a mischievous creature, ran into the linen room and stuck his nose in the box."

"Oh, dear!" exclaimed Polly and David together.

"And Towsle—"

"Was that his name?" asked Davie, pressing up to her black silk gown in great excitement.

"Yes, dear," said Miss Parrott, smiling down into his blue eyes. "Well, Towsle nipped that doll up in his sharp teeth and ran off downstairs with her. And Sister heard him coming and she called 'Towsle—Towsle' for she wanted him to come and play with her. But Towsle was going to have a great deal more pleasure he thought with the doll, so he hid behind one of the big carved chairs in the hall. And then when he thought she had gone safely by, he crept out. But she spied him, and she screamed, 'Oh, he's got our doll!' and Uncle John, who was in the sitting room with Mother, ran out with her. But Towsle—oh, there was no catching him then, for—"

"And didn't they catch him?" burst in Davie.

"Why, yes, dear," Miss Parrott pointed to the doll in her lap.

"Oh, yes," said Davie with a sigh of relief.

"But in flying down the long steps at last, Towsle caught one of his feet in the doll's dress, and over he rolled from the top to the bottom. But he wouldn't give up the doll. And then I heard the noise, and I ran out from the garden, and before Mother and Uncle John and Sister got there, I seized the doll, and Towsle pulled and I pulled—and there," Miss Parrott turned the doll over in her lap, "the silk gown was torn. You can scarcely see the place, for our mother mended it so neatly."

The Pepper children bent over to scan closely the rent in the back of the checked silk gown.

"I shouldn't know it was mended," declared Polly at last.

"No, would you?" said Miss Parrott, with bright eyes. "Our mother was a most beautiful sewer. Well, we couldn't help laughing, Towsle was so funny, and he tried to get that doll away from me after I had at last torn it from him. And then Sister cried right out, 'Oh, our poor doll!'—and then I cried over her, and we petted her up. And we said we'd love her forever after."

"That was nice," said Polly, smoothing down her gown in great satisfaction.

"And we called her 'Priscilla,' and we took her to bed with us every night," finished Miss Parrott.

XV

"And See My Slate"

"Was Towsle your very own dog?" asked Polly breathlessly.

"Yes, Sister's and mine," said Miss Parrott. "You see one day he belonged to me, and the next to her. And one night he slept on the foot of her bed, and the next on mine. And he never made a mistake—when he saw us get into our nightgowns."

"Oh!" exclaimed Polly, clasping her hands. David crowded up closely, almost forgetting the precious book in his hands. To own a dog, and to have him sleep on your bed at night!

"Would you like to see a picture of Towsle?" asked Miss Parrott, with a keen look into each face.

"Oh, *would* you show it to us?" cried Polly eagerly.

Davie drew a long breath. It wasn't necessary for him to ask, as long as Polly did.

"You hold the doll," Miss Parrott laid Priscilla in Polly's arm, "and stay there, children."

So Polly and David waited by the big sofa and watched Miss Parrott go over to a cabinet on the wall. And pretty soon back she came with an old-fashioned daguerreotype in her hand.

142

"You see, Uncle John wanted to have our pictures taken, and we begged to have Towsle between us. So there we are!"

Miss Parrott pushed up the little spring and there were two small girls in checked high-necked dresses, with ruffles around the necks, and hair brushed back and held by round combs. A small fuzzy-wuzzy dog with eyes like black shoe buttons sat primly up between the two.

Polly and David gazed perfectly absorbed at the picture. At last Miss Parrott asked, "Now which of these two little girls do you think is my picture?"

"Were you ever a little girl?" It was impossible for David to keep from asking the question now, although the instant it was out, he knew that a terrible blunder had been made.

"Oh, Davie!" exclaimed Polly, greatly mortified.

"It's no wonder that you ask, Davie," Miss Parrott smiled at him, so he raised his head, "so many years have passed. Well, which of those two little girls do you think I was?"

David considered slowly—then put his finger on one. There was something in the kind eyes that made him think of Miss Parrott when she smiled at him.

"Which do you think, Polly?"

"I don't know," she said, "but I think this one," and she chose the other little girl.

"Davie is right," said Miss Parrott, with another smile for him. And Polly beamed at him, for it really was nicer that he had guessed the right one.

"Did Towsle like to have his picture taken?" asked Polly.

"No," said Miss Parrott, with a little laugh, "not at first. He barked dreadfully at the man who was trying to take the picture, and he said at last that he couldn't let the dog be in it. And Uncle John said then nobody would have a picture taken at all."

"Oh, dear! What did you do?" cried Polly.

"And wasn't there any picture?" cried David, dreadfully worried.

"Why, yes—see—here it is." Miss Parrott tapped it with a long hand, on which shone several ancestral rings.

"Oh, I forgot," said Davie, looking down at the daguerreotype in her lap.

"Oh, Miss Parrott, what *did* you do?" begged Polly anxiously.

"Well, the man went out and told his little girl to come in. They had just been making some molasses candy, and she brought a piece. And he told her to hold it up, so that the dog could see it. And then he got back of his little black thing over the picture machine, and he stuck up his head, and said, 'All right—sit still, children,' and then something clicked, and we were all taken."

"Towsle was good to sit still, wasn't he, Miss Parrott," cried Polly, with shining eyes.

"Yes, indeed. You see he knew it was candy that the little girl held. That was the way Sister and I always made him keep still before we gave him any. So he never took his eyes off from it."

"And did he get the candy—did he?" cried David in great excitement.

"To be sure he did," laughed Miss Parrott, "and it took him ever so long to eat it, for he got his teeth all stuck together. And Uncle John paid the man, and then he said, 'Hasn't that dog finished his candy yet?' for there was Towsle whirling around, putting up first one paw and then another to his face to try to get his jaws apart. You see the candy was too soft." Miss Parrott burst into a hearty laugh in which Polly and David joined.

"And Towsle wouldn't take any molasses candy when

Sister and I offered it to him after that," said Miss Parrott, wiping her eyes. "Dear me, children, I don't know when I have laughed so. Well, now I must put the daguerreotype up."

When she came back to the big sofa, she looked at David, the book tightly clasped in his hands.

"Now I must tell you about this. So you chose a book, Davie?" as he laid it in her hands.

"Yes," said Davie, "I did."

"Well," Miss Parrott turned the leaves of an old First Reader. "Now this makes me very sad."

"Oh, don't tell about it, if it makes you feel bad," cried Polly in distress. "You don't want her to, Davie, do you?"

Davie swallowed hard, trying to say, "No, don't tell about it."

But before he could get the words out, Miss Parrott said quickly, "I really should like to tell about it, children. Well, you see, I wasn't quick about learning to read, as Sister was, and our governess—"

"What's a gover—what you said?" David broke in. He must know if he really were going to understand about the book.

"Oh, Davie!" cried Polly reprovingly, "you mustn't interrupt."

"A governess was the lady who taught Sister and me our lessons. You see we didn't go to school, but studied at home."

"Oh," said Polly and David together.

"Well, Miss Barton, that was her name, had a good deal of trouble with me, I suppose. And one thing that I was the slowest to learn, was spelling. I was quite dull at it. And one day—this is the part that makes me sad, children, I was very naughty. I was determined I would spell my own way, and I began at the word 'From.' " She turned the next page, and there in the midst of a little story was the word "From" beginning a new sentence, and around it were queer little crumpled-up places in the paper.

"Those are the tears I shed afterward," said Miss Parrott, pointing to them.

"Oh, dear!" cried both children, quite overcome to see these tears that were cried out of Miss Parrott's eyes so long ago.

"You see, Miss Barton would have Sister and me stand up before her while she picked out words for us to spell, and then she would have us read the story to which they belonged, and she gave me that word," Miss Parrott's finger pointed to "From" in the midst of the crumply spots, "and I spelled it 'Frum,' and I wouldn't spell it any other way, although she told me how. I kept saying, '*Frum — Frum*' over and over, and Sister tried to make me obey Miss Barton, but I shook my head, and kept saying, '*Frum*,' and at last our governess had to call Mother."

The room was very still now.

"Well, when our Mother came into the little room, I remember I longed to run into her arms and say I was sorry, but something inside of me held me back, and Mother led me away, and Sister burst out crying."

"Well, children," said Miss Parrott, after a pause, "I shall never forget how I suffered as I sat on the little stool in a room by myself, which was our punishment when we were naughty, and thought it all over. And I can never see the word 'From' that it doesn't come back to me. Well now, Davie, so you chose a book?" she added brightly.

"Yes, I did," said David, still keeping his eyes on "From."

"You like books pretty well, do you?" asked Miss Parrott, with a keen glance.

"Davie just loves books," declared Polly impulsively, as Davie raised sparkling eyes.

"And there was another thing that Sister and I had to help us with our spelling. We each had a slate."

"A *slate!*" screamed Davie. "Oh, did you really have a slate?"

"To be sure," said Miss Parrott.

"All to yourself?" cried Davie, quite gone with excitement.

"Yes, indeed—we each had one. Do you want to see them?"

Davie's eyes said "Yes" without the word. But he said it aloud nevertheless.

Miss Parrott went over to the same cabinet and put up the doll and the daguerreotype, bringing back two small slates, with a pencil and a little sponge hanging to each.

"Sister's had a green edge," she said, holding first one slate up to notice, and then the other, "and this one is mine —with a red border."

"May I hold it?" begged David, longingly reaching up his hands.

"Indeed you may," said Miss Parrott, giving it to him. "And, Davie, you may keep that slate. I can't give away Sister's—I shall keep that always—but that one is mine. I hope you like red best?" she asked anxiously.

"I do," said Davie, clasping the slate hungrily. "Is it mine —all mine?"

"It's yours to keep always," said Miss Parrott decidedly, "and I am so glad that you like it. Well now, Polly, I'm going to give you a little plant to carry home. I hope you like flowers."

For answer Polly clasped her hands. It was all she could do to keep from hopping up and down in delight. Seeing this, Miss Parrott took her hand. "We will go down and choose it," she said.

David, hanging to his red-bordered slate, followed them downstairs and out through the little green lattice door.

When they reached the little green plot with the stone seats, Miss Parrott sat down, for all the unusual happenings of this day made a little rest seem very sweet. But she looked at Polly's and David's dancing feet, and said, "You run about, children, and I will come presently and pick out a plant for Polly."

No need for a second invitation. Like little wild things, they were off up to the big green trees, David hanging to his red-bordered slate for dear life.

"Put it down, Davie, do," begged Polly, "under that tree. We can't play tag with any fun if you hold the slate."

"No—no," cried Davie in alarm, and grasping it tighter.

"Oh, well, never mind," said Polly. "Now, come on," with a pat on his shoulder, "you're it."

"She's all tired out," declared the housemaid, peering out of the green lattice door, "look at her a-settin' there. I sh'd think she would be with them children round her all day."

"Bad luck to 'em," exclaimed the cross cook, coming up to look over the housemaid's shoulder. "Well, I never—jest look at 'em a-racin' an' a-chasin' all over th' place! Did anybody ever see sech goin's-on in this garden before?"

The butler didn't dare, since his reproof in the dining room, to join this conversation, but he shrugged up his shoulders, as he kept on at his task of polishing up the family plate.

And Miss Parrott being nicely rested, more by hearing the happy voices and watching the flying feet than by sitting still on the little stone seat, got up presently. "Come, children," she called, "we must choose Polly's plant," and in almost no time at all they both stood before her.

Around and around the old-fashioned garden bright with hollyhocks and all sorts of blossoms and shrubs, they went, Miss Parrott with her finger on her chin, a way she had when she was thinking, and Polly holding her breath whenever a stop was made before a little plant.

At last Miss Parrott paused before a row of little yellow primroses, lifting their bright faces as if to say, "Take me—oh, do, take me!"

"I really believe, Polly," said Miss Parrott, looking down at them, "that you will like one of these. I am sure they were great favorites of mine when I was a little girl."

For answer Polly threw herself down on her knees and laid her flushed cheek against a small cluster of yellow blooms.

"You may pick out the one you like best," said Miss Parrott.

"Oh, this one—if you please," cried Polly, lifting a little pot. "I choose this one—and thank you, dear Miss Parrott."

"I really believe you have made a good selection, Polly," said Miss Parrott, the color rising to her sallow cheek. It was so long since anyone had called her "dear." "Well, now, I am sorry to say it is getting time for me to send you home, for I have much enjoyed the day, but your mother will never allow you to come again if I keep you too long," and she led the way into the house, where Polly got her hat and Davie his cap.

Miss Parrott led the way down the broad hall, with its rugs on the polished floor and the portraits of her ancestors lining the walls. She looked back as she neared the big oaken door to see Polly standing spellbound before the drawing room, and Davie by her side.

"Would you like to go in, dear?" Miss Parrott came back and pointed within the long apartment.

"Oh, if I may," said Polly, in an awe-struck little voice.

"Certainly, dear, and Davie, too." Then she followed, curious to see what would first claim attention.

Polly went straight to the big grand piano standing half across two long French windows, and stood quite still. David came softly after.

"If you can play, Polly," said Miss Parrott, not thinking of anything else to break the silence, "I am quite willing that you should, dear."

"Oh, I can't play," said Polly, coming out of her absorption with a little laugh at the very idea.

"She plays on the table," said Davie, looking up at Miss Parrott.

"Plays on the table?" repeated Miss Parrott in a puzzled way. "I don't understand."

"Just like this." Davie, having by this time quite forgotten to be embarrassed, went over to the big mahogany center table, and laying down his beloved slate, softly ran his fingers up and down the shining surface.

"Oh, you mean instead of a piano she uses a table."

"Yes," said Davie, picking up his slate and running back to stand by Polly.

Miss Parrott was quite still for a moment regarding Polly. Then she said, "Would you like to have me play to you, Polly?"

Polly drew a long breath, and tore her gaze away from the big piano.

"Oh, if you would!" she cried with shining eyes.

So Miss Parrott sat down on the music stool and drew

her long figure up just as the music master had instructed her years ago, and began to finger the keys, Polly, with her little plant in her hand, standing in rapt attention on one side, and David, with his slate, on the other.

At first the tunes didn't go very well, Miss Parrott observing, "I don't know when I have tried this before," and breaking into some other selection. But by degrees, the slender fingers began to run up and down quite at their ease among the black and white keys, and the long somber drawing room seemed to glow with the trills and quavers.

"My soul an' body!" exclaimed the cross cook to the housemaid, "ef she ain't playin' th' pianner. I'm scared to death, Mary Jane."

Mary Jane's florid face turned two shades paler. "I expect she's going to die," she whimpered.

And over in the big drawing room, their mistress was just beginning to blame herself for keeping them so long. She arose hastily from the music stool. "And now it is good-by." She laid a gentle hand on each head. "Run out and get into the carriage," for Simmons had been waiting all this time.

She opened the big oaken door and waited to see them off—then turned back with a curious light on her sallow face.

And Polly and Davie, being set down at the gate of the Little Brown House, raced up to the big green door, and burst in. "I've a plant—a dear, little plant," announced Polly, raising it high.

"And see my slate," Davie tried to reach higher than Polly, "and it's all my very own—it is, Mamsie."

XVI

At Grandma Bascom's

"Davie must go over and sit with Grandma Bascom," said Mrs. Pepper slowly. She looked worried as she glanced up from her sewing by the window; then she smiled brightly over to him.

"Oh, Mamsie," began Polly in dismay.

Davie laid down his slate carefully on the table and ran over to Mother Pepper's chair.

"You see, Davie," said Mrs. Pepper, snipping off a little thread hanging from the sleeve to the coat she was trying to finish, "no one else can be spared, and Grandma mustn't be left alone, now that she is sick."

Polly took two or three quick little stitches in the other sleeve, then she threw down the needle. "But Davie was going to help Mr. Atkins, you know, Mamsie," she cried.

"Mr. Atkins told Davie he was only to come when not wanted for anything else, you know," said Mrs. Pepper, not pausing in her work.

"But, Mamsie," began Polly again, at sight of Davie's face.

152

"No, no, Polly," said Mother Pepper firmly. "Davie must go to Grandma Bascom. And hurry now, child, for work as we may, it will be much as ever we finish the coat in time." She said no more to Davie, who stood silently by her chair, and the kitchen became very quiet except for the ticking of the old clock on the shelf.

"I'll—I'll go—Mamsie," said Davie, swallowing hard.

"That's Mother's boy," said Mrs. Pepper, beaming at him.

Davie wanted dreadfully to take his precious red-bordered slate along so that he could practice his writing, but since no one said anything about it, he didn't like to ask. So he took it off from the table, and going over to the shelf, he stood up on his tiptoes and deposited it behind the old clock. Then he went out and down the lane to Grandma Bascom's.

Polly looked up a few minutes after and saw that the table was bare. "Well, I'm glad, anyway," she said, as she stopped to bite off a thread, "that Davie took his slate. Now he can practice on his writing."

"Don't do that, Polly," said Mother Pepper reprovingly. "Never bite your thread. It's bad for the teeth, child."

"My teeth are awfully strong, Mamsie," laughed Polly, snapping her two rows of little white ones together.

"You never can tell how strong teeth are if they are used to bite threads," said her mother, "so be sure you never do it, Polly."

"I won't," promised Polly, stitching merrily away again; "only it's so hard to remember. I bite off threads before I think, Mamsie."

"That's about the poorest excuse a body can give—'don't think,'" remarked Mrs. Pepper. "Well, child, you sew better every day."

"Do I, Mamsie?" cried Polly, a warm little thrill running up and down her whole body, and the color crept into her cheek. "Do I, really?"

"You do indeed," declared Mrs. Pepper, "and such a help as you are to me!"

"Some day," said Polly, sitting very straight and sewing away for dear life, "I'm going to do every single bit of all the coats, Mamsie."

"And what should I do then?" asked Mrs. Pepper with a laugh.

"You would sit right there in your chair," said Polly, "but you shouldn't take a single stitch—not even the smallest, teentiest stitch."

"Oh, dear me!" exclaimed Mother Pepper, as her needle flew in and out.

"Because I'm going to do 'em all, every bit of every coat," declared Polly positively, and bobbing her brown head.

"Work isn't the worst thing that can happen to a body," observed Mrs. Pepper. "But to sit in a chair with nothing to do—oh, Polly!"

Her look of dismay as she said, "Oh, Polly!" was so funny that Polly burst out laughing, and Mamsie laughed, too, till the old kitchen became cheery at once, and the sun breaking out suddenly two bright little spots danced out on the floor to have fun by themselves.

Davie hurried down the lane to Grandma's and turned into the small patch before the kitchen door. The hens had found an old beef bone and were making an awful noise fighting bill and claw for its possession.

Davie hurried on over the sill into the bedroom. There was Grandma in bed, the gay patched bedquilt drawn up nearly to the big frill of her cap, showing eyes that were not in the least expressive of comfort. When she saw Davie, she pushed off the coverlet. "Oh, my land!" she said. "Grandma's glad to see you!"

By the side of the bed, sitting stiffly on the edge of a cane-bottom chair, sat the parson's elder son.

"My mother told me to ask how she is," he said.

Grandma beckoned to Davie, and patting the coverlet, he climbed up. "He's ben a-settin' there an' a-settin' there by the bed," she said.

"My mother told me to ask how she is," came from Peletiah in his chair, "and she won't tell me. My mother told me—" he began again.

"He won't go home," said Grandma, drawing Davie's ear close to her mouth. "Oh, dear me! an' he's th' parson's son."

"My mother told me—" began Peletiah once more.

Just then there was an awful cackle and clatter out in the kitchen. The beef-bone fight concluded, every scrap of a mouthful being gobbled up, the hens had come tumbling in over the sill all together to see what could be found, now that Grandma was sick in bed and couldn't drive them out.

Davie told Grandma this. He had to say it over several times, his mouth under her cap frill.

"My sakes!" she exclaimed, "you take th' broom an' shoo 'em out o' the kitchen, Davie, an' shet th' door tight after 'em."

So Davie slipped down from the bed, glad enough to have something to do.

"My mother told me—" began Peletiah.

"An' you go with him an' help drive out them pesky hens," cried Grandma, rolling over in bed to look at him. "An' I'm well enough, so you needn't come again, you tell your ma."

Peletiah never waited to hear more than the last sentence that told him what he had come to find out. He got off from his chair in great satisfaction and went out into the little kitchen where Davie was waving the broom over the wild fluttering tangle of hens, all squawking together, as he tried to drive them out of doors.

"Oh, dear! one's running into the bedroom. Keep her out, Peletiah—hurry!" cried Davie in great distress.

But Peletiah, never having hurried in his life, couldn't understand why he should do so now. So the hen had plenty of time to run around him and fluffed and squawked her way into the bedroom, where she ducked under Grandma's big four-poster.

"She's gone under Grandma's bed," announced Peletiah, coming up to where Davie, leaning under the big table, had seized one hen by the leg and was wildly trying to catch another. At last he had her, but she turned and gave him a vicious little peck on his hand as he backed out holding on for dear life to them both.

"There's a hen gone under Grandma's bed," said Peletiah again.

"Oh, dear—dear!" exclaimed Davie, trying to hold fast to the two struggling biddies.

But they flapped so violently that one got away, and thinking that where another Mrs. Biddy went, it was easy to follow, this one ran around Peletiah's slow legs, and there they were, two of them, under Grandma's big four-poster.

Davie shut the door on his vanquished fowl, and turned his hot tired face to the parson's son.

"We must get them out."

"We can't," said Peletiah. He might be slow, but he knew when it was impossible to accomplish a thing. "You can't get hens out from under a bed," he said positively.

"But they can't stay there," persisted David. "You stand

one side of the bed, and I'll stand the other with the broom, and drive 'em out." And he ran and laid hold of the broom again.

"I want the broom," said Peletiah, reaching a hand for it.

"Grandma told me to drive out the hens."

"Well, she didn't say with the broom."

"Oh, yes," cried Davie eagerly, "she said, 'Take the broom and shoo 'em out.'"

"She said out of the kitchen—she didn't say bedroom," declared Peletiah, who was nothing if not exact.

"So she did," said Davie, giving up the broom with a sigh. "Well, you drive 'em away from your side, but I must tell Grandma first."

So he climbed up on the bed again and put his mouth close to the big cap frill, and told what was going to be done.

"Land alive! What's come to your thumb?" cried Grandma in great consternation.

David looked down at his small thumb. The blood had run down and stiffened into a small patch of red where Mrs. Biddy had nipped it. "It doesn't hurt," he said, trying to stick his thumb away from the eyes under the cap frill.

"Now to think that you sh'd 'a' come over to take care of me, an' got hurt," moaned Grandma. "Oh me—oh my! what will your Ma say! Well, you must have some opodeldoc on, right away. Run out an' go to the cupboard, an' you'll find a bottle on th' upper shelf. I put it there to be handy, ef anyone gets hurt. My son John mos' had his leg took off one day when he was mowin' in th' south medder an' they come a-runnin' for me."

Grandma didn't think to tell that the same bottle couldn't be found on that occasion, but she had always been under the impression that it had saved son John's life.

"Can't we drive out the hens first?" asked Davie, slipping off from the bed.

"Mercy no—th' hens can wait—they're comf'table under th' bed. You run an' get that bottle."

So Davie ran out into the kitchen while Peletiah, leaning on the broom, waited by the side of the bed.

"You'll have to git up on a chair," called Grandma from the bed, "it's on th' upper shelf."

So David pulled up a chair and climbed up on it. But even on his tiptoes he couldn't reach, although he tried and tried until his face got very red.

"I can reach with a box—there's one," he said. And jumping down he ran over to the corner and emptied out a few apples and deposited the box on the chair.

"Maybe it's back of th' teapot," said Grandma. "I remember now that teapot got cracked, and I put it up there. Look behind it, Davie."

So Davie looked behind it, holding on to the edge of the shelf with one hand, and feeling around with the other. But no bottle was in sight. There were some papers of herbs, and, as they got stirred about, the little fine particles coming out of various holes made him sneeze.

"You're ketchin' cold," said Grandma, who was getting dreadfully nervous. "Mercy me! What will your ma say ef you got sick over here, an' she's had sech trouble with th' measles? Oh, dear—deary me!"

David by this time was in great distress at not being able to find what he was sent for. And to think of Grandma sick and worried—that was the worst of it—so he worked on.

"I remember now—it's come to me—'twa'n't on that upper shelf at all," said Grandma. "I took it down one day, 'cause thinks I 'twon't be so easy for me with my rheumatics to stretch clear up there, an' I put it on the one underneath."

"I'm glad it's on the one underneath," said Davie joyfully. So he got down from his heights, and put the box in the corner and the apples back in it again. Then he hopped up on the chair and peered all along the bottles and various things cluttered up on the shelf.

"Is it a very big bottle?" he asked, his blue eyes roving anxiously over the array.

"Oh, my land, no," said Grandma; "'tain't big, an' it ain't little. It's jest a bottle."

"Oh," said Davie, trying to think what he ought to leave out in the search.

"You better bring me one or two that you think is it," said Grandma at last.

So Davie picking off from the shelf some "jest bottles" hurried with them to Grandma's bed.

"My sakes!" she said, not looking at them and lifting up her hands, "what a sight you be, Davie Pepper!"

"You're all dirt," said Peletiah pleasantly.

"I didn't s'pose I had any cobwebs in that cupboard," said Grandma in a mortified voice. "An' you're all a-runnin' with sweat. Well, you've got to wipe your face—there's a towel there on th' bureau."

"Here are the bottles," said Davie. His eyes peered at her under his soft light hair where the herbs had drifted down.

"Oh, yes, so they be," said Grandma, taking them. "Well, 'tain't th' opodeldoc—none of 'em ain't. You wash your face, David, first, an' then you can look again. There won't be no cobwebs on the lower shelf."

So Davie took the towel and ran out to the sink, and

washed up. He shook his hair pretty well; but some of the little green things stayed in the soft waves. Then he took the bottles away from the bed where Grandma laid them, and brought away some more "jest bottles."

But no opodeldoc appeared, and at last Grandma lay back on her pillows dreadfully disappointed.

"Can't I look some other place?" begged Davie, climbing up on the bed to lay his mouth against her ear.

"No mortal man would know where to tell you," moaned Grandma.

"Oh, dear!" exclaimed Davie, laying his hot little cheek against her wrinkled one. "There's a bottle on that little table." He pointed over toward the big old bureau. "May I get it?"

"Yes, but it ain't a mite o' use," said the old lady hopelessly.

So Davie slid off from the bed once more, and went over to the small table by the side of the bureau and brought the bottle and put it in Grandma's hand.

"Land o' Goshen, now it's come to me! How glad I am I remember. I took that down from th' shelf th' other day when I cut my finger peelin' potatoes."

"Is that the—what you said?" gasped Davie.

"Yes—it's th' opodeldoc."

"Oh!" cried Davie, and his blue eyes shone, and he clasped his hands in bliss. He didn't have to go home and tell Mamsie he couldn't find Grandma's things when she was sick and he had come to help.

"Now you go to the lowest drawer in th' bureau," said Grandma, "and get a roll of old white cotton, an' I'll tie up your thumb."

David looked down at his thumb. He had forgotten all about it in the general turmoil.

"It doesn't hurt any," he said, "and I washed the blood off."

"That may be," said Grandma, who wasn't going to lose what she dearly loved to do: bind up any wounds that presented themselves, "but a hurt is a hurt, and it's got to be took care of. An' there's some blood a-comin' yet."

A tiny drop or two making its appearance to her satisfaction, she made David sit up on the bed again. And at last the little thumb was all bound up, and the cloth tied up with a bit of string she found in the little table drawer by her bed.

"An' now you must go right straight home—an' you tell your ma she don't need to tetch that bandage till tomorrow."

"We haven't driven out the hens," said Peletiah, still standing by his broom.

"Hey?" said Grandma. "What does he say, Davie?"

"He says we haven't driven out the hens. Oh, I forgot them, Grandma," said Davie in a sorry little voice. It was impossible to be more mortified than he was at this moment.

"Well, you can do it now," said Grandma composedly; "it's gittin' late, and hens knows better'n most folks when it's along about time to go to bed. They'll go easy—like enough."

David lifted up the calico valance running around the bed, and Peletiah got down on his knees and lifted up the part hanging down his side. There bunched up together were the two fat biddies. They turned sleepy eyes on the two boys. And when Peletiah inserted the broom under the bed, they got up, shook their feathers, and marched off to the kitchen, and so out of doors, much preferring to roost respectably on a tree than under a feather bed.

XVII

The Fishing Party

"I very much wish I could go," said David to himself, and he sighed clear down in his little heart. Then he crept out from behind the woodpile, his favorite place when he had anything to think out, and started to run as fast as he could down the lane into the highroad.

"Because if I don't hurry, Joel will ask Mamsie to let me go, too, and I promised Mr. Atkins I'd help him keep store today.

"And besides," as he panted on, "I should lose the ten cents he'd give me for Mamsie."

So he was all hot and tired out when he pushed open the door to the store. Mr. Atkins was behind the counter.

"You needn't to 'a' hurried so," he said. "You're all het up, Davie. Now set down an' rest."

David, without much breath to spare, said nothing, as he climbed up on the sugar barrel, his usual place when there was a chance to sit down, and folded his hands to wait for orders.

But before these came, the door was swung violently open and in rushed Joel.

"What made you run off?" he demanded. "Mamsie says you can go," and he plunged across the store to David on his barrel.

"Hulloa!" cried Mr. Atkins, "hain't you no time to say good morning? Your ma wouldn't like you to lose your manners."

Joel, very much ashamed, deserted David and ran over to the counter. "I'm sorry," he began, his face very red, and his black stubby head bobbing. "I didn't mean to forget."

"All right," said Mr. Atkins. "Well now, what's the rumpus, pray tell, Joel?"

"He can go," said Joel, pounding one fist on the counter. "Mamsie says he can."

"Who, Davie?"

"Yes, he can go. Mamsie says so, if you don't want him." Then Joel, fearing that one fist was not enough to emphasize his statement, now began with the other till the pieces of paper on the counter were all in a flutter.

"Hold on there, Joe," said Mr. Atkins, "or, first you know, you'll have us all a-blowing out the door."

Joel stopped pounding and looked anxiously over at the store door, while Mr. Atkins laughed and leaned over the counter.

"What's it all about—where do you want David to go?" he asked.

David, who up to this time had sat quite still, now hopped from his barrel and ran over to Joel. "Oh, I can't go," he cried. "I'm going to stay here and help Mr. Atkins."

Joel whirled around and seized Davie's calico blouse. "You can," he howled, "you can, Davie—"

"Where do you want David to go?" demanded the storekeeper, between Joel's howls and David's remonstrances.

"Fishing," said Joel. Then he turned a face of anguish. "Do make him," he cried, still hanging to David's blouse.

"Don't you want to go, Davie?" asked Mr. Atkins with a keen glance at him.

David stopped crying. "Oh, I can't go," and hung his head. He wanted dreadfully to say, "No, sir," but Mamsie had always told them all to speak the truth. So he said, "Yes," in a very low voice.

"Then I guess you better go," said the storekeeper.

"Oh, no, no," cried Davie, springing away from Joel. "I can't go. Don't make me, Mr. Atkins."

"You mean because you promised to help me today, David?" said Mr. Atkins.

"Yes, sir—and do make Joel stop." David was now in such a panic that Mr. Atkins came out from behind the counter. "See here, Joe," and he seized his arm, "you get up on Davie's barrel an' set still if you can." And before Joel quite knew how, there he was, and the storekeeper and Davie were settling matters by themselves.

"You see," Mr. Atkins was saying, "it's quite lucky that I want to set about some things today in the store where you can't help me, Davie."

"Can't I, Mr. Atkins?" cried David.

"No; fact is, I'd ruther you'd come tomorrow, 'nstead o' today," said Mr. Atkins decidedly. "You can go fishing as well as not. Hop down, Joe."

No need to tell Joel. He was off the sugar barrel and down by David's side in a twinkling.

"Got any fish pole, Davie?" asked the storekeeper. He was back by the counter now, and rummaging on his shelves.

Before David could answer, Joel piped, "Yes—we made 'em."

"An' fishhooks?" Mr. Atkins went on, bending over to get a small box on the lower shelf.

"Yes, yes," said Joel. "Mrs. Blodgett gave us some big pins. Come on, Dave."

"Well now, David," said the storekeeper, turning around, a fish pole in one hand and two or three fishhooks in the other. "Here's somethin' for you. You've ben a good boy an' helped me fust-rate."

Joel rushed over to the counter, his black eyes sparkling. David came up slowly.

"Hold your hands, Davie," said Mr. Atkins. "Now, says I, I guess you can ketch some fish. Hurry up, my boy," as David hung back.

"Can't—can't Joel have 'em?" asked Davie.

"No—no, these are for you. You've ben helpin' me real good in th' store." Mr. Atkins dangled the fish pole before the boys. Joel held his breath and crowded closely up.

"Joel could catch more fish with 'em," said Davie, the color dropping out from his little face.

"Well, maybe," said the storekeeper with a keen glance at Joel, who twisted his brown hands tightly together, trying not to say how very much he wanted that fish pole and those splendid hooks. "There, hold out your hands, Davie."

David put forth a pair of hands that shook so that the fishhooks tumbled out of them and down to the floor.

"I'll pick 'em up," cried Joel, scrambling after them. He held them a minute, trying the sharp points on his small thumb, and turning them over and over admiringly.

"Now it just comes to me, I do verily b'lieve I've got another fish pole like David's," said Mr. Atkins reflectively, and turning back to his shelves.

"Is it for me? Oh, is it, Mr. Atkins?" screamed Joel, and

he tumbled the fishhooks into David's hand and scrambled up on the counter.

"I wouldn't wonder," said the storekeeper over his shoulder.

"Oh—oh!" Joel hopped up and down on the counter, his black eyes shining in anticipation. "Dave, he's going to give me one, too—he is—he is!" he screamed.

David, both hands full of his treasures, gave a long blissful sigh, then hugged them to his breast, and he laughed aloud in glee.

"Mercy sakes! Get down off th' counter, Joe," said Mr. Atkins. "There," as Joel slid to the floor, putting a fish pole, just the size for a boy to swing, into the eager brown hand, "an' there's th' hooks. Be careful not to git 'em stuck into you."

"They're goin' to be stuck into the fishes," cried Joel, seizing fish pole and hooks. "I'm going to catch lots and lots. Come on, Dave," beginning to march to the door in great excitement. Then he remembered and ran back. "I thank you," he said, then dashed out.

"Now, run along, Davie," said Mr. Atkins, "or Joe will be down to th' brook an' catch every single fish before you have a chance to get up with him."

David stood quite still clasping his treasures, as he tried to speak. His blue eyes shone, but he couldn't say a word.

"I know," said the storekeeper kindly. "Now you run along. I shall need you tomorrow, for you are a great help to me, David."

David's happy feet scarcely seemed to touch the ground, as he hurried after Joel, almost catching up with him turning into the gateway of the Little Brown House.

It was some time before the boys could settle down from the excitement of showing their treasures, to the work of digging the worms. Polly came out and helped them with an old iron spoon. She couldn't work fast and her hand trembled, all her healthy young body longing for the fun of the expedition. But there was no hope that she could go —for she must help Mamsie to finish the coats brought home from the store the day before. And there were the Henderson boys waiting, Mrs. Pepper being willing, since the parson's sons could go, to let Joel and David have this pleasure.

At last they were off—all four of them—the worms wriggling about in an old tin can that Joel shook up and down at every step.

Polly hung over the old gate with Phronsie by her side, to watch them off.

"Oh, I wish I could ever have any fun," she said to herself. "The little path in the woods is just lovely, and the dear brook! Oh, dear, why can't I ever go anywhere!"

"Polly," asked Phronsie, giving a little twitch to Polly's blue checked apron, "what is the matter?"

"I'm not crying," said Polly, turning her face away.

"But your mouth looks like crying," said Phronsie, peering around anxiously at her.

"Oh, never mind, Pet," said Polly. Then she drew a long breath. "Let me alone, Phronsie. I'm bad this morning."

"You're never bad," said Phronsie decidedly. "Do let me see your face, Polly," she begged.

Polly swallowed hard. "I'll tell you, Phronsie, what let's do—we'll race down the road to the corner and then turn and race back. Catch me now."

Phronsie, all intent now on the race, forgot about Polly's face. When they came back and ran into the Little Brown House, Polly's cheeks were as rosy as ever, and Phronsie was laughing gleefully.

When the "lovely little path in the woods" was reached, Joel dashed ahead and Ezekiel at his heels.

"You're so slow," Joel said, looking back at Peletiah. So David had to hold back his feet, longing for a run, to keep pace with the parson's eldest son.

The consequence was, as they came up to the deep pool in the silvery little brook, Joel was fixing his best hook on the line hanging from his new pole. Ezekiel, too lost in admiration to do anything to get his own made ready, was hanging over him.

Peletiah sat down and calmly looked around. "My father says you mustn't splash the water when you fish," he said, as Joel made frantic flings with his fishline on which a long worm made curves in the air.

"I can fish," shouted Joel, standing on a big stone in the middle of the pool. "See— Come on, Dave!"

David, who never could bear to stick a worm on the hook, put his hand into the tin can, then drew it back again. "Perhaps a fish will bite without it," he said to himself. Then he went farther down the pool and behind some bushes, and cast in his line.

"Come here!" shouted Joel, from his big stone, and splashing the silvery surface on all sides. "Come, Dave!"

"My father says you mustn't splash the water when you fish," said Peletiah, beginning slowly to choose a worm from the tin can.

Joel turned a cold shoulder to the parson's son and continued to beat the water to right and to left. Ezekiel, seeing there was more fun to be gained than to stay with Peletiah, who was having difficulty with his worm, stepped gingerly across the steppingstones, holding his pole carefully aloft.

"I'm coming," he announced.

"No, no," cried Joel crossly, "this is Dave's place."

"I'm coming," announced Ezekiel pleasantly, as he picked his way along.

"You aren't going to get on," declared Joel, spreading his small legs apart defiantly.

"I'm the minister's son," said Ezekiel, "and you must let me get on."

"No, I shan't," said Joel. Yet he had an awful feeling down deep in his heart that he ought to; but he stood his ground sturdily.

"And that stone is mine as much as it is yours," said Ezekiel, drawing near and balancing his pole with great care.

"No, it's mine, I got it first." Joel squared his shoulders and gave a swish to his line that sent his worm away off among the shining ripples.

Just then came a cry from David. "I've got a fish—I've got a fish!" in a jubilant little voice.

Joel deserted his big stone and flew past Ezekiel on the steppingstones, who immediately in great satisfaction stepped on to the coveted place.

"I'll help you get him in, Dave," cried Joel, plunging along the bushes where Dave, with a very red face, was struggling to land a heavy weight on his hook. "I'll get him for you."

Joel threw aside his fish pole, the long worm still continuing his exercise, and dashing up, laid his little brown hands next to David's, and together they pulled so hard that over backward they went, and the fishhook with an old tangled root hanging to it flew straight up in the air.

"Oh, dear!" exclaimed David in great mortification, as they picked themselves up and began to untangle the root, "there wasn't any fish at all."

"P'raps you had one, and he ate off the worm," said Joel, seeing David's face.

David turned off to the bushes, leaving Joel to get the old piece of root off. "I don't need to tell him that I didn't have a worm on," he said to himself, and his hands worked nervously.

"I 'most know a fish stole your worm," Joel kept saying as his hands were busy. "Bad old fish!"

David's cheeks got so hot that he came out of the shelter of the bushes. Could he go home to Mamsie without telling Joel all about it? Without stopping to think, he plunged up to Joel's side. "I didn't stick a worm on."

"Didn't stick a worm on?" repeated Joel in amazement, dropping fishhook, tangle of root and all.

"No," said David in a miserable little voice. "I didn't, Joel." Then he sat down on the grass, and hid his face.

"Hoh!" sniffed Joel, "you can't fish—any more than—than—a girl."

"Oh, Joel, I can," burst out Davie, leaping to his feet. "I can Joel—and I will put on a worm," but he shivered.

"You needn't," said Joel, turning back to the root tangle. "I'll put 'em all on for you—I like to."

"I've got one!" screamed Ezekiel.

Sure enough! There was the minister's son having the greatest difficulty in his excitement to keep his footing on the big stone, swinging his line, at the end of which was a little speckled trout shining in the sunshine.

XVIII

Danger

JOEL threw the fish pole, root tangle and all, and rushed wildly over to Ezekiel on the big stone. "Let me see him—let me!" he cried.

"I shall take it home for my father," said Ezekiel in proud possession, holding up the little speckled beauty dangling from the hook, as he hurried over the steppingstones.

"And I shall catch one and take it home to my mother," announced Peletiah, where he sat by the side of the brook. He hadn't even chosen his worm, but was taking one after another from the tin can and laying them down on the grass.

"They're all running away," cried Joel, flying up with his own fish pole and David's, the root tangle still hanging. "Oh, they're all running away, Peletiah Henderson."

"They can't run," said Peletiah, still busy trying to decide which worm would be most likely to entice a nice fish, "because they haven't got legs."

"And there aren't but a teenty-weenty few," cried Joel, aghast at the loss. "Oh, you're a bad boy, Peletiah Henderson," he added wrathfully, as he examined the contents of the tin can.

"I'm not a bad boy—I'm the minister's son," said Peletiah calmly. And selecting the longest and the fattest of the remaining worms, he proceeded to fasten it on his hook.

"I don't care. You're the baddest of the bad boys, and you shan't have any more of these worms." With that Joel huddled up the tin can within his arms and marched off to a safe corner back of the bushes.

"See my fish," cried Ezekiel, coming up to swing his line so that all the others could have a good view. "I caught the first one."

"I don't care," said Joel, busy over David's tangled hook. "I'll catch the next one." Then he twitched off the piece of root, stuck on a worm—David hurrying off to cover his eyes—and jumped to his feet, and in a minute he was over on the big stone.

But he didn't get the fish. Instead it was Davie's worm that met the eyes of a fat old father trout that came lazily down the little purling brook. He had always warned his children, had this fat old trout, to beware of boys, and dancing bugs and worms. But he was tired on this day, and hungry, having eaten nothing since a breakfast of two flies. And the first thing he knew a juicy morsel was in his mouth. But alas! he couldn't swallow it—for something stuck fast and held him pinned. And one of those same dreadful boys was shouting, "I have got one, Joel!"

When the fat old trout was laid on the grass, all the boys stood around it in speechless admiration.

Finally Joel found his tongue. "Dave caught that," he announced proudly. "My brother Dave caught that all by himself."

"It was Joel's worm," said Davie.

"I caught the first one," said Ezekiel. He couldn't take his eyes from the big fish. At last he ran and tucked his little trout in the basket, and shut the cover down very tightly.

"Dave's is bigger," boasted Joel, strutting off. "Hoh!

your fish is a squinching little one, Ezekiel Henderson."

"I shall catch one now," announced Peletiah, going pompously off over the steppingstones, and carrying his fish pole with a careful hand.

Joel dashed wildly past him, reaching the big stone first. "This is my place," he declared. "I found it."

"I shall stand on that stone," declared Peletiah decidedly, and crowding up to get both feet on it.

As there wasn't room for more than one, the two boys couldn't raise their arms enough to swing the fishlines, so they whirled around and around, each trying to get the best place for their feet. At last Peletiah made an unlucky movement, his foot slipped and in he splashed, fish pole and all.

"I'll pull you out," cried Joel, in the greatest dismay, bending over the pool. Oh, dear, if the parson's son should drown!

"I don't want you to," said Peletiah, getting up and paddling to the steppingstones. Then he marched over them in great dignity, and dripping water dreadfully. "I am going home, and I shall tell my mother how you crowded me off the big stone."

Joel deserted the big stone by a single bound.

"Don't—oh, dear!—Mamsie will feel—don't, Peletiah," he begged, plunging frantically after him.

David deserted his big fish, having sat down on the grass by its side, happy in the thought of taking it home to Mamsie, to run up and mingle his entreaties with those of Joel.

"I shall stay and catch a bigger fish than David's," announced Ezekiel, preparing to select another worm.

"I am going home," declared Peletiah, stalking off. Instead of taking the wood path, he turned into a meadow where a number of cows were grazing.

Joel, with no thought of the fish pole he was leaving behind but only that he must prevent Peletiah from taking such a dreadful tale to the parsonage, plunged after him. And Davie, abandoning the big fish, followed in distress.

Peletiah kept swinging his fish pole and stalked on.

Suddenly there was a great noise. It was just like a roar of wind—then a queer sound, and that was a bellow, and an old bull, that didn't like anybody, least of all a boy, to come swinging things around in the field that belonged to him and to the cows, gave a snort and came charging down across the meadow.

Joel saw him first. "The bull—the bull!" he screamed.

Peletiah, quite lost to everything but the story he was carrying to the parsonage, kept on his dignified way, swinging his fish pole triumphantly.

Joel took a long breath. By turning off he could run by a crosscut and perhaps make the bull forget Peletiah. Then he swung his arms, and made an awful noise. The bull didn't like this a bit better, for here were two impudent boys instead of one. So he stopped just a second, trying to decide which one to go for first, and Peletiah, turning, for once in his life was anything but slow in the way he made for the fence. This decided the bull, who now gave his whole attention to Joel, and the small boy pattering after.

"Run for the fence, Dave," shouted Joel, zigzagging from right to left, trying to confuse the bull, who now was getting thoroughly mad.

David gave one dreadful scream in the direction of a man, off in the road where Peletiah was now safe. But he didn't run for the fence; on the contrary, he did just what Joel was doing, darted first to right, then to left, so that between the two boys the bull was troubled in his mind which one to toss up toward the sky.

The first thing either of them knew, somebody was saying, "I'll take care of the bull—run for the fence!" and a tall figure was dashing in to the thick of things and swinging his hat.

By this time, the bull didn't know where he was nor what course to pursue. And before any of them quite knew it, Joel and David were over the fence, and the tall man was bending over them where they had tumbled flat down on their faces in the grass.

"Well, little chap, I've paid my debt to you," he was saying, bending over David. But David was beyond hearing anything, having fainted clear away. So the tall young man took him and carried him across the road where there was a little thread of a stream of water that ran away by itself from the brook, Joel stumbling after, picking out the grass that flew in his mouth as he tumbled off from the fence.

"Now then," the tall young man smiled as David opened his eyes, "little chap, you're coming round all right," and he wrung the water out of his handkerchief, with which he had bathed the small, white face.

And David looked up into the eyes of the visitor who had come uninvited to Mr. Atkins's store, to go afterward to Cherryville jail.

The color came flying back into David's cheeks, and he sat straight.

"Did they hurt you there?" he cried anxiously.

"Not a bit of it," said the young man. "I'm just out today. Good luck for you," he said under his breath.

The old bull, very angry that the cows should see his discomfiture, was snorting and pawing the earth over in the meadow. David shivered and hid his eyes on the young man's sleeve.

Joel, who hadn't taken his gaze from the stranger, crowded up as closely as he could.

"Who are you, Mr. Man?" he demanded.

"Didn't you ever hear of a fellow who tried to rob the store in Badgertown?" asked the stranger.

Joel tumbled back, "Are you the burglar?"

"He didn't take anything," cried Davie hastily.

"Good reason why. This little chap wouldn't let me," said the young man. Then he laughed.

"And you—you jumped in front of the bull," gasped Joel.

"That was easy enough," said the young man. "I couldn't have this little chap hurt. He was good to me, and didn't want me to be hurt."

"I think you are a good burglar, Mr. Man," said Joel, crowding up closely. "I said I'd have smashed you if I'd been there in the store—but I don't want to now."

The young man burst into a hearty laugh.

"I could have done it," said Joel, very much nettled at the laugh—and he doubled up his small fists.

"Oh, I dare say," said the young man, wiping his eyes. Then he saw Joel's face. "Well, you have got a pair of fists, to be sure!" he declared admiringly.

Joel spread his little brown hands, then doubled them up again and flirted them in the air, very much pleased.

"Yes, indeed," said the young man. "Well, now, don't use them any more than you can help. Good luck to you, little chap," he turned to David, and was gone down the road.

"I wish he hadn't gone," mourned David, looking after him. "Perhaps he would have come with us to Mamsie."

That made Joel think of the two fish poles and the big fish. "I must get them," he said, springing up. Just then down the road that he had struck from the wood path came

Ezekiel, who didn't find it so pleasant, after all, being alone. He was carrying all the things, even the tin can that had one worm in it.

Peletiah, long before this at the parsonage, was sitting on the back steps. Having run every step of the way home, a thing he couldn't remember ever doing in his life before, he still sat thinking it all over. It didn't seem quite so nice a thing to do, to carry the tale into the parson's study, as at first it had appeared to him. And when he thought of the bull, as Joel's cry had warned him, he ducked his head down between his arms. And although he had seen the young man save the situation, he couldn't forget Joel waving his arms and telling him to "run for the fence."

Joel was occupied for the next few hours after reaching the Little Brown House and the story all through with, in pretending he was the bull and dashing after imaginary persons; and then when tired of that, he said he was going to be the burglar.

"Don't call him that," begged David, who had shivered all through Joel's performance. "Mamsie, please don't let Joel call him that."

"No, Joel, you mustn't," said Mrs. Pepper; "say, instead, 'How good he was!'"

"He said I had good fists," said Joel.

"Fists are to be used only when you are sure it is right to do so," said Mrs. Pepper. "Remember that, Joey."

"Oh, hello!" Joel, at last obliged to drop his imaginary performances as a bull, had run out to pick up some kindlings. By the woodshed stood Peletiah.

"I didn't tell my father and my mother you wouldn't let me get on my big stone," he said.

"It was my stone," declared Joel, squaring up to him. "I got on it first."

"You got off of it," said Peletiah, "and that made it mine when I got on."

"I was coming back when I got Davie's fishhook fixed," said Joel stubbornly. "It was my big stone."

"It was mine, and you came up and scrouged," said Peletiah, bobbing his tow head obstinately.

"I wish your father would preach at you, and preach at you every single Sunday," cried Joel vindictively, Kicking his rusty little shoe in the dirt.

"My father doesn't preach at us," cried Peletiah calmly. "He preaches at other people."

"Well, I wish a bear would come out of the woods and eat you," said Joel.

Peletiah looked all about him, his glance even taking in the hills ranging about Badgertown. "There aren't any bears around here," he said calmly.

"Well, maybe they could come from somewhere else," said Joel, his round face brightening.

Just then Mrs. Pepper appeared in the doorway, and David just behind her. "Peletiah, you are just the one I want to see," she cried. She had a blue plate covered with a napkin in her hand. "Now, David, you tell him," looking down at him. But David hung back. So Mamsie had to do it for him. "David wants you to take half of this nice big fish to your mother, as Ezekiel is going to give his to your father." She came down from the step and put the plate in his hand.

Peletiah, standing quite still, looked at the blue plate covered with the napkin. Then he moved off slowly. Joel ran after him.

"I don't want the bears to eat you," he said.

"And you can have the big stone if you want it," said Peletiah.

XIX

"Polly Kissed It!" Said Davie

"Yes, it beat all," said Mr. Atkins, "how he come in and begun looking around—"

"You mean th' doctor," interrupted Deacon Blodgett, reaching over for a scrap of cheese to put on his cracker. He knew the story, having heard it a good dozen times, but he wanted some of the other ears to be introduced to it.

"Who am I a-talkin' of, ef 'tain't Dr. Fisher?" said Mr. Atkins irritably.

"Of course," said the Deacon, helping himself to another cracker to top off the cheese.

It had just begun to drizzle, the light rain keeping customers within the store, and at such a time Mr. Atkins opened his cracker box and laid out his cheese knife. He was delighted at the chance of village gossip, and besides they would all more than make up by their orders for the price of the entertainment.

"Yes, he come in, and he looked around this way and that, an' I kep' still, for th' doctor, you all know, has a way

179

of his own, an' he would explain in good time, an' pretty soon he says, 'Ain't any Pepper children around, hey?' "

"An' I says 'No,' an' he took one more good look, for he says, 'I'm not so sure about Joel, for he can get everywhere in just about a minute,' an' I says, 'Yes, I know *that*, but Joel is to home, for he came tearin' in here half an hour ago, an' he said he must hurry an' git some corn meal, for he'd got to help Polly.' An' I waited on him quick, I tell you, an' he tore off.'"

" 'I guess I'm safe then—' said Dr. Fisher. 'Well, I want to see a stove.'

" 'A stove!' says I.

" 'I said a stove,' said Dr. Fisher, quite calm. 'Come now, let's see if you've got one to suit.'

" 'I've got a perfec' beauty,' says I, an' so I had—ordered a new one for old Miss Pringle an' then she didn't take it—said her old one acted better after all, an' she'd concluded to try it a spell longer. So me an' th' doctor went out to the 'Extension' [the shed where the storekeeper kept his stoves when he had any, and the pots and pans required by the village housekeepers]. 'Ain't that splendid?' says I, pointing to it.

"Th' doctor danced around that stove—you know how he steps off on the tips of his toes when he's pleased—an' set his spectacles a dozen times to get a better view, an' finally he says, 'Don't you s'pose she'd like it?' I never see him so anxious about anythin'.

" 'Why don't you get your sister to come an' pick it out for herself?' I says finally. He kep' a-dancin' around so.

" ' 'Tain't for my sister,' he says. 'It's for Polly Pepper.'

" 'Oh, my land!' says I.

" 'Yes, it would go to anyone's heart to see that little girl.'

"Dr. Fisher stopped dancing and faced me quite severe. 'Why—well, I don't know what to say when I think of her. An' now her eyes—'

"Well, then, th' doctor whips out that big handkerchief of his, an' he blows his nose—pretended he'd got an awful cold—till you'd 'a' thought 'twas Gabriel's trump, an' then he says, 'I'm goin' to send her a new stove in place of that broken-down old thing that Ben stuffs up with putty, an'—'

"An' I says, 'oh, my land, I didn't know that!' an' I was all struck of a heap to think I might 'a' give Polly a stove, an' eased up things a mite for the Little Brown House folks, an' th' doctor grabs my arm, an' he says, 'It's to be kep' quite secret. Be sure, Atkins, you don't let a soul know,'—an' I said I wouldn't, cross my heart, an' all that. An' then I put my foot in it, for I says, 'Let me give half o' that stove, doctor.'

"I tell you, he was real mad then. Did you ever see th' little doctor mad? Well, he swelled up till he actually looked big, an' his eyes—my gracious! they was so fierce, I says, ' 'Xcuse me,' an' then he ca'med down, an' told me th' stove was to go that afternoon. An' then he paid me, an' bolted out as if he'd ben caught doin' somethin' bad."

"Hem!" Deacon Blodgett snipped off another crumb of cheese, looking around to see the effect on the group.

A woman over behind the sugar barrel burst out, "He's awful good, Dr. Fisher is. He cured my Jenny of pneumony, an' he never took a cent o' pay for it." She wiped her eyes with her apron.

"Beats all how he takes care o' those old maid sisters o' his'n," broke in Farmer Jones. "It's bad enough to have one old maid fastened on you—but two—" he gave a long whistle, "that's worse'n pisen."

"Mebbe th' Lord'll let him shift 'em pretty soon—they

do say there's a rich wid'wer over to Stockton shinin' up to Sarah, an' that'll be a chance for th' doctor to get free."

"Hoh! well, Sarah ain't Laviny, an' she's homely as a hedge fence."

"Sarah Fisher always said whoever took her, must take Laviny, too. They hain't never ben separated, an' they never will be."

"Hoh!" said Farmer Jones again. "Well, th' little Pepper gal didn't go blind, after all."

Mr. Atkins pounded on the counter with his red fist, so that the group jumped. *"Blind!"* he roared, "Polly Pepper blind? Well, I guess not. Th' Lord wouldn't let sech a thing happen, an' so He got Dr. Fisher to take care of her eyes. Oh, my soul an' body! there's somethin' in th' world for that girl to do. I dunno what 'tis, but she's got to have a pair o' eyes to do it with."

"Hem!" said Deacon Blodgett again. "Well, now do tell us how th' stove got there, Atkins."

"You'd orter hear Davie tell it," the storekeeper chuckled with glee, and rubbed his hands together—then chuckled again. "I made him go over it one day—you know he helps me keep store."

"What, that scrap of a boy? You're jokin', Atkins," said one of the men.

"I ain't jokin', Tom," Mr. Atkins drew himself up and declared. "Davie may be a scrap of a boy, but he's worth more'n some men. An' it beats all how he can tell th' truth. An' I never see nothin' like it for manners he has—he can keep shop real elegant," the storekeeper wound up in pride.

"Somethin' different from Joel," laughed Tom.

"Well, now, Joel's all right," declared Mr. Atkins.

"I'd ruther have Joel," said Tom. "David is such a meek little mouse."

"David Pepper ain't sech a meek little mouse as you think," said Mr. Atkins decidedly.

"That's so," said Farmer Jones. "Remember the burglar in this very shop here, Tom."

"To be sure!" said Tom, "I forgot that he was th' boy."

"Them two boys is as diffrunt as can be," said the storekeeper, "but they can't be beat, neither one on 'em. And don't you never let anyone call David a meek little mouse, Tom Sanders. He's little, but he's got a mighty lot o' grit aboard. Why, here he comes now!" he cried joyfully.

Everyone whirled around as the door opened and David Pepper walked in.

"Well, well, Davie," said Mr. Atkins, as David went up to the counter, "so you came to help me keep store, did you? Why, I didn't 'xpect you today, as it rains. Well, I'm glad you've come though."

"I can sweep up the ell," said Davie, "that you said yesterday I was to do this morning," and he hurried off for the broom.

"So I did—so I did," replied the storekeeper, "an' that made you come in the rain?"

"Yes," said David, his mind intent on the broom and the dustpan.

"Well, see here—hold on a bit," called Mr. Atkins. "Come here, David. Now—" as David hurried back, "I want you to tell us how the stove Dr. Fisher gave Polly got to the Little Brown House as a surprise. Set up on th' sugar barrel an' tell us, Davie."

All the color in David's body seemed to rush into his little round cheek, as he stood there holding the broom. He looked helplessly around, and his eyes fastened on Deacon Blodgett pleadingly.

"I would, Davie," said the Deacon kindly. "It's a rainy

day an' we'd like to hear it— an' 'twould make us like th' doctor better."

To make everybody "like th' doctor better" seemed to Davie a thing to do. Every bit of the color went out of his cheeks. He set down the broom, and with a catch in his breath, he mounted the sugar barrel and folded his hands in his lap.

"Dr. Fisher gave Polly the stove," he began solemnly.

"Yes, yes," said Mr. Atkins quickly. "We all know that, Davie. Now tell us all about how it got into the Little Brown House an' was set up. Begin at th' very beginnin', Davie."

"I would, Davie," said Deacon Blodgett encouragingly.

David drew a long breath and began again—while the circle crowded up around the sugar barrel.

"Mamsie told us to stay in the bedroom, and to play something. She said we might make just as much noise as we wanted to, for Polly mustn't hear things in th' kitchen, and we mustn't come out until she called us. And Polly said, 'Oh, can't we play in the kitchen because the bedroom is so small?' and we wanted to play 'Old Father Dubbin,' because Phronsie—"

"Who's old Father Dubbin?" interrupted Tom, the young farmer.

"He isn't anybody," said Davie, shaking his head. "Polly made him up, and we play him when she lets us."

"Oh," said Tom, "I thought 'twas somebody in Badgertown—new folks, mebbe, who'd moved in."

"Go on, Davie," begged the woman, whose daughter Jenny had been cured of pneumonia by Dr. Fisher, and she pressed further into the circle.

"Mamsie said, 'No, Polly, you must all stay in the bedroom until I call you," and Mamsie patted Polly's head, on top of the bandage, and—"

"Bandage?" repeated another of the men in the listening group.

"Yes, don't you see Polly's eyes were tied up." Davie's voice trembled, and he had hard work, as the remembrance of it all swept over him, to keep the tears back.

"Oh, I forgot," said the man, "she was blind."

"Oh, no, no!" cried David in a sharp little cry, and he tried to spring from the barrel. Oh, couldn't he get home to Polly, and hold her close and forget that she had ever had her eyes tied up! Then the tears came.

Deacon Blodgett laid both large hands on the small lad. "Well, Davie, you know she wasn't blind," he said in a hearty voice.

"No, she wasn't," said Davie, smiling through his tears.

"Now tell how the stove got in," said Jenny's mother, with a black look for the man who had said "blind."

"Yes, tell us," they all took it up.

"Well, we were playing Old Father Dubbin," Davie had wiped his tears on the big handkerchief that Deacon Blodgett laid in his lap, "and Polly she was 'Old Father Dubbin,' " then he laughed, "and she had almost caught Joel, when we heard an awful big noise out in the kitchen, and Joel said he was going out there."

"I reckoned you wouldn't keep Joel in," laughed one of the men.

"Oh, he didn't run out," Davie hurried to say, and he shook his light waves of hair convincingly. "Joel stopped wanting to go out when Polly said 'No, you mustn't— Mamsie said we were to stay here.' And then Ben came in. Mamsie kept him in the kitchen, and he had a big stick—

oh, as big as this," David spread his arms, "and he said he wanted to be Old Father Dubbin, and Polly said she was glad, and Ben pounded on the floor, and chased us all, and I got under Mamsie's bed, and Phronsie, too." Here Davie gave a gleeful laugh that showed all his little white teeth. "And Joel chased Ben and tried to get the stick, and Polly laughed and clapped her hands and said, 'Old Father Dubbin will get you, Joey!'—and it was awfully nice." Davie drew a long breath and clasped his hands ecstatically.

"Well, now, the stove," Jenny's mother pressed closer. "Tell about Dr. Fisher's stove."

Davie's blue eyes shone as he continued, "And then the door opened, and Mamsie came in, and she said, 'Come, children—why, where are Davie and Phronsie?' and Joel said, 'They're under the bed,' and Mamsie laughed and said, 'Wait, till they come out, for we must all go into the kitchen together.' And Joel helped Phronsie out, and Ben said, 'Well, Old Father Dubbin has got you, Dave,' and he pulled me out by the legs." Here Davie laughed long and loud, and it sounded so gleeful that everybody joined in till the old store rang with the noise, and Mrs. Atkins ran in, her sweeping cap on her head, to see what could be the matter.

When she found that Davie Pepper on the sugar barrel was telling something, she joined herself to the group, in time to hear him say, "And Joel cried, 'It's a sto—' and Mamsie said, 'Hush, Joel!'—and Ben said, 'Don't you dare to say a word, Joe Pepper!'—and Polly said, 'Oh, what is it, Mamsie?' and Mamsie said, 'Children, be quiet.' And Joel stuffed the towel in his mouth, and we all were still as mice, and Polly said, 'Oh, I do wish I could see!' " Here Davie's face became very grave, and his voice fell.

"Well, she did see," said Deacon Blodgett in a loud voice. "Now, hurry and tell us, Davie boy."

"Yes, she did," said Davie, bobbing his light, wavy hair till it fell over his forehead again, and the smile ran up his round cheeks. "Mamsie said, 'Now, Polly, I'm going to take off your bandage.' And she did!" Davie drew a long breath and clasped his hands. "And the stove was there!" he cried; "Dr. Fisher's stove was there—it was—it was!" He sprang off from the sugar barrel, made his way through the group, and ran over to the farther end of the store, all the circle whirling around to watch him; "just like this, in the corner," he got down on his knees and patted the floor.

"What did Polly do?" cried Jenny's mother in an awe-struck voice.

David hopped to his feet, and flung back the soft waves of hair that had tumbled over his forehead again, and faced them all with shining eyes. "Polly kissed it!" he said.

XX

Joel's Company

"Now, Davie," said Mrs. Pepper, "you must be Mother's good boy and not feel badly because Joel cannot go."

"I very much wish Joel could go," said Davie, gazing out of the window disconsolately. "Oh, why couldn't good Mrs. Brown have asked Joel, too!"

"Joel must stay at home with Polly—you wouldn't have Polly left alone, Davie, when Ben is to help Deacon Blodgett."

• "No," said Davie, shaking his head, "but if Polly could go, too."

"That would be a big company on Mrs. Brown's hands," said Mrs. Pepper, with a little laugh. "Now, Davie, set to work and do all the things Polly wants you to do today, for tomorrow morning Mr. Brown is coming for us bright and early."

David turned away from the window. He was going to sigh, but seeing Mother Pepper's face, he smiled instead.

"What can I do, Polly?" he cried, running up to her.

Polly had her head all tied up in Mother Pepper's big sweeping cap. "Let me see," she paused on her way for the broom. "Oh, you might clean out the Provision Room, Davie."

"I will," said Davie, hurrying out to the woodshed to get the old broom, a rough wisp of a thing almost worn down to the handle. But it was good enough for the Provision Room.

"And I should think the potatoes needed looking over," said Mrs. Pepper, on her way to the bedroom.

"I'll do 'em, too," said Davie.

"You better do the potatoes first," said Polly, picking off her broom from its nail in the corner, "before you sweep the Provision Room out, Davie."

"I will," promised Davie, hurrying out to the woodshed.

"Come, Phronsie, you and I must stay in the bedroom while Polly sweeps up the kitchen." Mrs. Pepper picked up her big work basket from the table.

"I shall sew on my child's dress to wear to my Mrs. Brown's tomorrow," hummed Phronsie, gathering up Seraphina and some scraps of calico and getting up from the kitchen floor to patter after her mother.

"Oh, dear me!" Polly leaned on the broom handle as the bedroom door was shut, "why can't I ever go to spend the day somewhere?"

Two tears rolled down from the brown eyes and wet the broom handle.

"They've got chickens and pigs, Mrs. Brown said so— and there's a cunning little brook back of the farmyard. Why can't I go?"

Away went the old broom with a clang to the kitchen floor.

The bedroom door opened and Phronsie's yellow head appeared. "I thought I heard a noise—oh, Polly, are you hurt?" she cried.

"No," Polly rushed over to the broom and picked it up. Her cheeks were very red. "Don't come out, Phronsie. I'm all right."

"Are you sure?" said Phronsie anxiously.

"Sure as I can be," declared Polly. "Do go back—oh, dear!" With a glance to see that the bedroom door really was shut, Polly rushed over to Mamsie's old calico-covered chair, and flung herself, broom and all, down before it.

"I'm the worst girl that ever lived," she cried, stuffing her fingers up before her mouth. Suppose Phronsie should open the bedroom door again!

Just then a mouse over in the corner gave a scratch against the wainscot. Polly hopped to her feet, afraid it was the bedroom door, and wiped her eyes on the end of the sweeping cap, that flapped down over her shoulder. Then she tucked it up, and began to send the broom flying over the dust and crumbs on the kitchen floor. Joel ran in and found her so.

"Polly," he began wrathfully, "why can't we go to Mrs. Brown's house tomorrow? Why can't we, Polly?" He laid hold of the broom handle, so that she had to stop chasing the dust and crumbs.

"Because Mrs. Brown didn't ask us," said Polly coolly. "Let go of the broom, Joe. I can't sweep when you do so."

"Well, why didn't she ask us?" demanded Joel.

"Hush—Mamsie will hear you," warned Polly, pointing to the door. "Because she didn't want us."

"She ought to want us," Joel dropped his voice, but his black eyes blazed in indignation.

Polly burst into a little laugh. "When folks have company they can ask anyone they want, and not ask anyone they don't want."

"Not a single one?" persisted Joel, still hanging to the broom.

"No; not if they don't want to," said Polly. "Now, you must let go of the broom."

When Polly said "must" in that tone, the little Peppers knew that it was time to obey. So Joel's brown hands dropped from the broom handle and down to his side.

"Then they'll be very mad—the folks who don't get asked," he said slowly.

"Of course," said Polly lightly, and making some of the scraps from Mamsie's sewing on the coats fly neatly away from the broom, "but what good would that do, Joey—they couldn't go, all the same."

Joel stood quite still and swallowed the lump in his throat.

"Don't you want to go, Polly?" he blurted out.

Polly turned her head and tried to laugh. "Maybe," she said.

"You do," cried Joel triumphantly, "want to go awfully. There's pigs and chickens there, and lots and lots of things, Polly Pepper! I'm going! I'll get on behind the wagon when Mr. Brown doesn't know it. Oh, Polly, you come, too —I'll help you!" He spun round and round her, broom and all.

"Joel Pepper!" cried Polly, quite aghast and whirling with him, to lay hold of his jacket sleeve. "Stop! Oh, Joel, aren't you ashamed to want to go when you're not invited?"

"You said you wanted to," cried Joel, trying to get away. But she held him fast.

"I said 'maybe.'" The hot color rushed over Polly's face at the remembrance.

"Well, that's the same thing," declared Joel with another twitch.

"Joel," said Polly, and she threw down the broom. "Come outdoors—" and still holding his sleeve, she hurried him out and into the woodshed. "Now see here, I was a bad girl to want to go."

"I'm not a bad boy to want to go," contradicted Joel stoutly.

"Yes, you are; we're both bad," declared Polly. "Don't you see, it's naughty to want something that Mamsie can't get for us, and just think how she would feel if she knew it."

Polly drew a long breath, and her hand shook that held to the sleeve.

Joel scrubbed his rusty little shoe on the woodshed floor. "Mrs. Brown is bad," he said. "She ought to have asked us."

"Stop saying that," said Polly. "And when you have company, you can ask anyone you want to."

"I shall ask everybody," declared Joel with a generous sweep of his hands, "just every single bit of folks." His face brightened, "Polly, can't I ever have company?"

"Goodness, no!" cried Polly and she burst into a laugh. "The idea of our having company in the Little Brown House—Joey Pepper!"

"I wouldn't have 'em in the house—they could stay outdoors, in the orchard."

"Well, I think we'd both better get back to our work instead of standing here to talk about having company," said Polly gaily. Then she stopped. "Why, Joel, perhaps you *could* have some company tomorrow. I do believe Mamsie would let you, after all."

"Can I—can I?" cried Joel eagerly, and prancing all about her.

"I almost know that she will let you ask—"

"Who?" interrupted Joel with a gasp.

"Peletiah and Ezekiel."

"Oh, I don't want them," howled Joel, horribly disappointed.

"Well, now you see," said Polly. "Mrs. Brown doesn't want us, and you think she ought to. Now here's a chance for you to ask somebody you don't want to."

Joel puckered up his round cheeks and ran off to the corner of the woodshed. "Have I got to?" he asked, coming slowly back with a wry face.

"No," said Polly coolly, "only you think Mrs. Brown is bad not to ask us."

"Perhaps Mamsie won't let 'em come," he said, a comforting thought striking him.

"Oh, yes, she will," said Polly cheerfully. "I heard her only the other day talk about asking them some time. And the Parson and Mrs. Henderson have been so good to us, Joey! Come, let's go and ask her now."

She grasped his jacket sleeve and he had nothing to do but to follow.

"Oh, dear me!" exclaimed Polly, as she saw the broom lying just where she had thrown it. "Well, it won't take a minute to ask Mamsie about your company, Joe, and then I'll finish sweeping the kitchen," and she threw wide the bedroom door.

There sat Phronsie on the floor at Mrs. Pepper's feet, snipping up what she called the "trimming" to Scraphina's new calico gown, and humming softly to herself as Mamsie set the stitches in the coat, a happy smile on her face. For pleasure was coming to two of her little ones tomorrow through the kindness of good Mr. and Mrs. Brown. When she saw Joel's face, the smile dropped off a bit, as she remembered how he wanted to go on the beautiful visit. And Polly, too! Then the smile faded completely away.

"Mamsie," cried Polly, rushing in and towing Joel along, "can't Joey have some company tomorrow; can't he, Mamsie?"

"Some company?" repeated Mother Pepper, her work dropping to her lap.

"Yes," said Polly, "oh, it would be so nice—Peletiah and Ezekiel—can't he ask them?"

"Ugh!" said Joel. He couldn't help it, and he twisted up his face, just as if he'd bitten something sour.

"You said you'd like to ask them some time, Mamsie," went on Polly, still holding Joel's little calico sleeve fast, "and now Joey and I will be all alone—and he wants some company."

Mamsie turned her black eyes on Joel's face. "If Joel wants them to come, I shall be very glad. But not unless he does want them," she finished slowly.

Joel put his little brown hands together tightly and looked down on the floor. "Peletiah can't play anything," he blurted out suddenly.

"Well, Ezekiel can," said Polly brightly.

"Huh!" exclaimed Joel contemptuously.

"Well, we'll play 'Old Father Dubbin,'" said Polly; "that'll make him play, Joey," and she gave a little laugh.

"Will you play 'Old Father Dubbin'?" cried Joel, looking up, and he began to laugh too.

"Yes, indeed!" promised Polly, bobbing her head so that the two brown braids flew out, "and we'll have the best party that you ever saw, Joel Pepper!"

"I'm going to have a party, Phronsie," Joel twitched away from Polly's grasp on his jacket sleeve, and flew over to her, "all by myself—I am," he cried, dreadfully excited, and giving her a bear hug.

"Take care, Joel—mind the scissors!" warned Mrs. Pepper. Too late! Phronsie, having great difficulty in making one part of the scissors stay on her fat little thumb, was just holding them up, while she wriggled her fingers into the other part, when down came Joel upon them.

" 'Tain't anything—I don't care," he said, bobbing up, wiping away the blood with the back of one small hand. But it came dripping down his face just as fast. Mrs. Pepper with never a word, gathered him up to her lap. Then she said, "The bowl of water, Polly."

Polly had stood like a frozen little thing. "His eye—Mamsie!" she gasped.

"I said the bowl of water, Polly," repeated Mrs. Pepper.

How she got the bowl of water, and then a towel, Polly never knew. All she was conscious of was standing holding the bowl while Mamsie washed away the blood, Joel all the while saying, " 'Tisn't anything—I don't care—a single bit."

At last Joel's black eye shone out clear and strong. Mrs. Pepper gave a deep cry of joy—and clasped her boy tighter to her breast.

Down flopped Polly in a little heap on the floor, the bowl coming with a thud that splashed the water over the rim.

"You're spilling all the water, Polly Pepper!" exclaimed Joel, struggling away from Mother Pepper to look down at her, amazement all over his bloody little face. "Just see there, Mamsie, she's spilt the water all over the floor!"

"Oh, Mamsie," breathed Polly, clasping her hands on her mother's knee, "it isn't Joel's eye—it isn't!"

Mrs. Pepper's white lips moved. She tried to say, "God is good," but the words not coming, she smiled instead.

"It didn't hurt any," declared Joel stoutly, brushing off more blood from an ugly little cut just below one of those bright black eyes.

"Take care, Joey," said Mother Pepper, holding his

brown hands. "Now you must just sit still. Polly, you better run and see if Dr. Fisher can come."

"Oh, I don't want Dr. Fisher to come," cried Joel in great alarm. "He'll put me to bed, and make me have the measles all over again. Don't let him come, Mamsie!" he begged.

"Oh, you can't have the measles again, Joel," said Polly, getting up on her feet and picking up the bowl.

"Can't I?" said Joel.

"No, indeed," said Polly decidedly; "the very idea, Joel Pepper!" and she gave a gay little laugh. Joel's eye wasn't hurt, and Dr. Fisher was coming. Everything would soon be all right!

Phronsie, who didn't really know that the scissors had done anything naughty to Joel's face, was still struggling to keep them on her fat little hand enough to snip away at the "trimming." She began now, in a soft little voice, to talk to Seraphina lying on the floor by her side.

"You are going to have a new dress, my child, to wear tomorrow to dear Mrs. Brown's, and you may see the little chickies and the dear, sweet little pigs."

"Then he can come," said Joel on a high key, "if he won't put me to bed and make me have the measles again," while Polly sped out, and on the wings of the wind, over to get good Dr. Fisher.

The little doctor was soon there, and mending Joel's face, who kept saying it didn't hurt, as he twisted his hands tightly together. When it was all over, he looked out over the plasters and bandage on his round face, and announced very pompously, "I'm going to have company tomorrow."

"Are you?" said Dr. Fisher.

"Yes, I am," said Joel, with an important air, and begining to get down from Mrs. Pepper's lap. "Mamsie said I might, and I must go and ask 'em now."

"Hold on there!" the little doctor put forth a restraining hand. "I guess I'd put off that company of yours, Joe, to another day."

"I can't," said Joel, wriggling to get down to the floor. "I must go now and ask 'em. It's my party I'm going to have while Mamsie and Dave and Phronsie are over at Mrs. Brown's."

"Is that it?" said Dr. Fisher. "Well now, see here, Joe," he began, while he laid both hands on the struggling little legs.

"And we're going to play 'Old Father Dubbin,'" cried Joel. "Polly said we may—oh, let me *go!*" He kicked and squirmed, but it was no use; at last he sat quite still and glared at the little doctor.

"Whoever heard of giving a party with a head tied up like yours?" Dr. Fisher burst into a hearty laugh.

"Then I'll tear the things off," declared Joel vindictively, and preparing to begin the work.

"Look here, Joe," Dr. Fisher's eyes were now so stern behind their big spectacles that Joel's small brown hands fell to his lap. "Just look at your mother!"

Joel whirled around in Mrs. Pepper's lap, and peered at her over his plaster and bandages. "Mamsie, I won't have my company," he said humbly.

"Oh, yes, you will, Joey," she said brightly, "you shall have a beautiful time. It's only put off!"

XXI

At Farmer Brown's

So it was a whole week after when Farmer Brown got Mrs. Pepper and Davie and Phronsie into the big wagon all ready to start for Maybury. Mother Pepper sat on the back seat with the farmer's wife, who insisted on holding Phronsie on her lap; and Davie, who would have been in a state of bliss if only Joel were going, sat very straight next to Farmer Brown waiting till all the good-bys were over and he could say "G'lang" to the old white horse.

"I'm going to have company," announced Joel importantly, for about the fiftieth time, and climbing up on the wheel to tell it to Mr. Brown.

"So I've heerd," said the farmer dryly.

"I am—all by myself," declared Joel, his black eyes shining.

"Well, you better get off th' wheel then," said Mr. Brown, "for your comp'ny folks may be a-comin' down th' road."

At that Joel leaped down and ran till he could see the turn in the road; then came flying back.

"They're not coming—not a single bit," he declared in an injured tone.

198

"Well, you keep off th' wheel," said the farmer, "for if Jingo starts, mebbe your leg would be sliced off."

Joel, with no heed to such a direful warning, ran around to look with new interest at the old white horse.

"Is that his name?" he cried eagerly.

"Mebbe," said the farmer. "Sometimes when I want him to hoof it real fast, I say 'By Jingo.'"

"And does he—does he go real fast?" said Joel, trying to climb up on the old white back.

"You get off that horse" roared the farmer at him, in such an awful voice that Joel lost no time in slipping down on his two small feet. Mr. Brown cast a despairing glance over his shoulder.

"I'm a-goin' to start," he said, gathering up the reins.

"Wait a minute, Pa," Mrs. Brown leaned over Phronsie in her lap. "Be careful o' th' custard pie," she said in a loud whisper, "it's kinder soft."

"I will," said Polly, her brown eyes dancing at the thought of this splendid addition to Joel's party. "I put it up on the top shelf of the cupboard, so he can't see it till the time comes."

Mrs. Brown's large face beamed approval.

"G'lang!" cried the farmer, snapping his whip, and they were finally off, Joel clattering down the dusty road a piece to see if he couldn't beat them to the corner.

The old house at Maybury stood back a good bit from the road. Mrs. Pepper gave a sigh of delight as Jingo turned into the yard and stopped before the big porch. Honeysuckle rambled all over it, and hollyhocks shot up their tall stocks—and lilac bushes and poplars guarded the doorway, the approach being bordered by rows of box, years and years old.

A big dog got slowly up from the flat doorstone, shook

himself, and came up to the wagon. Phronsie gave a little cry and sprang over to get into Mother Pepper's lap.

The farmer's wife held to her. "He wouldn't hurt you," she said. "Why, you'll be playin' with him as soon as you get out o' th' wagon."

Phronsie looked doubtfully out of her brown eyes—but she settled back into the good lap.

"Won't he bite me?" she asked.

"Land, no!—he hain't got any teeth to bite with, neither," said Mrs. Brown.

"There now," Farmer Brown, having got down to the ground, came around to his wife's side of the wagon. "Come here, little gal," putting up his long arms.

Phronsie, one eye on the big dog, confidently held out her hands, and he swung her down, her small pink calico skirt puffing out in her descent.

"He won't hurt you, Phronsie," cried David, clambering over the wheel. "See," he patted the big dog's head.

"He won't hurt me," repeated Phronsie, but her little hand trembled on the shaggy head as she said it.

"I told you so," said Mrs. Brown, getting heavily out of the wagon. "Now you an' Towser is a-goin' to be reel comf'table together." She glanced at Mother Pepper standing quite still, drinking in the sweet air in long deep breaths as she gazed about her, and the farmer's wife smiled. "I'm reel pleased you like it," she said, quite gratified. "Well, come in an' take your bunnit off, Mis Pepper," she cried hospitably, as she ducked under the honeysuckle branches that drooped over the doorway.

But Mother Pepper stood quite still.

"Can't you let her be, Ma," said the farmer, stopping at the doorstone on his way to the barn to untackle Jingo. "When a person's comf'table, let 'em stay so, I say."

"I know how to take care o' my comp'ny," said his wife, "you look out for the boy, an' I'll see to Mis Pepper and th' little gal." Then to her great delight, Mother Pepper turned and came up to the big porch.

"Now you lay off your things in here," said Mrs. Brown, leading the way to the big bedroom in the ell. The chintz curtains swung in the breeze that carried a pleasant fragrance from the sweetbrier climbing over the windows. "Lay your bunnit an' shawl right on th' bed, Mis Pepper," patting the pieced bedquilt of a gorgeous "rising sun" pattern. "An', little girl, I'll take off your things for you," turning to Phronsie, who was holding her mother's gown.

"Oh, no, no," said Phronsie decidedly, "I want my Mamsie to take off my things."

Mrs. Brown's mouth dropped suddenly at the corners, and over her large face spread disappointment of the worst sort.

"I would let Mrs. Brown take off my things, Phronsie," said Mrs. Pepper.

Phronsie turned her brown eyes wonderingly up to her mother, and seeing that she really meant it, she dropped her hold on the protecting gown and put up her little face for the pink sunbonnet to be untied by the farmer's wife.

"Now that is the best child that ever lived," exclaimed Mrs. Brown joyfully. She got down to her fat knees and began to fumble with the pink calico strings. "It's jest like havin' a little girl of my own," she said, catching her breath.

"Haven't you any little girl?" asked Phronsie, patiently waiting till the strings that now got themselves into a knot under the nervous fingers could be untied.

"No," said Mrs. Brown, and despite all her efforts, the big tears would come, and down they rolled over the large face.

"Are you crying because you haven't any little girl?" Phronsie gazed in dismay at the tears, while the large hands fumbled at their task.

Mrs. Brown tried to speak, but it was no use. Down fell the pink calico strings, and she put her hands over her face and sobbed.

"Don't cry," begged Phronsie, dreadfully distressed.

"If you'd be my little girl," said the farmer's wife, "p'raps—"

Phronsie scuttled over to Mother Pepper on frightened little feet, the pink sunbonnet flying off to the floor.

"I mean jest for today," cried the farmer's wife after her, scared out of her tears, and wiping them off.

Mrs. Pepper laid her hand soothingly on the yellow hair. "She wants you to let her do things for you, Phronsie—just as if you were her own little girl."

"And can I go back to the Little Brown House?" asked Phronsie, clutching fast her mother's gown, and casting fearful glances at the big women who had forgotten to get up from her knees.

"Yes, dear, you can go back with me and with Davie," Mamsie smiled reassuringly.

"Then you may do things for me," said Phronsie, going back to the big woman.

"You sweet lamb, you!" cried the farmer's wife, quite overcome. And she unbuttoned the little calico sack, and getting up, she laid it neatly on the bed by the side of Mrs. Pepper's bonnet and shawl.

"I've baked a little pie for you," she leaned over and whispered, when that was done, taking Phronsie's hand as she did so. "Come, and I'll show it to you."

"For me?" cried Phronsie, showing her little white teeth in her delight.

"Sure, all for you. And I curlicued th' edge, all round."

Phronsie gave a little gurgle at that, although she didn't know in the least what "curlicued" meant. It must be something to make her little pie very splendid. And she gave a sigh of great satisfaction and smoothed down her pink calico gown.

"An' then, says I, you shall see th' chickies." By this time Mrs. Brown, holding Phronsie's hand, was well on the way to the big kitchen where certain smells proclaimed very unusual things going on in preparation for the company dinner, Mrs. Pepper following, a happy smile lighting her face.

Meanwhile Davie, lost to everything but the bliss of being allowed to help take off Jingo's heavy harness, was on his tiptoes and working with all his might to do as much with the buckles and straps as the farmer on the other side of the old white horse.

"I declare ef you ain't as smart as th' next one," declared Mr. Brown admiringly over Jingo's back. "You've helped me a whole lot."

"Have I?" cried Davie in delight. The streams of perspiration were running down his hot little face, and his fingers trembled over their struggles with a refractory strap.

"I should jest say you have!" cried the farmer. "Well now," and he slouched around Jingo. "There, that's an' awful plaguy strap—it bothers me somethin' dretful."

"Does it?" cried Davie, quite pleased to find that the big man didn't blame him for his failure to undo it.

"You better believe it does," declared Mr. Brown, laying hold of the strap. "There, you set down on that box a spell."

Davie, wanting dreadfully to ask, "Can't I help some more?" did as he was bidden, and silently watched the farmer get Jingo out of the harness and into his halter. "Don't you want to lead him into th' stall?" asked Mr. Brown, when that was all done, and turning suddenly.

"Oh, can I—can I?" cried Davie, springing from the box, his little hot face beaming with delight.

"There ain't nothin' to hinder you," said the farmer, with a chuckle. "There now," and he put the halter strap into David's hand. "Come this way," he was going to say, "Little boy," but coughed and gave it up.

"You're handy as you can be," said Mr. Brown, when Jingo was munching his oats. "Now says I, let's go down an' see th' pigs," and he put out his big hand.

"Phronsie loves pigs," began Davie. Then the color ran over his face—Mamsie had told them not to show that they wanted anything while on this visit. In his anxiety that Phronsie should see the pigs, he had forgotten that.

"You needn't to worry about th' little gal," said the farmer composedly, "Miss Brown'll look out for her."

"Will she let her see the pigs?" asked Davie, turning an anxious face up to the keen eyes under their shaggy brows. "Sure!" said Mr. Brown. "There won't be nothin' that little gal ought to see, but what she'll see it today. Ma'll look out for that," and he gathered up David's little hand in his big one.

David trotted along in great contentment, trying to keep step with the farmer's big strides as they left the sweet-smelling old barn, fragrant with its generous haylofts.

"You see Mis Brown has got th' little gal, an' I've got you," said the farmer in great satisfaction. "You're my boy."

Everything swam around before David's eyes. He stopped in silent terror, dragging on the big hand, and his cheeks grew quite white.

"Whew!" exclaimed Mr. Brown, aghast at the storm he

had raised, "wouldn't you like to be my boy, pray tell?"

"Oh no, no," cried Davie, finding his tongue, "I'm Mamsie's boy—I must go to Mamsie." But all his pulling wouldn't get his hand free.

"You see this place," Mr. Brown went on as fast as he could talk, and he swept his other big hand around, "there's everythin' here,—and I'd get you a pony, all for yourself, just think, David, an' a calf, you may have the pick of all the bossies, an' a pig—two of 'em, if you want 'em."

"No, no!" cried Davie, quite gone in his fright that he was never going to see the Little Brown House again. "Do let me go—oh, do let me go, please!"

The farmer gave a long sigh. He still clutched the small hand.

"Davie," he said, and his voice broke, "I hain't never had a little boy, not a single one," he added mournfully.

"Haven't you ever had one?" gasped Davie.

"Never!" declared Mr. Brown. His face twitched, and if ever a big man did cry, he looked as if he were going to that very minute.

At seeing that, Davie began to lose his fright in his distress over the farmer.

"Seem's as ef you could now—" began Mr. Brown. "*Hem!*" he brought up suddenly at sight of the little face. "Well, we can pretend you're my boy jest while you're here today," he begged.

"I'm Mamsie's boy," said Davie stoutly.

"I know—I know," said the farmer reassuringly, "but jest while you're a-visitin' me today, you can make b'lieve you live here on the farm."

"I'm going home when Mamsie goes, and Phronsie," said Davie.

"Of course," said Mr. Brown, slapping his big hands together. "Well now, you an' me'll keep together, Davie, to-day. Mis' Brown's got th' little gal, an' I've got you. Come on, they're hayin' down in the medder, an' you can ride on th' cart ef you want to."

Davie slipped his hand into the big one extended, and snuggled up to the farmer.

"I'm sorry you haven't ever had any little boy," he said, a worried look spreading all over his round face.

"Don't you let that make you feel bad," said Mr. Brown, trying to smile. "Hem! We'll have to hurry ef we git on to that cart before it leaves for th' barn! Now says I, your little legs has got to run to keep up with me."

XXII

The Beautiful Day

"HEY there look out for that boy!" roared the farmer.

It was all done in a minute. The mass of hay, with David in its center, slid neatly off the top of the cart to the ground. Bill, the hired man, pitchfork in hand, leaned over the edge in a state of great consternation, the rest of the laborers, the loading all completed, watching to see the cart start off for the barn.

"Jehoshaphat!" Mr. Brown pushed them all aside, and threw himself over the landslide of hay. "Get him out! Get th' boy out!" he roared, pawing frantically to right and to left to reach David. The laborers fell to with such energy that hay flew in every direction, and at last David was pulled out white as a sheet, and gasping for breath.

"Land o' Goshen!" Farmer Brown rose up tall and straight. "You dumb lummux, you!" and he shook his fist at Bill, "to let this happen!"

Bill cowered down on top of the hay out of sight. David tried his best to speak, but he hadn't any breath to start the words.

"Ye ain't hurt, be ye?" cried Farmer Brown, in an anguish. Then he felt David's arms and made him take a step or two to try his legs.

David shook his head and said, "No,"—while the men picked out the wisps of hay from his soft light hair and dusted off his little calico blouse.

"Well, that's a mercy," breathed the farmer at last. "It's th' biggest luck I ever see in my life."

"He didn't make me fall," said Davie, drawing the first long breath since the tumble, and pointing up where Bill's head showed on the top of the load of hay, "I did it myself."

"Well, never mind—you ain't none th' worse for it, I reckon. But you scaret me most out o' my boots, Davie." The farmer's big black eyes began to settle back into their natural places. "Well, pitch back this hay, boys, and drive off."

"Put me up," cried Davie. "Oh, I want to get up there again. Do, Mr. Brown," he begged.

"You sure you can stick on, Davie?"

"Oh, I will—I will stick on," promised Davie, dreadfully excited, "if you'll only let me get up there."

"All right. H'ist him up, boys."

So the hired men, two of them, seized David and swung him up to the shoulders of the third, and in "a shake of a lamb's tail," as the farmer said, there he was on the top of the load, and laughing with glee, and the men below were pitching up the hay that had taken a slide carrying him along with it.

"Keep away from th' edge," shouted the farmer after him, as the big horses began to pull the load off across the meadow.

"You mustn't stand up when we get to th' barn," said Bill, not intending to take any risk with this visitor to the farm. "You've got to set, an' duck your head, when Job drives in."

"I'll lie down," said Davie.

"That's a good idee," said Bill approvingly. "Well, how'd you feel when you was a-goin' off th' load ker-slap."

"I didn't feel," said Davie, "I just slid."

"Warn't you scared none?"

David longed to say, "No." Instead, he hung his head, "Yes, I was," he said.

"So sh'd I have ben," said Bill, picking up a wisp of hay to chew it.

"Would you?" cried Davie eagerly, and lifting his head suddenly, while his blue eyes shone.

"Sure," declared Bill, chewing his wisp. "I don't like no sech sudden removals. 'Tain't my style."

"Oh, I'm so very glad that you'd have been scared," said Davie, clasping his hands.

"Well, you better set, or you'll go again," said Bill, as the big wagon toiled over a lump, and then swayed on to level ground once more.

"I'm not going again!" said David, all in a glow to think that the big man would have been scared, just the same as a little boy. And he settled himself comfortably in a hollow in the middle of the hay load.

"Well, you're goin' to stay here a spell, ain't you?" asked Bill, regarding the small figure curiously.

"Oh, no, no," declared Davie in terror. All his glow was gone, and he looked so very miserable that Bill hastened to reassure him.

"We get awful good things to eat. Ever seen any o' Mis Brown's pies?" And he smacked his lips.

But David's thoughts were away off from Mrs. Brown's pies, or any other pies, and he shook all over and folded his hands tightly together.

"He'd set by you," Bill pointed with his big thumb to Farmer Brown and the hired men following to help unload the hay, "he said you was a-comin' an' he meant to keep you."

"I can't stay—I can't!" exclaimed Davie wildly, and springing up, he stood as straight as he could for the jolting cart.

"Take care!" Bill put out a big hand and grasped the little calico sleeve. "You better set," and he put him back in the hollow of the hay. "Thunder! You needn't feel so bad about stayin' here," he added in a dudgeon. "It's a bang-up good farm. 'Tain't every boy would get a chance at it, I can tell you."

But Davie shivered, and didn't half hear while Bill rattled on about Mr. Brown, and Tom, Dick, and Harry, Mr. Brown's hired men, and how they all hoped to spend their days there. At last he got talked out, and stopped and looked at David.

"Say, youngster, where'd you come from, anyway?" he asked.

"The Little Brown House," said David faintly, without looking up.

"Gosh!—I thought you'd say a palace, to the very least," said Bill, "after turning up your nose at this place."

David unfolded his hands and put one up to feel of his nose. It never had been turned up at the end, and he was relieved to find it still the same.

Bill burst into such a guffaw that two old crows flying over the field stopped their own hoarse croakings to listen in amazement.

"Got any more like you over there to the Little Brown House?" asked Bill, when he came out of his amusement. "Say, boy, I'd give a dollar ef you would stay here."

This made David's distress very dreadful.

"You can cry, ef you want to, though 'tain't very polite,

after an invitation like you've got," said Bill, "an' not set there tying your face into knots. You ain't a-goin' to be kep here agin your will. Don't get scared, youngster."

"Won't you keep me?" breathed David in a shaking voice.

"Me? My land o' Goshen, I sh'd say not," declared Bill, slapping his overalls with a red hand. "What do I want with a boy, pray tell?"

"I'm so glad," exclaimed Davie in delight, "that you don't want a boy, Mr. Bill," and his face shone, as the cart rolled up to the barn door. David flung himself flat on his face, just in time before they bumped over the sill.

As "Mr. Bill" didn't want a boy under any consideration, David reached the hayloft in a comfortable condition, and by the time that Farmer Brown and Tom, Dick, and Harry came up, he was shouting and laughing at a great rate as he helped to pack the sweet-smelling hay on the big loft.

Meanwhile Phronsie was having her visit with good Mrs. Brown. Mother Pepper, seeing how things were, had begged to be left in the big old kitchen to see to the dinner. There were a pair of ducks roasting away in the oven, and a big chicken pie, for the farmer's wife was determined to do things up well, and there were potatoes and onions boiling away, with cranberry sauce and ever so many pies in the cupboard waiting their turn to be invited to the table. And Mrs. Pepper, with one of Mrs. Brown's checked aprons tied over her neat calico gown, moving about, in all the mysteries of "seeing to dinner," had such a happy smile on her face that the big kitchen, although it was just as different as a kitchen could be from the Little Brown House one, began to seem cheery and homey at once.

"Phronsie," said the farmer's wife, "I tell you what let's

you an' me do—we'll go an' see th' chickens first—an' get them off'n our minds."

"We'll go and see the chickies," hummed Phronsie, and putting up her small hand for the farmer's wife to take it, which so pleased Mrs. Brown that her head went quite high in the air as she picked up her black alpaca gown and stepped off.

"I see them," cried Phronsie, on a high key, and she tried gently to pull Mrs. Brown along faster as they neared the chicken yard.

"Yes, yes, child," said Mrs. Brown, who wasn't accustomed to much walking out of doors, "you don't need to hurry so."

"They're going off," said Phronsie in a worried way.

"Oh, no, they ain't. Hens always has to be steppin' round important. They ain't doin' nothin', only they like to be on the move all the while.

"Will they wait for us?" asked Phronsie, anxiously watching the incessant movement in the chicken yard.

"My soul an' body!" exclaimed Mrs. Brown, with a little laugh, "you'll find 'em fast enough when we get there." But she redoubled her pace, lumbering on till she was quite red in the face.

"Can we go in?" cried Phronsie, very much excited, as a whole bunch of fluffy little yellow chicks tumbled over each other to get away from the noise of their footsteps.

"Well, that's what we've come for," said the farmer's wife, pushing up the hasp of the big gate.

"We're going in!" cried Phronsie, clapping her hands and hopping up and down. This made the little fluffy chicks tumble over each other worse than ever, till they looked just like one big yellow ball.

"Can I take one—can I?" begged Phronsie, running after the big ball as Mrs. Brown pulled to the gate.

"You wait, little girl," said the farmer's wife, "an' by 'n' by, you'll have your lap full."

Phronsie stopped and regarded her pink calico gown. To have her lap full of chickens was something that had to be thought out carefully. And she was standing there quite still when Mrs. Brown, who had hurried into the shed, came out with a tin pan in her hand.

"There now, says I," she took Phronsie's hand. "You come along of me," and she led her to the other end of the long chicken yard. "Now we can set, an' I'm sure I'm glad to," and down she went heavily on a low bench under some currant bushes.

"Chick—chick," called the farmer's wife. "Set down, Phronsie. There, don't you see 'em runnin' fit to break their necks," as she put her hand in the tin pan and brought it forth full of corn and fine grain to fling it far and wide.

"Oh, don't let them break their necks—please," begged Phronsie. She had sat down by Mrs. Brown's side, but now hopped to her feet in distress.

Mrs. Brown gave a comfortable laugh. "They hain't got any necks hardly to break—only a bunch o' feathers."

So Phronsie, seeing that the chickens' necks were to be perfectly safe, sat down on the bench and filled both small hands with the corn and grain.

Chickens of all sorts and sizes came sweeping down in flocks till the ground all around the bench was covered, and the first thing she knew, one or two hopped up on the end of the bench and jumped into Phronsie's pink calico gown to get nearer to the old tin pan. When the other chickens saw that, a whole fluffy crowd followed.

Phronsie gave a little squeal and threw herself over into Mrs. Brown's arms, thereby upsetting a couple of the more adventurous ones.

"There—there," chuckled the farmer's wife, "didn't I tell you you'd have your lap full. Well, see here," to the chickens, and she pushed off the biggest ones, " 'tain't polite to scrouge so—you'll all get your turn. Now, Phronsie, let that littlest one eat out o' your hand."

Mrs. Brown shook some grain into the little calico gown. A small fluffy ball plumped right into the middle of it, holding on by its little claws to Phronsie's small thumb.

Phronsie squealed in delight. And the little yellow chick, not caring in the least how much anyone squealed as long as there was this sweet grain, hung on to Phronsie's thumb and pecked away, the farmer's wife scaring the other chickens off.

It seemed impossible for Phronsie to tear herself away from this enchanting party in the old chicken yard. The farmer's wife might talk and talk over the charms of the pigs who were supposed to be waiting to be visited. Phronsie had no eyes nor ears for anything but the "chickies" and their soft little "peep—peep."

At last Mrs. Brown said, "They'll be sick if they eat any more," and getting up from the bench, she went off, tin pan and all. And Phronsie, slipping down to the ground beneath, sat down in the by-no-means-clean spot, and put her arms around the fluffy bunch that swarmed into her lap.

"Gracious!" exclaimed Mrs. Brown, coming back, having disposed of the tin pan. "I don't know what your ma'll think! My senses! just look at your dress, child!"

Phronsie huddled up two of the chickens in the front

breadth of her pink calico gown, as Mrs. Brown got her up to her feet.

So they didn't get to the pigs after all, Phronsie having to be led back to the farmhouse for the messy little back breadth of her gown to be washed clean. And of course, while that was being done, she must have on a calico wrapper of Mrs. Brown's and sit in the rocking chair by the kitchen window. But she didn't care, for the farmer's wife let her bring in one of the little yellow fluffy chickens.

And then all the merry getting ready of the big dinner was going on, and the little pink calico gown had to have its back breadth smooth, so Mrs. Brown set a flatiron on the stove, and got out the ironing board.

"It's jest 'xactly as if I had got a little girl," she kept saying to herself with happy throbs of the heart.

And then, Phronsie had to stumble to the door as well as she could for Mrs. Brown's big wrapper catching her feet, and put the little chicken out.

"I'm afraid he won't find his way home," she grieved.

"I'll carry him back," said Mrs. Pepper.

So Phronsie put the little yellow fluffy chick into Mamsie's hand and went into the big bedroom. And when she came back, the little pink calico gown all clean and smooth, and buttoned on by Mrs. Brown, why, there was Mamsie back again, and the old clock in the corner said as plain as a clock could say, "Time for dinner!"

And then after that big splendid dinner was over, and the ducks' backs didn't have any covering on to speak of, Farmer Brown took Davie off to see the "bossies," and Phronsie crooned a little song of delight—for wasn't she going to help Mrs. Brown and Mamsie to wipe the dishes?

And then she never could remember what was done next.

For the first thing she knew, somebody was saying over her head—and that was Mrs. Brown, "It's a pity to wake her!" And Phronsie rolled over on Mrs. Brown's big bed and opened her brown eyes, and there was Mother Pepper—and she said, "But we really must start for home now."

And then the pink sunbonnet was tied on, and Davie came running up, his hands full of treasures that Farmer Brown had given him. And there was the old wagon with the big white horse waiting by the porch. And then she was lifted in and put on Mrs. Brown's lap, a basket of goodies on the floor, and the farmer took up the old leather reins.

"Let 'er go, Bill," he said.

And the beautiful day was over.

XXIII

The Uninvited Guest

"'THEY'RE coming!" announced Joel, with a wry face. Oh, dear me!"

"How fine!" exclaimed Polly brightly. It was quite elegant to be waiting for company, but it began to be a bit tiresome. Now they had really come! "Hurry and open the door, Joe."

Joel deserted the window and the green door being opened, in walked Peletiah.

"Where's Ezekiel?" cried Joel, looking past him.

"Oh, Joel," exclaimed Polly in great distress, for she dearly loved fine manners, "you must shake hands." Then she put out her hand, and said, "I'm glad you've come, Peletiah."

Joel stuck out his little brown hand, then drew it back. "He won't do it," he said, as Peletiah, having to think about it first, wasn't ready.

"Never mind," said Polly. "Isn't Ezekiel coming?"

"My mother said he would come in half an hour," said Peletiah, "and I'm going to stay until five o'clock."

"Oh, dear me!" said Joel, turning off in great disgust, "perhaps it's half an hour now. I'm going out to look for him," and he danced out to the flat doorstone.

"Nonsense!" exclaimed Polly with a little laugh and hurrying after him. "Why, it isn't any time yet, Joey."

"Why, Polly Pepper!" declared Joel, hopping up and down impatiently, "it's an awful long time, and he keeps saying things over and over."

"Well, never mind," said Polly again. "Now, you must come in and we'll begin to play something."

"He can't play," said Joel, "and he keeps saying things over and over."

"Well, you're just doing that yourself, Joel Pepper." Polly burst into a merry laugh. "Now, come in."

"I'm going to watch for Ezekiel," said Joel obstinately.

"Oh, no, you mustn't," cried Polly decidedly. "I never heard of such a way to have company. You must come in and make him have a good time at your party." And she laid hold of his sleeve.

"There isn't any good time," grumbled Joel, stumbling along, Polly still holding his sleeve.

"Well now, boys," said Polly, shutting the green door. "I think the first thing we'll do, will be to march."

"That'll be fine," exclaimed Joel, clapping his hands. "I'm going to lead."

"Yes, you may," said Polly. "Get the broom, Joel."

So Joel ran over and pulled the broom down from its hook in the corner, to stick it up by his shoulder and prance off. "Come on," he shouted.

"Come, Peletiah," said Polly, "you must march next."

"I don't want to march," said Peletiah, not moving.

"Oh, yes, you do," said Polly. "You've come to Joel's party, and this begins the party."

Peletiah, not being able to contradict this, stepped slowly forward. Then he stopped. "Folks don't have to do everything they don't want to at a party," he said.

"Yes, they do," said Polly, bobbing her head decidedly, "when the party is in the Little Brown House. Come now, you must get into line."

So Peletiah, seeing no help for it, found himself back of Joel marching off with his broom, as best he could, while Polly brought up the rear.

"Come on," shouted Joel, prancing wildly off. Then he looked around.

"He isn't marching—he's just an old mud turtle crawling," he cried in disgust.

"Oh, Joel!" cried Polly. "Now, Peletiah, you must go faster."

"He called me a mud turtle." Peletiah stopped in his tracks, his face red clear up to his tow hair.

"Joel oughtn't to have said that," said Polly, "but you must go faster. Don't you see I can't march at all unless you do."

"I'm not going to march," declared Peletiah, deserting the ranks to go across the kitchen and sit down in one of the chairs backed up against the wall, "and he called me a mud turtle, and as soon as I'm rested, I'm going home."

"Oh, no," said Polly, "you couldn't do that. Why, you are at a party. Well, now, don't let's march. We'll play something else till Ezekiel comes. I know," she clapped her hands and spun around once or twice in the middle of the floor.

Joel threw down the broom wrathfully.

"You must hang it up first," said Polly, coming out of her spin.

"I don't want any party," declared Joel, "not a single snitch of one."

"Oh, yes, you do," said Polly, running up to him. "Hang

up the broom, Joel—that's a good boy. I've thought of something just too splendid for anything."

If Polly had thought of "something just too splendid for anything," that altered matters, and after all, the party might be quite worth while. So Joel ran and got the broom back on its nail—then he was back.

"What is it—what is it?" he cried, his black eyes sparkling.

"He called me a mud turtle," said Peletiah over in the chair backed up against the wall, "and I'm going home."

"Oh, no," Polly ran over to stand in front of him. "Company never goes home from a party till it's over. Besides, we're going to play perfectly splendid things, and there's the refreshments."

"Refreshments!" howled Joel, "are there going to be refreshments! Oh, I do want a party, Polly, I do," and he swarmed all over her.

"Don't, Joel," she said in vexation. Oh, dear, and it was to be such a surprise, and now she'd told before it was time!

"They're in the cupboard, the refreshments are," said Joel, springing off to the corner. "I know they are."

"Joel, you mustn't," cried Polly, flying after to stop him. But she was too late! He flung open the door of the old cupboard, and there on the shelf was the custard pie, and beside it three cups and a pitcher.

"A pie!" screamed Joel, his nose wrinkling up, and he stood on his tiptoes to reach it. "Oh, I want some now. Do let me, Polly."

"For shame, Joel," cried Polly angrily. "Come right straight away." She seized his calico blouse.

But Joel hung with both hands to the edge of the shelf. And the green door opening, in came Ezekiel.

"There now, just see, here's the rest of your company

coming," cried Polly, quite lost in her vexation. "Now I don't believe I shall let you have any pie at all."

"It's my party," howled Joel, still hanging to the shelf and looking over his shoulder at her, "and I'm going to have the refreshments, Polly."

"How do you do, Ezekiel," said Polly.

Ezekiel had on a new calico blouse, pink and white striped, that the minister's wife had sat up the night before to finish for the party. And he was hardly able to take his thoughts from it, until he saw the pie, and underneath it Joel hanging to the shelf. Then he stared out of big eyes.

"I'm going to have some refreshments," cried Joel over to him.

"Oh, no," contradicted Polly. "Joel has been naughty," she said to Ezekiel, "and he ought not to have any pie."

"He called me a mud turtle," said Peletiah, over in the chair by the wall. He concluded not to say anything about going home since he heard "refreshments and pie."

"Oh, dear!" exclaimed Polly, her cheeks very hot.

"Can't I have any pie?" gasped Joel, dropping suddenly to the floor, his face working dreadfully as he tried not to cry.

"I don't see how you can," said Polly slowly. She hated to say it, but when a boy was naughty, why of course he ought not to have goodies.

Joel threw himself flat on the floor and sobbed as if his heart would break.

"And I can't have any, either," Polly leaned over him to say it, "because I got angry."

This was so very dreadful that Joel raised his head to look at her, the tears dripping off from his round cheeks. And the old kitchen became so very still, you could have heard a pin drop.

Peletiah slipped off from his chair and came slowly up. "And I was naughty, too," he said, "'cause I was going home."

"Then Ezekiel will have the whole pie," cried Joel, and down went his head again to the floor, where he kicked and screamed so that all the pins in the world dropping couldn't possibly have been heard.

Did ever anybody see such a party! Polly clasped her hands tightly and said to herself, "I won't cry! Oh, if Mamsie were only here!"

But it wouldn't do any good to keep saying that to herself. She must *do* something. She swallowed very hard. "I'm going to play 'Old Father Dubbin,'" she cried, and spun out to the middle of the old kitchen floor.

Up came Joel's head. "Are you really going to play 'Old Father Dubbin,' Polly?" he cried, blinking through his tears.

"Of course, I am," cried Polly gaily, running into the bedroom to kneel down before the bottom drawer of Mamsie's big bureau. Here Polly kept the things for that much-prized play of "Old Father Dubbin." Phronsie's red-topped shoes were there, too, and the other few treasures possessed by the Five Little Peppers. All except the fishhooks, and the dried bugs, and such choice possessions that Joel and David exulted in. Those Mother Pepper said must be kept up in the loft.

Polly dragged out "Old Father Dubbin's" queer little hat, and the rest of his things. Her heart beat dreadfully and one or two tears dropped into the drawer. "I mustn't cry—anyway, not until the party is over," she said, shutting the drawer.

Out in the kitchen Joel was prancing about, screaming, "We're going to play 'Old Father Dubbin'—we are!" until

Ezekiel ran up to him. "I'm going to play it, too." So Joel seized his arms and they spun around together.

Peletiah fidgeted first on one foot, then on the other. At last he said, "I will play it, too." And he tried to get in between the two boys. But he was so slow, they only bumped into him, almost knocking him over.

"You don't know how," Joel was just going to scream at him, as they spun past him. Then he remembered, "Well, come on," he said, opening his arms.

Before he knew it, Peletiah was being danced about till he thought his head would fly off. Then he was quite sure it would. He tried to say, "Stop," but he didn't get breath enough.

"My goodness!" exclaimed "Old Father Dubbin," coming out of the bedroom, as they whirled past. The minute they caught sight of the old gentleman, Joel gave a squeal and the dance came to such a sudden stop that Peletiah's feet flew out from under him and down he sat on the floor. Ezekiel sank panting down beside him.

"Well now," "Old Father Dubbin" looked through his big spectacles, which were nothing but holes and a pasteboard frame tied around his head, "you must all rest before we begin the play."

"Oh, no, no," roared Joel, "I'm not tired, not a single squinchy bit."

"But the company is," said Old Father Dubbin, resting on his staff.

Joel looked down impatiently on the two boys. "You aren't tired, are you?" he said, "not a bit, are you?"

"I'm most dreadfully tired," declared Peletiah, taking up one foot to rub it. "And you stepped all over me, and wouldn't let me stop, either."

"Humph!" said Joel disdainfully, turning on his small heel. "Well, when can we begin?" he teased, going over to Old Father Dubbin.

"Just as soon as the company is rested," said the old gentleman.

"Begin with me—do begin with me," cried Joel, circling around him, "please, Old Father Dubbin."

Polly was just going to say, "It isn't polite to begin before company is ready," and then when she thought what a dreadful time they had all had, she said, "All right. Now come on."

And they did come on, Old Father Dubbin and Joel; and Ezekiel forgot how tired he was and screamed with delight, and Peletiah let his foot take care of itself, and pretty soon the two boys hopped up and said they were "plenty rested," and then the old kitchen was in an uproar.

So of course no one heard what was happening in the bedroom.

There was a string of thin old gold beads that Mrs. Pepper kept rolled up in soft paper in the little drawer at the top of the bureau. They used to be worn on Father Pepper's grandmother's neck, and were to be Polly's some time, as the one treasure that was left. Now they were spread on the old patched bedquilt, and somebody in a black hat pulled down over his eyes, stopped to gaze at them. Then he turned off to pull things over in the bureau once more, every now and then pausing to listen to the babel going on in the kitchen. But as the window was open, he didn't care very much if the noise did stop, for couldn't he spring out at the least warning just as easily as he jumped in, pray tell! So he rummaged on.

At last, Old Father Dubbin held up his staff. "All done," he said, "the play is over." And Joel might tease and tease—

there was to be no more for that day. Everybody must sit down to draw a long breath.

Then the person in the bedroom took his hand out of the bureau drawer, and stepping over to the bed he gathered up Father Pepper's grandmother's gold beads, slipped them into his pocket, and jumped out of the window.

"Oh, dear, I'm so hot!" cried Joel, seeing that there was to be no more "Old Father Dubbin," no matter how he teased, "I'm going to get Mamsie's fan. Can't I, Polly?"

"Yes," said Polly. It was Joel's party and they'd had such a dreadful time—and a sorry little look came into the brown eyes—Mamsie surely would let him take it. So Joel dashed into the bedroom to get the big palm-leaf fan that was stuck into the frame of the looking glass over the bureau.

Then they heard a dreadful scream that brought Old Father Dubbin into the bedroom, and after him the two Henderson boys.

There was Joel, his black eyes wide with excitement, and swinging his arms. "A burglar!" he shouted, "I'll catch him," and he dashed to the window and jumped out.

Old Father Dubbin took one look all around; then flew over to the bed. There was the roll of soft old paper that had held Father Pepper's grandmother's gold beads, but empty. Polly dashed wildly out through the kitchen, flung the green door wide and rushed after Joel.

XXIV

Great-Grandmother Pepper's Beads

"THERE's the Little Brown House!" cried Davie, just as if he had never seen it. "And Joel has had a party!" all in the same breath.

"Joel has had a party," hummed Phronsie in Mrs. Brown's lap, "a beyewtiful party," her pink sunbonnet flying back with the jolts of the old white horse over the rough road.

Mrs. Pepper's eyes grew suddenly bright. "You have been so very good to us, dear Mrs. Brown," she said, leaning over to whisper the words.

The farmer's wife held Phronsie closer, but did not trust herself to speak.

"At least," she said, clearing her throat, "you'll come again."

"Yes, indeed," Mrs. Pepper was about to reply, but David screamed, "There's Joel— Oh, do let me get out!"

"Whoa!" cried the farmer, and Davie was out, over the wheel in a twinkling, and rushing up to Joel sitting on a big stone by the roadside, and the very picture of woe.

"Oh, Joel!" cried David, flinging himself up against him, "what's the matter? Mamsie—he's sick," flying back to the wagon and wringing his hands.

"Don't worry your ma. She'll get out as soon as she can," said Mrs. Brown.

Mrs. Pepper was already out at her side of the wagon, and reaching Joel on his stone. The happy expectant look had gone from her eyes, but she still smiled.

"He's sick, Mamsie," cried Davie frantically, and kneeling down to seize Joel's hands.

"I'm not," declared Joel in a dudgeon, "sick one single bit. I didn't catch him and he's gone."

"Who has gone, Joel?" Mrs. Pepper put her hands on his two shoulders. "Look up and tell Mother."

Joel raised his black eyes and cried wrathfully, "And he took your gold beads, Mamsie."

"Oh, Joel, not those!" For once Mother Pepper forgot herself and her hands dropped to her side. The little thin string of gold beads was all she had to hand down to Polly as a link from the past.

"I'll go after him some more," screamed Joel wildly, and jumping from his stone. He had an awful feeling at his heart, for Mamsie had never given up like that before.

"No, no, Joel," Mother Pepper managed a smile, and seized his sleeve.

"What's the matter?" asked the farmer's wife, clumsily picking her way up to them over the thick uneven grass, and still holding Phronsie's hand.

"Nothing so very bad," said Mrs. Pepper.

"Nothing so very bad!" echoed Joel, turning big eyes up to his mother.

"No," said Mrs. Pepper cheerfully, "as long as nobody is sick. Where is Polly?" she asked, a white line beginning to show itself around her mouth.

"She's gone after Ben, and she told me to stay here and tell you," said Joel gloomily, "and I was going after the burglar some more," he added in an injured tone. "I'm going now." He leaped away, and in another second would have been around the bushes and out of sight.

"Joel!" Mother Pepper's voice was low, but it brought him back. "I need you now." She took his little brown hand, "You can help me so much."

"I'll help you, Mamsie," said Joel, feeling very tall and important. "You don't have to come, Davie; Mamsie's got me," he said over his shoulder, as Davie crowded up.

"Oh, I want Davie; we shall both need him," said Mrs. Pepper.

"You can come," said Joel patronizingly, and striding off, clinging to Mrs. Pepper's hand.

Davie lifted his face that had become quite downcast with this dreadful trouble coming to Mamsie, and then, too, not being wanted to help, and trotted after.

The farmer's wife, not having heard the word "burglar," grasped Phronsie's hand tighter yet. "Come, child," she said, "an' you an' me'll find out what's ben goin' on."

"We'll find out," Phronsie cried with a little gurgle of delight, skipping along by the clumsy footsteps, "and I'll show you my Little Brown House."

"So you shall, you sweet lamb, you," exclaimed Mrs. Brown, yet with a heavy heart against the hour when she and the farmer would be in the big wagon and on the Maybury road, going home, just those two.

Once in the old kitchen, the story came out, with many jerks from Joel, as he often stopped to bemoan the loss of a chance to capture the burglar, and the positive assurance that he could have beaten him to nothing if he had only been there.

"My senses!—your gold beads!" exclaimed the farmer's wife. She had sat down in Mrs. Pepper's calico-covered rocking chair, and now she lifted both hands in dismay. "How you can, Mis Pepper, take it so easy!"

"Just think, all the children are well," said Mrs. Pepper with a smile.

"I know," said Mrs. Brown, "but gold beads is gold beads."

David, seeing Mother Pepper's smile, brightened up a little, as he sat on the floor at her feet, as the story went on. Phronsie was going about, patting everything with loving little fingers, and humming softly to herself, so she didn't hear how Joel's party had been interrupted by an uninvited guest in the bedroom. And how Polly had run out in "Old Father Dubbin's" rig after Joel in hot chase to catch the visitor, who had jumped out of the window, without anyone's getting a sight of him.

"And then Polly made me go and watch for you, while she went for Ben." All Joel's injured feelings now blazed out again. "And she told me not to stir till you came, or she got back. I could have caught him just as easy." Joel doubled up his little brown fists manfully.

"Polly was just right," said Mother Pepper, "and you are a good boy, Joel. Mother is so glad she can trust you."

Joel's indignation changed to a smile that showed his little white teeth—just as Farmer Brown, having tied Jingo to a post in the fence, walked in. "Well, did you have a good party, Joe?" he asked breezily, not knowing anything about burglars or any other trouble.

"And did you like th' custard pie?" cried Mrs. Brown, gazing about for any evidences of the feast.

Joel ran up to the big chair. "We haven't had it."

"Oh, well, you've had other things to think about beside custard pie," said the farmer's wife. "Well, I s'pose likely that Polly put it away."

"I know where she's put it," Joel pranced over to swing the door of the old cupboard wide open. "Here 'tis!" He stood on his tiptoes, clinging to the upper shelf where the big custard pie, with a pitcher of weak lemonade and some teacups stood, ready to be summoned when Polly should decide that the proper time for refreshments had arrived.

"I'm going to get it down now!" cried Joel, jumping up to reach it with wild little hands.

"No, no, Joel," said Mrs. Pepper.

And the farmer's wife cried, "For mercy's sake, Mr. Brown, lift that pie down, or that boy will smash it." So the big custard pie was safely taken from the shelf and set on the table.

"Dave, see—the custard pie!" screamed Joel, waving frantically for David to come.

"There's somethin' in th' pitcher," said the farmer, handing down the lemonade. "I guess that's for th' party." So he set that on the table, too.

"Yes," said Mrs. Pepper. "Mr. Atkins gave Davie a couple of lemons the other day. And Polly has made this for Joel's party."

"I want it now—my party," cried Joel, and pulling out the table drawer to get the big knife. Then he suddenly stopped. "I've got to wait for Polly," he said.

"You better wait till your big brother gets here, too," said the farmer, pointing with a thumb over his shoulder in the direction he supposed Polly and Ben would appear.

"They're never coming," declared Joel, in anguish at any proposed postponement of the cutting of the pie. Still he must see Polly before it was cut.

"I wouldn't wonder ef they was comin' down th' road this very minute," said Mrs. Brown.

"You better run an' see," added the farmer.

So Joel tore himself away from the pie, and dashed out and down to the gate, Davie at his heels.

"Ef we can help you, Mis Pepper," said the farmer, "we'll stay—but ef so be there's nothin' my wife an' me can do, why, we must be streakin' it for home."

"We don't need to start jest yet, Pa," objected his wife, all her eyes following Phronsie.

"Now, Ma, you won't be a bit sprier to go, ef you set for another hour. I'm a-goin' ef we can't help Mis Pepper."

"Maybe we can help her," said Mis. Brown, clinging to any straw that might delay the setting out for home.

But Mrs. Pepper shook her head—so far as any assistance was concerned. "I wish you could stay," she said. But this Mr. Brown wouldn't do, so the farmer's wife, seeing that there was no help for it, got slowly out of her chair, and the leave-taking began. And just as they were finally in the big wagon, up rushed Polly and Ben and Joel.

"Anybody seen th' feller?" asked the farmer of Ben.

"No, sir," said Ben, setting his teeth together hard.

"Sho now, that's too bad," said Mr. Brown sympathetically, and flicking his whip over Jingo's back. "Well, I s'pose th' Badgertown folks'll keep on th' lookout for him."

"Good-by." Mrs. Brown, with no eyes for anyone but Phronsie, looked back until the turn of the road made it impossible to see any one, or even the Little Brown House.

"Now we must have the party and Joel's pie," said Mrs. Pepper, when the disconsolate little group was back in the kitchen. "And you may get the knife, Joey." But first, there was a little talk between Polly and Joel and Mother Pepper. When it was all over, she said, "Yes, Polly, you and Joel may have some of the pie, and Joel must cut it now." And no one peering in at the window would have thought that the chief treasure of the house had been seized that afternoon by a cruel hand.

They didn't want any supper that night because of the custard pie and the lemonade. And after Phronsie was fast asleep in the trundle bed, and the two boys were tucked safely away in the loft, Polly and Ben curled up on the floor, either side of her big chair.

"I can't think, Mamsie," began Ben, "who it could be." He wrinkled up his round face in distress.

"No," said Mrs. Pepper, "we can't think. But, oh, Polly child." She put her hand on Polly's brown hair and her voice trembled.

"Mamsie," cried Polly, "don't feel badly. I don't mind— so very much." She longed to put her head on her mother's lap and cry, for she felt no bigger than Phronsie. Oh, the years that she had loved those beads, ever since she was a little girl and Mrs. Pepper had taken them out and told her that she was to have them when she was grown up, and then every time that this was done, and before the beads were wrapped up in the soft paper and put back in the drawer, the words of the father, who had died when Phronsie was a baby, would be said over again.

"Always remember, child," Mrs. Pepper would say, "what your father told you. 'You must be good, Polly, to be worthy to wear Grandma's beads.'"

And Polly had always said, "I will." And now the beads were gone—oh, could she bear it!

But she looked at Mother Pepper's face, and what father had said meant, she very well knew, "help Mother," so she swallowed the sobs that were almost out. And Ben, as he looked at her, set his teeth and concluded to do the same thing.

"Tell us about Mr. Brown's farm," said Ben, as soon as

he could speak. "We want to hear about it, Mamsie."

So Mrs. Pepper began, and set the whole day before them from beginning to end.

"Oh, I am so glad," said Polly, with a long breath, "that Davie had a good time—because he didn't want to go without Joel."

"Joel is going to have a chance," said Mother Pepper, "and you, Ben, and you, too, Polly, for we're all invited to spend a day there before very long."

"Isn't that fine!" cried Polly, forgetting for a moment her dreadful trouble, and she clapped her hands. And Ben was so pleased at that, that he actually smiled.

"And now you must get to bed, both of you." Mother Pepper looked up at the old clock on the shelf. "Dear me, who would think it was so late!"

It was all of an hour after, and Mrs. Pepper, who had been sewing by the light of the candle, to make up for the time spent in the visit of that day, let the work drop in her lap, and she was lost in thought.

Suddenly a noise like a little mouse at work in the corner, struck upon her ear, to be followed by another not at all like one to be laid to a mouse, and then a distinct, though soft, rap was heard.

She got out of her chair and went over to the big green door and opened it.

"Why, Jimmy!" she exclaimed, "is your mother sick?"

An awkward, overgrown boy leaned against the door casing and covered his face with his hands.

"Tell me about it," commanded Mrs. Pepper, "or I can't help you."

The boy caught his breath, then gasped, " 'Tain't that—Mother's all right."

"Then it is something about yourself," said Mrs. Pepper

kindly. "Now, Jimmy, you want me to help you, or you wouldn't have come at this time of the night."

"I've been walking up and down," said Jimmy. "First, I waited till they were all abed, 'xcept you, and—" then he broke down.

"Well, now that you have come, you must tell me your trouble, or I can't help you," said Mrs. Pepper decidedly.

For answer, he ran his hand in the pocket of his shabby jacket, and pulling out something, timidly presented it— and Mrs. Pepper's fingers were over Polly's gold beads that Great-Grandmother Pepper had left her.

"Oh, Jimmy!" all the gladness over their coming back couldn't stop the pain, "how could you!"

"I don't know," he gasped, and he looked so distressed that Mrs. Pepper hastened to say, "You didn't think, Jimmy, you didn't, how—"—"wicked," she was going to say, when he burst out, "Yes, I did—I saw you through the window take 'em out of the bureau one time, and roll 'em up again and put 'em back. And I—I—wanted to go to the circus—it's coming to Cherryville next week, and—and—"

It was no use, he couldn't go on with Mrs. Pepper's black eyes on him, but cowered worse yet against the door casing.

"But you've brought them back," at last Mrs. Pepper made herself say, "that was good of you, Jimmy."

"I—I couldn't keep 'em. You've been awful nice to Mother. Don't tell her," he brought himself up in sudden terror. "You won't—oh, you won't, Mrs. Pepper!" he begged, shaking all over.

"I won't, Jimmy," promised Mrs. Pepper. "Now see here, my boy, you're almost a man—and I'm going to see you make a man that we all in Badgertown will be proud of." She put her hand on his shoulder. "Now run home and hop into bed."

XXV

Jimmy

THERE was a sound of somebody hurrying along the road back of her, who wasn't accustomed to running, and who couldn't walk fast. And then that somebody gasped, "Mrs. Pepper!"

Mrs. Pepper turned, "Why, Mary Pote!"

"Well," said Mary Pote, bringing her short roly-poly figure to a standstill and putting her hand to her side, "I'm mortal glad you stopped, for I couldn't have held out much more. I've been chasin' you clear from Atkins's store." She brought this all out in gasps.

"Now that's too bad," exclaimed Mrs. Pepper sympathetically.

"You see— My! but I'm hot." Mary Pote twitched off her leghorn hat, and began to fan herself furiously.

Mrs. Pepper looked about. "There's a big stone," she said, "let us sit down."

"I'm sure I'm glad to," said Mary Pote, going off to the roadside after her, and sinking down under an old scrub oak, over which blackberry vines scrambled at their own sweet will. Mrs. Pepper sat down on the other end of the stone, and placed the bundle of coats Mr. Atkins had given her, on the grass at her feet.

"When I get my breath enough, I'll tell you," said Mary Pote, "what I was following you for."

Mrs. Pepper folded her hands in her lap and let her gaze wander off to the hills encircling Badgertown. It was hard to remember when she had done a thing like this, idling of a morning on a roadside stone.

"Well, now," said Mary Pote, "I'm getting my second wind and I'll begin. Miss Parrott sent me down to say that she wanted to have you and the children go to the circus tomorrow at Cherryville."

"*To the circus!*" Mrs. Pepper hastily turned her gaze from the hills and turned to Mary Pote in blank amazement.

"To the circus, I said," Mary Pote nodded and picked off a spear of grass to break into small bits and scatter in her lap, "though if all is told, I b'lieve it's a sight more of a menagerie than any other show. Anyway, Miss Parrott told me to tell you that she was going to send you all to it, if you'd go."

"Not all of us?" said Mrs. Pepper incredulously.

"Every single one of you. I'll give you her very words— 'Mary Pote, you go down and say to Mrs. Pepper that I want her and all the children to go to the circus tomorrow. Mind, Mary Pote, Mrs. Pepper and every one of the Five Little Peppers.' There you have it." She picked off a second spear of grass and sent the bits after the others.

Mrs. Pepper drew a long breath. "Oh, I don't think I can," she said.

"I wouldn't think, if I was you," said Mary Pote, "I never do when Miss Parrott says a thing, but I just get up and do it."

"It's so good of her," began Mrs. Pepper. Oh, to have Polly see the animals that she was always making up into stories to keep the children quiet, and Phronsie—only think of her delight over the monkeys. And there was Joel—well, Mrs. Pepper by this time was so excited that she turned a face on which two red spots were coming in her cheeks. Mary Pote had the good sense to let the thing work itself out, and kept quiet.

And Davie, could Mother Pepper ever forget his face when the circus came to Cherryville last, and almost all Badgertown folks went over but the Little Brown House people? And Davie, his eyes on her, had tried to smile when Joel howled in his distress at missing it. And there was good, faithful Ben, who wouldn't even show that above all things he had longed to see a circus.

"I would like to have the children see it," she said slowly, her eyes alight.

"Well, if I was you, I wouldn't sit on that stone considering it any longer," said Mary Pote. "Miss Parrott is one to speak her mind, and if she asks you, you might take it for granted that she wants you. Well, I must get back—she took me off from that black silk basque I was finishing, to come down. Simmons is going to pick me up at Mr. Beebe's shoeshop, so I must get there as soon as I can." Mary Pote rose from her end of the big stone and shook her front breadth free of the grass bits. "Well, is it yes or no?"

"It is yes," said Mrs. Pepper, her voice trembling with happiness, "and oh, Mary Pote, will you tell her how I thank her. She is so good to ask us."

"I'll tell her." Mary Pote pushed back her little corkscrew curls on either side of her round face and clapped on her leghorn hat.

"Oh," turning back, "she said, 'tell Mrs. Pepper to be ready at eleven o'clock.'"

"Yes," said Mrs. Pepper, scarcely realizing the bliss that was actually in her grasp.

"And one thing more," Mary Pote looked over her shoulder. "She said you'd find the lunch basket in the carriage."

Mrs. Pepper tried to say something; but Mary Pote was moving off intent on reaching old Mr. Beebe's shoeshop, for Simmons didn't like to wait for anyone sent on errands, and he could make it very unpleasant for days if thus detained.

Suddenly Mrs. Pepper started, took a step forward—then another and faster, all her effort being to overtake the little roly-poly figure hurrying over the dusty road.

"Mary—*Mary Pote!*" Her voice was so clear that it carried well, and her steps so rapid that she soon stood beside the little woman.

"Now you aren't going to say 'No.' " Mary Pote regarded her with disfavor.

"I've come for something else—to ask you to beg a favor of Miss Parrott." The color flew suddenly out of Mrs. Pepper's cheek, but she went on bravely. Mary Pote stared with all her eyes.

"It's this," Mrs. Pepper went on rapidly. It was best to get it out as soon as possible. "To beg her to let me take another boy with my children."

"What boy?" asked Mary Pote abruptly.

"Jimmy Skinner."

"What—that woman that lives on Fletcher Road—her boy?"

"Yes," said Mrs. Pepper.

"He's an idle, good-for-nothing boy," declared Mary Pote, shaking her head decidedly till the corkscrew curls flew out. "No, I don't b'lieve Miss Parrott would ever countenance his going in all this world."

"His mother works so hard—it would please her," began Mrs. Pepper.

"That's true enough, but the boy, no, he ain't worth doing things for. I shouldn't think you'd want him along with your children, Mrs. Pepper." She regarded her curiously.

"Jimmy thinks a great deal of his mother," said Mrs. Pepper. She fastened her black eyes on the little woman's face. "That's enough to save any boy. Won't you ask Miss Parrott to let him go?"

"What? Me ask her? Oh, I couldn't." Mary Pote started back and put up both hands. "I'll do anything to oblige you, Mrs. Pepper, but I couldn't do that. Besides, she'd only say 'No.'"

"Well, good-by," said Mrs. Pepper. She turned and went rapidly back to the big stone, picked up her bundle, and sped home.

Polly ran out to meet her and take the bundle of coats. "I'm going on an errand, child," said her mother, "and I may be home a little late, so don't worry."

Polly's brown eyes looked questions, but Mrs. Pepper only smiled, as she turned off.

She didn't give herself much time to reflect all the way to the Parrott estate. And at last Hooper was ushering her into the solemn drawing room with its rich furniture and heavy brocaded hangings, and presently Miss Parrott was before her—and the thing was to be done.

"Now, Mrs. Pepper, do take off your bonnet, you look so tired, and I will give you some tea." And Miss Parrott's heavy black silk gown was trailing across the room to the bell cord.

"Oh, no, please," Mrs. Pepper put up a protesting hand. "I must speak to you—please, Miss Parrott."

It was so pleading a tone, very like Polly's, that Miss Parrott turned back and sat down in the high-backed chair, regarding her vistor curiously.

"You are so good to me and to my children that I cannot thank you enough, Miss Parrott," began Mrs. Pepper.

"There—there," returned Miss Parrott, raising a protesting hand, only it sparkled with ancestral rings. "Mary Pote brought back your thanks, so say no more about that."

"Miss Parrott." Mrs. Pepper hesitated a bit, then took the plunge, "I very much wish that a boy might go to the circus with me and my children." It was all done in one sentence.

"A boy?" Miss Parrott gazed at her. It seemed like a long time, but it was really only a breathing space. "What boy, Mrs. Pepper?"

"Jimmy Skinner."

Miss Parrott's long face dropped. If Mary Pote had been there, she could tell the "signs of the times" it gave. Mrs. Pepper could guess, but her black eyes did not droop, and now she went on steadily.

"His mother lives on Fletcher Road, a hard-working woman, glad to do anything."

Miss Parrott's brow wrinkled. "Go on," she said, "if you please, Mrs. Pepper."

"And Jimmy thinks a great deal of his mother," Mrs. Pepper considering it wise to bring this point to the front as speedily as possible, went on pleadingly.

"If I remember rightly," said Miss Parrott dryly, "that Jimmy is considered by the village people to be an idle, good-for-nothing boy, Mrs. Pepper."

"Yes, he's idle," confessed Mrs. Pepper, "but I believe he will work, for he thinks so much of his mother."

"And you want him to go to the circus with your children, and in my carriage!"

It was perfectly dreadful the silence that followed. At

last Mrs. Pepper said in a low but distinct voice, "Yes, Miss Parrott."

"I am sorry—but I am obliged to say I consider it unwise to draw that boy into the company." Miss Parrott drew herself up stiffly against the high-backed chair, till she looked exactly like the portrait in the wide hall, the most disagreeable of all the ancestors whom she possessed.

Mrs. Pepper opened her lips, thought better of it, and closed them. Then she got off from her chair.

"Do sit down," Miss Parrott waved her long fingers. "I want to oblige you, Mrs. Pepper," she said, struggling to throw a little cordiality into her manner and tone, "but I cannot see my way clear to grant this request."

Again there was silence, cold and dreadful; then Mrs. Pepper moved toward the door. Miss Parrott got out of her chair, "Don't go." She took a step or two, astonished at herself. When had she ever capitulated to anyone, and here was a plain woman from a little brown house making her experience such a strange desire to yield to the distasteful request!

"I really wish you would tell me," she laid the long fingers on Mrs. Pepper's shawl, "all about it—why you wish that boy to be drawn in to the company, with your children. It is most astonishing. I cannot understand it."

So Mrs. Pepper suffered herself to be led, and she presently found herself sitting, this time on the brocaded sofa, and Miss Parrott by her side.

"Jimmy is going to be a man," she said, just as she had told the boy, only she never whispered a word of his wrongdoing, "if Badgertown people take hold and help."

"And would it help to take him to the circus?"

"I think it would be the greatest help in all this world."

Mrs. Pepper leaned forward, her eyes sparkled, and she was as eager as Polly now. "Don't you see, he longs to go? Every boy does. And if he can be invited by you, Miss Parrott—"

"And go with you and the Five Little Peppers," interrupted Miss Parrott. "Yes, I begin to see."

"And once he thinks that he's a boy that people believe has got something worth while in him, why, he'll see it himself."

"Yes, yes," said Miss Parrott, finding herself thawing all over.

"And then when he sees that, he'll take hold and work— if it is found for him." Here Mrs. Pepper went more slowly and looked fixedly into the long face.

"You mean that perhaps I might find some work for him," said Miss Parrott. "Well, perhaps so, but I haven't got that boy to the circus yet. Let us settle that matter first," and a grim smile stole over her long face. "Now proceed, please, Mrs. Pepper."

"And a boy who has something worth while in him can't help but grow up to a man," Mrs. Pepper said with emphasis, "a *real* man, can he, Miss Parrott?"

"I suppose not," said Miss Parrott, a bit grudgingly, as all her defenses were thrown down. Then she smiled, "Oh, you may take the boy—that Jimmy," she said, "with you tomorrow. I can't say I believe all the good is to result that you think; but you can try the scheme. He'll probably worry the life out of you—tease the animals almost to death, and get into innumerable scrapes—and I should think you had enough trouble without calling this down on your head. But you can take him."

Miss Parrott shut the door after Mrs. Pepper, feeling extraordinarily light of heart. "I wish I were going to the circus, too," she said. Then she brought herself up, "What has come over me at my time of life? How I act!"

Mrs. Skinner, down on Fletcher Road, had just lighted her oil lamp. It gave out a pleasant twinkle through the window, as Mrs. Pepper knocked at the door.

"I was just a-packin' up th' wash for them boarders over to the Hill," she said, lifting a flushed face from the basket at her feet. "An' Jimmy is goin' to carry it over." A proud smile ran up to her eyes that she turned on the big awkward boy.

"That's fine," said Mrs. Pepper. Then without more ado, she gave Miss Parrott's invitation. It had two different effects. It sent Mrs. Skinner down on a pile of clothes waiting in a chair to be sorted and washed. She raised both red toilworn hands. "Glory!" was all she was able to utter. Jimmy stood perfectly still, but his eyes burned into Mrs. Pepper's face.

"And now be at the Little Brown House tomorrow, Jimmy, by eleven o'clock," Mrs. Pepper made speedy work of it, and got herself out to carry the joyful news home.

Could it really be true that her children were to see a circus at last, or was she dreaming?

XXVI

The Circus

When they were all packed into the big Parrott coach, ready to start for the day at Cherryville, things couldn't have been better for a beginning. There was Mrs. Pepper with Phronsie on her lap, then Davie next, and in the corner, Jimmy fixed up in the jacket his mother had worked on as to patches, up to the last moment.

And over on the other seat were Polly and Joel and Ben —just a good half dozen and one of Badgertown folks going to their first circus.

For once Joel could say nothing. The wonderful expedition had stunned him, and he sat with folded hands, and eyes big with suppressed excitement. Ben was the one who did the talking, and he bubbled over in the most unusual fashion, so that Polly kept bobbing her smiles and delighted appreciation over Joel's head, at intervals all through the ride. It was so good to see Ben merry, and to know that he was going to have a good time for once in his life.

But once the circus ground was reached, Joel found his tongue. He sprang out the first, and a volley of questions were fired, sometimes to the Peppers, and just as often as not into the air. It made no difference, for Joel couldn't wait to get the answers.

Mother Pepper kept her brood together, and waited while Simmons carried out the instructions of Miss Parrott, and bought the tickets, and got the big lunch basket down. Then he considered his duties were all done, until after the performance he should pick the party up for the return trip.

"I'm going to carry the things to eat," cried Joel, tugging at the big basket as it was set on the ground.

"You let that basket alone, Joe," commanded Ben.

Joel dropped the handle as if it were hot, then he whirled around to make a beeline for the string of red carts where the animals had been.

"See here," Ben gave a dash, seized him and brought him back. "You stay here with us."

"Now, children," Mother Pepper smiled on the eager-eyed group, "there are two things to remember—we must all keep together, and we mustn't crowd nor push other people."

"I'm going to see things," began Joel.

"We can see a great deal more if we don't push," said Mamsie, "and we can enjoy it better."

"I'll take care of Joel," said Ben, his fingers holding the small calico sleeve, "so you won't have to look out for him, Mamsie."

"Oh, I don't want Ben to take care of me!" Joel howled and squirmed to get free, but as Ben's fingers only gripped the tighter, it wasn't much use.

"Joel is going to be a good boy, I'm sure," said Mother Pepper, smiling down at him.

Joel drew himself up. "I'm going to be good," he said proudly.

"Well, in the first place, we must think what we will do with the lunch basket," said Mrs. Pepper. "Ben can't carry it around until it is time to eat."

"Let's eat the things now, Mamsie," begged Joel, tearing off his gaze from the beautiful red carts and other entrancing equipment of the show scattered over the big field.

"Why, Joel Pepper!" exclaimed Polly, with a little laugh, "we haven't hardly begun the day. The idea of eating!"

"I can eat," said Joel in an injured tone. "I'm awful hungry."

Just then up came Simmons. He even touched his hat to Mrs. Pepper, a courtesy he was just beginning to observe, for the Little Brown House people didn't at all appeal to him. He scraped his throat, "Miss Parrott said I was to take care of the lunch basket." He was about to say, "I forgot to tell you," but he couldn't quite make up his mind to utter such a story, although he had planned it all out, intending to keep the whole day to himself without the bother of such people on his mind. Instead, here he was saying, "She said I was to bring it to you when you were ready for it."

So there was that trouble settled. And the tickets being in Mother Pepper's hand, up she went with all her brood to the little narrow walk between the stakes of the tent, where a big man, his hat on the back of his head, sat in a chair.

"Seven," he said, taking them to count, and he tore off the numbers, and pushed them into her hand, "that's right. Step in, mar'm." And into the tent they all stepped, Joel and Ben crowding together, for the small calico sleeve still had to be held, of course.

The grass was all trodden hard beneath their feet, and everything seemed to smell of peanuts that boys were carrying about in baskets, bawling out their wares—people eating out of the bags they had just bought, and scattering the shells to right and to left.

No one of the Peppers said a word about "peanuts" and

they all tried not to look at the baskets, for they had settled that matter when they knew they were going to the circus.

Polly began it, and Ben helped her, getting the children together in a corner of the kitchen, "You know we haven't any money to spend, and it will make Mamsie feel just dreadfully if we look as if we wanted things," so they had all promised they wouldn't look at the things. But now it was pretty hard work with so many baskets, and boys poking them in their faces. Didn't the peanuts smell good though! At last Joel had to hold his little stubby nose tightly with his fingers. Then he suddenly dropped them.

"I'm going upon top," he screamed, as several boys dashed by scrambling over the rows of boards that encircled the big ring, and he twitched himself free.

"No, you don't," said Ben, dashing after, "we've got to sit where our tickets say."

But Joel wildly protested that he was going where those other boys were, who now on the tiptop seat were laughing and jeering people down below, and acting dreadfully.

One of the circus men passing by, said "Jiminy! I wouldn't want to hold that eel," to Ben.

Joel turned his wild gaze down to the man, "I'm not an eel," he said, and his black eyes blazed.

"You are," said the man, looking back as he hurried off, "a slippery, squirmy old eel and I've a good mind to douse you into the fish tank."

"He shan't," roared Joel, and he beat his small fists together, "and I'm going after him, and smash him."

"You'd get smashed yourself," said Ben. "Now aren't you ashamed, Joel; everybody's looking at us. Mamsie will have to take us home if you act so."

Joel's fists flew apart, and he glanced quickly around. "There isn't anybody," he began, but an old woman in a poke bonnet came up. "Is the little boy sick?" she asked in great concern.

"No," said Ben, "I'm afraid he's naughty."

"That's very bad," said the old woman severely and shaking her poke bonnet at him. "I sh'd take him right home if I was you. Folks want to enjoy a circus and th' animiles in peace without having boys act like Kedar."

"I think he's going to be good," said Ben. His face was very red, and he would have given a great deal to have the old woman pass along. Oh, if Mamsie and the others were to come up! But she stayed. "I d'now," she said, "I don't set no gret by boys. You never know what they're up to unless they're sick. Sure he ain't?" She peered at Joel's little scowling face and drew out a small bottle from a black silk bag dangling on her arm. "Now two or three drops of this," and she pulled out the cork.

It smelt dreadfully as it was put under Joel's little nose, and he bobbed his head back and threw up his arm. Away went the bottle with the black stuff, and the old woman with the poke bonnet ran after it, as it fell on the sawdust just inside the rope ring.

"Here, keep out of there!" roared a circus man, tearing along up, and leaping the rope, he seized her shawl.

"I'm getting my bottle," she said angrily, "that boy there," she pointed to Joel, "threw it over here, and he's spilt most all of my med'cine." She held it up to the light.

"Oh, no," said Ben, hurrying over, "my brother didn't throw it—it was an accident."

"She stuck it up to my nose," said Joel, hurrying up wrathfully, "she hadn't any business to. She is a bad old woman."

"Joel—Joel!" Ben's face was scarlet. The circus man took the bottle and gave it a good smell.

"*Phew!*" he said, giving it back hastily. "Well I'd 'a' throw'd it to Halifax. Now get out o' here," he helped her over the rope, "we don't want no old women with bottles makin' trouble. I've a good mind to put you out." He kept hold of her shawl.

The old woman, with a trembling hand, put the cork back into the little bottle. She began to whimper. "Oh, don't do that. I've never ben to a circus, an' I've saved my money for ever so long. Don't put me out, Mister."

Joel swallowed hard; then he plunged over. "You mustn't put her out. I shan't let you."

"Hello!" the circus man looked down at the small figure, then he whistled.

"No, I shan't," said Joel, tossing his head and his black eyes flashed. "She thought I was sick."

"That's it," the old woman mumbled, "I thought he was sick, and—"

"And I didn't want medicine," Joel hurried on, "and it smelt."

"I sh'd think it did," the circus man rubbed his nose. "Well, that's another thing, if you want her to stay. But I thought you said she was bad."

Joel hung his head, and the hot color rushed all over his little face.

"She didn't mean—" he began.

"All right," said the circus man. "You can stay, old bottle woman," he turned to her. "I've got something more to do than to hang around here to straighten out a fuss when there don't seem to be none."

"Mister," said the old woman, as he was slouching off, "that boy didn't 'xactly throw my bottle, not 'xactly—"

He laughed and snapped his fingers at her, and now he was gone for good.

"Why, there's Mamsie—and the others," cried Ben, looking off to a middle row of seats, where Polly was standing up and beckoning with all her might. "Come, they've found our places."

"I'm sure I don't know where my seat is," said the old woman helplessly, and she began to fumble in her black silk bag, "th' man give me somethin' an'—"

Joel was dashing off to the others, but thinking better of it, turned back. "I'll find it for you," he cried, "give me the bag," and not waiting for permission, he seized it and getting down on his knees he emptied it of all its contents on the grass.

It was all done before Ben could do more than cry, "Joel!"

The old woman sank down on her knees beside Joel, as he pawed among the collection of articles spread on the grass. Strange to say she seemed more curious to see if he would find it than disturbed at the way her bag was emptied.

"Here 'tis!" he held it up joyfully.

"You're a real good boy," exclaimed the old woman gratefully. "Now I'll put the things back."

"I'll help," said Joel, falling to on the work. So together everything was all snug and safe once more in the black silk bag, and the old woman hung it on her arm again, and got up to her feet.

"It's Number 12," said Joel, squinting at the little piece of pasteboard. "I'll find it for you," and he pranced along, Ben and the old woman following, his black eyes eagerly scanning the seats. "21—20," he ran on, "15—14—why—it's next to Mamsie!"

Sure enough. They helped the little old woman, her poke bonnet settling over her eyes on the ascent, up to the middle row, and down she sat by Mrs. Pepper. When she found who it was in the next seat, she leaned forward and said in a loud whisper, "Your boy, the littlest one, is an awful good boy. He helped me consid'able." She had not then learned that there was a third Pepper boy, still smaller.

Mrs. Pepper beamed on her, and was just saying, "I am so glad," when Joel, on her other side, burst out, "Oh, I was bad—her bottle flew off—and it smelt bad, and I'm sorry."

"It was an accident," said Ben hastily. And the old woman, when she saw Mrs. Pepper's face, hurried to say, " 'Twarn't much spilt, an' anyway I've got enough left," and just then, so many people came hurrying in that there was such a great commotion in finding seats, as to absorb all attention. And the first thing Joel knew, a trembling hand was laid across Mrs. Pepper's lap. "There's a dime," said the little old woman, "I brought it for peanuts. And you can buy some for us all."

Joel hopped to his feet, his eyes sparkling.

"I'll go with him," said Ben.

"No, no," roared Joel, clutching the dime. "She said me —I'm going alone," and he began to wriggle out of his seat.

Ben looked at Mrs. Pepper in dismay, as she said quietly, "Yes, you may go, Joel, by yourself. I can trust you."

"She says I may," Joel was already working his way over the rows. He turned to send a delighted smile back, and Mrs. Pepper nodded. "I can trust you," she said again.

"All them children yours?" asked the little woman presently, craning her neck to see the row of heads the other side of Mrs. Pepper.

"All but one," said Mrs. Pepper, "and he is a Badgertown boy."

"My sakes! hain't you had a sight o' trouble though, to bring up such a lot o' young ones."

Mother Pepper turned clear around in her seat. "Trouble?" she repeated, and her black eyes shone, "why I never should think of such a thing! Why, they are my *children*."

"Yes, that's jest what I say—and such a lot o' them," affirmed the little old woman, bobbing her poke bonnet with emphasis, as Joel came rushing back swinging a big bag of peanuts.

"You see I thought I'd get peanuts. There's a sight o' nourishment in chewin' of 'em," she said, taking the bag, "so I didn't bring nothin' to eat." She emptied out a small handful into her lap. "There, boy," and she handed the bag back to Joel, "you an' your folks can have th' rest, an' we can sit an' chew on 'em together."

"And we have a great deal of luncheon," said Mrs. Pepper, "and it will be very nice to have you eat with us."

And just then the band marched in, smart in bright red coats and gilt helmets—with a blare of trumpets, to announce the approach of the grand procession.

XXVII

More About the Circus

"I HAIN'T never ben to a circus," said the little old woman, after the splendor of the grand procession had swept around the ring, and she caught her breath.

"We have never been to one," said Mrs. Pepper, looking down the length of her row of absorbed faces.

"Is that so? Why, I thought ev'rybody had had a chance at one, 'xcept me— An' I says, 'Now, next time it comes to Cherryville, I'll go.' I'd ben a-savin' up for it, for circuses don't wait for folks to turn back an' grow young. Look at them ponies—did you ever see sech mites!"

She leaned forward, her withered face suddenly looking as if she had indeed "turned back to grow young."

"You're pokin' me in the back somethin' dreadful," said a woman in front, with an indignant face over her shoulder. The head was surmounted with a hat topped off with a big pink bow wound around a higher bunch of yellow roses.

"I s'pose so," said the little old woman, "but I have to poke, to get the best of that contraption on your head—I've got to see; that's what I come for."

The woman with the hat flounced back and threw her head up higher yet.

"I guess I'll have to stand up," said the little old woman, tired of twisting first one side and then the other.

Mrs. Pepper, her mind down the line where Phronsie, in absorbed delight over the ponies, was sitting between Polly and David, had no eyes for her neighbor's distress. Now she laid her hand on the rusty black shawl. "I'm so much taller," she said, and before anybody quite knew it, the little old woman was in the seat next to Joel, and Mother Pepper's black eyes were gazing over the "contraption" of a hat.

And, then, after the ponies, came the elephants—the big one and the little one. Phronsie shivered when the old one marched ponderously into the ring, and threw herself over into Polly's lap.

"He won't hurt you," whispered Polly, her arms about her.

"And he isn't half as bad as Polly's rhododendron," said Ben, leaning forward to talk across.

Polly turned a cold shoulder to Ben. "See the little elephant, Phronsie—see him!"

"Is there a little one?" said Phronsie, uncovering one brown eye fearfully.

"Yes, indeed," said Polly, "and he's such a dear little elephant, Phronsie. Do look!"

"He's a dear little el'phunt," cooed Phronsie, bringing both eyes into view. But she sighed after the ponies, now careering on the other side of the big ring, drawing the little chariot gay with ribbons and flags, and a small boy and a smaller girl riding in state.

"I wish they'd come again," she said, pulling Polly's head down to whisper in her ear.

"Perhaps they will," said Polly encouragingly, "and if they don't, there'll be something else just as splendid."

Phronsie folded her hands in her lap and sat quite still.

Could anything be as splendid as those sweet little ponies? And she sighed again. But Polly had said so, and it must be true.

Meantime David, who had scarcely dared to breathe through the whole show, screamed right out.

Everybody turned and stared, and a nervous woman down in the front said, "Gracious! somebody's sick—get th' doctor." And one of the funny men in a white coat with red spots all over it, and a hat with holes where his eyes came, looked up as he was walking down beneath the seats saying things to make people laugh.

"Toss me that boy," he roared, snapping a little whip he carried under his arm, "and I'll eat him up."

And at that, Joel screamed, "You shan't eat my brother— I'll smash you!" And everything was in a commotion. And a man in a red coat, with a good many brass buttons on it, rushed up and said: "You're disturbing the show—I'll put you out if you make any more trouble."

And Mrs. Pepper leaned over past the little old woman. Polly caught one glimpse of Mamsie's distressed face, and she swept Phronsie over into Ben's lap.

"Oh, Davie—what is it?" she cried, huddling him up against her, as he buried his face in her neck.

"The bears! Joel has always wanted to see some—they're coming!"

Joel, with no heart for bears or anything else, was still shaking his little brown fists and declaring that he wouldn't let anyone eat up his brother, while Big Bruin and Mrs. Bruin and two small Bruins were doing their best down in the ring to make the parade lively.

"Oh, Davie!" cried Polly, so mortified that she forgot herself, "you shouldn't have screamed. We're so ashamed!" While Mother Pepper said quietly, "Joel," and down went his little fists, and he stopped right in the middle of a word.

David was so still that Polly bent her hot cheek over him. "Why, Davie, are you sick?" she cried in sudden fright.

Davie tried to say "No," but the word wouldn't come. And before he had time to begin again, Mrs. Pepper had quietly worked her way past the little old woman and Joel, and there he was in her lap.

"There, it's all right, Davie," she said, "Mother knows all about it."

"I've made—I've made—you all—ashamed," said Davie in little shivery gasps, throwing his arms around her neck.

"You will make us very much ashamed," said Mrs. Pepper, "unless you sit up now, and be Mother's good boy."

"Will I?" David raised a little face that was quite white. The soft waves of light hair tumbled over his forehead.

"Yes, indeed," Mother Pepper brushed them back soothingly.

"I will be your good boy, Mamsie," said David, sitting up in her lap, his miserable little face brightening a bit.

"He better take some o' this med'cine." The little old woman tried to pass the small bottle she picked out of her black silk bag. "I always carry it everywhere's I go, ef I sh'd be sick."

But Mrs. Pepper shook her head. And Joel being now absorbed in the bears that somehow were determined not to march with the others, but to get up a show all by themselves, till the trainer with his little whip had to get them into line, everything became quiet once more.

Well, after the grand parade, there was the big show when the animals did the most surprising things, and the men and the women in spangles and satin and velvet jumped from horses going at top speed—or through hoops, or swung in the air like big birds.

And then there was a great to-do, everybody clambering down from the seats—all trying to get out of the tent at once.

In and out of the crowd Miss Parrott's coachman worked his way with the big lunch basket.

"I thought you would like to have it now," he said. And he didn't forget to touch his hat to Mrs. Pepper.

"I think it is time," said Mrs. Pepper, "for I believe everybody is hungry," with a smile that included the little old woman next to Joel.

"I'll show you a place where you can sit and eat, and not have many people around," said Simmons, going off with the big basket, and all the Peppers hurried down from their seats to follow. But not before Mrs. Pepper took hold of Joel's little calico sleeve. "Help her down, Joey," she said, nodding her head toward the little old woman.

"I want to go with Dave," grumbled Joel.

"Help her down, Joel," said Mother Pepper distinctly.

"And I'll help her, too," cried Davie, turning back.

"So you shall," Mrs. Pepper beamed at him, so that he forgot for the first time how he had made them all ashamed.

And Joel on one side and Davie on the other made the little old woman say when she was safely down from her seat on the middle row, "My sakes, I never had no gret likin' for boys before. What's your name, anyhow?"

Joel, who was frantic to hurry along, as the others and Miss Parrott's coachman were well ahead, had no time to answer questions. So Davie said, "He's Joel Pepper, and I—"

"Pepper? What a name!" interrupted the little old woman with a snort.

Davie's face got very red.

Luckily Joel didn't hear; all his mind was bent on getting

along faster as he beat his hands together aching to pull the little old woman on by her rusty shawl.

"Joel is a good enough name," said the little old woman. "My husband's father was Joel, but Pepper is a perfectly dreadful name."

"Pepper is just a perfectly splendid name!" David stopped short by her side and looked at her out of flashing blue eyes.

"My sakes alive!" exclaimed the little old woman, stopping aghast, "I sh'd as soon 'xpect a hummin' bird to dare me, as you. Now ef it had 'a' ben him," she shook her black silk bag at Joel, who was marching on. Joel looked back and screamed, "Come on!" which they did, redoubling their speed.

"Now, my name is a sensible one," said the little old woman, "Jones. But Pepper—I sh'd as soon think of salt and mustard."

David, finding it harder and harder to escort a person determined to find fault with his name, had all he could do to keep himself from deserting altogether. But knowing that Mamsie would feel badly if he did, and remembering how he had made them all ashamed, he marched on by her side; but his head was tossed up, and his cheeks were very red.

But in the excitement of getting into the corner of the field around the big lunch basket that Simmons put in their midst, no one noticed him but Mother Pepper.

"Tell Mother," whispered Mrs. Pepper, under cover of getting the good things unpacked.

"Mamsie," said David desperately, "that lady is a bad old lady. Don't make me sit next to her," he begged.

"Why, Davie boy!" exclaimed Mrs. Pepper in surprise. "I think she is quite a nice little woman."

"Oh, no," Davie shook his head. "She's been saying awful things. She doesn't like us to be called Pepper."

Mrs. Pepper burst into a cheery laugh. "Well, that's not being bad," she said. "Now perhaps I shouldn't like her name, if I knew what it was."

"I know it," said Davie, "she told me—it's Jones."

"Well, I don't like it. I never did like it," said Mrs. Pepper, "so you see, Davie, it isn't so much matter if people's names don't suit other folks. But the people themselves have got to be just right. Now run along and be nice to her. She is poor and old. Remember that, Davie boy."

There was everything in that fine big lunch basket. First came a tablecloth and napkins as fresh and sweet as if they had been packed away in lavender, as indeed was the case. Then seven little cups—and a big jar of lemonade, piles of bread and butter and cold chicken, cake, and biscuits. Was ever such a feast spread out for hungry people at a circus!

Jimmy, who hadn't said a word all through the show, but had absorbed it with all his eyes and ears, now hung back from the group and leaned up against the wall of a shed a little distance away. He was watching the merry party with longing.

Ben, helping Polly to spread the tablecloth on the grass, looked off and saw him.

"Give us a hand, Jimmy," he said.

Jimmy started, then stopped, hanging back.

"Come on," said Polly, "and take hold of this other corner, please."

So there Jimmy was, and the tablecloth being spread, the articles from the basket were soon in place, everybody being handy at getting them out, Joel and David especially so, while Phronsie got in between, laughing and crowing happily under the impression that she was helping very much.

"I think I will visit with you," said Mother Pepper, sitting down on the grass next to the little old woman. There was a happy look in her black eyes, and a soft color began to come on her cheek, "and let the children take care of things."

The little old woman raised her withered face and regarded her curiously. "You ain't a bit of a fussbudget," she said.

"No?" replied Mother Pepper. Then she laughed and said, "Why should I be?"

"La! you shouldn't be. But a woman who's got a raft o' young ones most generally is."

"They are my *children*," said Mrs. Pepper softly, and her happy eyes roved over the little bunch of Peppers. Bursts of laughter came from the group, in which Jimmy's voice could now and then be heard.

"Who's that boy?" abruptly demanded the old woman.

"That's Jimmy Skinner, a Badgertown boy," said Mrs. Pepper.

"Oh, then he ain't a Pepper?"

"No. Well, children," Mrs. Pepper got up to her feet, "you are all ready now, aren't you? We better begin, for we want as much time as we can spare to see the animals, you know."

At mention of the "animals" there was great excitement, Joel beating his hands together and shouting, "Let's begin —let's begin!"

"Oh, Mamsie, please sit here," cried Polly, patting one end of the tablecloth, "and Mrs.—"

"Jones," said Davie, coming to the rescue, "that's Mrs. Jones," and he held out a hand to help the little old woman up from the grass.

"Jones I am—but I ain't no Missis," said the little old

woman, getting up stiffly to her feet. "My! but I feel like a wooden-jointed doll! I'm Susannah Jones—that's th' handle to my name. Well, where'll I set?"

"Right next to Mamsie," said Polly.

Miss Susannah Jones let her pale eyes rove all around the circle. "What?" she said in a puzzled way. "Where?"

"Why, here," said Polly, with a little laugh, and leading her to Mrs. Pepper. "This is Mamsie," and she laughed again.

Miss Susannah opened her thin lips. She was just about to say, "Well, of all the queer names, *that* is!" when, glancing at Davie's face, she thought better of it. And besides it was no worse than Pepper. So she sat down and the feast began.

Mrs. Pepper, glancing across the tablecloth at Jimmy, saw something that made her say, "Come here a minute," and as he shuffled around to her side, she whispered to him, "What is it that makes you afraid to save your cake?"

Jimmy's freckled face got very red. He scrubbed his rusty shoes back and forth in the grass. Then he said, "I didn't want you folks to see."

"You want to give it to somebody?"

Jimmy nodded his tow head, glad enough that he didn't have to speak any more.

"You may," said Mrs. Pepper kindly, "do just as you like with it."

"May I?"

"Indeed you may," declared Mother Pepper. "So don't hide your cake under the tablecloth—but keep it on your plate, and you shall have a paper to do it up in when we all get through."

"I don't want no paper," said Jimmy bluntly.

"Oh, Jimmy, you can't carry it home in your hand."

"I ain't going to carry it home—and the boy won't mind."

"The boy?" Mrs. Pepper looked very puzzled.

"There's a boy over there," Jimmy pointed off in the direction of the big red cart standing in the field, "and he keeps looking and looking at us—and I guess he's hungry."

Mrs. Pepper turned a swift eye in that direction. "Jimmy," she said, "I think you are right. Wouldn't you like to carry your cake to him now?"

"Wouldn't I just!" exclaimed Jimmy, finding a ready tongue, and springing off on just as ready feet.

"Oh!" screamed Joel, "look at Jimmy—running off with his cake! See, Mamsie, Jimmy is—"

"Joel!" Mother Pepper didn't need to say more, as everybody whirled around to see the Badgertown boy skim over the grass clutching his slices of cake that he had been tucking under the tablecloth.

Joel ducked, and everybody else was quiet except Miss Susannah.

"That Badgertown boy is jest as bad as th' rest o' you," she said, between the bites on her own piece of cake, as Jimmy slipped back and into his seat, but not to eat any cake.

"Well, now," said Mrs. Pepper, when everything was cleaned up neatly, and the big basket had been handed to Simmons, who appeared at the right time, "we'll start to see the animals."

Joel screamed, "The bears—the bears! Oh, let's see the bears first."

"We will take them all in order, Joey. If the bears are at the beginning of the line, why we will see them first."

"The monkeys," cried Phronsie, pulling at her mother's

hand. "Oh, I want to see the dear sweet little monkeys, Mamsie!"

"We are going to see the monkeys, Phronsie, and all the rest of them," said Mrs. Pepper in a happy voice.

Polly couldn't help jumping up and down and clapping her hands in joy, her two brown braids flying out.

"I think we ought to visit your rhododendron, Polly," said Ben, catching hold of her to stop her and say it over her shoulder. But Polly pretending not to hear, the words were lost in the babel of delight that ensued. And Mrs. Pepper was asking the little old woman if she would like to go with them to see the animals.

"Indeed I would," cried Miss Susannah. "My! I was wonderin' how in th' world I'd ever get around amongst those animiles an' reptiles. Say, do you Peppers family always go about th' world lookin' out for other folks?"

"We don't go about the world," said Mrs. Pepper, with a little laugh. "Well, now, we must start."

As it happened the bears were first in the line, so Joel had his wish, and he crowded up plastering his face close to their cage, in which the beasts had been put on their return from the parade in the ring.

"That boy will get his nose clawed off," said a man in the crowd. Mrs. Pepper turned, "Joel!" she cried, just in time! Out came old Father Bear's paw with its five cruel claws as sharp as knives—and a sudden scratch went sizz on the iron bars just where Joel's face had been.

"He didn't get me," said Joel vindictively, staring into the wicked little eyes of the bear snapping angrily at him.

"Now look here, Joe," Ben broke through the crowd to him, "you'll keep away from the cages, or I'll hold you every single minute."

"Oh, I don't want to be held," howled Joel, squirming to get free, "don't hold me, Ben; I'll be good."

"I shall hold you," said Ben firmly, "unless you'll promise not to touch the cages. Aren't you ashamed, Joel?" he said in a lower voice. "Everybody is looking at you."

"I want to see the bears," roared Joel. All the world might be looking at him. He was in such an anguish that he didn't care. He *must* see the bears!

"Well, promise," said Ben, "and I'll let you go."

"I can't see 'em," fretted Joel, "unless I go close."

"Yes, you can; nobody else touches the cages."

Joel swept the crowd with his black eyes, disdainfully.

"Just look at Mamsie," Ben leaned over and whispered this into Joel's ear. Mrs. Pepper, holding Phronsie's hand, was looking at him. Her face was white, but she smiled.

"I won't go near those bears," said Joel. "Oh, dear!" He tried not to cry, but it was no use. The tears dripped down through the fingers clapped up to his face and trailed all down his calico blouse.

"Now that's all nonsense, Joe," said Ben, releasing his hold. "You can go just as near as I do, and all the other folks. I'll trust you," and Ben slipped away to prove his words.

Joel felt somebody tugging at one of the hands over his wet little face. "There's a good place over there," said Davie, pointing to a little space where two men, who hadn't been able to forget that they had once been boys, were holding it open for him. They spread it out a little further so that Davie could slip in, too.

It was some time before Joel was willing to leave the bears. Father Bear, who couldn't forgive the boy who made him miss such a well-aimed scratch, kept pacing up and down, growling and showing his teeth at him—and altogether being so very fascinating that a crowd was continually in front of the cage, staring with open mouths and eyes. At last Mrs. Pepper gave the word to move on.

They had the big snakes, and a lion who was old and tired out, and half asleep in the corner of his cage, so that he wasn't at all interesting, and almost everything else in the animal line that the circus had afforded, before they came to the monkeys. Phronsie saw them first.

"There they are, Mamsie!" she gave a joyful little cry.

Mrs. Pepper hurried to keep up with her, and the others followed in close ranks, being kept in line by Ben, who brought up the rear.

A small boy, who was just as anxious to see monkeys as Phronsie, rushed in between, knocking off the pink sunbonnet. It had been so hot in the crowd that Phronsie had untied it, and now away it went, and a big clumsy man set his foot right on it. Jimmy saw it and tried to rescue it, pulling at one string; but the people pushed about so that he was knocked down and the string came off in his hand. Then the big clumsy man saw what he was stepping on, and he got off.

"Oh, I'm so sorry," Jimmy's face was full of distress, as somebody picked up the poor little sunbonnet, and he held out the string.

"It couldn't be helped," said Mrs. Pepper, only glad that Phronsie was so absorbed in delight over the monkeys that she wouldn't know that she had lost her sunbonnet.

And the monkeys seemed to think that something special was expected of them, for they at once set to on so many antics that there was nothing but crowding and pushing as everybody came up to see, and stopped to laugh. At last a great hulking boy came up suddenly back of David and pushed him against the cage.

This was apparently just what one of the monkeys had been watching for. He swung himself down from his perch, reached out a long arm, and grabbed off David's little cap. Then up he leaped back again, squatted down to bite and tear it to his heart's content.

David clapped his hands to his head, and turned very white, as a cry went up from the crowd.

"Oh, that's too bad!" "He's got the little feller's cap." "Oh, what a shame!" And one mother elbowed her way in through the crowd to Mrs. Pepper, who had her arms around her boy trying to comfort him. And she herself needed sympathy, for how could she scrape together the money for another cap? "I know who the boy is that pushed him, and I'll tell his father—he'll give him a good beating."

"Oh, no," said Mrs. Pepper, "don't do that. Davie doesn't want you to. Do you, Davie dear?"

"No, I don't," said Davie, through his sobs. Then when he saw his mother's face, he wiped away the tears and managed to smile through them. "I can go without a cap," he said.

XXVIII

David's Cap

Mrs. Pepper turned away for a moment, not trusting herself to speak.

"I don't mind it—much," Davie pulled at her shawl and looked anxiously at her face as she turned back.

"Well, now," she said comfortingly, as she led him out of the crowd. "Mother will see how she can fix it up for you, Davie boy."

"The monkey's spitting out the pieces of your cap," cried some boys after him, and they laughed and doubled up in glee.

"Shame on you for laughing," cried the woman who wanted to tell the boy's father. But it was no use to stop the crowd—they cheered and guffawed as they pressed up closer to the cage, where the monkey on his high perch was biting out pieces of David's little cap, and throwing them off toward the bars, grinning dreadfully between each bite.

Joel rushed up to see the fun. He had stayed as long as he could at the cage of big snakes, Ben finally hauling him away, and now, with Polly and Jimmy, they hurried up to join Mrs. Pepper and Phronsie.

"What is it?" cried Joel, thrusting in his hot little face wherever he saw a crack of space to get it in. "Oh, what is it he's got?"

"A boy's cap bein' et up," said a man, stopping his laugh long enough to shoot this out.

"Oh, I want to see!" By a way Joel best knew would secure a good place, he was pretty soon worked in, till there he was in the front row with the other boys still screaming with the fun of the thing.

There the monkey sat on a high perch, biting very slowly now in order to make the cap last as long as possible. His little eyes were twinkling, and his paws were kept busy to hold the cap, and fight off the other monkeys, who now swarmed and chattered around him, in order to seize the beautiful thing that was making the people so noisy with delight.

"What is it he's got?" cried Joel, wrinkling up his face trying to see the wad in the monkey's paw.

"A boy's cap—he twitched it off his head. Oh, Jiminy— see!"

The monkey, fearing that the other monkeys might be too many for him to hold his prize, took a last big bite from it, spit out the pieces, and threw them derisively right at the bars, and into Joel's face pressed against them. One piece fell out at his feet; it said "—vid Pepper" just where Mamsie had marked it on the rim of the cap.

Joel's brown hand closed convulsively over it, and he looked wildly around. Then he put down his head and bolted right through the middle of the crowd.

"Mercy sakes!" the woman screamed—the boys who had laughed skipped nimbly out of the way—and nobody thought the case quite so funny as it had been.

"Mamsie, where are you?" screamed Joel. He almost threw Polly over, for he was beyond seeing anything or anybody in his mad rush, and Ben wasn't quick enough to catch him. It was Jimmy who did it.

"Let me go," cried Joel frantically, and he kicked Jimmy's shins. But Jimmy's hand was just as tight, for all that, on Joel's arm.

"He's chewed it all up," cried Joel wildly, as Polly and Ben ran up. "Let me go!"

"No, you don't," and Ben got hold of the other arm, "what's that in your hand, Joe?"

"Dave's cap," Joel flung open his hand. There it was, with "—vid Pepper" on what remained of the rim.

"Oh, Mamsie!" and the horrified little group looked up into Mother Pepper's face. And there was Phronsie, who hadn't understood anything only that she must leave the dear sweet little monkeys—and Davie, his light hair in soft waves over his forehead, crowded up to Mrs. Pepper's side. His hands were tightly clasped and he closed his eyes to squeeze back the tears.

"No, no, Polly," said Mrs. Pepper, for Polly was just beginning, "Why, Mamsie, what—" "we won't have the story now, and see—there is Simmons coming for us. It's time to go home."

When they were once in Miss Parrott's big coach, the story all came out. Simmons on his coachman's box, alternately drew himself up straighter then ever, and then shrank down in a way he couldn't remember doing when on duty as befitted holding his aristocratic position in the community.

"I won't tell her—the missus acts bad enough as 'tis over them poor children. What if he did lose his cap!" Away he drove in great form down a hundred yards or so. Then he pricked up his ears.

"Oh, Davie," Polly was saying mournfully within the coach, "it's too bad! Mamsie, what shall we do!"

Simmons didn't hear Mrs. Pepper's reply. Down his

shoulders went and he drooped, letting the reins slacken. And then he straightened up again, quite determined to let matters alone. But as he drove up to the Little Brown House, and watched them all get out, he couldn't help but see Davie's face.

He looked back over his shoulder to watch them go up the path, not taking his gaze off till they were all in, and the green door shut.

"I s'pose I'd felt pretty bad when I warn't no bigger'n him, to lose my cap, if I didn't know where to get another. Thunder!"

And before he even put up his horses, Miss Parrott had the whole story.

"I presume they keep boys' caps down at the store, Simmons?" said Miss Parrott quickly.

"That they do, ma'am," said Simmons.

"And perhaps you could tell Mr. Atkins the right size?"

"There wouldn't be no trouble about that, ma'am."

There was a little transaction with money that came out of Miss Parrott's black silk bag, and Simmons hurried out to take care of his horses, before he attended to the matter that now began to appear quite important to him.

Jimmy, his hand thrust into the pockets his mother hadn't been able to make quite whole, turned down to the little cabin on Fletcher Road called "Mrs. Skinner's house." The loss of David's cap bothered him dreadfully on top of the other matter connected with the circus boy. Jimmy wasn't able to get him out of his mind. While the cake was rapidly disappearing, he had heard the story of being "starved and beaten," the boy looking for more, in a way that struck Jimmy harder than the loss of his own treasured part of the feast.

"I can't help him none," he declared, with a reckless

twitch of his shoulders, "no more'n I could get a new cap for Mis Pepper's boy."

He stopped suddenly, "Can't I help get a cap for David Pepper?"

He took off his own cap and scratched his head. That did no good, and he flung the cap back. He hadn't a penny in his pocket. He knew that without the trouble of turning the pocket inside out. But—couldn't he get some work? Where?

It was a pretty small prospect before him, as all Badgertown people had a poor opinion of his desire or ability to work.

"What's th' use?" he said, kicking off some small stones in the rough road. Then he picked up one and shied it at a bird. He was astonished to find that he was relieved after all that he hadn't hit it, and he kicked and scuffed more stones. That gave him an idea.

Away back, almost a year before, a farmer in the north end of the township had asked him to "pick rocks" in a barren field to be cleared for cultivation. Jimmy had said "Not much!"—and turned off with a laugh. Suppose the farmer wanted him now! It wasn't a pretty job, Jimmy knew, breaking one's back, and hauling and piling the stones. But—well, he could ask; it wouldn't do any harm to do that.

Jimmy turned in at the door. Mrs. Skinner lifted a hot red face from the steaming washtub. All hours of the day were her work times.

"Well," she beamed in great and unusual contentment, resting her hands on the tub rim, "and was the circus fine?"

"Prime," said Jimmy, "I'm coming back," slamming the door.

"I want to hear—" began his mother in terrible disappointment. But he was already halfway down Fletcher Road.

"No," said the farmer, just getting up from his supper,

"you're too late. Them rocks was all picked, an' I'm plowin' th' field."

"Tell him about Badger's land," said his wife, gathering up the remains of the supper.

"Oh, yes, see here," called the farmer. "Badger wants th' rocks picked from his land. I guess you can get a job there."

When Jimmy dragged himself back from Badger's, the lamps and candles had been lighted for some time in the cottages along the road. He looked for Mrs. Pepper's as he passed the Little Brown House. There she was over by the table sewing. Jimmy had a pang as he thought how many stitches she would have to set before Davie's loss could be made good. He didn't know that a brand-new cap had been handed in, and that after the jollification over it had spent itself, Davie had taken it up into the loft to hang by the side of the shakedown, the first thing his eyes would rest upon the next morning.

That next morning, the old kitchen was just the jolliest place, full of the circus and its delightful memories. Davie, with his new cap on his head, was prancing around, the center of observation.

"It's a perfectly beautiful cap!" declared Polly, for nobody knows how many times, and stopping on her way for the broom to sweep up.

"I wish the monkey had eaten mine up," said Joel discontentedly.

"You may wear mine." David stopped prancing and twitched off his cap.

"No, no, Davie," said Polly, "Miss Parrott sent you that cap, and she wouldn't like you not to wear it."

"And if a monkey should eat mine," said Joel, just as well pleased, "I guess Miss Parrott will give me one. I don't want yours, Dave." With that David clapped on his cap again, and Joel seizing him about the waist, they spun round and round the kitchen, getting in the way of Polly's broom, and hindering dreadfully. All of a sudden, down fell David, and Joel on top of him.

"I didn't make him," cried Joel, in dismay and hopping up, as Polly threw down the broom and ran over.

"He didn't make me," gasped Davie, getting up. The new cap had fallen off long before, and Polly had picked it up to hang it carefully on a nail. "It was my shoe."

"Your shoe?" repeated Mrs. Pepper over by the window. "What is the matter with your shoe? Come here, David." She laid down the sewing in her lap, as David scuffed across the floor.

"Well, that does need mending," she said, as David put his small foot in her lap.

"I'm so sorry," he began.

"Well, now, Mother is so glad that you didn't get hurt with your shoe so bad as that," she said cheerily. "Now you must go down to Mr. Beebe's and ask him to sew it up."

"And mine needs mending, too," cried Joel, hopping over on one foot to her chair. "I want to go to Mr. Beebe's."

"No, Joel," said Mrs. Pepper, with a laugh, "your shoes are perfectly sound. There now, Davie, go right down to the shoeshop and ask Mr. Beebe if he will please to sew it up now—because you haven't any other shoes—and walk carefully, child, else you might fall."

"Now isn't it nice that Davie has a new cap?" cried Polly, going to the window, broom in hand, to watch him as he passed down the road. Joel had run out to go as far as the gate with him, then he had turned back to the woodshed, for Mrs. Pepper had said he must pick up some kindlings.

"I do think folks are awfully good to us, Mamsie," said Polly, turning away from the window, to pause a minute before beginning to sweep again. "Just supposing Miss Parrott hadn't let us see that circus!" and her cheeks paled at the very thought.

"Yes," said Mrs. Pepper, and her busy needle stopped. "Miss Parrott is good, and God is good to let her do it."

"Isn't He?" cried Polly, with shining eyes. "And now to think that Davie has a new cap, too!" as the busy needle now went hurrying in and out. "But I never shall get this floor swept up, if I stop all the time."

Davie hurried as fast as he could, because the shoe must be mended as soon as possible. But he had to step carefully else a bad matter would be made worse. At last he was over the cobblestones of the narrow street in front of the shoe-shop, and lifting the knocker on Mr. Beebe's door.

"Well, well," cried the little shoemaker, turning away from a box of bed slippers he was sorting to rub his hands together delightedly, "if here doesn't come Davie Pepper!"

"Yes," said David, "I've come."

He took off his new cap—he didn't want to, but Mamsie had said "Never keep a cap on when you go to see people," and to enter the little shoeshop was far more than to do business; it was to visit friends.

"And now what can I do for you, Davie?" asked little Mr. Beebe, coming forward. "What has your mother sent you for?"

"It's to mend my shoe," said Davie, holding up his foot to show where the leather flapped.

"So?" cried the little shoemaker, setting his spectacles straight. "Well, now, you come over an' set on th' bench, an' we'll see what we shall see about that shoe."

So Davie hobbled over and sat on the bench, and the little shoe was drawn off and submitted to a close examination, Davie following every movement with anxious eyes.

"The whole o' th' shoe is pretty bad," said little Mr. Beebe slowly, pinching the well-worn leather critically.

Davie drew a long breath. "And Mamsie said would you please sew it up now, as I haven't any more shoes."

"Sho!" exclaimed the little shoemaker. Then he thought better of what he was going to say. "Yes, I'll get right to work on it," and pretty soon he was stitching away and cobbling at a great rate, Davie swinging his stocking foot, and the other one in its rusty shoe, while the work went on.

"Where do you suppose I went yesterday, Mr. Beebe?" asked Davie in the midst of it. For the little shoemaker always expected the Pepper children to entertain him when they came to the shop. "It makes work go easier," he said.

"Now I never can guess," said Mr. Beebe, waxing his long thread again.

"I went to the circus," said Davie.

"You didn't, though!" The little shoemaker was genuinely surprised now, and he dropped his needle to peer over his spectacles at Davie.

"Yes, I did," said Davie, with a jubilant little crow, "and every single one of us did, Mr. Beebe," and he clapped his hands in delight at the remembrance.

"Now do tell!" The little shoemaker was so overwhelmed with the news that he forgot to pick up his needle. "Well, how did you get there?"

"In the big coach," said Davie, bobbing his head. He didn't think it was necessary to designate whose vehicle, as Badgertown boasted only one.

"Not Miss Parrott's! exclaimed Mr. Beebe.

"Yes," said Davie, bobbing his head again.

"Well, I never! She didn't go, did she?" exclaimed the little shoemaker.

"No," this time Davie shook his head.

"I thought not. I sh'd as soon 'xpect one of th' tomb-stones in th' buryin' ground to get sociable as her. Well, well—" here Mr. Beebe picked up his needle and began to pull it briskly in and out of the leather. "Now you must tell me all about it. Begin at th' beginnin', Davie, an' reel off."

So Davie began, and the little shop got very merry, Davie stopping every now and then to laugh at the antics of the bears, and the little ponies and the elephants and the funny men who wore white clothes with red spots over them, and who had holes for eyes, and who kept walking up and down saying things to make people laugh, or who were tumbling off all the while from the donkeys' backs. And the little shoemaker wanted dreadfully to stop cobbling to hear the better, but he knew Mrs. Pepper expected her boy home, so he kept on with his work, every now and then grunting out, "Well I never!" and "Who ever did!" and the like.

So of course no one heard the door open, and the big woman who walked in, exclaimed, "Goodness, Mr. Beebe, what's th' matter!"

"There ain't nothin', as I know of," said the little shoe-maker, looking up composedly, "an' please to shet th' door, Mis Goodsell."

Mrs. Goodsell pushed the door to with her foot. "I thought you was havin' a party by the noise," she said, coming over to sit heavily down on the bench by David's side. Then she whipped the shawl ends over across her lap and stared first at the little shoemaker and then at Davie.

"We was," said Mr. Beebe, "us two. We made quite a nice party; just big enough."

"Who is the boy?" Mrs. Goodsell turned her heavy body as far as she could and stared worse than ever at Davie.

"That is David Pepper sitting on the bench," said Mr. Beebe. "Now what kind o' shoes do you want, Mis Goodsell? You can be tellin' me, an' then I'll be ready to get 'em when I'm through with this piece o' work."

"I d'no's I want any shoes," said the big woman. "I thought I'd drop in an' see what you'd got."

"Well," said the little shoemaker, "my business is to show folks who want shoes, not to show 'em shoes ef they don't want any."

"But I may want 'em ef you've got some I like," said Mrs. Goodsell tartly.

As Mr. Beebe said nothing to this, but kept on with his cobbling, Mrs. Goodsell concentrated her attention on the small boy by her side.

"Who's your folks?" she demanded. She had faded greenish eyes, and Davie could think of nothing but gooseberries. He tried not to look at them, and at last turned such a helpless glance on the little shoemaker that Mr. Beebe came to the rescue. He had opened his mouth to ask, "And how is your folks, Mis Goodsell?" when an organ-grinder suddenly struck up a tune just outside the shop door.

Davie sprang from the bench and hopped close to the little old man still cobbling away.

"Oh, I must go," he cried. "Do give me my shoe, Mr. Beebe," holding out a frantic hand.

"There, there, Davie," said the little shoemaker, "you wait a minute, an' I'll have your shoe done."

"Isn't it done enough?" said Davie, all in a tremble, "please, dear Mr. Beebe, let me go!"

"What's th' matter with th' boy?" cried Mrs. Goodsell, "I never see anybody act so."

"Don't you fret yourself, Mis Goodsell," said Mr. Beebe, "I'll take care o' Davie. You set an' be comf'table."

"Well, I can't be comf'table—who could be, seein' him carryin' on so?" said the big woman.

Mr. Beebe, not hearing her, for he was now divided over his attempts to soothe Davie, and to see the little shoe repaired as it should be, bent his gray head to hear Davie, who was by this time in a frenzy to get home, and as he kept saying, "be with Phronsie."

"So you shall, Davie, in a minute or two, an' don't you worry, th' organ man can't get by your house in a long while with that thing on his back. And mebbe he ain't goin' that way at all."

"Oh, he will—he will!" cried Davie, in his terror guilty of contradicting, and he beat his hands together and hopped from one foot to the other in his distress.

Suddenly the organ man stopped the tune and twitched a chain that rattled on the cobblestones. Up ran a monkey, and as the man slung the organ on his back, the monkey followed to perch himself there, pull off his cap and bow to a baker's boy and a small girl with a paper bag of groceries, both hanging on his every movement with wide open mouth and eyes.

Davie saw all this, as he plunged over to the small-paned window, when the tune stopped, and peered out between the rows of shoes and slippers that were strung across it.

"He's going!" he gave a sharp little cry. Hearing this, and seeing his face, little Mr. Beebe stopped his work nearly as suddenly as the tune. "There now, I'll put on your shoe. 'Tain't done as good as I want to, you tell your Ma, an' ef you come over tomorrow, I'll finish th' job up good an' splendid." He was saying all this as he tied the shoe on Davie's small foot. "An' don't you worry a mite."

Davie, only waiting till the string was tied, shot out and over the big flat doorstone to the cobblestones of the narrow street.

XXIX

The Story in the Shoeshop

"My! How he acts!" exclaimed Mrs. Goodsell, nervously drawing her shawl ends closer over her lap. "Who is that boy, anyway?"

"Why, that's David Pepper," said the little shoemaker.

"David who?"

Mr. Beebe was craning his short neck to see through the small-paned window what progress David was making over the cobblestones and he didn't pay much attention to the big woman sitting on the bench. So she got clumsily up to her feet and came over to him.

"Who'd you say that boy was?" she demanded.

"Pepper—David Pepper, I told you," said little Mr. Beebe, turning away from the window.

"You said David—I didn't catch the last name."

"Well, it's Pepper."

"Pepper? Well, that's a funny name. Who be his folks?"

"Now, Mis Goodsell," exclaimed the little shoemaker in exasperation, standing quite still to regard her, "do you mean to say that you don't know Mis Pepper? I thought all Badgertown knew her."

"Well, my fam'ly ain't Badgertown folks, you must

remember," said Mrs. Goodsell, getting back to the bench and flapping the shawl ends again across her lap, "an' I don't get over from Four Corners only once in a dog's age. How am I to know your Pepperses, pray tell?"

"Well, you've missed gettin' acquainted with an awful nice woman," observed Mr. Beebe. "I tell you, we set by her in Badgertown, her an' her childern."

"Well, ef they're as queer as that young one"—Mrs. Goodsell indicated with her large hand the departed small boy—"I guess I hain't anythin' to cry over 'cause we ain't more acquainted."

"Ef you mean 'cause David got scared an' run off," the little shoemaker stopped half across the shop on his way to begin a cobbling job and faced her with a gleaming eye, "I can tell you why. 'Twas enough to make him run, I says, says I."

"What was?" the big woman hitched forward on the bench. It was worth coming in from Four Corners—a journey she detested—to hear the little shoemaker go on like this, for generally he only passed the time of day, and then got down to the business of selling shoes.

"Why, when he heard that organ man strike up so suddint."

Mrs. Goodsell turned and stared at the small-paned window in a puzzled way.

"I don't see nothin' to that," she said.

"Well, but there was a monkey."

"S'posin' there was—there warn't nothin' to that, neither."

"Well, it might 'a' ben like th' other monkey—mebbe 'twas th' same one!" the little shoemaker slapped his fat thigh, "I wouldn't wonder; an' David guessed it."

"Ef you could stop talkin' about your monkeys, an' begin

again, mebbe I c'd make head or tail o' what you're tryin'
to tell me, Mr. Beebe," cried the big woman in irritation.

Little Mr. Beebe kept slapping his thigh and declaring,
"I do b'lieve Davie guessed it," then he suddenly waddled
over to the corner, got out a box of dilapidated shoes, picked
out a pair, and sat down to work, "Yes, I verily b'lieve he
guessed it."

Mrs. Goodsell heaved a long sigh. It was no use to ask him
to begin, for she knew he wouldn't do it till he was ready,
so she folded her large hands over the shawl ends.

"You see," said little Mr. Beebe, holding up a man's
shoe to thumb it critically, "it's just this way, about David
—oh, dear me! it beats all how th' parson does wear out his
shoes. I'm afraid that's too far gone to mend."

He set the minister's shoe on his lap and regarded it
mournfully.

"I guess I must be goin'," Mrs. Goodsell made as if her
mind were on Four Corners.

"No, no," cried the little shoemaker, tearing off his gaze
from the parson's footgear, "I must tell you about Davie,
for you ain't a-goin' away until you understand about th'
boy. You see, th' littlest of th' Pepper childern is a girl, an'
she ain't much more'n a baby. You ought to see her!" He
pushed up his spectacles and beamed at her.

"Never mind," interrupted Mrs. Goodsell, "I know about
babies. Had plenty o' my own. Go on, Mr. Beebe."

"Well," the little shoemaker swallowed his disappointment at being held up in his description of Phronsie, "everybody in the Little Brown House looks out for everybody else.
That's th' way they do; an' although Mis Pepper is a hard-
workin' woman, it just beats all how pleasant they keep. You
never'd know to look at 'em how they scrimp an' pinch."

The big woman unfolded her hands from the shawl ends

and slowly regarded them. But she said nothing, and Mr. Beebe went on.

"Yes, they just hang together, an' look out for each other."

"I warrant so," exclaimed Mrs. Goodsell with a sniff, "an' do nothin' for nobody else."

"There's where you're wrong." Little old Mr. Beebe fairly snapped it out. "Ef there's a fam'ly in Badgertown that does more for other folks, I hain't, so far, heerd th' name."

"I thought you said they was obleeged to scrimp," said Mrs. Goodsell.

"What's that go to do with it?" The little shoemaker brought this out with such a roar that old Mrs. Beebe threw open the door into the shop. She was just mixing bread, and her sleeves were rolled up, and little flour dabs had flown up as far as her cap.

"Mercy me, Pa. I thought you was sick!" she exclaimed. "Oh, how do you do, Mis Goodsell."

"I ain't sick, Ma," replied the little shoemaker, turning his round red face to her, "but I shall be unless you come in an' 'xplain things about th' Peppers."

"What about th' Peppers? There hain't nothin' happened to 'em!" cried Mrs. Beebe in alarm, and trotting in.

"My land, no!" declared the little shoemaker. "I wouldn't be a-settin' here so ca'm-like, ef any trouble had 'a' come to them, Ma."

"Oh, well, if they're all right, I'll come back as soon as I've mixed my bread," and Mrs. Beebe trotted out again.

Little Mr. Beebe began to work briskly on the minister's shoe. As long as Ma was coming back, it wouldn't pay to get flustered. Meantime the big woman plied him with questions till she had a pretty fair idea of the Little Brown House people, and all their ages and names.

Then she drew out her big hands again from the shawl ends and held them up, "They'll tell the story. I've worked some in my life," she said, "an' I never got no time to do for other folks."

"Prob'ly not," said the little shoemaker dryly. "Well, here's Ma," and he drew a long breath of relief.

Little Mrs. Beebe had put on a fresh cap, and was now tying the strings of a clean white apron around her ample waist, as befitted sitting down in the shop.

"Tell about how Phronsie run off after th' monkey," said Mr. Beebe.

"That always makes me feel bad whenever I tell it," said Mrs. Beebe, with a sigh, " 'cause it brings back what a dretful thing it was. Why, we thought we'd lost her!" She leaned forward suddenly in her chair, and the color in her cheek, like that of a winter apple, seemed suddenly to fade.

"You!" exclaimed Mrs. Goodsell in astonishment. "Why, she warn't noways related. Why did you take on about it, pray tell?"

"Don't you understand," began Mrs. Beebe.

"No, she don't," declared the little shoemaker irritably, "and what's more, she won't ef you sh'd set there till the day o' judgment."

"But she must." Mrs. Beebe pointed off her words with the fingers of one pudgy hand marking them off on the palm of the other. "We all—everybody in Badgertown sets a sight by those Pepper childern, an' Phronsie—well there," she lifted up a corner of her apron and wiped her eyes.

"Well, go on," said Mrs. Goodsell.

"An' one day, we don't 'xactly know how, Phronsie followed an organ-grinder—he had a monkey an' he stopped an' played in th' Peppers' yard—th' Little Brown House, you know."

Mrs. Goodsell nodded. "Yes, go on."

"An' when he went down th' road, Phronsie went after him. Polly had hurried back to work, an' Mis Pepper was down to the parson's helpin' Mis Henderson, an' the boys was a workin'."

"Seems to me they was mighty little childern for all of 'em to be workin'," broke in Mrs. Goodsell incredulously.

"Th' Peppers warn't never too little to work," the little shoemaker said quickly. "They was up an' at it, I tell you, 'nstead o' playin'."

"Well, go on," said Mrs. Goodsell.

"Oh, I can't, hardly," gasped little Mrs. Beebe, clasping her fat hands, "it brings it all back. You see, she—she didn't come back, an' then we all knew she was lost." With that, Mrs. Beebe threw her apron over her head and burst out crying.

The little shoemaker deserted the parson's shoe and skipped over to her. "There, there, Ma," he patted her cap with a soothing hand. "You know she didn't stay lost. We got her back."

"Well, I think you're th' queerest folks," exclaimed Mrs. Goodsell, "to carry on so over somethin' that never happened, an' besides 'twarn't to your folks, neither."

"'Twas our folks, I keep tellin' you." Little Mrs. Beebe brought her flushed face out from the apron and wiped off the tears. "They was 'our folks' to all Badgertown. An' ef Phronsie had 'a'—" and her mouth trembled.

"You see," the little shoemaker hastened to say, "we was all a-lookin' through th' whole o' Badgertown for her—an' then to think 'twas an out-of-town one who found her, after all."

"Who?" cried the big woman.

"A boy, an' he didn't live in these parts, neither—him an'

his big black dog got her away from th' organ-grinder an' th' monkey."

"Is that so? Well, go on."

"Yes—now you tell th' rest, Ma." The little shoemaker ambled back to his work and picked up the parson's shoe again.

"Well, that boy was stayin' over to Hingham," explained Mrs. Beebe, pointing with her fat finger.

"Hingham don't lay in that direction," said Mrs. Goodsell critically, "it's over there," and she waved her big hand to the opposite corner of the shop.

"Never mind," said Mrs. Beebe easily, "I ain't partic'lar about Hingham now. I'm tellin' about th' boy, he was stayin' there with his father."

"Who was his father?" Mrs. Goodsell was for getting all the particulars, if she got any.

"Oh, he was an awful big man. I guess he was born big," and Mrs. Beebe shuddered. "I hain't seen him but twice. An' then Badgertown seemed so little when he was drivin' by, I was afraid he couldn't get through. But the boy"—here a smile ran up Mrs. Beebe's round face—"you never'd know from him that he was rich."

"Was he rich?" asked Mrs. Goodsell in an awed tone.

"*Rich?*" the little shoemaker's wife brought it out almost in a scream, "why he could buy us all up, an' you Four Corners folks, an' everywhere's around for miles and miles."

"You don't say!"

"But th' boy—why, he'd come over an' play with th' Pepper childern ev'ry chance he got. You see th' father didn't care about havin' young folks round, so Jasper got lonely."

"Jasper?" interrupted the big woman.

"Yes, that was th' boy's name—Jasper King."

"Oh! Well, go on."

"He got lonely, I was sayin', with nobody but his big dog for comp'ny, so over he'd come to Badgertown. You just ought to hear what times they had in th' Little Brown House."

Here Mrs. Beebe laughed. The little shoemaker laid down his work, and joined, both of them shaking their fat sides at the remembrance.

"I've heerd Polly tell about them times—I tell you, she's the one to set off a story good," chuckled old Mr. Beebe, "ain't she now, Ma?"

"You'd ought to have seen 'em as I seen 'em—Pa an' me both did," said the shoemaker's wife, "that boy with one o' Mis Pepper's big check apuns on tied around his neck, an' rollin' out bits o' dough—an' then stickin' 'em in th' old stove. That was before Dr. Fisher give 'em th' new stove— an' him as rich as Crocus."

"Dr. Fisher rich!" cried Mrs. Goodsell, raising both hands. "Why, he's as poor as Job's turkey, an' with them two old maid sisters on his hands. Now I know you've ben stuffin' me right along, Mis Beebe," she added in an injured tone.

"Oh, I didn't mean Dr. Fisher was rich, I said th' boy," cried Mrs. Beebe in a loud voice.

"Well, go on."

"An' then, he had to go—th' boy did, for his father went back home, an'—"

"You hain't told about th' gingerbread boy, Ma," old Mr. Beebe began to laugh again.

"That was th' funniest of all," said Mrs. Beebe, and she began to laugh, too.

"What was it?" cried the big woman impatiently. "You

do so much laughin', you an' Mr. Beebe, it's kinder slow work gettin' along."

"I know it, an' you must 'xcuse me, Mis Goodsell," said Mrs. Beebe, "but them childern—well, you see Phronsie always takes it to heart when she hears anybody's sick, so she made a gingerbread boy an' made 'em send it to Jasper's father."

"My goodness!—to a rich man—a gingerbread boy!" gasped Mrs. Goodsell.

"Yes, an' you'd 'a' thought 'twould 'a' made him mad," said Mrs. Beebe.

"Well, it did, didn't it?" said Mrs. Goodsell.

"Mad? Why, he just took to that gingerbread boy like a duck to water! An' he come over to see Phronsie. An' now you can't think, they're a-writin' back an' forth, Jasper an' th' childern."

"Polly gits th' letters," said old Mr. Beebe.

"Yes, an' they hope he's comin', an' th' father, over to Hingham again this summer," said Mrs. Beebe. "Well, I could tell lots more, but I shan't, 'cause I've got to get back an' git on my other apun an' red up my kitchen," and she waddled off.

"It's th' most remarkable story *I* ever heerd," said Mrs. Goodsell, getting off from the bench, seeing there was no more to be gained.

"So you see why David Pepper run so like lightnin'," cried old Mr. Beebe, "he was afraid th' organ man was goin' down by th' Little Brown House, an' he wanted to get home an' see that Phronsie didn't get took off."

"Well, I don't blame him," said Mrs. Goodsell, with a nod from her large head, "an' I don't myself much like organ-grinders snoopin' round. Why, there he is now—an' th' monkey's comin' in th' door!"

XXX

The Letter

THE little wrinkled face of a monkey appeared, dragging a chain at the end of which came his master. He had set the organ up against the little shop.

Mrs. Goodsell, not knowing how she got there, was standing on the bench, her calico gown whipped tightly around her, the shawl ends wound over that, and screaming loudly. Old Mrs. Beebe hurried in with both hands raised, while the little shoemaker, trying to drive out both the monkey and the man, didn't succeed in doing either, but got tangled up with the chain.

"Pa—Pa, let him go!" cried Mrs. Beebe, wringing her hands. "I'll get th' broom," disappearing to come back with it, when she found things in a much worse state. For the monkey, shaking the chain free from both the little shoemaker and his master, was now on the upper shelf in the row that occupied one side of the shop, twitching off the covers of the boxes, and throwing down the shoes and rubbers and slippers in a heap to the floor.

In the midst of all this confusion, David Pepper opened the door.

"Oh, my senses!" screamed Mrs. Goodsell from the

bench, where she was constantly hopping from one foot to the other in terrified distress, "here's that boy again—ah— oof!" as the monkey stopped his work a second to fasten his little eyes on her.

Davie quickly closed the door and stood on the big flat stone, his heart beating wildly. Then he opened it again. "I'll help you," he said, going in.

"Davie, he'll bite you!" screamed old Mrs. Beebe, waving her broom.

Davie shut his eyes, as he thought so, too. Then he opened them and began to climb the lowest shelf to reach the end of the dangling chain. The monkey stopped regarding the screaming woman on the bench, whom he had almost made up his mind he would leap for, and peered over at the boy, and as quick as lightning, he twitched up the chain and grinned in Davie's face.

"Now, you've done it," exclaimed the organ man, with a word that wasn't pretty at all, and he glared at Davie.

"Oh, I'm so sorry," said Davie, sliding to the floor. His face was very red, and his blue eyes went down in shame.

"Don't feel bad," old Mr. Beebe gasped out the words, and leaned, quite spent, against the counter where he did up his bundles for customers.

"Get something to eat," the organ man growled it out at the shoemaker's wife, "then he'll come down and I'll lick him 'most to death."

"Oh, you mustn't," cried Davie, forgetting his shame to rush over to the organ man.

"Mustn't, hey? You stand out of th' way, you beggar boy, you," looking down contemptuously at Davie's little patched shoes, and he pushed him roughly off.

"You let that boy alone," commanded old Mr. Beebe,

puffing up. The man laughed in the fat little shoemaker's face. "Get somethin' to eat, I tell you," he roared.

"Oh, I will—I will." Old Mrs. Beebe trotted off, and came back with two doughnuts in her trembling hands.

"You hold 'em up," said the organ man. "He won't come down for me."

"Oh, I can't," Mrs. Beebe shook all over.

"Let th' boy hold 'em," said the man; "he butted in there an' lost us th' chain, and now he can git him down."

David cast a wild look up at the little beast, whose sharp eyes were roving from his master to the small boy that had interfered with the chain.

"No, no, Davie," began the little shoemaker—but intent only on the organ man's charge that he was to blame, Davie took the doughnuts out of old Mrs. Beebe's hands before she realized it.

"You mustn't whip him," he said, looking back at the man, before he held them up.

But he didn't need to, for there was a sudden leap from the high shelf, the end of the chain rattled off, and the monkey came down on Davie's little shoulder, knocking him to the floor in among the shoes and slippers and rubbers scattered about.

They never knew quite how it all ended, but when Davie picked himself up, the organ man was dragging the monkey, swallowing the last piece of the second doughnut, out of the shop.

"He mustn't whip him," cried Davie, gasping from his fright, and darting after.

"You come back," commanded the little shoemaker. "See!" and David having nothing to do but to obey, he was led over to look out of the window. There was the monkey perched on the organ slung on the back of the man, who was getting over the cobblestones at a lively rate. "Now you can help me to pick up these," added old Mr. Beebe, pointing to the havoc made in his merchandise sprawled over the floor.

Old Mrs. Beebe had sunk down in a chair, and clasped her hands.

"I'll help you," cried Davie, springing to the work, yet with a heavy heart as he thought of the monkey.

Mrs. Goodsell stood quite still on the bench, her surprise not allowing her to take her eyes off from Davie. Now she peered down at him, gathering up the shoes, rubbers, and slippers. "I thought you was scared of monkeys," she said slowly. Then she put one large foot down and began to descend to the floor.

"Did you go home, Davie?" asked the little shoemaker quickly.

"Yes," said Davie, handing him two or three rubbers; "I did, and Mamsie sent me back to ask you to please finish mending my shoe."

"So I will," said old Mr. Beebe, "as soon as we get these things gathered up. Your ma will look after Phronsie, I s'pose she told you."

"Yes," said Davie, "she did."

"Well, now, I'm glad you went home an' told your ma there was an organ man in Badgertown 'cause there ain't no Jasper here now with his big dog. Heard anythin' from him lately?"

"Yes," said Davie. "Mr. Atkins gave Mamsie a letter yesterday."

"Sho now!" exclaimed Mr. Beebe, much gratified. He ached to ask what was in it, but for all the world he couldn't bring himself to such a thing.

"What did the letter say?" demanded Mrs. Goodsell.

Davie turned his blue eyes up to her. "It was Mamsie's letter," he said simply.

"Yes, yes, I heerd you. Well, what did it say? I ain't cur'ous, but I jest thought I'd ask. Hey?"

But she got no answer, David being busy handing the shoes, slippers and rubbers up to old Mr. Beebe's waiting hands.

"Well, of all the impident boys I ever see!" exclaimed Mrs. Goodsell, slapping the shawl ends indignantly around her big figure, "you beat 'em all!"

"There—there—" declared the little shoemaker, straightening up, "my shop ain't big enough to hold folks who talk against th' Peppers. So, good mornin' to you, Mis Goodsell."

"An' I shake th' dust off from my feet," cried Mrs. Goodsell, shaking her shawl ends instead, "an' I wouldn't demean myself by stayin', Mr. Beebe—what with your Pepperses an' monkeys an' letters." She slammed the door, and disdaining the flat stone, strode over the cobblestones.

Davie, to whom her words brought a memory he was trying to put in the background, sighed.

"Now you're gettin' all tired out," said Mrs. Beebe in a worried way. "Don't let him work any more, Pa."

"Oh, no, I'm not tired," said Davie, raising his flushed face. "I want to put all the things back. Do let me, Mr. Beebe," he begged. He longed to say that it was old Mr. King's letter to Mamsie that was bothering him. But that belonged to Mamsie.

How could they ever let Polly go from the Little Brown House to visit in the city! Mamsie had written "No" twice before to Mr. King; but yesterday after reading this particular letter, Mother Pepper had looked very sober. "She must think about it," she had told the children. Think about it!

Davie didn't imagine that it needed a second thought. They couldn't let Polly go! even if Jasper was sick, and the doctor said there must be some little friend invited to cheer things up. Oh, no, they couldn't!

When the shoes and rubbers and slippers were all neatly put back in their respective boxes, and on the shelf once more, old Mrs. Beebe, who had gone off into the kitchen, came back with a blue plate on which were two doughnuts. "Now while Pa is a-mendin' your shoe, you can set an' eat 'em," she said.

Davie, well pleased, curled up on the bench and munched the sugary things slowly to make them last. He wanted to ask if he couldn't take one home for Phronsie, but then that was as good as begging one—for old Mrs. Beebe would trot out to her big stone pot and get him another. So he watched his shoe having the finishing touches put to its repairs, while he ate.

"Now says I," the little shoemaker held up the completed work, as David swallowed the last crumb of the doughnuts, "that job is done as good as th' next one, if I do say it. Now, Davie, that will last you a long spell."

"I am so glad." Davie hopped off from the bench, and sitting down on the floor, he pulled on the shoe with great satisfaction.

"That string ain't very strong," said Mr. Beebe, "I guess I better get you another." He went across the shop and pulled out a drawer.

Davie stopped trying to tie the shoestring. "Mamsie didn't say that I was to get a new string," he said.

"Oh, you ain't goin' to buy this," said old Mr. Beebe, coming back. "I'm goin' to give it to you. Give me the shoe, Davie, and we'll see about that string."

So Davie pulled off his shoe, and old Mr. Beebe sat

down and pretty soon there was a brand-new shoestring in it, and the old one lay on the floor.

"I think th' mate to that string is pretty poor," said the little old shoemaker, peering at Davie's other foot critically; "give me that shoe, Davie," and when it was in his hand, he pulled out the shoestring. "Yes, it's wore in spots," he declared.

At last Davie was on his way home. Didn't the shoes feel good though; the mended one all strong and just as good as ever, and with new shoestrings, too! He wanted to dance —but stopped suddenly. There was Polly—was she going away for a visit to the city? He went slowly up the path leading to the Little Brown House and opened the green door. There were Mamsie and the others, and David knew by her face what she was going to say.

"Children," she began, "you know how good Jasper has been to us! And think of Phronsie!" She gathered her up in her arms to hold her tightly to her breast, and her voice broke. "What can we ever do for him!"

"But, Mamsie," began Ben, "Polly—we can't—" He couldn't get any farther, and his head went down to hide his face on his knees.

"Oh, I'm not going!" cried Polly passionately, a little red spot coming on either cheek. "You needn't think of it, Ben," and she threw her arms around his shoulders—while Joel roared, "She isn't going—she isn't!" and he ran over to throw his arms across Polly's—till Ben was nearly smothered. David longed to add himself to them, and he started, but catching Mother Pepper's eye, he settled back and held his hands tightly together in dread of what was coming, for Mrs. Pepper was speaking.

"Don't say that, Polly," she said reprovingly. "You must think, child, before you speak."

"Oh, I don't want to think, Mamsie!" cried Polly wildly, and deserting Ben, she plunged over to Mrs. Pepper's chair and threw herself on her knees. "Mamsie, don't make me go!" she begged, burying her face on Phronsie's small feet.

"I never should make you go, Polly," Mrs. Pepper stroked the brown hair. "Mother feels badly enough to think of your going. It must be as you say, Polly."

So there it was left. And every now and then Polly would break away from whatever she was doing, even if setting the supper table, and rush up in a torrent of tears. "Oh, I can't go—Mamsie, I can't!" And then she would fly back to her work to creep up presently with "Jasper saved Phronsie for us, Mamsie!"

"I know, Polly," Mother Pepper would say softly, and Polly would know that all Mamsie's objections to the visit had not only flown away, but that instead, there would be an approval of it if Polly should decide to go.

"Now, children," after the supper dishes were cleared away, and everything was spick and span again, and Mother Pepper had sat down to get a little more of the waning light to sew by before the evening really set in, "I think," she said, "you better have that day in the woods tomorrow, for you have been waiting for it so long."

"Mamsie," cried Davie, looking up at his mother with shining eyes, "can we really go to the woods tomorrow?"

"I think so, Davie." Mrs. Pepper smiled at him. "Don't scream so, Joel. Yes, you may all go tomorrow." She looked around for Polly—who had drawn off in a corner with Ben, their heads together and filled with sad thoughts, as she very well knew. The day in the woods was the only thing she could plan by which she might divert the sadness, at least for a time.

"Mamsie," Davie crowded up to her chair, "can we stay when we get there in the woods—can we?" he asked, dreadfully excited.

"Yes indeed—a whole long day if you want to," said Mother Pepper decidedly. "Now run over and tell Polly and Ben how glad you are about it."

"And can we carry things to eat?" demanded Joel precipitating himself upon her, his black eyes waiting impatiently for her answer.

"Of course, you can take your dinner," and Mother Pepper laughed. "Who ever heard of spending a day in the woods without anything to eat! And I expect you'll be very hungry, Joel."

"I'm hungry now," said Joel reflectively.

"Oh, Joey—you've only just finished your supper," said Mrs. Pepper. At his words, she began to sew away brisker than ever.

"There wasn't half enough," said Joel, looking over his shoulder at the cleared table set up against the wall. "Why isn't there ever any more to eat, Mamsie?"

"Never mind," said Mrs. Pepper, stitching fast. "Well, now, tomorrow you shall have a good deal. You will like the basket I shall pack for you," she added cheerily.

"What's to be in it?" cried Joel, smacking his lips, "candy and a pie?"

"Oh, dear me! Joe—not those things," said Mrs. Pepper. Then some cake," said Joel, hanging over her knee, so that his small elbows dragged her work down.

"No, indeed," she slipped the sewing away, but let the elbows remain, "cake isn't the best thing for children to eat in the woods. But, Joel, just think, Mother is going to give you some nice thick slices of bread and—butter."

"Not butter?" cried Joel, quite overcome.

"Yes," Mrs. Pepper nodded.

"And spread it thick, do, Mamsie," cried Joel, dreadfully excited, "as thick as that." He took off his elbows to put his little brown hands a good distance apart.

Mrs. Pepper laughed. "You never would relish butter again if you had it as thick as that, Joey," she said. "Now run over and tell Ben and Polly all about it."

Her work fell down for a minute, as he dashed off—and a shadow swept across her face; but it was gone as quickly, and the needle flew all the faster.

Joel rushed up to the two in the corner. "We are going to have butter tomorrow, Polly Pepper," he announced.

"Nonsense!" exclaimed Ben, pulling himself out of his gloom. "You've been dreaming, Joe."

"I haven't, either," retorted Joel indignantly. "Mamsie said so." He darted across the kitchen. "Didn't you, Mamsie?" he cried, plunging up to her chair. "Ben says I've been dreaming."

"Didn't I do what, Joel?"

"Didn't you say you were going to give us butter tomorrow to eat in the woods?"

"I certainly did, Joey," said Mrs. Pepper. She looked over his head and nodded to the three in the corner. "Come over here, children. Wait a minute; Phronsie."

Phronsie, who had been undressing Seraphina for bed, always a slow process, laid the rag doll on a chair and came up wonderingly to her mother's knee.

"Now it's just this way," began Mrs. Pepper, looking at them all, "tomorrow must be the very happiest day of the whole year. And in order to get ready for it and make it happy—why, we must all begin tonight. Now, Joel and Davie, you'd better run off to bed, so that you can hop up bright and early in the morning."

"I don't want to," Joel grumbled. But seeing his mother's face, he finished, "All right—come on, Dave." Then he ran back when halfway up the loft stairs. "Please spread it thick, Mamsie," he begged.

"Come, Phronsie," Polly held out her hand. She tried to make the sad little smile a brighter one, but it was a sorrowful face, after all, that she carried off.

"Oh, no, no," cried Phronsie in distress. "My child hasn't her nightie on," and she ran back to the chair where Seraphina waited to be gotten ready for bed.

"I'll help you," said Polly, "for you must get into your own nightie. There, you run back and kiss Mamsie, and I'll get Seraphina ready."

So Phronsie, well pleased to be cuddled by Mamsie, ran back and scrambled into Mother Pepper's lap.

"Be a good girl, Phronsie, and don't trouble Polly, but hop right into bed," said Mrs. Pepper.

"I'll be a good girl," cooed Phronsie, her lips against Mother Pepper's neck. Then she slid off from Mamsie's lap, and was soon fast asleep in the trundle bed, Seraphina huddled up in her arms.

And Polly, down on her knees by the big old bed, her head on the gay patchwork quilt, was saying, "I'll go."

XXXI

Working Hard to Keep Cheery

PARSON HENDERSON walked slowly between the hollyhocks, his hands folded behind his back. His wife hurried down the narrow path to join him.

"Oh," she said breathlessly, "we are all going to feel dreadfully when Polly has really gone."

"We mustn't think of ourselves," said the parson. "Poor Mrs. Pepper!" and he sighed.

"I know it, and yet you did right to advise her to let Polly go," Mrs. Henderson peered anxiously up into his face.

"I'm not a bit sorry that I did so advise," declared Parson Henderson firmly. "Mehitable, it is a clear case of the working of Providence for that girl to have the chance." He stopped short on the garden path.

"I know it," cried his wife gleefully, "think of the music! Oh, Jotham, how Polly has longed for a chance to learn to play."

She clasped her hands and the smile ran up to capture the anxiety in her face.

299

"I do think. I think of all the good that will come of the visit." The parson began his walk once more, this time with a stride. Mrs. Henderson trotted by his side, trying to keep up with him.

"Don't go so fast, husband," she begged.

"Yes," as he slackened his pace, "and another thing. We ought to consider how much the Peppers are indebted to Jasper. If it hadn't been for him—just think." She ran her hand within his arm.

"That's the reason I was able to persuade Mrs. Pepper to let Polly go," cried Mr. Henderson. "She put aside everything else, when she saw that she could do this for the boy."

"Yes—yes. Oh, I'm so glad. But, oh, dear," she couldn't for the life of her keep from adding, "those children—can you imagine what they are going to do without Polly!"

The parson's face fell gloomily.

"There's Ben—it will come desperately hard on him," he said.

"Ben will make up his mind to bear it—he is the oldest —and he is such a strong boy," said Mrs. Henderson quickly. "The one I am worrying about the most is Davie."

"Poor Davie will take it pretty hard, I am afraid."

"And he will keep it all in on account of Mrs. Pepper, and it will wear on him terribly. Oh, dear me!" Mrs. Henderson now looked so very miserable that her husband lost thought of the Peppers and turned to comfort her.

"See here, Mehitable," he cried, "we are acting badly, both of us. What sort of example, pray tell, are we to the Little Brown House people. We've simply got to cheer up."

"So I will," cried his wife, trying to smile; "I'm ashamed of myself. And now that Polly is really going, I mustn't stay here talking any longer, when I could help to get her ready. There's that old brown merino dress of mine; it's been up in the attic for I don't know how long. I shall make it over for her." She drew her hand away from his arm and ran down the path ahead of him. "I've a fine chance to get the pattern of Polly's calico gown, now that the children are all away in the woods today."

"The children all away in the woods!" repeated the parson in surprise.

"Yes, Mrs. Pepper told me yesterday that she was going to let them have that treat. Polly has been wanting it so long. And it would help to cheer things up. Oh, I am so glad I took over that little pat of butter. Oh, dear!" for a sudden turn in the path, and there was Miss Jerusha, a scowl on her face.

"Of all things on this earth," she exclaimed, lifting her long hands, "the silliest is to send that Pepper girl to the city."

"Don't let us talk about it, Jerusha," said the parson's wife, trying to get by.

"Talk about it! It's time for someone to talk." Miss Jerusha's angular figure successfully blocked the way. "Such goings on! Jotham," as her brother came up, "what on earth did you put such a notion into that girl's head for! The idea of her going into those rich folks' house! She'll be snubbed to death—that's one comfort," and Miss Jerusha gave an unpleasant little cackle.

"Polly Pepper will never be snubbed, Jerusha," declared the parson decidedly. "On the contrary—"

Miss Jerusha interrupted him, "We'll see," she cried, the cackle becoming a shrill laugh. Mrs. Henderson stepped off into the grass, and hurried up into the attic, leaving the parson to get away as best he could.

And now all Badgertown knew that Polly Pepper was going to the city on a visit to Mr. King's house.

Mr. Atkins took down a roll of gingham from his shelf of dry goods. "I'll give her enough for two dresses," he said. "Land o' Goshen! she needs somethin' to help her out. I wouldn't be in th' same house with that old Mr. King for a hundred dollars—no, not by a long shot."

And the little shoemaker called Davie in one day, as he was running by. "You tell Polly that I've got a splendid pair o' shoes waiting for her," and then he turned to old Mrs. Beebe. "She'll set by those shoes when she's in th' city," he said complacently, "an' goes a-walkin' with Mr. King."

And Mrs. Beebe shuddered again, and said, "I can't never imagine her walkin' with him, Pa."

And then one day Mr. Tisbett drove his stage up with a great flourish to the Little Brown House and Polly's hair trunk was strapped on—and she was almost off—when out she sprang.

"I can't go!" she cried, "oh, I can't!" and dashing between them all, she flew back through the kitchen to throw herself down in a torrent of tears by Mamsie's bed.

No one quite knew how they got her back again—but the stage at last, with Polly inside, rolled off, and Mother Pepper and the four little Peppers went into the Little Brown House and shut the green door.

Davie ran fast as he could, for the first time in his life not wanting Joel, his mind intent on reaching the spot where the day in the woods had been spent. There, under a clump of oaks on a little mossy bank, were bits of leaves and flowers, the remains of the wreath Polly had made to carry home to Mother. When David saw them, he threw himself down and buried his face, in an agony of tears. "I want Polly!" he cried.

A little bird hopped along the branch over his head to

turn a sharp eye down at him. The sun shone, and he had eaten several worms and was perfectly comfortable. What anyone could cry about, he couldn't understand. For his part, he felt much more like singing. And accordingly he did, and such a lively air, all trills and high notes, as quite astonished himself. But that only made Davie cry worse, for it brought back the story that Polly had told them as they all sat around her while she made the wreath, of a little bird —why, it must have been that very one now singing over his head.

So of course the little bird, very much hurt in his feelings, at last stopped his song and flew away. And the wood became quite still.

All of a sudden, a whoop and a shout—and a boy's feet came tearing through the bushes, and between the trees.

"Joel!" gasped David to himself. There was no time to run, and besides Joel would see him. The only thing to be done was to burrow deeper in the mossy bank.

"You ran away," cried Joel in great displeasure, and precipitating himself on him.

David couldn't very well say he hadn't, so he said nothing.

"And it was mean of you," cried Joel wrathfully, and rolling him over to stare into his face. "Oh—oh—you've been crying!"

"Let me alone," cried David crossly, and twitching away, he rolled back again. "Go right home, and let me alone."

"You ran away," Joel repeated loudly, so astounded at such a reception that all he could do was to repeat it again, "you ran away." This time his round face became very sober —and in a minute down he went flat on his face by David's side.

Davie by this time was quite gone in misery, and he burst out, "I want Polly!"

Joel didn't say anything as Davie cried on. And everything was so still that Davie forgot that he was there—until a queer little rustle made him poke up his head. Joel was stuffing the end of his calico blouse into his mouth and making frantic efforts to hold back his sobs. It was now David's turn to precipitate himself on Joel.

"I want Polly," came in gusts from Joel, and he rolled over and over trying to stop.

"Oh, don't, Joel," begged Davie, very much frightened.

"I want her," screamed Joel, "and I'm going right straight after her to Mr. King's house to bring her home." With that he hopped to his feet. His face was dreadfully red, but he had stopped crying. "They shan't keep her there," he declared, and his black eyes flashed defiantly.

"Oh, Joel, you wouldn't do that!" David, in his terror, gripped Joel's sleeve.

"I would, too," declared Joel stoutly. "I shall start this minute," and he tore himself free, and darted down the mossy bank.

David, without stopping to think of the impossibility of such a plan ever coming to completion, dashed after him, screaming, "Don't, Joel," with all his might, and catching his foot in a rambling vine, over he pitched headlong down a steep descent in the bank.

Joel heard him go, and rushing back to scramble down after him, he found David picking himself up from a heap of dried leaves.

"I'm not hurt," he said.

Joel, who had been shaking with terror, now laughed till his little white teeth shone. "They're all in your hair, Dave," he said. "I'll get 'em out," pawing the soft light waves, in which the little dried wisps were sticking.

"You won't tell Mamsie I cried," said Davie, looking up anxiously.

"I don't know," said Joel. Then he stopped picking the leaves out of the soft hair. "If you won't tell her that I did," he began.

"Oh, I won't—I won't," promised David eagerly, "not a single bit of it, Joel."

"We both cried, and we both won't tell," decided Joel in a matter-of-fact way.

"And Mamsie will worry if we don't get home," said Davie, "and we mustn't want Polly to come back." He twisted his small hands together, as he regarded Joel nervously.

"But I do want Polly to come back," declared Joel obstinately, shaking his head.

"It will make Mamsie sick." Davie could think of nothing better to say, so he repeated it in a despairing voice, "It will make Mamsie sick."

Joel scuffed the heap of dry leaves with his rusty little shoes, then he blurted out, "I don't want my Mamsie to be sick," he said slowly.

"Then you won't go after Polly to bring her back?" David didn't dare to breathe, as he asked it, but hung on Joel's answer.

"No," said Joel magnificently, "she can stay."

Times were pretty hard in the Little Brown House about these days, and Mother Pepper had all she could do to have it look as if any ray of sunshine had ever hopped in. If the work hadn't pressed so, it would have been much worse. But night after night the three boys dragged themselves up to bed in the loft, too tired to do anything but tumble on to the shakedowns and get ready for the next day. For there was all Polly's work to do, and as much of it as they could accomplish to save Mother was eagerly sought by them all.

And Phronsie, lost to everything but that Polly was gone, refused to be comforted, and hung around her mother's chair, or mourned for Polly when Mrs. Pepper went down to the store, or was away to help Mrs. Blodgett.

David, who took upon himself the task of amusing her, was almost in despair. He had given up going to help Mr. Atkins in his store to stay at home and take care of her. He even tried to tell stories, and racked his brain to think how Polly would relate one. But he couldn't make any headway in getting her to stop crying, "I want Polly."

At last one day Grandma Bascom waddled in.

"Oh, me—oh my!" she exclaimed, sitting heavily down on the first chair. There sat Phronsie on the floor, the very picture of woe, and crying into her pinafore. David was squatting in front of her, frantically trying to draw a picture on his slate and explain it by a story.

Phronsie got up and went over to Grandma's chair.

"I want Polly," she said, the tears trailing down her little cheeks.

"Yes, I know," said Grandma, who seemed to understand, even if she couldn't hear very well, and patting her yellow hair. "Oh, you poor creeter, you!" she said to Davie.

"She doesn't like my stories," said Davie, getting up from the floor, his cheeks very much flushed. He came over and put his mouth close to Grandma's cap. "And I can't tell any good ones."

"Well," said Grandma, "that's because she's heard Polly's stories. Ef I was you, I wouldn't try to tell 'em."

"What can I do?" cried Davie in despair. The flush died

off, leaving his cheeks quite white, and he twisted his small hands in distress.

Grandma Bascom gave him a keen look, then bobbed her cap wisely till the frill quivered. "Now, Phronsie," she said, "you must take care of Davie. He'll be sick if you don't."

"Oh, Grandma," exclaimed David, quite horrified at such a turn of affairs, "I'm not sick." He tried to shout it into her ear, but she kept on, "Davie will be sick ef you don't take care of him, Phronsie."

"I'll take care of Davie," said Phronsie, wiping away the last tear on her pinafore, "and I shall put him to bed, so that he won't be sick."

"That's my good little lamb," said Grandma, her cap frill bobbing worse than ever. "Now, Davie, you go an' curl on your ma's bed, an'——"

"Oh, no, no," cried Davie. "Why, I'm a big boy, and I don't want to go to bed in the daytime." He was in such distress over the idea that his voice was very sharp, and Grandma heard every word.

"You ain't as big as the parson," said Grandma coolly, "an' Mis Henderson said she put him to bed last week right in the middle o' th' day." It was a long speech for Grandma to make and she wheezed so at the end that Davie forgot everything else and ran and got her a cup of water.

"An' I'm goin' to stay here a spell, an' Phronsie must set by th' bed an' watch you," beginning again when she got her breath, and the cup was taken back.

Phronsie, feeling very important that she was to take care of David and keep him from being sick, now clamored for him to get on Mamsie's bed and let her tuck him up. And nothing would do but that she should take his hand and lead him off to the bedroom.

Grandma chuckled to see them go. It presently became so still in the old kitchen that she dozed in her chair, waking up with a start.

"I declare ef I haven't lost myself jest for a minute," she said. "Now I'll see how them blessed childern is gettin' along."

She opened the bedroom door softly and peeped in. Davie, with the patchwork quilt drawn up to his chin just as Phronsie had tucked him in, and with one arm thrown over his head, was sleeping as he hadn't been able to do since Polly went away. And Phronsie, curled up on the floor, her yellow head on the old braided rug, was dreaming that she was watching Davie and keeping him from getting sick.

Ben and Joel found them so, when they came home from Deacon Blodgetts where they had been piling wood. Joel rushed past Grandma Bascom like a whirlwind. "*Sh!*" she said, raising her hand. Too late! Into the bedroom flew Joel waving something over his head. "*Hoh!* in bed!" he cried. "Get up, Dave!"

"Look out!" cried Ben, "you almost stepped on Phronsie!" and he picked her up, as Joel jumped on the bed.

"It's for you," he cried, shaking the arm thrown over Davie's head. Then the old patchwork quilt was twitched down and something white was thrust in its place.

"What is it?" asked Davie, his blue eyes dewy with sleep, and he rolled over to show very pink cheeks.

"A letter from Polly," cried Joel, waving it impatiently.

Davie flew up to sit in the middle of the bed. "*Oh!*" he cried hungrily, "a letter from Polly!"

"Yes—yes, and it's for you," screamed Joel, sticking it into his hand.

Davie threw off the patchwork quilt and, tumbling off the

bed, ran out into the kitchen. "A letter from Polly—and it's for me!" he shouted.

Just then the door opened and Mother Pepper came in to meet Ben coming out from the bedroom with Phronsie on his shoulder. She kept saying, "I watched Davie all the while—I did."

It took Davie so long to open the letter with trembling fingers, that Joel impatiently kept crying, "Do hurry, Dave!" beating on the table for emphasis.

"Hush, Joe," cried Ben, "we couldn't hear the letter if it were open, you make such a noise."

"I'll stop when he opens it," said Joel. "Oh, do hurry, Dave!" and he ran across the kitchen with Mamsie's big bread knife. But Davie already had the letter out of its envelope, and spread in his hand.

They all held their breath to catch every word, and Grandma Bascom put her hand behind her best ear, and Davie began:

"Dear Davie:

"I just wish I could hop into the Little Brown House and—(Oh, dear me! I wrote that crooked) see you all. To-morrow I'm going to write to Joel."

"Hooray!" screamed Joel. He rushed up to Grandma and shouted in her ear, "Polly's going to write to me tomorrow!"

"Come back," cried Ben, "if you want to hear the rest. Go on, Dave."

"Wait for me," roared Joel, skipping back. "Have you read any more, Dave?" he cried anxiously.

"No," said Davie, "I haven't read a bit more."

"Well, I want to tell you how kind dear Mr. King is. (He wants me to call him Grandpapa.) He has a music teacher for me. Just think, I'm really going to learn to play on the

piano—really and truly! Oh, Davie, I was almost afraid to touch the piano, it is so magnifesent (I haven't spelled that right I know) but Grandpapa said I must not feel that way, so I don't now, for of course if I were afraid of the piano, I never could learn to play.

"And, oh—little Dick is too cunning for anything. Phronsie would like to play with him."

"I should," said Phronsie, smoothing down her pinafore, "very much indeed."

"Oh, and Prince, this morning, when Jasper asked him if he didn't want to send his love to Phronsie, said just as plain as could be, 'Bark—Bark!'"

Phronsie screamed so with delight that it was some time before Davie could go on.

"And now you must write to me, Davie, and tell Phronsie to write to me, too, all by her own self. And, oh, tell Mamsie I mended my stockings last week 'cause two big holes came. I must save some room for Jasper wants to write.

"Polly, with love to all in the Little Brown House."

"Dear Dave:

"You must write to Polly, all of you, because I want her to like it here, and she won't unless she hears often from the Little Brown House.

"Polly just practices every chance she can get. The music teacher says she is the best—Polly is stopping me, so I can't tell the rest.

Jasper"

Davie stood quite still, not minding when Joel twitched the letter out of his hand, then he marched straight up to Grandma and said under her cap frill,

"Now I know what Phronsie would like to do—write a letter to Polly every day."

Then he flew over to Mother Pepper. "You don't need to take care of Phronsie, I'm going to do it every single day, Mamsie, all by myself," he said, his blue eyes shining.

Pelosi Doan